WALK
IN THE
FIRE

Copyright © 2018 by Steph Post
Cover and jacket design by Georgia Morrissey
Interior designed and formatted by E.M. Tippetts Book Designs

ISBN: 9781943818839
eISBN: 9781943818969
Library of Congress Control Number: 2016952315

First hardcover edition January 2018 by Polis Books, LLC
1201 Hudson Street, #211S
Hoboken, NJ 07030
www.PolisBooks.com

POLIS BOOKS

WALK
IN THE
FIRE

STEPH POST

For Vegas and Mr. Sweaters,
Unique in All the World

"Behold, all ye that kindle a fire, that compass yourselves about with sparks: walk in the light of your fire, and in the sparks that ye have kindled. This shall ye have of mine hand; ye shall lie down in sorrow." –Isaiah 50.11

CHAPTER 1

RAMEY CLOSED HER eyes, leaned back against the glass and, for a moment, wished it all away. The heat from the sun-blasted windshield stung her shoulder blades and the backs of her bare arms. She pressed her palms against the shimmering hood of the silver Cadillac and lost herself in the feverish sensation. The burn was like a calescent itch she was finally able to scratch. There was not a breath of movement around her, and the stillness of the salvage yard in the late evening was both suffocating and reassuring. Ramey languidly opened her eyes, looked up at the impossible cobalt of the sky, deep and cool, far away from the pillars of crushed cars radiating heat all around her, and sighed.

"Lesser, I know you're there. What do you want?"

Ramey sat up and rubbed her hands along the thighs of her jeans. She slid down to the edge of the Cadillac's hood and coiled her long dark auburn hair around her wrist. She twisted it up off her neck while waiting for the embarrassed seventeen-year-old to come around a stack of plywood pallets.

"Sorry. I didn't want to just come up on you like that. Though, I guess I did anyway, huh?"

Lesser grinned, but then quickly looked down as he pushed his stringy blond hair back behind his pierced ears.

"I know you come out here sometimes to get away. Probably from me, I bet. Or Benji and his moods. I wasn't spying on you or nothing, I swear."

Still keeping his eyes on the ground, Lesser nudged a piece of rubber hose with the toe of his dirty Converse sneaker. Ramey waited until he glanced up at her and then she shrugged her shoulders expectantly.

"Lesser. What do you want?"

"Oh, sorry. Judah's here. He's back. Just got back. He's up at the garage. Said he wanted to talk to you."

Lesser raised his head and smiled at her before jamming his hands into his pockets and turning on his heel. Ramey tried not to laugh as she called out her thanks. Lesser had been working at Cannon Salvage for more than a month, but he still stumbled over himself every time he was alone with her. The kid was good, though. A high school dropout, sure, but a halfway decent mechanic, and Ramey didn't know what they would have done without him. She took a last look around at the little niche of seclusion she had made for herself in the back corner of the lot before heading back up to the garage.

Ramey emerged from the maze of stripped, derelict cars and heaps of twisted scrap metal and debris to find Benji finally out of the sagging aluminum lawn chair he had installed himself in early that morning. She figured Judah being back probably had something to do with it. He was leaning awkwardly against the bumper of a turquoise Firebird, with one of his crutches rammed up under his armpit and the other discarded in the oily gravel at his feet. Benji glanced up at her as he unscrewed the oil cap and underneath his flop of blond bangs she could see that his eyes were distant and glazed. Ramey picked up the fallen crutch and set it against the car's dented fender as she walked by. Benji only grunted.

She stepped through one of the large, roll-up doors into the cool shade of the double bay garage. Judah was standing with his back to her, staring hard at the mess of papers spread out across a metal desk in the corner. Ramey crossed her arms and leaned against a metal storage cabinet just inside the door.

"Want to take a crack at it? It's tons of fun, let me tell you."

Judah poked at a stack of curling yellow legal pads before turning around.

"Are you kidding?"

Ramey raised her eyebrows as she grinned at him.

"Come on. It's only a lifetime of Sherwood's twisted accounts and cooked books. There's probably only thirty steps in each transaction to make sure they all come out clean in the wash."

Judah's lips cracked into a lopsided smile. There was a flickering spark in his gray eyes as he came across the garage toward her.

"Well, it's a good thing I've got you in my life, Ramey Barrow. You're the only one smart enough around here to make any sense of it."

"That the only reason you want me in your life?"

Judah put his arm around her waist and leaned into her.

"It's one."

He kissed her collarbone and Ramey cupped the back of his neck, running her fingers up into his dark hair. Judah needed a haircut. He always needed a haircut. She leaned her head against his as he looked over her shoulder and surveyed the salvage yard.

"How's he doing today?"

Ramey knew he meant Benji. Judah put his hand on her hip and she could feel the tension in the way he moved his body. But there was a weariness, too, in the slump of his spine. In the slackness of his fingers. The way he rested his chin against the curve of her shoulder as he took in Cannon Salvage, the front for the criminal enterprise he had so desperately wanted to escape, but had now circled back around to, like a snake devouring its own tail. Judah couldn't seem to break free of it. Ramey only hoped he still wanted to.

"He's the same. I moved out here to the garage so I could keep an eye on him."

"And how many pills, you think?"

Judah stepped away from her, but kept his eyes on his younger brother. Ramey shook her head.

"Hell if I know. He's been up and out of bed for two weeks now. I can't control what he takes anymore."

"I know."

Judah frowned and screwed his palms into his eyes as if trying to scour the dust of the day away. He walked over to the poker table and collapsed into one of the metal folding chairs. Ramey followed, grabbing her cigarettes and lighter from the desk and dropping them on the stained green felt in front of Judah. He lit two and handed her one as she sat down next to him.

"So. How'd it go today?"

Judah tapped his cigarette on the edge of the orange plastic ashtray.

"You really want to know?"

Ramey nodded, waiting. Judah leaned back in the chair and stared down at the table.

"I spent all day riding around with Gary, trying to track down Lonnie Able."

She frowned around her cigarette.

"All day? I thought the bar was just over in Keystone Heights."

"Turns out, when Lonnie isn't running bets for us over at The Drunk Goat, he's selling weed to middle schoolers down in Alachua. Who knew we had such a winner working for us?"

"Well, Sherwood knew how to pick 'em."

Judah wedged his cigarette in the ashtray and laced his hands behind his head.

"You have no idea. Between Lonnie and the old bag behind the bar at The Goat who, I swear to God, must use cat piss for perfume, I've never wanted to take a shower so bad in my life. And then being stuck in Gary's van all day. Nothing but Big Mac wrappers and balled up sweat socks rolling around. Porno mags in the floorboard. And the smell. Jesus, I tell you, something died in the back of that van. I mean, what the hell's wrong with these people?"

Ramey shook her head.

"Did you at least get the money?"

"The bartender had the cash for the cigarette load the Daughtry boys brought down from Alabama last month."

"That's good. But the rest? The take from the last two weeks? There wasn't too much going on, but the Brickyard should've brought in some action. It did up at The Ace and over at Ponies."

She watched the lines in Judah's face tighten.

"Lonnie was a few thousand light."

Ramey blinked the smoke out of her eyes. She tried to bite back her frustration.

"I guess everyone's trying to get theirs now that Sherwood's gone. Even Burke is talking about keeping a bigger cut of the vig. They're all a bunch of damn buzzards."

Judah nodded slowly.

"Yep."

Ramey picked at a scratch on the edge of the table.

"We need to get that money over to The Ace. With that big fight on pay-per-view coming up this week, Burke's gonna need it to start making loans now. We've already moved all the free cash around."

Judah nodded again.

"I know. I think we got Lonnie back in line, though. He's not real trouble, he's just trying to skim. Testing the waters now that Sherwood and Levi are out of the picture. That kinda shit. He just about had a heart attack when Gary moved in to make the point a little clearer. Started hyperventilating or something."

"Jesus."

She rolled her eyes and crushed out her cigarette.

"That hundred and fifty grand we put back in the ground sure would come in handy right about now."

Judah rested his chin on his hand and cut his eyes up at her.

"You know we can't touch it."

Ramey shot him a wry smile.

"I know. But a girl can dream, can't she?"

Judah scratched at the stubble on his cheeks, ignoring her comment.

"Lonnie's calling some guys. The rest of the money should be at The Goat tonight."

"So you gotta go back down there?"

Ramey could see the shadows hanging underneath Judah's eyes, the skin tight, the color of healing bruises. It was getting to be too much. No, it had been too much all along.

"Can't. I'm sending Gary back with Alvin. I got to meet Nash tonight."

Ramey frowned.

"Alone?"

Judah twisted his cigarette in the ashtray and then stubbed it out. He shoved the ashtray away from him and turned in his chair to face Ramey.

"Shouldn't be a problem. Nash is just handing over the take from Sipsy's."

Ramey chewed on her bottom lip while she picked at the felt tabletop.

"Yeah, but Nash has been operating all the way out in Putnam County on his own. You've never even laid eyes on the guy before. You don't know a thing about him. Or what he thinks of you taking Sherwood's place."

She abruptly turned toward Judah.

"I don't think you should go alone."

She started to reach for his hand, but realized that he wasn't looking at her. He was looking past her. Benji's gruff voice echoed across the garage.

"I'll go with you."

Ramey twisted around in her chair. Benji was leaning on his crutches in the open bay door behind her, his left leg jutting out awkwardly in front of him. Lesser was standing a few feet behind, cleaning grease out of his nails with a rag. Like Judah and Ramey, he was staring at Benji's grimy cast. Judah stood up and shook his head.

"No, Benji. Not yet. Give that leg a little while longer."

Ramey glanced at Benji and saw the bitterness stinging in his eyes. This wasn't the Benji she had known all her life, with blue eyes sparkling, an irrepressible smile and a joke for everyone. He had been the only Cannon who didn't have a tightness in his jaw or lines permanently creasing his brow. Didn't have devils of some kind or another always gnawing at his heart. She missed the old Benji who could bring light into a room just by crossing over the threshold. Her eyes settled on the tracks of puckered scars running down the left side of his face and she wondered if she would ever see that man again.

Lesser stepped forward, wringing the rag in both hands, and cast an uneasy side glance at Benji.

"I can go. I mean, if you need someone to go. I can do it."

Judah stared hard at Lesser for a moment, but finally turned to Benji.

"What do you think?"

Benji hopped a little as he adjusted himself on the crutches. He wouldn't meet anyone's gaze.

"Sure, send him. Why not. Gotta bust his Cannon cherry sometime."

Ramey looked up at Judah standing next to her. His eyes were locked with Benji's.

"All right."

Judah broke his gaze and turned to Lesser. He nodded toward the raised lift on the far side of the garage.

"But get the transmission in that Honda finished first. That stupid parking lot racer has been up there all week, taking up space. Ray's coming by in the morning to pick it up."

"Oh, right. Sure thing, I'm on it!"

Lesser grinned and darted away. Ramey waited until he was on the other side of the garage before turning to Judah.

"You sure about this? I can go."

Benji stumped forward on his crutches, his lips curling up into an ugly sneer.

"Give him a break, Ramey. Quit trying to be his mother."

Ramey stood up.

"Are you serious?"

Benji shrugged.

"Just let the kid go. We're gonna need him sooner or later to do more than just swing a monkey wrench."

"Oh, is that so?"

Ramey turned to Judah, but his face was expressionless, his eyes flat, telling her nothing. When he saw the look on her face, though, he gave her a half smile.

"It's fine. Benji's right, it'll be good for Lesser. He's just going along for the ride. Nothing to it."

Benji smirked at her before pivoting on his crutches and hobbling away. Judah watched him go and then turned back to Ramey. He put his hands on her shoulders and shook her lightly.

"Stop worrying. Lesser will be okay."

Ramey put her hands over Judah's, gripping his fingers in hers.

"Lesser's not the one I'm worried about."

Judah's face fell into a frown.

"Ramey, I need you to keep holding on just a little longer."

"Yeah, you keep saying that."

She averted her eyes, but there was no masking the sharp edge of accusation in her voice. Judah squeezed her shoulders and dipped his head, trying to make her look at him.

"I'm doing everything I can here. I know it was only supposed to be a week."

Ramey turned her head, still keeping her eyes away from him. A rough laugh caught in her throat.

"And then two. And then it was just a month. Just until Benji got out of the hospital. And then it was just until he got back on his feet. Well, his feet are under him, but it looks like we're still here."

Judah shook his head.

"You know it's not that simple."

She knew. They had been over it a hundred times before, but that still didn't make it any easier. Judah let go of her and took a step back.

"So, you just keep holding on. Okay? I need that from you. I've never let you down before and I'm damn sure not about to start now."

That wasn't entirely true. But Ramey wanted to believe it. She wanted to and needed to. Her chest heaved.

"Okay."

"And I'll be fine tonight."

Ramey finally turned to him and met his eyes.

"I know."

LESSER GLANCED OVER at Judah, relaxed behind the wheel, and then purposefully slouched down on the other end of the F-150's maroon vinyl bench seat. He cranked the window down and resisted the urge to brush his chin-length hair of out his face. It whipped across his eyes, but he tried to ignore it as he slung his elbow up on the edge of the window and squinted through the streaked windshield into the lowering twilight. He rode in silence for a few miles, trying to watch Judah out of the corner of his eye, but not be noticed doing so.

In the luminous green glow from the dash, Judah seemed so at ease, his arm half out the window, fingers just barely touching the steering wheel, a lit cigarette burning down in the other hand, resting lightly on the gearshift. The wind seemed only to graze his hair. Judah appeared to be completely engrossed in the monotony of the road ahead of them. Or maybe he was preoccupied with some kind of deep thoughts, of Ramey most likely, and Lesser was startled when Judah suddenly tossed his cigarette out the window and picked up the pack from the dash console.

"Go ahead, kid. It's not as glamorous as it looks."

Judah held the pack out to him. Lesser ducked his chin, embarrassed for staring. He quickly looked out the window and brushed his hair back behind his ears.

"No, thanks, Judah. That shit will kill you."

He heard Judah laugh and toss the pack down.

"You sound like Ramey."

Lesser fiddled with the fake diamond studs in his ears and then turned back to Judah.

"Yeah. Well, Ramey's something else, ain't she?"

He regretted it as soon as he spoke, but Judah only smiled, his eyes still on the road ahead.

"She sure is."

Lesser couldn't help himself.

"I mean, I meant that in the way, you know. I ain't moving in on your girl or nothing."

He regretted that even more. Lesser sat up straight and pushed his hair back again. He wished to God that it was long enough to pull back into a ponytail. He glanced nervously at Judah again, but Judah was still smiling.

"I didn't think you were, Lesser."

"I mean, I know, you and her. You're like the king and queen of the Cannons now. I would never even look at her that way. Though, I mean, it's not like I wouldn't neither. I mean, Ramey's like every guy's dream. Back when I was in school, me and all the boys, we—"

"Lesser."

Lesser clamped his jaw shut.

"I think you should probably stop talking about Ramey now."

Lesser bobbed his head emphatically.

"Yep, you got it."

He felt like an idiot. He'd been working at Cannon Salvage for almost two months now and yet he still constantly felt like he had to prove himself to Judah. Lesser knew he'd been hired as a mechanic only, just until Benji could get back on his feet, but he was determined to stick around. Benji had always been like an older brother to Lesser and most everything he knew about working on cars and bikes had come from him. Starting at about age twelve, Lesser had hung around the salvage yard, doing anything he could to make himself useful to the Cannons. First to Benji—running for tools, cleaning up, finishing jobs when one of his girlfriends stopped by and needed to be shown the inside of the office trailer—and then to Sherwood and the oldest Cannon brother, Levi. Sherwood had made it clear that he had absolutely no use for Lesser, and usually gave him a look like he was a stray dog about to get a kick in the ribs, but Levi had occasionally noticed him and let him make a run for sandwiches.

When Judah Cannon, only a few months out of prison, walked into Pizza Village and offered him a job, Lesser had stripped off his sauce-spattered apron right then and there. Lesser hadn't been able to believe his luck. Not that he'd wanted Benji to be hurt, he'd just about lost his lunch when he visited Benji in the hospital and saw the raw hamburger his face and left side had been ground into, but he knew that working as a grease monkey at the scrap yard was the surest way for him to become part of the Cannon crew. And that was all Lesser had ever wanted.

He watched Judah light another cigarette, his mouth pinching into a frown around it. Judah turned toward Lesser.

"What did you mean by king and queen?"

Lesser spread his hands out on the thighs of his jeans and looked down at his knuckles. Even in the dim light of the truck's interior he could see that they were still webbed with grease and grime.

"Well, you run the Cannons now that Sherwood's dead and Levi ain't nowhere to be found, right?"

Judah's eyes were back on the road and he didn't say anything.

"And the Cannons, well, it's like a kingdom."

Judah nodded slowly.

"I never quite thought about it like that."

"That's probably 'cause you're on the inside. Everybody else is on the outside, looking up at the castle. Either wanting to get in or scared you guys will come charging over the drawbridge with your army and shit."

Judah cut his eyes at Lesser.

"You pay attention in history class or something?"

Lesser grinned.

"Nah, this all comes from my old man. Back when he was still around, he'd talk about you guys like that. He was the one into history. Had all these books laying around that he liked to read."

"Your dad worked for my dad back in the day, didn't he?"

Lesser sat up straight.

"Yeah. He did a few things. He drove for Bullet Freight all his life and sometimes he'd call Sherwood about a load he was carrying. Cigarettes, or maybe TVs or something. He'd let himself get jacked so Sherwood could steal whatever he was hauling. We'd always know when Dad had been on a job for the Cannons 'cause he'd come home with a black eye or two. I don't think we kids were supposed to know, but 'course we did. They'd have to rough him up a little when they stole his load so the company wouldn't think he was in on it."

"Sounds typical."

"I don't think he minded. He'd always get paid afterward and take me and my sister to Chuck E. Cheese's down in Gainesville. A month or so after, he'd always buy us something big, too. New bikes or a Super Nintendo. Dad was good, he always waited until the heat was off him before spending the money. We even got kicked out of a place once and Dad had the cash for us to stay, but he wouldn't use it. Mom wasn't too happy about that."

Judah put both palms against the steering wheel and stretched.

"I bet not."

"Once he started spending a payout, though, he'd go on a binger. Never at home, but he'd be gone for a week or so up at my uncle's. That's how he died. Was so drunk one night, he stood out in the middle of a railroad crossing, playing his stupid harmonica, carrying on, I guess, and didn't even see the train coming."

Judah winced.

"That's a rough way to go."

Lesser looked down at his knuckles again.

"Yeah. I think he always thought he'd get it in the back of the head one night. Instead of just breaking his nose, Levi'd put one in him to keep him quiet. Or just because, you know. So, that's what Dad meant when he said you Cannons were like a kingdom. He'd say that he wasn't part of the inner court like some of the guys were. Like Leroy, Ramey's dad. My old man said he was just a soldier. And soldiers could never know when their time was gonna be up."

Judah drummed his fingers on the steering wheel.

"Sherwood was a king, huh? That's how people saw him?"

Lesser nodded.

"And now you've taken his place."

"I wouldn't say that, Lesser."

"And you're gonna be an even greater king than he was. Because you've got Ramey."

Judah's mouth twisted into a smile, but it was an ugly smile.

"Because I've got a queen."

Lesser couldn't tell if what he was saying was doing him any favors with Judah or not. He probably shouldn't have said anything in the first place. Judah's face had fallen into an unreadable mask and Lesser grew more and more uncomfortable as a mile, then two, passed while they rode again in silence. Judah had said that they were meeting Nash somewhere out near Carraway and Lesser reckoned they were getting close. He was already nervous about acting right on his first run with Judah. Now he was worried he'd pissed Judah off before they'd even gotten there. The silence in the truck was killing him and suddenly he blurted out the first thing he could think of, just to hear the tone in Judah's voice and know where he stood.

"So, how did Sherwood really die, anyway?"

Judah glanced over at him sharply and Lesser cringed. Why, why couldn't he just keep his damn mouth shut? Judah turned his eyes back to the road without answering him and Lesser continued, stumbling over his words.

"I mean, everyone says he died in the fire up at that church in Kentsville. That he was in a shootout with those biker dudes. They torched the place and Sherwood was caught inside."

Judah turned the wheel with both hands, guiding the truck off the highway and onto a narrow side road. The crumbling pavement was rough underneath the tires, but Judah didn't bother to avoid the potholes. Lesser gripped the door handle as they bounced along without losing any speed. Judah didn't look at him.

"If that's what everyone says, then that's what happened."

"But why did it happen?"

Judah's mouth was set in a grim line.

"If you'd paid more attention in school like you should've, then you'd know. Every king has their day, kid. And every king falls. No one can reign forever."

THE GLOW FROM a buzzing orange street light heralded their arrival and Judah swerved the truck around the last bend in the road. He rolled to a stop in front of the two gas pumps outside Jedidiah's Food and Fixins and cut the engine. He kept the headlights on, illuminating the rest of the road as it disappeared into the near primordial swamp and lowland woods. Judah sat for a moment, just watching the road, listening to the night. Bullfrogs. Crickets. Insects droning away. The birds that swallowed them whole in midair, calling out to one another in the dark.

"What is this place?"

Judah turned to Lesser, wide-eyed and leaning out the window.

"Jedidiah's. Last stop for beer, ice and bait before you hit Kettle Creek down that a way."

Judah gestured toward the empty road and then reached for the .45 under his seat. Lesser was still eyeing the store front with its two neon beer and ice signs flickering in the windows. Paper signs lettered in black marker covered the rest of the glass: *Red Worms Sold Here. Boiled Peanuts. Cash Only. Lotto Cigs Sandwiches.* It looked like any other country store, with a low, sloping tin roof hanging down over the two wooden benches and tin bucket full of sand and cigarette butts on the porch. Judah's truck was the only vehicle in the dirt lot. Lesser leaned back against the seat.

"Those gas pumps still work?"

Judah dropped the clip in the gun to check the bullets. He glanced up at the two pumps, their nozzles hanging haphazardly against the sides. Peeling rust spotted the face of the chest-high dispensers. Judah shrugged.

"Probably. This place does some business during the daytime. Benji and I used to drive down here when we were about your age. You go a mile or two more down the road and you'll hit some of the best catfish spots this side of the St. Johns River. You gotta drive the forty miles from Silas, but it's worth it. At least, it used to be."

Judah slammed the clip back into the gun and yanked the slide. He jutted his chin toward the compartment in front of Lesser.

"In there."

Lesser thumbed open the glovebox and pulled out a .38 Special. He was holding it awkwardly by the barrel. Judah suddenly thought that bringing Lesser along might not have been the brightest idea after all. But he had needed Alvin and Gary to be sure that Lonnie came through with the cash. And even if Benji had just stayed in the truck, he was a risk. Judah wasn't sure he'd have been able to stand the drive with his brother, anyway. These days, he did as much as he could not to be alone with Benji and the misery that tinged his every glance and word. Misery and silent accusation.

Only twice had Benji outright blamed Judah for his involvement in the robbery whose retribution had caused him to be dragged down County Road 225 behind a Harley for a quarter of a mile. Once in the hospital, a few days after Benji had woken up, and once right after Judah and Ramey had taken Benji home to live with them in the house they had just rented at the end of Redgrave Road. Judah had tried to cut through the Oxy haze and explain to Benji that their father, who had led the robbery on the outlaw motorcycle gang and then betrayed his own family, was dead. Only Ramey knew, and would ever know, exactly what had gone down between Judah, Sherwood, Sister Tulah and the Scorpions, but Judah had wanted to make it clear to Benji that things had been settled. That he and Ramey were determined to take care of Benji until the broken bones in his leg and the massive lacerations all up and down his body had healed. Neither conversation had gone well, and both times Ramey had been forced to pull Judah from Benji's bedside before he said something he would regret. She had known Benji was half out of his mind with pain and the seeds of resentment worming their way up to the surface, like shards of embedded shrapnel.

Now, three months after Benji had first been admitted to the ICU, there were no more raving accusations. No more spitting tirades. Only hollow glances or deep, seething glares, depending on how long it had been since Benji had swallowed his last pill. No, Judah much preferred Lesser's guileless chatter to an hour car ride with his brother.

Judah pointed to the gun resting in Lesser's lap.

"You know how to use that?"

Lesser picked it up and stretched his arms out, pointing the gun straight at the windshield. Judah slammed Lesser's arm down.

"Jesus. Why don't you get out and wave it around some?"

Lesser dipped his head and looked down at the gun he was now cradling with both hands.

"Sorry."

Judah shook his head.

"Just stick it in your waistband and leave it there. You're not gonna need to use it."

"Okay."

Judah turned back to his own gun. He should have brought Ramey, really. He didn't need backup, he just needed someone beside him. Someone who could keep a cool head if Nash decided to be difficult. But things were tough enough already with Ramey. She probably wouldn't have said anything, but she would have been thinking it the whole time. They were supposed to be getting out. Hell, they were never supposed to be in. And yet here they were. Every day being swept out further with the tide; every day watching the shoreline become more and more hazy in the distance. Judah should have listened to her. He should have kept his foot on the gas until Florida was nothing more than a rearview mirror memory.

Ramey had been hell-bent on running. Especially since they were in possession of the hundred and fifty thousand dollars that had first been stolen from Sister Tulah and Jack O' Lantern Austin, leader of the Scorpions motorcycle club, and then from Sherwood himself. During the shootout at the church, Judah had killed Jack with a wild shot. He had also stood up in front of Sister Tulah and all but admitted that he had her money. He and Ramey had fled the scene of the burning church, and the chaos and uncertainty of who was still alive and who was dead, with the intention of collecting the money buried in Hiram's minefield and hightailing it. The plan had been to leave Bradford County for good. To disappear completely. Use the cash to start a new life together, one that wasn't shadowed by the reputation and deeds of the infamous Cannon clan.

Doubt, however, had soon crept into his mind. Doubt and guilt, all tangled up with the image of Benji lying motionless in a hospital bed, his face and body mangled, his mind lost somewhere in the depths of a coma. Before they had even made it across the Florida-Georgia line, the guilt had given way to shame and Judah had felt its weight pressing down upon him, forcing him into a mire of degradation. If he had fled, if he had abandoned his brother, Judah knew he would have never forgiven himself. He would be a coward. He would be contemptable.

As expected, Ramey hadn't seen the situation in quite the same light. She had, however, agreed to stop and stay the night at the Peacock Inn in Valdosta so they could talk it through. Judah's mind had already been made up, though, and he had set to work trying to convince Ramey before they'd even walked through the motel room door. Judah had been determined: he wasn't going to leave Benji. But he certainly wasn't going to leave Ramey, either.

Thankfully, the TV news had been on his side. After an hour of arguing, with Ramey alternating between reason and panic, and Judah single-mindedly appealing to her conscience, Ramey had turned on the television in frustration. According to the Channel 6 Evening News, the remaining Scorpions had been arrested only a few miles from the church. Sister Tulah had lost an eye, but had made it out of the fire alive. In her interviews, Judah and Ramey hadn't been mentioned. Neither had Sherwood. Sister Tulah had assumed that the man who had gouged out her eye, and whose remains had been found in what was left of the church, was one of the outlaw bikers. When the body was identified as Sherwood Cannon, Tulah had appeared astonished and then bemused. Judah had scrutinized Sister Tulah's placid face on the fuzzy television screen as she stood next to the shell of her church, her idiot-looking nephew beside her, and responded with shock in learning that she had innocently stumbled into a feud between rival gangsters. Sister Tulah had offered no idea as to why her humble church had been the stage for so dramatic an encounter.

Over takeout pizza on their lumpy motel bed, Judah had laid out his case with a clear finality to the woman he was confident would stand by him. Sherwood was dead. Levi was missing. The Scorpions, or most of them anyway, were locked up. Shelia, the crazy bitch who had set up both Benji in the bar and Judah at the church, had disappeared into thin air. And Sister Tulah was claiming she had nothing to do with either the bikers or the Cannons. Judah had figured that she most likely believed Sherwood had lied to her about having the money in the first place, and Judah rolling up on the scene was a just a family matter. Even if she did suspect that Judah had the money, he had doubted Tulah would do anything about it. With all of the media and police attention on her now, she was too exposed. Sherriff Dodger had been on the Cannon dime for years, so Judah didn't expect any trouble from that quarter. They would be safe. They would be there when, and if, Benji woke up. Judah had assured her; they would only stay in Silas as long as they absolutely had to.

But once Benji had woken up, once he had been assured that his brother would survive, Judah couldn't just forsake him. Not after what he saw burning behind Benji's eyes. The resentment. The silent castigation. So one week had turned into two. And then three. Then they had brought Benji home. Meanwhile, Sherwood's ghost had been haunting their every step. Judah had quickly discovered that the criminal enterprise Sherwood spent his life building would not simply crumble with his death. There were too many people involved, too many ongoing deals with strings attached, and, by necessity, Judah had begun the convoluted process of attempting to unravel, and extricate himself from, his father's notorious legacy.

It was easier said than done. Every time Judah thought he was close, another unforeseen strand slipped around his neck like a noose and threatened to strangle him. Three weeks had become three months and they were still no closer to being free. And he could see it in Ramey's eyes: she was beginning to doubt him. She was beginning to lose faith.

Judah opened the truck door and stepped out into the sweltering night. He came around to the passenger's side and hooked his wrists over the lip of the open window.

"Let's go, Lesser."

Judah stepped back and ran his thumb over a deep gouge in the red two-tone paint job and then yanked the door open, waiting. Lesser slid out of the truck and jammed the .38 into his pants. He stood up straight and flung his shoulders back. He didn't look as awkward as he had in the truck and Judah nodded his approval. Lesser put his fingertips in the pockets of his baggy jeans.

"We're the only ones here."

Judah glanced around the empty parking lot, even though it was obvious they were alone.

"We are. I'm going inside to check things out."

"What do you want me to do?"

Judah started walking toward the store.

"Just wait out here on the porch."

Lesser caught up to him and Judah clapped him on the shoulder.

"And relax. This isn't a big deal. He's just handing over some cash."

"It sounded before like you ain't even know this guy, Nash."

"I don't. But he worked for Sherwood for years. Collects from Sipsy's out here in Putnam and the couple of mom-and-pop operations we sell cigarettes and booze to."

Judah pointed toward the front of the store.

"This being one of them. Nash is kinda on his own all the way out here, which is why I haven't met him until now."

Judah jerked the store's door handle and a bell jangled. Lesser was still right at his heels.

"So he's one of ours, then? There shouldn't be no trouble, right?"

"Right. Just stay out here a minute."

Judah left Lesser standing conspicuously outside and walked into the brightly lit store. The setup of the place was exactly as he remembered it from fifteen years ago. Two sets of shelves running down the middle of the narrow building displayed everything from canned dog food to bug spray to boxes of instant macaroni and cheese. Plastic bins lined up against the windows housed crickets and worms. Judah walked to the back cooler next to the ice machine and slid open its metal lid, reaching in to pull out a glass bottle of RC Cola. The fluorescent light over his head sizzled as he popped the top against the opener screwed into the wall and slowly made his way toward the front of the store. The single restroom had an Out of Order sign taped to the door. Judah took his time, sipping the soda and keeping his on eye on Lesser, still standing out on the porch. Judah set the half-empty bottle on the counter and waited for Jedidiah to look up from the local Mugshot Magazine he had propped up against the cash register. The old man finally raised his eyes and puckered his mouth. He didn't appear to recognize Judah.

"That it?"

Judah took out his wallet.

"That's it. How's business?"

Jedidiah shrugged his shoulders. His faded Marine Corps T-shirt hung loosely around the wattle of his neck.

"It's business."

Judah pulled out two dollars and laid them on the counter. He took another swallow of cola as the old man picked up the bills and replaced them with three quarters. He stared at Judah with vacant eyes and Judah stared back. He remained standing in front of Jedidiah, slowly finishing the bottle. Judah had one sip left when the bell tied to the door clanged and Lesser poked his head inside the store.

"Judah, someone's pulling in."

Judah tilted his head back and then set the empty bottle on the counter. He scooped the quarters into his palm and nodded once at Jedidiah.

"Good talking to you."

The old man grunted and crossed his sagging arms over his chest. Judah followed Lesser out onto the porch and stood next to him, watching the SUV roll in to a stop, facing Judah's truck. Immediately, two men got out and the one with his dark hair slicked back and a patchy mustache sprouting over his thin lips came straight toward Judah. His bedazzled cowboy shirt winked in the glaring light and he stopped fifteen feet away from the porch, waiting. Judah turned his head slightly toward Lesser.

"Just stay here. Don't do anything, don't say anything. Just keep your eyes open and your mouth shut. And watch Mr. Clean over there."

Judah cut his eyes to the barrel-chested bald man standing next to the SUV and didn't wait for Lesser's response. He came down the porch steps, but still kept some distance between himself and Nash. They looked at each other for a good long moment and then Judah narrowed his eyes.

"Let me guess. You don't have it."

Nash reached into his pocket and pulled out a single toothpick wrapped in plastic. He peeled it open and stuck it in the corner of his mouth. Judah would have bet anything it was mint flavored. Nash scratched at his mustache.

"Hey, what do you know? You're smarter than your daddy always said you were."

"Pretty sure Sherwood never said two words about me to you."

"Well, now that there's the truth."

Judah glanced over Nash's shoulder at the man still standing by the SUV. He was making no secret of the pistol tucked into the front of his pants. The gun's grip was jammed up into his overhanging gut. Judah fought the urge to turn around and just hoped Lesser was keeping his cool. It was obvious now that this wasn't a cash handoff; it was a pissing contest. Nash was here to size him up in the wake of Sherwood's death, that was all. Judah suddenly felt more tired than he had in weeks.

He took a step forward. Judah knew the exhaustion was showing on his face, but he didn't care. He shook his head slightly.

"Do you not have my money or are you just not giving me my money?"

Nash pinched the toothpick from his lips.

"Whoa. You don't mince words, do you? Sherwood would be halfway into some pointless story right about now. Talking my damn ear off."

Nash gave a forced chuckle and stuck the toothpick back in his mouth. He turned to the man behind him, who didn't even crack a smile. The bald man looked bored and Judah took note of this as he crossed his arms.

"I guess you just figured out that I'm not like Sherwood, then. So which is it? The money?"

Judah watched the lines wrinkle across Nash's forehead.

"You in a hurry or something? We don't even know each other yet and you're rushing straight into things. You got something better to do? Somewhere you need to be? You got a girl you need to get back to?"

He heard Lesser inhale and huff behind him, but Judah didn't blink.

"Let's just say that I've already met my asshole quota for the day."

"Are you calling me an asshole?"

"Yes. And one I don't have time for. If you hadn't noticed."

Nash rolled the toothpick from one side of his mouth to the other and then curled his lip up in a smirk.

"Ramey, right? Good looking, but got a mouth on her, I hear. That the piece you're so anxious to get home to?"

"Trust me, she's got even less time for you than I do."

Nash gave a laugh that ended in a sneer.

"I bet."

Judah sighed and then pointedly looked over his shoulder at Lesser. The kid's face was pale, but he was standing tall, just taking it in. He realized that Lesser might not be too bad at this after all. Judah turned back around and set his gaze squarely on Nash.

"Okay. We're done here."

Judah took a few steps in the direction of his truck, but Nash put out his hands to stop him.

"Wait, now, just wait a sec. Don't you want to hear what I'm offering?"

He stopped walking, but didn't look at Nash.

"Not really."

"So you already know that I could double what Sherwood was bringing in every week out here. You already know all about that, huh?"

Judah turned to Nash.

"Selling more than untaxed cigarettes, I'm guessing."

"Much more."

Judah exhaled heavily.

"Look, Nash. You want to run dope, go right ahead. I ain't stopping you. Good luck. Godspeed. Have at it. But you are not selling through Sherwood's bars and using his connections. Got it?"

Nash grinned wide, displaying uneven, yellow teeth.

"But they ain't Sherwood's no more, are they? Last I heard, Sherwood had hopped on his last rattler and Levi had gone underground. So it's just you. And your gimp brother. And your girl."

Nash set his gaze directly on Lesser for the first time.

"And this Boy Scout over here."

Judah shook his head.

"Not interested, Nash. So I'm going now. Get me the money you owe me and then get the hell off my payroll. I think you understand my policy on assholes now and where you fit into it. You and I are done."

Nash spit the toothpick out into the dirt. He put his hands on his hips.

"So, you're telling me that I gotta go back to Weaver with nothing but that?"

Judah had no idea who Nash was talking about, but he didn't miss a beat.

"Looks like it."

He took another few steps toward his truck and then heard a buzzing in his ears. The air pressure seemed to drop all around him and, in a split second, Judah knew what was going to happen.

"Judah Cannon, wrong answer."

Judah barely caught the light glinting off the barrel of the gun as he dove behind the gas pump. He slid in the dirt and had his .45 in hand when the second shot went off. He aimed over the pump and fired, winging the bald man as he climbed into the SUV. Another bullet whizzed past Judah's head, but he kept firing, missing Nash both times as he flung himself into the passenger's seat. The SUV swung around and peeled out of the parking lot with a squeal. Judah stood up and emptied the clip, even though he knew it was pointless. He stood panting for a moment and then slung the empty gun on top of the pump. He rubbed his forehead violently, trying to process what had just happened and trying to get his heart to stop banging around inside his chest. He took a deep breath, holding it in for as long as he could.

"Goddamn it."

Judah stared down the empty road.

"You okay, Lesser?"

There was no answer.

"Lesser?"

Judah slowly turned around. The realization was like slamming into a brick wall.

"Jesus, no."

Judah tilted his head and bit down hard on his lip. He clenched his fists and looked away, up into the yawning mouth of the night sky.

"No. No, no, no, no."

He slowly brought his gaze back down to Lesser's body, splayed out awkwardly in the dirt. Judah brought his wrist up to his mouth, trying to keep his emotions back behind his teeth. He walked over to Lesser and squatted down beside his twisted torso. Judah looked the body up and down. One bullet had gone into Lesser's face, just beneath his right eye, and the other into his chest. Judah wasn't sure which shot was the one that had killed him. He touched Lesser's neck, slick with warm blood, and pressed hard. The life must have gone out of him almost instantly. Judah pulled his fingers back and let his hands dangle between his knees. He rocked back on his heels and looked up at the sky again. He was vaguely aware that his face was wet.

Jedidiah came out onto the front porch of the store and stood with his arms crossed, gazing down at the scene before him. Judah found the old man's face and blinked it into focus. He choked out the words.

"Call 9-1-1. Now. Please."

Jedidiah's face was completely devoid of expression.

"Why? I didn't see nothing."

CHAPTER 2

BROTHER FELTON KNELT down on the thin, bristly Astroturf lining the floor of his camper and pressed his nose against the glass. The unblinking eye of a scarlet kingsnake was only a few inches from his own. Felton rested back on his thick haunches and considered the snake, motionless, coiled up in a knot in the corner of the terrarium, its narrow head resting on a dead branch, its black eye fixed in space. He wasn't sure if the snake could see him through the glass or not. Felton smiled to himself and murmured in a sing-song voice.

"Red on black, friend of Jack. Red on yellow, kill a fellow."

Felton was proud of himself. Most of the snakes in his collection were dull in color. Black racers. Rattlers. Garters. He had caught a yellow rat snake a few years back, but it hadn't survived long in captivity. In comparison to the rest, this new find with its colorful banding was a showstopper. Felton hoped the snake was happy with its new home.

He rose to his knees again and jerked a damp handkerchief out of the back pocket of his polyester pants. Despite the rattling box fan jammed into the corner, the camper was sweltering. The exposed bulb overhead was switched off, but the seven heat lamps for the terrariums were still blazing away, their carmine glow creating stark, eerie shadows on the walls. Even over the whirr of the fan and the burble from the turtle tank, Felton could hear the lamps, buzzing above the snakes. He pressed the handkerchief to his moist upper lip and then dragged it across the top of his balding head. Felton wadded the handkerchief up and stuffed it back in his pocket before patting down the fringe of brown hair circling the back and sides of his head. He tugged at his pinching collar, but didn't undo the top button of his dress shirt. Still on his knees, Felton straightened his back out and clasped his pudgy hands tightly in front of his chest. He bowed his head.

The sweat continued to trickle down the sides of his face and neck. He didn't have to pray surrounded by the sizzling heat lamps, he had a new camper now, set up only a few yards from the one housing his reptiles, but old habits die hard. Felton scrunched up his face and squeezed his eyes tightly shut as he pleaded for God to forgive him.

Three months ago, Brother Felton had taken a life. He had lifted the heavy wooden crucifix from the back wall of the church and bludgeoned Sherwood Cannon in the head. Yes, Sherwood was a bad man. Yes, Felton had killed him to save his aunt's life. And no, Felton would never be blamed for it, never be punished for it, because no one would ever know what he had done. No one except for Sister Tulah. And God, who had seen it all. And the snakes and turtles in the stifling camper, the secret keepers of all his whispered sins.

Soon after the church fire, Felton had moved out of Tulah's house. He had emptied his savings account and bought the second camper, this one with a window air conditioning unit, a stand-up shower and a miniature kitchen where he could microwave his Lean Cuisines in peace. Sister Tulah had been furious. Although she had temporarily banished him from her house in the wake of his botched attempt to intercede in her affairs with the Cannons and the Scorpions, she had obviously expected him to move back into his child-sized bedroom at the top of the stairs. She had been livid when Felton had refused. He knew it wasn't because she cared for him or would miss him, but because he was doing something on his own. Independent of her. Felton would no longer be always within shouting distance, no longer directly under the grind of her thumb. Though it sickened him to admit it, Sherwood's death had in many ways been a blessing for Felton. It had given him confidence. It had shown him that he was capable of action. And it had given him the courage to look his aunt in her one, pale, remaining eye and not give in when she demanded that he return to her house.

Brother Felton thumped his clenched hands against his forehead. It was wrong to think of death that way. As a means to a positive end for him. It was wrong and it made him writhe with shame. He opened his eyes and stared up at the low, cobwebbed ceiling of the camper, beseeching God to have mercy on him. But God was quiet. Outside of The Last Steps of Deliverance Church of God, away from the centrifugal power of Sister Tulah and her direct line to the Holy Spirit, God didn't even seem to exist. Felton let his hands drop to his sides and his head sink. He had been concentrating so hard that he'd made himself dizzy, but it didn't matter. Praying on his own was futile.

He started to stand up, but froze when his eyes fell on the terrarium in front of him. The kingsnake had moved. It was no longer locked in repose on the branch in the corner of the tank, but had slithered up to the glass and raised its body up unnaturally. It was swaying back and forth, but its obsidian eyes were fixed on Felton. The snake's split tongue flickered. Brother Felton leaned forward, curious but also wary. When the snake eventually spoke, Felton fell backward on his ass.

"Rise up."

Felton trembled and his eyes darted around the camper. The door was closed, the shadows against the low red light were still. He was alone. Felton glanced back at the kingsnake. It flicked its tongue again.

"Rise up."

He carefully got to his knees and brought his face closer to the glass. The snake tilted its head, almost as if it was considering Felton for a moment.

Brother Felton licked his dry lips and tried to speak.

"Snake?"

The kingsnake righted its head. Felton looked around the camper again; he was still alone.

"Snake? Did you say something?"

"Rise up. The time has come. The time is yours."

The snake was definitely talking to him. Felton's whole body was shaking now. He pressed his palms to the glass and nodded to the snake. He didn't know what else to do.

"Yes? What time? What has come?"

The snake rose up another few inches and Felton followed it with his eyes.

"*Behold, I have refined thee, but not with silver; I have chosen thee in the furnace of affliction.*"

Brother Felton gasped. The snake was not only talking to him, it was quoting scripture. From the Book of Isaiah.

"What does that mean? What are you saying?"

The snake blinked at him.

"Rise up. Your time has come. Your task will be revealed. Rise up."

Felton shook his head.

"I don't understand. I don't understand what that means."

The snake dropped back to the base of the terrarium. Felton yelled at it through the glass.

"Snake! Snake, I don't understand!"

The kingsnake slithered back to the branch. It looped its body around and buried its head underneath one of its coils. Felton mashed his face up against the glass. The outside of the terrarium was slick with sweat. He waited, but the snake didn't move. Finally, Brother Felton collapsed backward onto the floor. A dull headache had settled in a band across his temples and he closed his eyes. He drew his knees up to his chest and whispered.

"I don't understand."

THE FRONT DOOR creaked open and startled Ramey awake. She had been sitting at the kitchen table in the dim light, trying to wait up for Judah. Ramey lifted her head from her folded arms and stretched her shoulders, trying to shake off the sleep. She started to brush the tangle of hair back from her eyes, but then caught herself. No one had stepped into the hallway. Ramey glanced across the kitchen. There was a .45 in the drawer next to the stove, but she'd have to make it all the way around the table to get to it. A double-barrel was leaning in a corner of the pantry behind her, but again, she'd have to get up and open the door first. Ramey scanned the table in front of her. Ashtray. Squashed pack of cigarettes. Bic lighter. Two empty Bud bottles. Ramey got her feet under her and leaned forward, reaching for the neck of one of the bottles. Her fingers closed around the smooth glass and she was just about to smash the bottle against the edge of the table when Judah stepped out of the shadows and into the kitchen doorway. Ramey almost choked.

"Jesus Christ, Judah."

Judah remained standing in the doorway, lit faintly from behind by the hall light above the stairs. Ramey let go of the bottle and fell back in her chair. She braced herself against the table, forcing herself to breath evenly.

"You have got to stop doing that to me. One of these days it's not gonna end well."

Judah didn't say anything. His hands were deep in his pockets and his head was tilted down. His face was shadowed in the umbral light, but Ramey could tell that something was wrong. The way his shoulders were hunched. The tendons in his neck. Something had happened.

"Sit down. I'll get you a beer."

Ramey started to stand up, but Judah took a step forward and held out his hand to stop her. He shook his head slightly. Now that Ramey could see his face, she was stunned. The usual ghostly shadows of the last few months were still there, but his eyes were now also swollen and bloodshot. Judah had been crying. Ramey lowered herself back in the seat. The last time Ramey had seen

Judah cry, he had been sixteen and spitting nails with angst and hatred toward his father. Ramey spoke carefully.

"What is it? What happened?"

Judah's gaze roamed around the kitchen, alighting on anything but her. He turned to look over his shoulder into the darkened living room. Ramey knew he was trying to compose himself, that he would want to speak without his voice cracking. She could tell from the way he kept blinking and widening his eyes that he had decided to be done with crying.

"Where's Benji?"

Judah's voice came out steady but sharp. He still wouldn't look at her. Ramey nodded toward the downstairs bedroom.

"Asleep."

Judah seemed to think about this a moment. Ramey watched his eyes, shifting back and forth. She wanted to go to him, but knew this way was better. He needed her to wait. Finally, Judah exhaled, long and loud, and raised his eyes. They were haunted.

"Lesser got shot."

"What?"

Ramey stood up and clapped her hands over her mouth. Judah didn't seem to register her reaction at all.

"He didn't make it."

"Oh my God."

Ramey dropped her hands and leaned against the edge of the table, staring down at the scratched woodgrain. Her vision went blurry for a moment. Lesser, who was just a kid. Who had spent the last month and a half trailing behind her at the salvage yard, being extra polite, earnest and smitten in his teenage way. Lesser, who had sat at this very kitchen table just the morning before, eating biscuits with molasses, telling her and Judah about this girl he had his eye on. She was chunky, but cute. He was taking her to a concert down in Gainesville next Saturday night. Ramey had swatted at him and told him he'd better behave.

"Judah, what happened?"

He looked away from her, intent now on studying the bubbling linoleum at his feet. Judah's voice was hollow.

"The guy we were meeting. Nash. He was aiming for me. He went to shoot me. I got out of the way, but Lesser didn't."

Ramey started to come around the table toward him.

"Oh, Judah…"

He held out his hand again.

"Don't."

Ramey stopped herself. She stood awkwardly in the middle of the kitchen and wrapped her arms around her ribcage. There was something harrowing behind Judah's eyes. Something that had been shredded. Shattered. Ramey knew Judah needed this distance. She knew, too, that later, in the early morning, with the mockingbirds whistling outside the open window and the ceiling fan clicking and swaying above them, she would turn to him in the dark and they would hollow out a space for one another. The rumbling fault lines cutting between them would be stilled.

But for now, Judah only looked at her with eyes smoldering and teeth grinding back and forth as he worked at something she wasn't yet a part of. He dipped his head slightly, almost in apology, and turned his back to her.

CHAPTER 3

SPECIAL AGENT CLIVE Grant snapped his sunglasses off and pinched the bridge of his nose. He started to lean back against the side of his midnight blue Charger, but caught himself. Clive turned and ran a finger over the outside of the back window. He had driven it through a Soap-N-Splash on the way down, but already the car was coated in a thick, sticky layer of pollen, road dust and lovebug guts. Clive had been in Kentsville less than an hour and already he hated it. He hated the suffocating heat and the slow-ass traffic, crawling through the speed traps lining Highway 301. He hated the good old boys, chewing on beef jerky and spitting Skoal outside the gas station, staring at him like they'd never seen a black man in an Armani suit before. It was 2011, for Christ's sake. Had they never turned on the news and seen who the president of the United States of America was? Clive plucked at his collar, damp with sweat, and glanced down at the open notebook in his hand. More than the weather, the roads or the locals, Clive hated the case he had been assigned.

The sooner he could wrap up his report, though, the sooner he could return to civilized Atlanta, and hopefully on to something with potential. Clive slipped the notebook back inside his gray, pinstriped jacket and buttoned it awkwardly;

he was still getting used to carrying the Glock again. He hadn't even fired it since basic training back at Glynco. Clive flapped the front of the jacket and ran his fingers up and down the length of his silk tie to regain his composure. He put the past year out of his mind and forced himself to concentrate on the task at hand.

The address he had punched into the car's GPS had taken him to a strip mall on the south side of town. A coin laundromat and a Payless shoe store bracketed the ends of it and the middle was taken up by a vacant store front, a nail salon and a used furniture store. That's all the white lettered sign above the unit proclaimed: *Used Furniture*. No name, no brand. His car was the only one parked in front of it. The number was correct though, 3800, and Clive strode up to the glass front door. A wrinkled Hispanic woman sitting in a plastic patio chair outside the laundromat gave Clive a vacant stare. The wilted Chihuahua at her feet didn't even bother to raise its head, let alone yap. He tried the door, but it wouldn't budge. Clive rapped his knuckles hard on the door and cupped his hands around his face to peer inside. He couldn't see much more than vague shapes and shadows through the dusty glass. Clive stepped back and pounded on the door again.

"This is Special Agent Grant. I need you to open up."

The Chihuahua flopped over on its side, panting in the heat. Clive banged a few more times and then put his face up against the glass again. He could see movement inside; a slender figure was slowly coming toward him. When the door swung out a few inches, Clive had his badge ready. He snapped it open and shoved it forward.

"ATF. My name is Special Agent Grant. I need to speak with Tulah Atwell. Is she here?"

The door opened wider and an old man shuffled forward. He was skeletal, with a few shreds of limp, colorless hair combed over his age-spotted skull. His cheeks were deeply sunken in and, oddly enough, considering the dimly lit interior of the store, he wore large, dark, wraparound sunglasses. Clive thought maybe he was blind. The man didn't respond to his introduction and only stood there, blocking the entrance. Maybe he was deaf, too. Clive raised his voice.

"ATF. That's a federal organization, in case you hadn't heard of it. Now let me in."

The old man didn't move. Clive put his badge away and braced his hand against the doorframe.

"This is the business address for Tulah Atwell, correct? So, whether you like it or not, I'm coming in to check the premise. That okay with you?"

The old man retreated back into the shadows of the store and Clive decided to take that for a yes. He wrenched the door open all the way and stepped inside to follow the man through the maze of clutter. When they reached the middle of the store, the old man turned abruptly to him and pointed to a beige leather armchair surrounded by spindly floor lamps. Clive eyed the chair.

"All right. But you'd better be getting Mrs. Atwell for me. I don't have time for games. Especially not in a place like this."

He thought the old man nodded slightly before disappearing, but it was hard to tell. Clive gingerly lowered himself into the armchair, trying not to think about what sort of bugs were probably scuttling around in its crevasses. There wasn't really anywhere to stand, though, without bumping into or tripping over something. Now that he had a chance to look around, Clive realized that the store wasn't cluttered, so much as stuffed to the gills. Kitchen tables were stacked on top of dining room tables and loveseats were balanced on top of couches. Everywhere he looked there were chairs, bookcases, lamps and desks crammed one on top of the other. There was only one narrow, crooked path leading from the front of the store to the back.

As Clive peered through the gloom, he became aware that it wasn't just every inch of the floor that had been taken up. He couldn't see any of the paint on the walls, either. Clocks, paintings, photographed portraits and framed velvet string art covered every available space. There appeared to be no rhyme or reason to anything, as hotel beach scenes were crammed right up against maps of the Soviet Union and life size cardboard cutouts of old movie stars. Clive dared to lift his head and then wished he hadn't. Suspended from the ceiling were rows and rows of seashell wind chimes, potted plant hangers and macramé fruit baskets. Clive, whose own apartment back on Peachtree Street was minimalist to say the least, shut his eyes and tried not to notice his skin crawling beneath his suit.

Clive was still being punished and he knew it. He had only been with the ATF two years, but he was already at the top of his supervisor's shit list. Last summer, with just about a year under his belt, Clive had been assigned an undercover bit in a sting operation to bring down a gun ring running out of Bankhead. All Clive had to do was go along with two other undercover agents who had been working the case for the past nine months. All he had been required to do, Lopez had bellowed at him over and over, was to walk into The Honey Club with the other agents, sit in a booth with them and look like a thug. That was all. Just be muscle. Eye candy. But ten minutes into the meeting with Papa Smurf and Shakey G, Clive had blown it. He still wasn't exactly sure how it happened. Clive had been antsy from the get-go and he was positive that he saw one of Smurf's guys pull something out of his pocket. Something that could have been a gun. Next thing he knew, he was yelling "Special Agent Grant!" and trying to tackle a teenager with a pack of Twix in his hand. His cover, and the case, was blown and Clive had been relegated to desk duty ever since. If it wasn't for his father up in D.C., Lopez reminded him about once a week, he would have been terminated. Apparently, he should be grateful that he'd finally been let out of the basement records room and given assignments again. Like this one. Whoop-de-do.

When Clive opened his eyes, he realized that the old man was standing at the back of the store, staring at him. Or in his direction; it was hard to tell with the glasses. Clive stood up and picked his way over and around the ottomans and coffee tables. He got tangled up with a tricycle just as he reached the old man.

"Goddamn it! This place is a funhouse."

The old man seemed to inhale sharply at this, as the shrunken, puckered hole that was his mouth became even smaller. He extended his arm and pointed down a short hallway to a door marked *No Admittance*. Another man, almost identical in appearance to the first, was standing next to it with his hands clasped and his head bowed. Clive rolled his eyes as he stomped down the hallway. He ignored the second old man altogether and drummed his knuckles on the door. Clive was surprised to immediately hear a muffled voice telling him to enter. He figured that with all the rigmarole he'd already been through, he'd be standing out in the dank little hallway for another twenty minutes. Clive opened the door and finally came face to face with Sister Tulah.

"Good afternoon, Special Agent Grant."

Clive stood awkwardly in the doorway, not sure if he should enter the cramped, claustrophobic office or not. He had seen photographs of Sister Tulah, of course, and he'd viewed the two television clips of her responding to the church arson, but he still wasn't quite prepared for meeting her in person.

"You look a little scared standing there like that in the doorway, special agent. Why don't you sit down?"

Clive swallowed and lowered himself into the chair across from Sister Tulah. In the images he'd seen, taken soon after the fire, Tulah's missing eye had still been bandaged. Since then, the wound had healed into an ugly, sagging gouge on the left side of her face. He wished she would cover it up. Her other eye was no less disconcerting, however. It was large and colorless, but seemed to pierce right through him. Even taking her eyes out of the question, Clive found the preacher unnerving. Her gray hair was pinned back severely and her thin, pale lips were tightly pursed. She was a large woman, yes, but seemed to take up even more space than she should, almost as if the immaculately pressed blue and pink flowered dress with the white lace collar couldn't contain all of her presence. Tulah narrowed her eye at him and clasped her bloated hands on top of the messy spread of papers littered across the desk. She was waiting for him. Clive cleared his throat.

"Ma'am, my name is Special Agent Clive Grant."

Clive couldn't look away from her drooping eye socket. Sister Tulah nodded curtly.

"Yes, I think we've established that."

"Right. I'm with ATF, up in Atlanta. The department of Alcohol, Tobacco and Firearms."

"Yes. I am aware of what ATF stands for."

Clive swallowed again. Sister Tulah tilted her head slightly.

"Does my eye, or lack thereof, bother you, Mr. Grant?"

Clive immediately shook his head, but was relieved when Sister Tulah slid open a desk drawer and pulled out a black eyepatch. She fit it over her head and adjusted the elastic band carefully. Tulah slammed the drawer shut and gave him a repelling smile.

"Better?"

Clive adjusted himself in the uncomfortable metal folding chair. It was better, but he ignored her comment.

"Ma'am, I'd like to get right down to business."

"Oh goodie."

Clive opened his jacket and slid the thin, spiral notebook out of his pocket. He flipped it open to the scrawl of notes he had hurriedly made about the case.

"This shouldn't take too long. I was sent down here from the Atlanta Field Division to help wrap up a few things about the incident at your church this past May."

"All right."

Clive glanced down at the scribbled notes he had taken. It was hard for him to read his own handwriting. Sister Tulah opened another desk drawer and took out a carton of snack cakes. She slid out a Ding-Dong and ripped open the cellophane. She didn't offer him one.

"I know that local law enforcement is handling the case, but due to the nature of the incident and the parties involved, I need to make a few inquiries for a report. I'm just here to determine whether or not the arson in question was a hate crime and can therefore be prosecuted at the federal level. I've only got a couple of questions."

Sister Tulah broke the Ding-Dong in half and stuffed one of the pieces in her mouth. She didn't say anything, so Clive squinted down at his notes again.

"According to statements from both you and your son, Felton—"

"Nephew."

"Pardon?"

Tulah spoke through a mouthful of cream, but her tone was dangerously adamant.

"Brother Felton is my nephew."

"Okay, nephew. Anyway, according to statements you both gave, you had no prior relationship with either Sherwood Cannon or the outlaw motorcycle club known as the Scorpions."

"I have no relationship with them now, either. Nor will I ever, I suspect. You do know who I am, don't you, Mr. Grant?"

Clive fidgeted with the peeling edge of the notebook. He could hear Sister Tulah smacking as she chewed and he kept his eyes on his notes.

"So you had no previous contact with Mr. Cannon or the Scorpions before the incident at your church on May tenth?"

Sister Tulah crumpled the cellophane in her hand and dropped it in the wastebasket next to the desk. She spread her hands out across the papers in front of her.

"That's correct. I believe I've said that now more times than I can count. Why anyone would believe that the upstanding preacher of The Last Steps of Deliverance Church of God, and a noted and respected spiritual and community leader, would be consorting with denizens and motorcycle hellions is beyond me. I have been asked this question quite enough and, to be honest, I'm insulted than an outsider like yourself would have the gall to raise it to me again."

Clive dipped his chin and smoothed down his lilac tie.

"I'm sorry, ma'am. It's just the standard line of questioning. I'm just confirming information."

Sister Tulah drummed her thick fingers on the desk.

"Well, confirm away, Mr. Grant, but hurry up about it. In case you were not aware, today is Sunday. This establishment is closed. And I have only a few hours to spare between the morning and evening services. I don't know what folks up in Atlanta do on Sundays, but down here, we respect the Lord's time."

Clive looked away from her narrowed eye and rushed through his next question.

"So, you don't have any ideas as to why the shootout between Sherwood Cannon and the Scorpions took place inside and around your church?"

"No."

"And you don't have any information to offer as to why the confrontation occurred in the first place?"

"No, I do not."

"And the reason for the Scorpions igniting the building as they fled the scene?"

Tulah huffed.

"Are you asking me to do your job for you?"

Clive swallowed hard and rested the notebook on his knee.

"Why don't you just tell me what happened?"

Sister Tulah banged her palms down on the desk, startling Clive. She leaned toward him ominously. Her voice was low and gave Clive strange, sick flickers in his stomach. Her pale eye seemed to be boring into him.

"Listen to me, Mr. Grant. Here is all I know. I walked into my church and found a man I had never seen before. This man turned out to be Sherwood Cannon. I asked him his business. He spoke to me threateningly. I asked him to leave and he attacked me. I fell unconscious. When I awoke, the church was

filled with smoke and flames and my nephew, Brother Felton, was pulling me
to my feet. No, I did not see the body of Sherwood Cannon. No, I did not see or
hear any of the gunshots or see any of the members of the Scorpions. No, I don't
know why the fire was set or if it was a hate crime and I don't care. I lost my eye.
I lost most of my church. I nearly lost my life. That is all I know. If you want to
poke around, find out more information for your little ATF book report, you're
going to have to ask someone else. Do you understand me?"

Clive slid the notebook back into his pocket and stood up. He nodded to
Sister Tulah.

"I understand. I suppose that's all, then."

Tulah didn't bother to stand up.

"Yes, that is all."

Clive stepped away from the desk and smoothed his tie again.

"Well. Thank you for your time."

Sister Tulah leaned back in her chair and looked Clive up and down
pointedly.

"Let me also give you a piece of advice, special agent. People around
here don't take too kindly to folks coming in, sticking their noses where they
shouldn't and asking questions. Stirring things up unnecessarily. If I were you,
I'd write your report and skedaddle back to where you belong. There's nothing
here for you."

"So, that's it."

Judah crossed his arms and leaned back against the porch railing. He was
talking mainly to Ramey, who was mirroring him by leaning against the side
of the house, in between the front door and the window box spilling over with
geraniums. Benji had stumped his way to the swing on the other side of the
window, but Judah had largely ignored him as he tersely related the events from
the night before. He was watching Ramey's downturned face as she listened

while tracing a crack in one of the peeling porch boards with the toe of her bare foot. She nodded slowly.

"What about the body? The funeral?"

From the slightly swaying porch swing, Benji snapped at her.

"Do you gotta be so goddamn practical all the time?"

Judah's instinct was to turn on his brother, but he knew Benji was hurting. He had only just now found out about Lesser. Judah kept his eyes on Ramey, unable to look at Benji's already ruined face, at the angry, puckered scars now slick with tears.

"I guess his aunt is taking care of everything. She's coming down from Jacksonville today and she made it pretty clear that she doesn't want any of us involved."

Benji sniveled and wiped his nose on the shoulder of his T-shirt.

"Figures."

"As far as she, or anyone else, knows, it was a drive-by shooting. That's how Jedidiah called it in and I think the cops went for it. Right now, it's probably best just to stick with that story."

Ramey nodded again and looked up at him. He could see her working through the event in her head, what the repercussions were going to be, the problems, and what to do next. Benji was right, Ramey was practical, but Judah needed that right now. He wasn't sure if she had cried yet for Lesser or not. He had fallen asleep with her still downstairs in the kitchen and hadn't seen her face when she had finally slipped into bed beside him. Judah had been turned away from her and he'd stayed that way.

"So this guy, this old man at the store. Jedidiah. He's working for Nash."

"Yes."

Benji coughed loudly and then snorted.

"And he sure as hell ain't working for us no more. Or, excuse me, for you. You, Judah Cannon."

Judah kept his eyes on Ramey and widened them in question. She shrugged her shoulders and shook her head. Judah pulled his keys out of his pocket, but Benji was on him before he could make a move.

"Where do you think you're going?"

Judah finally turned to Benji and sighed. He pushed himself away from the porch railing.

"I think Ramey and I need to go for a drive."

Benji's face was still wet in places, but he had stopped openly crying. He jammed the crutches under his arms and hauled himself up.

"Oh, no."

Benji leaned toward him, wobbling.

"No way. This is your fault. You're not gonna do this to me and then just leave me out of it."

Ramey's voice was quiet but firm.

"That's not fair, Benji."

Benji stumped forward and looked back and forth between Judah and Ramey.

"Tough titty. Life ain't fair. Who knew?"

Judah was trying to be patient with his brother, but he could feel the weight of everything pressing down, threating to crush him. To suffocate him. It was all too overwhelming: Benji's accusations, Ramey's disapproving silences, Lesser's face. He couldn't seem to get the image of Lesser's bloody, dirty face out of his mind. The dull cast of his eye. Judah took a deep breath, doing his best to keep his voice level and the rise of anger at the back of his throat in check.

"Don't do this, Benji."

"Don't do what? Put this on you?"

Benji spat a thick clot over the railing of the porch.

"He was just a kid. He was my friend. I taught him to take apart an engine. I talked to him about girls. School. You came along and used him. Out of nowhere, he's suddenly looking up to you like you're something. Somebody. And you just used him. You're no better than Daddy was."

Ramey's voice cracked like a whip.

"Benji, shut up."

Benji swung on his crutches toward Ramey.

"And you…"

"What? What now?"

Ramey jumped in front of Benji with her hands on her hips and a threat on her face. Judah knew she'd been dealing with the brunt of Benji's moods for the past few months, but he had never seen her this confrontational toward him. She turned and shot Judah a look over her shoulder and he realized she was not so much venting frustration as taking control of an otherwise volatile situation. Everything about his relationship with Benji had changed since he had gotten out of the hospital. He wasn't sure exactly if it was the guilt still chewing away at him or his growing disappointment in his younger brother. He needed Benji to be on board with him. He needed him to step up, be a Cannon, even if he was still hobbling around and popping pain pills like Tic-Tacs. Benji had always been exempt, protected. He'd been too nice and good-natured for Sherwood and Levi to ever pressure him into risky situations. To ever beat him down in a parking lot. While Judah had been stewing in prison, taking the rap for the Cannon family, Benji had been free of it all, chasing girls, working on cars, doing whatever he wanted. Benji was right: life wasn't fair. It hadn't been fair then and, despite Benji's condition, Judah didn't think it was fair now. He and Ramey were sacrificing. Benji should be, too.

Ramey looked from Judah back to Benji and then stepped away, putting her hands up. They all stood together in awkward silence until finally Judah spoke.

"We can't be at each other's throats like this."

Ramey turned to him, arms crossed now, but back to focusing on the problem.

"What are you thinking?"

"Well, we know that Nash is against us, right?"

"No shit."

Judah ignored Benji as Ramey nodded along with him.

"Right. But do we know why?"

"He wasn't just Sherwood's man out in Putnam County. He's running drugs on the side."

Ramey frowned.

"But I think a lot of the guys are. That Lonnie screw-up you sent Alvin and Gary after last night, for instance. Even Sherwood looked the other way on that."

"Yeah, but I don't think Nash is just pushing weed on school kids. He's part of a bigger operation."

Benji piped up again.

"He tell you that?"

Judah begrudgingly glanced at Benji.

"He made it pretty clear that he wanted to use our infrastructure. I told him no. That's when the shooting started."

Ramey bit her lip and tilted her head.

"It doesn't make sense, though. Is he just a stupid hothead? If he wanted to use our network, why ruin his chances by doing what he did last night? Why not back off, try to feel you out, negotiate or whatever?"

Benji sat back on the porch swing with a heavy thud.

"There's Ramey, thinking all rational again."

Judah shook his head.

"I said want, not need. I'm not sure that he wasn't going to try to shoot me one way or the other, to tell you the truth. I think he was two-timing Sherwood all along. Or, at least he's working for someone else now."

Ramey jerked her head up.

"Who?"

"Don't know. He mentioned somebody named Weaver. That name ring a bell?"

Both Ramey and Benji gave him blank expressions. Judah's mouth twisted into a frown. He'd been hoping that one of them had at least heard the name before.

"I asked Jedidiah and he looked at me cross-eyed. Either he was covering, or he honestly didn't know. I'm not sure which is worse."

They were all quiet for a moment. Judah looked down at his hands. He rubbed at the calluses on his palm, trying to think. Finally, Ramey huffed. He looked up to see her blowing strands of hair out of her face. It was another bright, scorching day, but a small breeze had picked up over the past hour.

"So, that's where we're at?"

Judah met her eyes. Since they had made the decision to stay in Silas, it seemed like they were still only dodging bullets, facing down one issue after another. Taking care of Benji. Untangling Sherwood's network. Dealing with the bookies and enforcers. The consequences. The repercussions. He had told Ramey that they were all just steps toward the end goal: getting out. That everything they were doing was so they could have a shot at having a life together. A normal, possibly happy life together and one where they wouldn't have to always be on the run.

He had believed it. Judah thought Ramey had believed it. But it was quicksand; the more Judah worked to pull them out, the faster they were dragged back under. And now this with Lesser. Sherwood wouldn't have let it happen. Sherwood wouldn't have been caught off guard. Judah had spent the night staring into the darkness, wondering over and over. Could he really keep trying to balance on the edge of a razor? Could he really keep telling himself that there was hope?

Judah studied Ramey's face. He wished he knew what she was thinking. He had thought about grabbing her hand while she poured him a cup of coffee earlier and putting it to her straight—did she still have faith in him? Judah hadn't said a word, though. He already knew her answer. He had made her a promise. Judah knew she expected him to keep it.

"That's where we're at. That's the question we've now got to answer. Who the hell is Weaver?"

"So, I TOLD her, I says right there, with my shorts in one hand, my pants in the other, standing right on her front porch, bare ass as the day I was born for all the world to see, I says, if you think you're getting a dime of child support from me, then you're barking up the wrong tree, lady. What do you think of that?"

Shelia tugged at her bottled-blond ponytail, tied up high with a leopard print scrunchie, and popped her eyes wide. Her mascara kept getting gunky on her and making her eyes water. She picked up the empty plastic cup on the edge of the high top table and rattled what was left of the ice.

"That's something, Harry. You want another sea breeze?"

Harry peered into the empty cup Shelia was still holding and stuck the gummy end of a cigar into the corner of his mouth.

"You sure there's actually vodka in these things?"

Shelia shrugged and snapped her gum.

"They're only a dollar fifty on happy hour. You want a double?"

Harry scratched his bristly mustache and frowned.

"What's that gonna cost me, three dollars?"

"Well now, I never was very good at math."

Shelia winked and headed back to the bar, taking the plastic cup with her. She slung it in the trashcan behind the bar and rang in a double. Mike, the bartender who was busy flexing for a pug-faced blonde across the bar who looked like she had just left cheerleader practice, rolled his eyes and shot Shelia a dirty look when he heard the ticket print. Shelia blew him a kiss and then made sure to give the perky co-ed a pointed onceover. The girl looked away in discomfort and Shelia smiled to herself. She turned to her reflection in the bar mirror and adjusted her see-through tank top, screen printed with three purple palm trees that drew the eyes just where they needed to be. She straightened her denim mini-skirt, but tried not to look down at her scuffed Keds. They only reminded her of the endless hours she was clocking as a cocktail waitress at The Salty Dog.

Shelia picked up the sea breeze, now in a slightly larger plastic cup, and sauntered back to the row of high tops cutting through the smoky haze in the center of bar. She slid the drink over to Harry, the only customer she had at four o'clock in the afternoon, but turned away before he could start telling yet another story about one of his ex-wives. Out of the corner of her eye, she caught a slice of blasting sunlight as Frank came stomping through the door. Shelia wandered over to the end of the bar where she usually hung out and waited for her uncle to come over and bitch at her about something.

Shelia didn't think she had spoken more than four words to Frank since she had been old enough to wear a training bra. She had always remembered him as a slick jerk, the kind of asshole who got off on telling perverted jokes around kids and flashing a wad of cash in a gold money clip whenever he got the chance. Now that Shelia thought about it, he hadn't changed much over the past thirty years, only grown a paunch and acquired a pair of gold-rimmed aviator glasses that made his already creepy, heavy-lidded eyes even creepier. He had lost half his hair, but wore what was left in a straggling, greasy ponytail. Sometimes Shelia couldn't believe that she was actually in Daytona Beach, in Frank's shithole of a bar, trying to make a buck.

And lay low. After the shootout and fire at that crazy preacher lady's church, she and Slim Jim didn't have too many options. It had been Tiny, Legs and Ratface who'd been caught, tearing down the highway away from the scene, Tiny and Legs both spattered with blood and Ratface still reeking of gasoline from the Molotov cocktail he'd launched through the church's window. Of all things, they'd been pulled over by a state trooper for speeding, though it didn't take long for them to be arrested for everything that had gone down at the church. In his panic to get away, Slim Jim had managed to flood his engine, putting him about a mile behind the others. He had told Shelia that he was sure his bike acting up would be the thing that did him in, but it turned out to have been his saving grace. He'd seen the flashing lights up ahead, pulling the others over, and been able to turn around in time.

When Slim Jim showed up at her trailer, sweating, out of breath, gunpowder still on his hands, Tiny's blood on his leather vest and neck, she hadn't even asked for the whole story. She had opened the rattling screen door, tossed him a roll of paper towels and begun to pack a bag. He'd been too out of sorts to make a decision, too busy standing around in shock, so she'd taken matters into her own hands. She was getting the hell out of Bradford County and Slim Jim was welcome to come along. When he started blubbering about Jack and Toadie, about the club, she'd given him a quick choice: stay and wait for the cops to show up or get his skinny ass in her car. They had managed to skip town before the sun set.

Ending up at her uncle's bar three counties away wasn't exactly what she'd had in mind, but Shelia had learned long ago that beggars had no place being choosers. Not if they wanted to stay alive or out of jail. After some convincing, Frank had agreed to let her and Slim Jim stay at the Sundaze, one of the two rat trap motels he owned along with The Salty Dog. After even more convincing, Frank had hired Shelia at his bar and taken Slim Jim on as a maintenance worker for the motels, paying them both under the table, of course. Shelia knew Slim Jim was less than thrilled about the arrangement, but it gave them a place to hide out and jobs without paperwork. As far as Shelia was concerned, if Slim Jim didn't like it, he didn't have to stay. Shelia was a cat; she knew she'd land on her feet anywhere and it was Slim Jim's skin she was saving, not her own, after all.

Frank swaggered over and rested his hairy knuckles on the edge of the bar. As always, he was standing too close and reeked of Brut cologne.

"Not exactly banging in here, huh?"

Shelia inched away from him.

"It's Sunday afternoon. What kinda high rollers were you expecting?"

Frank turned around so that he could survey the bar with her. Harry was busy chewing on his cigar and checking his phone. The blonde had been joined by a brunette who couldn't bother to put a shirt on over her bikini top, but they were the only ones sitting at the bar. The girls were snickering over their Smirnoff Ices and the sportscasters on the fuzzy TV were droning on about the race, but otherwise The Salty Dog was as silent as a tomb. Frank scratched at a large mole on the back of his sunburned neck.

"Well, you could at least have some music playing. Turn the lights down some. It's as bright as a damn grocery store in here. You think this type of atmosphere makes people want to come in and drink?"

Shelia shrugged.

"I think if people want a drink, they're gonna come in regardless of the lighting."

Frank gave her a disgusted look. He turned down the lights and the room became bathed in the neon glare from the beer signs hanging behind the bar and along the back wall. The two girls looked uneasily around them, as if just now realizing what a dive they'd wandered into. Frank shoved a CD into the sound system and turned the volume up. He grinned at Shelia.

"See, ain't that better? Atmosphere. It feels like a bar now, not a damn hospital."

Shelia was concentrating on blowing a bubble as Cindy Lauper came screeching through the speakers. When the front door banged open, Shelia let the gum pop and whirled around. Frank whistled.

"Well, lookie, it's your boyfriend Slimmy Jimmy. I'm pretty sure he's supposed to be over at the Tropix. You know, working. Like I pay him to do."

Shelia rolled her eyes at Frank as she watched Slim Jim stomp the plaster dust off of his boots in the doorway.

"He's not my boyfriend."

"What, did you marry him or something?"

Shelia pursed her lips but ignored Frank as he walked away down the bar, chuckling to himself. Slim Jim stormed up to her and Shelia sighed. What would it be this time?

"Have you seen the motel room lately?"

Shelia narrowed her eyes.

"You mean the one we live in? Yeah, I think I know what it looks like."

Slim Jim shook his head and rested his grimy elbows against the edge of the bar.

"It looks like a bomb exploded in there."

"So clean it up."

Slim Jim grabbed her wrist and looked as if he was going to say something, but Frank came around the bar and crossed his arms over his chest. Slim Jim let go of Shelia and turned to Frank.

"What?"

"Since it's still daylight out there, but you're in here, I'm going to assume that you finished patching up the walls in 101 and 102."

Shelia watched Slim Jim's jaw tighten. One of these days it was going to come to blows between the two of them. She'd love to see Slim Jim take a swing at Frank, belt him one right in the kisser. Over Frank's shoulder, Shelia could see Harry holding up his empty cup and waving it at her. Shelia rang in another drink and then dropped it off. By the time she made it back to Frank and Slim Jim, both of their voices were raised. Frank slapped his hand down on the soggy bar mat.

"So, what? You're just not going to do the pool at Tropix?"

"There's a pool?"

Slim Jim's mouth was twisted in ugly sarcasm.

"Oh, you mean that hole in the ground out back of the motel? The one that all the kids pee in?"

Frank stepped in closer to Slim Jim.

"You need to watch your mouth, sonny boy. Or you and your old lady here are gonna find yourselves out on your asses. I'm doing you a favor and you'd best not forget it."

Slim Jim balled up his fists, but just shook his head in disgust.

"Whatever. I don't have time for this shit."

He backed away from the bar and cut his eyes at Shelia. She tried to give him a sympathetic look, but Slim Jim only smirked at her and then bolted out of the bar without saying goodbye. He nearly crashed into several guys coming through the door and they all looked each other up and down for a tense moment. Shelia shook her head and jammed the ice scoop further down into the bin. It amazed her sometimes that men could even manage to take their own pants off without a woman doing it for them. Jesus, how did they survive?

Frank nudged her hard and she looked up from the ice.

"Girl, you'd better get a smile on that mug."

"Oh, really?"

"Really."

Frank's voice had taken on a strained tone that Shelia hadn't heard before. He quickly popped out the '80s mix and put in a Dwight Yoakam CD. He carefully adjusted the volume and then grabbed her shoulder, shaking her roughly.

"What the hell, Frank?"

Frank nodded toward the corner booth. One of the men who had just come in was sitting there alone. The other two were standing around one of the high tops, but it didn't look like they wanted a drink. They were shifting their eyes around as if surveying the bar from all angles. Frank leaned in close and whispered.

"You see the guy sitting alone in the booth?"

Shelia snapped her gum loudly.

"So?"

The man was haloed in red light from the Budweiser sign above his head. He had a beaked nose and straight black hair that fell along the sides of his face like curtains. Despite the heat, he was wearing a bomber jacket, the brown leather scuffed and mottled. He was sitting up perfectly straight with his fingers steepled on the table in front of him. Shelia had never seen him before. Frank nodded solemnly.

"Take special care of him, okay? I mean it."

Shelia tried to wriggle out from underneath Frank's hand.

"Why? Who is he?"

Frank shoved her shoulder.

"Just do it. And spit that wad out or he's likely to smack it out of your mouth for you. He doesn't like gum chewing. I'll be in the office for a minute. Just make sure he has everything he needs and don't be a smart-ass about it."

"Okay, okay."

Shelia waved him off and spit her gum out in the trash before crossing the bar to the man sitting at the booth. She was aware that the other two guys were eyeballing her, but she didn't look their way. She tugged on her tank top so that her cleavage was more prominent and then flashed the man in the corner a flirtatious smile. He didn't smile back.

"Can I get you something, sugar?"

His voice was like gravel and this close up Shelia could see that his eyes were an unexpected, startling light blue. She rested two fingers on the edge of the table and arched an eyebrow. The man's stagnant expression didn't change.

"Mai Tai. No fruit."

"Sure thing."

Shelia waited a second to see if the man wanted to make small talk, but it was obvious he wanted nothing to do with her. She cocked her hip out and winked anyway.

"I'm Shelia, by the way."

His eyes narrowed slightly and though Shelia knew she could hold her own with any man, she felt the chill of someone walking over her grave.

"Weaver. Now get me my goddamn drink."

CHAPTER 4

SISTER TULAH HEAVED herself into the driver's seat of her sleek, black Lincoln Navigator and wrenched the door shut. She started the engine and adjusted the air conditioning vents. They were already pointed directly at her, exactly where she wanted them to be, but she fiddled with them anyway to calm her frustration. Yesterday, it was the ATF agent harassing her; today, it was the claims adjuster. Didn't these people have anything better to do with their time than bother her with their nonsense and incompetence? The cold air blasted her, prickling the mustache of sweat hanging above her upper lip, and Tulah let her head drop back against the headrest. She brushed her fingertips across the arch of the tan leather steering wheel and tried to relax. At least she had the cool, quiet interior of her Navigator to escape to.

Like clockwork, Sister Tulah bought a new Lincoln every year in the fall, when the new models rolled out. She had been doing so ever since she had first slid the letters across the marquee in front of the church to form the words: Pastor Tulah Atwell. That had been back in 1982, and during that first year there had been a few rumblings from the congregation. Sister Tulah was preaching hellfire and damnation on swimsuits, movie theaters and Coca-Cola, and a few of the brothers and sisters had taken issue with their preacher zipping around Kentsville in a brand new Continental. The dissenters had soon been taken care of, though. Sister Tulah couldn't always govern the few outliers, the few backsliders who hovered at the fringes of her church, new spouses and friends of her true believers, but she could certainly shut them up in a hurry.

And not even those heathen Baptists up in Starke at Holy Living Waters could fault her purchase this time. Sister Tulah fingered the fine leather stitching on the steering wheel. Her last Navigator had ended up looking like a piece of Swiss cheese, riddled with bullet holes from the shootout in the church's parking lot three months ago. At least the insurance on her vehicle had come through quickly. The church, however, was another headache altogether and half the reason she was still using that mouse hole in the back of the furniture store for an office.

The Last Steps of Deliverance Church of God was still functional after the fire, but barely. Sister Tulah continued to hold Wednesday night and Sunday morning and evening services in the crumbling building, but there was no way she would still use it to do business. The back of the church where her office was located had been relatively untouched by the destruction of bullets and flame, but the entire incident had opened the church's doors wide to police and investigators, none of whom she needed poking around in her business. While the fire was still roaring, and she was trying to hold the goopy remains of her eye against her face, Tulah had ordered Felton back through the choking smoke to retrieve a folder of documents from the safe in her office. If discovered by the wrong people, its contents would have had her in prison for the rest of her life. Fortunately, she had known everyone who arrived at the scene and they hadn't dared to rifle through her office. In her mind, though, it had still been too close a call.

Sister Tulah had moved her base of operations from the back of Last Steps to the back of the Elders' lair: the used furniture store on the other side of town. She hadn't bothered to ask if they minded her sudden takeover of their sacred space. The Elders, four men who had been with the church since it had been under the steerage of her grandfather, would not hesitate to slit their own throats if Sister Tulah commanded it. Or anyone else's, for that matter. It was almost impossible to tell them apart, and while Tulah suspected that the ancient men were brothers, she couldn't be sure. Not that it mattered. The Elders were more loyal to her than dogs, and though she would never share her deepest secrets with any living being, she trusted the old men. More than she had her limp-wristed husband Walter and certainly more than she did her moon-brained nephew Felton.

A squabble of voices pierced the sanctuary of the Navigator and Sister Tulah snapped her head around. Two women tumbled out of the laundromat, screeching at one another in Mexican or some other gibberish. Sister Tulah scowled at them. She had been enjoying her respite before heading home, but it seemed she would never find a moment's peace. Tulah glared at the women, one now shoving a pink towel in the other's face, and was about to put the Navigator in reverse when it was suddenly filled with the eerie sound of a phone ringing. Sister Tulah was startled, but then primly corrected herself, even though she was alone. She peered at the Navigator's stereo as the car phone continued to ring. Sister Tulah pushed a button.

"Yes?"

It kept ringing. Sister Tulah pursed her lips and jabbed at another button.

"Hello?"

She twisted the radio dial back and forth and poked at more buttons, feeling as though she were in the cockpit of an airplane. Tulah had been hesitant about the car phone feature, but the slick man at the dealership had finally persuaded her that it was about time she joined the technological revolution. She had taken no time in informing him that the only revolution she needed was that of God's angels smiting down the rest of the world, but she had gone in for the luxury package anyway. Sister Tulah mashed one more button and a voice finally came through the speakers.

"Hello? Sister Tulah?"

Tulah sat back in her seat and took a few deep breaths before answering.

"Yes. Who is this?"

"Um, this is Cary Lane."

The man calling her acted as if she should know and then Tulah remembered that the stereo was supposed to tell her who was calling. She looked at the display: First National Bank. Tulah turned away from the stupid car phone and gazed across the mostly deserted back parking lot.

"Yes, Brother Cary. I know that. What do you want?"

Cary coughed a few times and cleared his throat.

"I'm sorry to bother you, Sister Tulah. I know you're probably busy…"

She interrupted him.

"Yes. I am. What is it?"

The voice hesitated a moment and Sister Tulah smiled to herself, picturing the squat, bald bank manager squirming in his wingtips.

"Well, I just thought you would want to know. That is, a man just walked into First National and started asking Julie at the counter some questions."

Tulah frowned and put the car into reverse. She craned her neck over her shoulder and began to back out of the parking space.

"What kind of questions?"

"Questions about the church fire. The shooting."

"Why would someone be asking your counter girl about my church?"

Cary coughed again.

"Well, I don't know exactly. To tell you the truth, he was mostly asking questions about you."

Tulah's frown deepened.

"Me?"

"I hurried over there as soon as I saw Julie talking to this fella. I made sure he was talking to me."

Sister Tulah pulled out in front of a minivan. She responded to the squeal of brakes with a menacing look in the rearview mirror.

"And would this happen to be a dark-skinned man? Not from around here? A little ahead of himself?"

"That's for sure."

"And the questions?"

"Well, he was just asking general things about you. How long you'd been preaching in town. How long the church'd been around. If you had any enemies. Were you well liked in the community."

Sister Tulah's eye widened and she raised her voice to a near-screech.

"Am I well liked?"

She could imagine Brother Cary cringing on the other end.

"I just gave him basic answers, you know. Nothing specific. I would've told him to leave right away, but he had a federal badge."

"I know, a Fischer-Price one. ATF."

"It's still federal."

Sister Tulah snapped.

"Yes, I know that. I am aware, Brother Cary. So this man, his name is Special Agent Grant, by the way, came into First National Bank and was asking questions about me. Anything else?"

There was a pause and Sister Tulah sighed. Sometimes it was hard with Brother Cary. Because he handled so many of her business accounts, because he had a few crumbs of inside information, he sometimes felt he was above the rest of her flock. Yet because of what he knew, Tulah was obligated to occasionally humor him and let him believe that he was. Sister Tulah hated negotiating. She hated tact. It was so tiresome.

"I stepped next door after the man left and talked to Barney. The ATF guy was asking questions in the barber shop, too. Barney said he'd seen him across the street, coming out of the hardware store earlier. I think this guy's asking questions all around town about you."

Sister Tulah nodded slowly and turned off the main road.

"All right. If you hear anything else you think I should know, call me."

It was the closest to a thank you that Tulah could muster.

"Will do, Sister Tulah."

"And, Brother Cary, while I have you, I need to know the status of the one eleven account."

Sister Tulah waited patiently through the awkward pause. When Cary finally spoke, he sounded flustered.

"I'm still working on it. I've had to transfer some money around, shift the holdings for a few of the other accounts. If the insurance for the church had come through already, I'd have a lot more to work with."

"The one eleven account is never supposed to be touched, Brother Cary."

Cary stumbled over his words.

"It hasn't. Usually, you have a lot more, um, cash flow going into other accounts that can then be diverted. It's just that all of your accounts have been a little low lately. The, uh, the issue with the mine…"

"Yes, Brother Cary, I am aware."

"Anyway, you're going to need to give me something more to work with if you want the account at a hundred."

Sister Tulah rolled through a stop sign.

"How much more?"

"I'll have to double check, but I think it was only a few thousand short. I'll need the money by the ninth, though, if you want to make the transfer by Friday."

"You'll have it. Hang up now."

Brother Cary started to say something, but obviously thought better of it and the stereo beeped that the call had ended. Sister Tulah pursed her lips. She was certainly not going to explain that she had no idea how to hang up the car phone. Tulah turned down the sandy driveway and finally parked the Navigator in front of her tall white house. She glanced in the rearview mirror, eyeing the husk of her church, just down the road and on the same property as her home. Sister Tulah smirked to herself and adjusted the elastic band of the patch over her eye. She might have to lay the brimstone on a little thick this week, and send the Elders knocking on some doors, but coming up with a few extra thousand dollars would be like shooting fish in a barrel.

CLIVE PRIED THE cap off his sweating bottle of Heineken and flipped his laptop open. The sudden brightness cut through the gloom of the motel room and Clive leaned back, staring at the screen on the table in front of him. He had only allowed himself to turn on the buzzing fluorescent light above the bathroom mirror so that he could fill the sink with cold water and dunk his six pack of beer. If the state of the room was anything like that of the hallway, with its thin, moldering carpet and bubbling, water-stained walls, he figured it was best just to not look too closely. He gripped his steadily warming beer and held it out next to him, directly in front of the rattling air conditioning unit, which didn't seem to be producing much more than a musty odor. The ice machine was broken. Of course.

There were only two hotels to choose from in Kentsville, and The Pines had seemed like the better option compared to its competitor down the road. Clive had gotten one glimpse of the palmetto bugs contentedly dozing in the corner of The Travel Inn's lobby and backed out the door immediately. At least the woman at the front desk of The Pines had assured him that "they sometimes sprayed for those damn dinosaur critters," so Clive had felt a little better about staying there. He wouldn't be getting under the sheets anytime soon, though. Or turning on all the lights. Clive chugged half his tepid beer and rapped his knuckles on the particleboard tabletop. He needed to decide what to do about the report.

It should have been simple. All Clive had to do was declare whether or not he believed the arson committed at The Last Steps of Deliverance Church of God was a religiously motivated hate crime. If it was deemed so, then the crime would come under the Church Arson Prevention Act of 1996 and be deemed a federal offense. ATF would need to conduct a full inquiry and the Scorpions would have to be tried in federal courts. If the church location was merely incidental, then ATF could check the arson off its list and let the state's attorneys handle the whole mess. All Clive had to do was make the determination.

He had spent the entire day up in Starke, a town he had quickly realized contained not much more than the state prison and a couple of bad buffet restaurants. Clive had been shuffled back and forth across the short length of the Bradford County Sheriff's Office, and in and out of cramped rooms and cubicles badly in need in of wastebaskets and filing cabinets, before he was finally able to find one of the investigators who had been on the Kentsville church case. Clive had grown up surrounded by government bureaucracy. Back at home in Washington, D.C., his father was a retired commander of the fifth district of the Metropolitan Police and his mother was the long-standing principal of Longview Public High School. Still, he was amazed by the lackadaisical attitude that confounded his every attempt to locate the basic information he needed. By the time Clive had finally found himself at the desk of Detective Gail Pricter, an actual person who supposedly knew something about the case, he felt like he had spent the morning running a marathon through streets of molasses.

Considering the Wonder Bread composition of the office, Clive had felt relieved at the sight of Gail and figured that he had lucked out. The feeling was short lived, however, as Gail made it clear that Clive's skin color wasn't going to win him any favors with her.

"You're not from around here, are you?"

Clive had been waiting beside Gail's vacant desk for forty-five minutes and it was the first thing she'd said when she pushed past him and settled herself, plunking a plastic bag down on the mess of coffee and ketchup stained papers in front of her. She had only briefly glanced at him before pulling a foot-long sub out of the bag. Clive had rested his elbow on the desk and given her a winning smile.

"Is it that obvious?"

Gail didn't respond. She slid the sub out of the paper wrapper and opened it up on her desk to inspect it. Clive cleared his throat, waiting for her to ask what he needed, but she was busy picking the banana peppers off the lumps of lunchmeat with her long, turquoise nails and then flinging each one into the trashcan at Clive's feet. Clive finally took out his notebook and flipped it open to a blank page.

"So, you and Detective Isen were the investigators working the arson and homicide at the Last Steps Church down in Kentsville, correct?"

Gail didn't look up from her sandwich.

"Goddamn peppers. If I wanted peppers, I would've asked. I don't know why they gotta go and put them on everything over at Lou's. It's disgusting."

Gail dug around in the plastic bag and pulled out a handful of mustard packets.

"And I don't see why they can't put the mustard on the damn thing for you. They pile the peppers on, but then you ask for mustard and they give you these Mickey Mouse servings. Don't make no sense."

Clive clicked his pen a few times, trying to get the detective to focus on him and not her lunch.

"Is that right? You were on the church case?"

Gail ripped open a packet with her teeth and then spat the triangle of plastic out onto her desk. She cut her eyes over at him as she squeezed out a curl of mustard.

"That's right. You need to see my badge or something? You don't believe me?"

Clive shook his head and tried to laugh.

"No. I just, I spent an hour this morning waiting on Detective Isen and then ten minutes talking to someone I thought was him, but who apparently is in charge of animal control."

Gail obviously didn't think this was funny. She squeezed on more mustard.

"Yeah, Bob's out on leave. Gave himself a hernia trying to move some of those file boxes out of the way. Clean the place up a bit."

She waved vaguely across the office and Clive followed her hand. The entire room was a maze of stacked cardboard boxes bursting with paper. He turned back to Gail.

"But he was on the case with you."

"Yeah."

Gail, finally satisfied with her sandwich, squashed it closed. She licked the mustard off her fingers and took a bite. Strings of pale lettuce fell to the desk when she pulled the sub away from her mouth. She was chewing loudly and Clive, who hadn't eaten since a snack machine candy bar five hours earlier, felt faint for a moment. He needed to get the hell out of there.

"All right. That doesn't matter. I'd like to ask you a few quick questions about the case, if you don't mind."

Gail slid open her desk drawer and pulled out a warm can of Shasta. She tapped the top of it and then pried it open with her fingernail.

"Who are you, anyway?"

Clive almost rolled his eyes. He'd figured the woman taking up space behind the front desk would have already told the detective who he was and what he was doing there. He tossed the notebook onto the desk, next to the pile of empty, twisted mustard packets.

"Special Agent Clive Grant. I'm with ATF. They sent me down from Atlanta to look into the church fire in Kentsville."

Gail took another bite and spoke with her mouth full.

"Why?"

"Because the arson was in a church. There's this federal hate crime law on the books..."

Gail slurped her soda.

"Okay."

The word "federal" had obviously made her tune out, so Clive decided it was best not to go into detail.

"Anyway, I'm just down here trying to determine the reason the fire was set in the first place. If the location was purposeful or incidental. Because with the shootout and the homicide in the mix, it makes the whole thing more complicated."

"Why?"

Clive rubbed his forehead. He was starting to feel like he was talking to a two-year-old.

"Because from the information we already received from the state's attorney's office, it seemed as if the shooting was the focus of the event. It sounded as if the location was inconsequential and the arson almost an afterthought."

"Okay."

Clive looked up at Gail. Her large brown eyes were pretty, if framed by too much mascara, but they definitely had a dull cast to them. He wasn't sure he was getting anywhere.

"So. I just need to know what your thoughts are. Based on the investigation you've conducted over the past few months, and the evidence you've been able to collect since, do you think the arson was indicative of a religious hate crime?"

Gail dropped her sandwich and rubbed her hands together. She leaned on her elbows and seemed to consider what he was actually saying for the first time.

"A hate crime? Like, against the church?"

Clive did everything he could not to groan.

"Yes. That's what I'm asking. When a member of the Scorpions..."

Clive flipped back a page in his notebook.

"A, um, man known as Ratface, when he threw the incendiary device through the church window, was he purposefully committing an act of arson motivated by intolerance of the religion practiced there?"

Gail glanced up toward the ceiling, thinking.

"No. I don't think so."

Clive waited for her to continue, but she took another bite of her sub instead. He was really beginning to hate that sandwich.

"Can you tell me why you think that?"

"Well, when we first questioned the Scorpions, right after they were arrested, the one who threw the bottle of gasoline at the church said he did it because he was pissed off. The whole club has pled not guilty to everything, but I remember he said that when we were hauling the boys in. Bob about slugged him. He don't tolerate language like that."

Clive jotted this down and then cocked his head.

"He said he was pissed off? So, he was angry. Was he angry at the church?"

Gail gave him a blank stare.

"Angry at the church? Why would he be angry at the church?"

Clive slapped the notebook back down on the desk. He was fed up.

"That's what I'm asking. That's what I'm trying to find out. Was this motorcycle gang against the religion practiced at the Last Steps Church? That's all I need to know. It's simple."

Gail whistled and then looked away.

"Boy, you need to watch that attitude. Talking like that won't get you nowhere around here."

Clive grit his teeth.

"Listen. I'm not trying to be disrespectful."

"Uh-huh. You come down here from your big city of Atlanta, thinking you're all that and a bag of Ruffles. That we don't know what we're doing down here in little old Bradford County. You're trying to show off, I guess. Educate us a little. Teach us a few things we don't know. Is that it?"

Clive shook his head vigorously.

"No. That's not it. That's not it at all. I just need some information so I can make my report. That's it. What can you tell me?"

Gail was apparently as fed up with him as he was with her. She picked up the last bite of her sandwich and answered him dismissively.

"No."

"No?"

"No, I don't think the fire was a hate crime. I don't see no reason why anyone involved would have something against the church or Preacher Tulah. I think the arson location was, what did you call it? Incidental. And I think the ATF needs to keep their nose out of other people's business and let people do their own damn jobs. That's what I think."

Clive scribbled this in his notebook, but then caught himself. He looked up at Gail and narrowed his eyes.

"Preacher Tulah? Do you know her?"

He watched Gail's eyes dart away from him.

"I know of her. Sure, everybody in the county knows of Preacher Tulah."

Clive leaned forward.

"What can you tell me about her?"

It was like a door had slammed shut in his face.

"Nothing. I can't tell you nothing."

"But you know who she is."

Gail shook her head stubbornly

"Like I said, everybody knows who she is. She's just an old preacher lady down in Kentsville. Does a lot for the community. That sort of thing."

"Her church is a little different than most, though, right? I met her yesterday and then spent some time looking into a few things. Last Steps is one of those old time religion churches. Pentecostal. Like, whooping and hollering, rolling on the floor services."

Clive bit his tongue as soon as he said it. He wasn't back in the office in Atlanta. Probably everyone down here was part of some kooky church. Gail's vacant expression turned venomous.

"You, Mr. Smarty Pants, might not have respect for God where you come from, but down here, we do. And if you had any brains in that fool head of yours, you wouldn't be talking about no preacher like that."

"Even Preacher Tulah?"

Gail stood up from her desk and crumpled the paper sandwich wrapping in her hands. It was obvious that the conversation was over.

"Especially Preacher Tulah. If you know what's good for you."

Clive stared at the laptop screen; he still hadn't touched the keyboard. He stood up and grabbed another beer bottle out of the sink. He struggled to open it and then threw the cap against the wall above the television before sitting down on the edge of the bed. Clive tried not to imagine what could be crawling around between the sheets.

After his meeting with Detective Pricter, the rest of the day had been a landslide downhill. He had spent the afternoon trying to track down the fire marshal, only to discover that he was on vacation in the Bahamas. He'd eventually been able to get his hands on the fire investigation report, but it hadn't told him much more than the fact that, yes, there had indeed been a fire in the church. By the time he'd finished up at the courthouse, Clive had been ready to wash his hands of Starke for good. He'd driven back to The Ramada Inn and the news that a pipe had broken on the second floor and his room, and most of the hotel, was under an inch of water. All of the other guests had already been moved to The Best Western, which was now full. The manager had only shrugged and told him to try Kentsville. Hence, his current situation of sitting in the dark in a $29.99 room at The Pines.

Clive rolled his shoulders, trying to work out the bunching knots, and then glanced over at his laptop. All he had to do was type up the damn report. It was obvious that the incident didn't fall under the CAPA law and wasn't a federal matter. It was a local case and not worth the ATF's time. Period. End of investigation. End of story. The report would take him less than half an hour to write and send. He didn't even have to stay the night if he didn't want to. He could be on the road north by ten and back in Atlanta before the sun came up.

Clive pulled his BlackBerry out of his pocket and stared at it. But then there was Sister Tulah. Clive couldn't figure it out. Sure, she was unnerving. With her one lurid eye and her steely, commanding voice. With her office in the back of the creepy furniture store and the silent old men surrounding her, looking for all the world like geriatric FBI agents. But it was more than that. Detective Pricter had made it clear that he shouldn't be asking questions about Tulah, and she hadn't been the only one. Clive had made sure to mention Tulah's name to others on his way out of the sheriff's office, and at the courthouse, and the responses had been similar: either silence or praise. When he'd come back down to Kentsville, Clive had decided to ask some of the locals, too, just to see what would happen. From the bank manager to the teenage girl at the checkout of the Save-A-Lot, the reactions had been the same. And behind each comment about Tulah, Clive detected traces of the same emotion: fear. Though he was sure no one would admit it, he was certain that everyone he spoke to was terrified of Sister Tulah. It didn't make sense. She was old. She was a woman. She was a preacher, for Christ's sake.

Clive ran his thumb over the smudged screen of his phone and took a deep breath. He dialed the number for his supervisor, not sure if he wanted the call to be answered or not. It was picked up on the first ring.

"Special Agent Grant."

As always, she said his name like it was some sort of sarcastic joke. Like she was amused that he still existed. Clive swallowed the rest of his beer and set the bottle between his feet.

"Vickie."

Clive knew that his boss hated to be called her by her first name. He assumed she even made her boyfriends call her Special Agent Lopez in the sack. Last year, the office had all chipped in to buy her a cake with *Happy Birthday Victoria!* written across the top in purple icing. She'd been so pissy about it, she hadn't even blown out the candles.

"What do you want, Grant? I'm busy."

She sounded out of breath and Clive figured she must be at the gym. Lopez was the type to keep her cellphone stuck in her sports bra while doing miles on the treadmill. Clive rolled his eyes.

"I wanted to ask you if I can take a few more days here."

"Where are you again?"

"Florida."

"Florida?"

Clive grit his teeth.

"Yeah, Florida. A podunk town in the middle of nowhere. You sent me here to look into that church fire for a CAPA report remember? You owed some friend at the Tampa office a favor or something, so we picked up the case? He couldn't be bothered to send one of his own agents all the way out here."

"Oh, yeah, that's right. You need more time?"

Clive knew he couldn't tell Lopez that something about the town and Sister Tulah was needling at him. She'd think it was ridiculous and order him back to the office immediately.

"Just a day or two."

She sounded bored with him already.

"Grant. It's not rocket science. Talk to the detective on the case, talk to the fire marshal, write up the report. Sending you down there was just a formality. The state's attorney we already talked to made it clear—this isn't ATF's jurisdiction. Just dotting Is and crossing Ts. Got it?"

It sounded like Lopez was still running. Clive could imagine her high, perky ponytail swishing with every step. He ground his teeth and swallowed his pride.

"I just, um, I'm still not sure. I think I should stay and talk to a few more people before doing the report. I'd like to talk to one or two of the bikers awaiting trial and track down some of Sherwood Cannon's relatives. See what they have to say. Just to be sure, so I know exactly what to put in the report. And I still need to go out to the church site and look around."

"Are you kidding me? Do I need to come down there and hold your hand through this?"

"The case doesn't seem as clear as the state's attorney made it. I just want to look into a few things."

"You know that if you say this arson is federal, Krenshaw's going to shit a brick. There's a list a mile long of cases with a higher priority. You know, cases that actually matter."

Clive stood up from the bed.

"I know, I know. I'm not going to rock the boat. I just want to be sure that I do this right."

Lopez snickered.

"Don't want to screw this up and get sent back down the dungeon, huh?"

Clive squeezed his eyes shut and grimaced.

"Yes. Exactly."

"You'd better not be staying at a Hilton. That'll be a pain in the ass to explain on the expense reports."

He hoped Lopez's shoelace got caught in the treadmill belt. He hoped she fell flat on her sweaty face and broke her nose.

"Don't worry. I'm pretty sure there's nothing above a two-star hotel for a hundred miles in all directions."

"Jesus. All right, do what you got to do."

Clive started to say thanks, but Lopez had already hung up on him.

CHAPTER 5

For Judah, Lesser's absence was more noticeable than his presence had ever been. Judah had never really paid too much attention to Lesser at the salvage yard, but now he kept expecting to see the kid pass through the bay doors, the sunlight haloing his lanky silhouette, on his way to grab a soda from the minifridge or change the station on the boom box. Ramey had turned on the radio when they came in that morning and it now occurred to Judah that the classic rock station had stayed the same all day. Lesser hadn't been there to twist the dial over to a new station every half hour.

Judah craned his neck to peer up at the underside of the Impala on the lift. He was trying to cut out the catalytic converter but was making a mess of the job. Judah knew his way around a car, but it was taking him two hours to do what he knew Lesser or Benji could have knocked out in fifteen minutes. Even on crutches, Benji was still a magician with anything sporting wheels. But Benji had ignored Ramey's poundings on his door that morning and had elected instead to spend another day holed up in his stuffy bedroom with his pain pills and PlayStation games, his resentment and his grief. Judah hadn't laid eyes on his brother since he had explained what had happened to Lesser on the front porch. He was worried, but Ramey had cautioned him to just let it be.

Judah was about to throw the damn Sawzall across the garage, the converter wasn't coming off for shit, when Alvin's bright orange Jeep, all jacked up on monster tires just as its owner was on steroids, swerved into the back lot. A dusty cloud swirled around the knobby tires as Alvin climbed down from the driver's side with a wide smile plastered across his broad, tan face. Alvin, Gary and Judah had been best friends back in high school, which, even almost twenty years later, created an unbreakable bond between them. Gary swaggered around the front of the Jeep with a Four Loko in hand, draining the last of it. He pitched the can into the trash barrel next to the whirring industrial fan and shouted.

"Well, shouldn't be no problem now, Judah!"

Judah's eyes darted to the other side of the garage where Ramey was perched on the edge of the desk, cellphone cradled against her shoulder and yellow legal pad in hand. She had her back to him and Judah watched her nod her head as she wrote something down. Ramey had been on the phone most of the day it seemed, trying to sell part orders to mechanics across the county. She had only briefly glanced up when the Jeep pulled in. Judah tugged an oily rag out of his back pocket and jerked his head, indicating for Gary and Alvin to follow him outside and around the corner of the garage.

When they were safely out of sight and earshot, Judah turned to Alvin and Gary.

"All right, so what's the plan?"

Judah scrubbed as much grease off of his fingers as he could and then stuffed the rag back in his pocket. Gary shook out a cigarette and passed the pack around.

"Everything's gonna go just like we said before."

Gary lit his cigarette and exhaled a stream of smoke.

"It shouldn't be no sweat at all to get Nash."

Judah looked down at the Parliament in his hand. Who the hell smoked p-funks? Judah almost tossed the cigarette to the ground, but his own Marlboros were on top of a tool cabinet in the garage. He took a drag of the weak cigarette.

"Run the plan by me. I want to know the details before you go through with it."

Gary shrugged his bony shoulders.

"All right, boss."

Immediately after he had explained the circumstances of Lesser's death to Ramey and Benji on the front porch, Judah had called up Gary and told him to drop everything else and find out who the hell Weaver was. Last night, Gary had checked in saying that Weaver was still a question mark, but that he and Alvin had managed to stumble upon the location of Nash.

"So, it's like this."

Gary sucked on his cigarette.

"Nash is still holed up somewhere in Palatka, like we said last night, but after I talked to you, this little opportunity fell right into our laps."

Alvin crossed his bulging arms over his chest and rolled his eyes.

"Or rather, she fell into my lap."

Gary punched Alvin in the arm.

"That's true, that's true, man."

Judah felt like he was in trapped in a locker room. He raised his eyebrows expectantly.

"The plan, Gary?"

"Oh, right, right. It's like this."

Gary flicked his half-smoked cigarette to the dirt.

"See, last night, since we were already over in Palatka, we met up with this cousin of Alvin's. We were over at his place, just partying a little, you know, and he introduced us to his friend, who introduced us to his sister, Kristy, and her friend, shit, I can't even remember her name."

Gary scratched at the back of his neck.

"What was her name, Alvin?"

Alvin shrugged.

"Beats me. All I remember is that it looked like she fell out of the ugly tree and hit every branch on the way down."

Gary covered his face with his hand.

"Oh man, yeah. I'm gonna have nightmares about that one. But now this Kristy girl, I'm telling you, Judah, she was a real piece of work."

Alvin turned to Gary and shoved him.

"How would you know?"

Gary bounced back and clapped Alvin on the back.

"Well, she didn't have eyes for me. But she did for our man Alvin over here. Eyes, ears and everything else. Stuck to him like a fly in honey. And then, I guess, they were in the back bedroom and..."

Alvin interrupted him.

"And it turns out she's the bartender over at Betty's, this little joint out on the edge of town. And your buddy Nash is a regular there."

Judah nodded, relieved to finally be getting somewhere.

"Okay."

Gary grinned.

"So this Kristy girl, she's so gaga over Alvin that she's on board with helping us out. I guess Nash's been laying low and she ain't seen him in a couple days, but Kristy's sure that he'll be in sometime soon. When he shows up, she's gonna give Alvin a call and we'll be on our way."

Judah narrowed his eyes.

"And then?"

Gary smacked his palms together.

"Then we show up. Kristy said Nash always has this big fella with him, ain't hardly speak, but always seems to have Nash's back. Sounds like the guy you said was in the car with Nash at the gas station. Got a head like a bowling ball."

"Yeah."

"And so Kristy's gonna send Nash out to the car for some blow and work her charms on the gorilla to keep him in the bar. Grabbing Nash shouldn't be a problem."

Judah stuck his hands in his pockets.

"All right."

He looked past them, out to the salvage yard lot. Last night, before the call, Judah had shared a beer with Ramey, sitting out on the back steps, just watching the heat lightning roll in. They hadn't said much to each other, half the time they didn't need to, and for a few moments, with the fireflies floating lazily in the trees and the sky quivering and pulsing overhead, it had felt like that first night. Before the church shootout, before Sister Tulah, before the biker cash, before Sherwood had slid the envelope across the table to him in the back of the Mr. Omelet. When, for a single night, the only thing that had mattered was the challenge in Ramey's eyes and the heat of her hand over his. The tangle of sheets, the hum of the ceiling fan, the words whispered into the cloud of her hair as it fell over his face.

And then his brother, Levi, had come knocking the next morning with a message from Sherwood and Judah and Ramey's path had changed direction. The spell had been broken. The pieces had been had scattered.

"When Kristy calls, are we good to go, then?"

He turned back to Gary, bouncing on the balls of his feet from too many energy drinks. Judah thought of Ramey in the garage, probably still on the phone, trying to keep things together. Keep them going. Judah hadn't told her that they had found Nash and he wasn't planning to. He set his mouth in a grim line and nodded once.

"Good to go."

CLIVE BLINKED THE sweat out of his eyes and studied the marquee before him.

Last Steps of Deliverance Church of God

Pastor Tulah Atwell

"God Before the World!"

Considering the building it was standing in front of, Clive would have expected the sign to be missing a few letters, but it was pristine, the white background blinding in the afternoon sun, not a weed in sight or even a stray woodchip out of place at its base. Clive raised his eyes to the church behind the marquee; it wasn't in nearly such good shape. The frame for the front door was still standing, though it was blackened in parts, and thick sheets of plastic had been draped and stapled to the casing. What was left of the walls on either side of the doorframe had been nailed over with sheets of plywood and hand painted with two large black crosses.

Clive took out his notebook and flipped it open. He glanced at his notes and then turned and surveyed the parking lot next to the church. Aside from his Charger and a dusty, gold Buick, the lot was empty. He walked out into the center of the asphalt and turned slowly around in a circle, trying to match what he was seeing with the fire and police reports he had studied in his motel room the night before. Right about where he was standing, the body of the Scorpions' president, Jack Austin, had been found. Clive turned to the front of the church; there was definitely a clear sightline from the door. He took a few steps toward the woods that backed up to the parking lot. Sister Tulah's Lincoln Navigator, peppered with bullet holes, had been found with its back tires in the dirt at the edge of the asphalt. Clive frowned. This wasn't noted as unusual in the police report, but it didn't seem to add up. Sister Tulah didn't seem like the type to leave her vehicle badly parked. And she definitely wasn't the type to park across the lot just so she could walk a few extra steps and get some exercise.

Clive squinted down at his notes as he traced out what had once been a crime scene. Sherwood's truck had been haphazardly parked over there, in the middle of the lot. Clive glanced at the diagram he had hastily copied out on the page and moved a few yards over, closer to the road. He stared down at the sunbaked asphalt. Another one of the bikers' bodies had been found here. Sprawled out, shot in the back. He lifted his head and held the crude sketch out as he scanned the rest of the parking lot. Clusters of shell casings had been marked there, there, there. Blood spatter by the walkway, over there. Clive scratched his forehead with his thumbnail. Unless the Scorpions had turned on themselves, it seemed like an awfully chaotic crime scene for them to have been in a shootout with only Sherwood Cannon, holed up inside the church. Clive crossed the parking lot to the edge of the woods. The diagrams accompanying the police report hadn't extended past the trees. Clive frowned. That didn't make any sense either. Not one stray bullet had made it into the woods?

Clive ducked his head under the low branch of a yellow pine and crunched through the brush of brittle needles and scrubby twigs. He walked parallel to the parking lot, scanning the ground as he moved gingerly through the swishing saw palmettos. The serrated edges of a Spanish bayonet snagged against his ankle and Clive tripped and cursed. Did everything in Florida hate him? He bent down to examine the rent cuff of his trousers, but something much more interesting caught his eye. He squatted and picked up the shell casing for a .45 bullet. Clive held it up and watched it glint in the sun. He stuck it in his pocket and then inched along, sifting through the detritus of dead oak leaves, pine needles and sandy soil. Clive found another. Then another, this one smaller, a .9mm shell. And then, of all things, a .308. Clive picked up the rifle casing and rolled it across his palm. He stood up and shoved it in his pocket. What the hell had happened that day? Clive wiped his sweaty face on the arm of his suit jacket and extricated himself from the palmettos. He brushed himself off and headed back to the church. It wasn't the scene that bothered him so much, but rather the lack of attention given to it in the reports. There had been no mention of casings in the woods. No mention of .308 or .9mm shells found in the parking lot. Only a few .45s and the .223s from the Scorpions' assault rifles. Something was off. Clive shook his head. No, something was wrong.

Clive parted the sheets of plastic and stepped into the dim church. The sun filtering down through more clear plastic stretched across parts of the roof appeared to be the only source of light. Some sections of the missing roof had been draped with blue and green tarps, strung across the scorched beams with twine, and the faint light coming down through these areas gave the room an eerie, watery ambiance. Instead of pews, rough benches of plywood and two-by-fours, bristling with shiny, new nails, were lined up to face the low stage. A pulpit, charred on one side, stood conspicuously in the center. Clive thought about what it would be like to sit on one of those hard, backless benches for the marathon Pentecostal services he had heard about, but then he figured most of the people in attendance didn't do much sitting to begin with. Clive had only ever been to a few bland Methodist Easter events as a child, his parents didn't have much use for religion, but he had heard stories about how rowdy the holy rollers could get.

The air in the empty church was stifling as Clive slowly crept around the perimeter, examining the walls. They were a mottling of plywood and sheets of particle board, tacked over one another to cover the gaps in the burned-out walls. Some of the squares of wood had clusters of small black crosses painted in the corners. Two hand-lettered cardboard signs had been taped to the wall, one proclaiming *In My Name Shall They Cast Out Devils* and the other simply *God is Watching*. Underneath this statement, two round eyes with long lashes had been crudely drawn.

Clive turned in a circle, surveying the rest of the room. Portable work lamps stood in the corners and something large, it looked to be a piano, took up part of the far wall and was draped with a heavy canvas sheet. Clive had read in a newspaper clipping that church services had resumed almost immediately after the fire, with the worshipers down on their knees in the still warm rubble praying and giving thanks to God. Apparently, come rain or shine, with or without walls and a roof, the Last Steps Church would not be closed.

He was just about to leave when the door on the back wall next to the stage swung open wide and a man with a push broom in his hands stood gaping at him like a goldfish. Clive turned to the man and smiled, relieved that he was finally having some luck.

"Brother Felton?"

The pasty man with a fringe of brown hair crowning his sweating skull gripped the broom tightly in both doughy hands and nodded slowly. Clive wasn't sure exactly what he was dealing with. He had watched a few local news interviews with Sister Tulah, and while Felton always seemed to be standing somewhere in the background, Clive had never actually heard him speak. From the terrified look Felton was giving him now, Clive wasn't sure he even could.

"Brother Felton, my name is Special Agent Clive Grant."

Felton nodded again, still clutching the broom out in front of him as if it could somehow ward off evil. Clive was beginning to wonder if Tulah's nephew had a couple of screws loose. He came down the aisle parting through the benches and sat down on a bench in the front row, trying to show Felton that he was harmless. Brother Felton eyed him warily and then leaned the broom carefully against the back wall. He remained standing in the doorway with a frightened expression on his face.

"What do you want?"

Felton's voice was a little high-pitched and wheezy, but otherwise he sounded normal. Somewhat intelligent. Clive started to reach inside his jacket, but then thought better of it, thinking that the notebook might scare Felton off. He rested his hands on his thighs instead and looked around the church as if seeing it for the first time.

"So, the place is still standing, huh? After the fire, I mean. Looks like you guys are putting some work into fixing it back up."

Felton narrowed his eyes and folded his arms across his chest. Clive could see the pit stains spreading through the man's pale yellow polo shirt.

"Yes."

Clive jerked his thumb over his shoulder.

"Sign out front looks new, though."

"It is."

Felton didn't offer anything else and Clive decided he'd better jump right in while he had the chance.

"Brother Felton, I'm with ATF. I talked with your aunt the other day. Since you're here, do you mind if I ask you a few questions?"

Felton's eyes drifted around the church as he seemed to think about this. Finally, he let his gaze fall warily back on Clive.

"What kinds of questions? I already gave my statement back in May."

"I know, I know. Don't worry, I'm not with the police. I'm just investigating the fire. That's all. So can I ask you a couple of questions?"

Felton came forward out of the doorway and stood awkwardly next to the edge of the stage.

"I suppose."

Clive still didn't take out his notebook.

"So, just to kind of go over what you already told the detectives and the fire marshal, you entered the church when the fire was already underway, correct?"

Felton nodded.

"And when you came in, what did you see?"

"I already made my statement."

Clive put up his hands defensively.

"Okay, don't worry. We don't have to go back over it. So let me ask you this, do you think either the Scorpions or Sherwood Cannon had anything against Sister Tulah?"

"Against her? Why would they?"

"Well, I don't know. That's why I'm asking."

He could see Felton working it out in his head, trying to figure out the best way to respond. Clive wouldn't have been surprised if he was trying to remember what Tulah had told him to say. Felton's lips were trembling slightly, like a child trying not to cry, and he spoke slowly and haltingly.

"I don't think, I mean, I don't know why anyone would have anything against Sister Tulah. She's a preacher."

"So then you think Sherwood Cannon liked Sister Tulah?"

Clive almost felt bad for Felton as he squirmed under the questioning.

"Well, I don't think he liked her exactly, no."

Clive stood up and casually walked a few paces around the base of the stage.

"I mean, he did put out her eye. With his thumb. That's not the sort of thing you do to somebody you like, is it?"

"No."

"So you think that maybe Sherwood Cannon hated your aunt?"

Felton looked down at his brown loafers.

"I guess. I mean, maybe he hated her. To do something like that."

Clive turned and took a few steps in the other direction, trying to keep his gaze on the church around him and not on Felton.

"It's funny, though. In my experience, it's hard to hate someone, really hate someone, so much that you'd try to strangle them to death and then screw your thumb into their eye socket, if you don't know them. Doesn't that sound about right?"

"I guess so."

"So what do you think Sherwood had against your aunt? Why do think he hated her so much?"

Felton twisted his hands together in front of him and stumbled over his words.

"I don't know. I mean, I guess he had a reason."

"And to have a reason, he'd probably have some history with her, right?"

Felton jerked his head up and the worried expression on his face began to disappear. Clive knew he had pushed it too far and Felton had figured out what he was getting at.

"Aunt Tulah said that when she asked the man to leave, he attacked her. She didn't know who he was. She'd never seen him before."

Clive came back around the stage again and stood directly in front of Felton.

"But what was he doing here in the first place, Brother Felton? That's what I really want to know. Why here? Why this church? Why did Sister Tulah just happen to be here at the same time as Sherwood and the Scorpions?"

Felton shook his head back and forth emphatically.

"I don't know."

"Okay, okay."

Clive decided to change tactics. He pointed to the space on the stage in front of the pulpit.

"That's where they found Sherwood's body, right?"

Felton had his mouth clamped shut, his resolve clearly being not to answer any more questions, so Clive just kept going.

"He had his head smashed in. You said you didn't see what had happened to Sherwood. You said that you only remembered there being a person there, but that you couldn't see who it was with all the smoke."

Clive pointed to the empty back wall.

"There used to be a cross there, right? A big, heavy cross that was found on the ground next to Sherwood's dead body. The forensics team on the case said they're pretty sure the cross was used to bash in Sherwood's skull. That's what killed him."

Clive put his hands in his pockets and rocked back on his heels.

"But you know what's funny, Brother Felton? No one knows who actually killed Sherwood Cannon. Now, the bikers claim they never even entered the church. When questioned, one of them said there were people they couldn't see shooting at them from outside of the church, and yet Sherwood was found dead inside. The bikers said that maybe it was Sherwood's son, Levi. He's been MIA ever since the shootout, I hear. His wife and kid apparently skipped town, too. So maybe it was Levi who killed him. Or maybe it was someone else."

He stared hard at Felton.

"What do you think?"

Clive was surprised to see Felton staring back just as hard. Maybe there was a little backbone in him after all.

"I think you should leave."

Clive smiled and took a step back.

"All right. I suppose I've outstayed my welcome. But thank you, Brother Felton. I appreciate it."

Felton continued to stare. Clive turned to go, but then raised his eyebrows and pointed to the pulpit on the stage. A glass jelly jar half full of clear liquid was perched on the corner of it.

"Mind if I ask? What's in the jar?"

Felton looked at the jar and then back to Clive.

"Strychnine."

Clive jerked his back around to Felton.

"Poison? What for?"

Felton seemed genuinely surprised that Clive didn't know.

"For the faithful, of course. To demonstrate our certainty that God will protect us."

Clive was shocked.

"You people drink that? Don't you know it will kill you?"

A smug smile played at the edge of Felton's lips.

"Not if you're one of us."

CHAPTER 6

RAMEY SHIFTED THE Cutlass into fifth and leaned back, dangling one hand over the top of the ragged steering wheel. It was late and they were driving west; the highway was glazed over with shimmering copper, and in the last rays of sunlight the trees and brush along the roadside seemed to swell and shiver with viridescence. This was Ramey's favorite time of day. The world became quiet, soft and lush, but reveled in a moment of brilliance before winking into twilight. It was a stepping out of time, and if Ramey caught it right, for a few seconds, she could slip away with it.

Beside her, Judah pitched his cigarette out the open window.

"See? Isn't this what normal people do? Get off work, go grocery shopping, come home and make Hamburger Helper?"

"Tuna Noodle."

Ramey kept her eyes on the road.

"And most folks don't go to the Winn-Dixie armed to the teeth, watching their backs in the cereal aisle."

Judah slung his arm behind her headrest and stretched out in the seat.

"In Silas? Where you been, woman?"

Ramey finally cut her eyes over at him. His grin was infectious and Ramey could feel the smile tugging at the corners of her mouth.

"Busy trying to run a criminal empire. Or not run it, that is."

Judah tugged at a wind-whipped snarl in her hair and then slid his hand up behind her ear. His fingers pressed lightly against her neck.

"But you're so damn good at it."

Ramey glanced over at him again and this time she couldn't help but return his look. This was the Judah she always wanted, with a sly smile and a devilish spark behind the eyes. A man with the world at his feet, or at least the sureness to think so. Ramey was acutely aware of the fact that she was the only one who could bring this out in him, and even then, it was rare. She hungered for this side of him. Craved it. Too often, by the end of the day, there wasn't much left for her but the raw scraps of his ruminations. And since Lesser's death, she had felt her narrow window to the inner workings of his heart closing fast. She didn't know why; she didn't know what was happening, only that at times over the past week she had met Judah's eyes and sensed that the breath was being sucked out of her, sharply, leaving her empty and hollow. They were so very far away from one another.

Judah dropped his hand to her thigh and picked at a loose thread on her jeans.

"It's gonna be okay, Ramey."

She knew that if she turned her head to look at him, she would hear the subtle change in his voice reflected in the cast of his eyes. Ramey focused on the nimbused tree line ahead.

"I know."

"I mean it. I get it, things are crazy. And getting crazier every day, it seems. But we will come through this. And I will take care of you through it all, understand?"

Ramey shook her head.

"I don't need you to take care of me. I just need you to be with me."

Judah removed his hand and twisted in the seat so that he was fully facing her.

"All right. I can do that."

Ramey turned off the road and eased the Cutlass down the sandy, washboard driveway. As she came jolting around the curve, she could see the house up ahead, shaded by live oaks and slash pines in the dusk. The porch light was on and a warm glow came from one of the twin dormer windows on the second story. The house appeared to be winking at them and Ramey smiled. From this view, it could almost be a home.

"And don't you ever keep things from me. Don't you ever shut me out, you hear?"

"Ramey."

Judah sighed and ran a hand through his hair before shaking his head.

"I never have. And I never will. You and me, we're in this together, all the way, right?"

"Right."

Ramey pulled up next to Judah's truck. She yanked the keys out of the ignition and sat staring at them in her hands for a moment.

"I just…"

She raised her eyes to Judah's. The spark was gone, replaced now by smoldering ash. His eyes held hers for a moment and then Judah leaned forward, cupping his hands around her chin and then sliding them down to her collar bone.

"Don't worry, Ramey. Trust me."

He pulled her to him and kissed her forehead lightly. Ramey closed her eyes.

"I trust you."

"Now come on, let's get this food in the house. I don't know about you, but I'm so hungry my stomach thinks my throat's been cut."

Ramey shot him a half smile and slid out of the driver's seat. She lifted a paper bag of groceries out of the back and kicked the door closed. The bag was heavy and she hitched it up on one side as she climbed the porch steps and fumbled with getting her keys in the door lock. She heard the passenger's side door of the Cutlass slam behind her and Judah called out.

"You got it?"

Ramey wrenched her keys out and pushed the front door open with her shoulder.

"Got it."

She hiked the grocery bag back up on her hip and blew a stray strand of hair out of her eyes. The living room was dark, but the kitchen light was on and she rushed through the hall, anxious to put the bag down before she dropped it. She came around the corner but froze, stunned, in the kitchen doorway.

"What in the holy hell?"

Gary, sitting on the kitchen counter, raised his beer up to her and grinned stupidly. Alvin had been leaning against the refrigerator, also with a beer in hand, but he stood up straight when he saw her and ducked his eyes to the floor. Benji was sitting at one end of the kitchen table, his crutches propped up against the wall behind him, and at the other end of the table sat a man with a gash over his right eye and a shiner around his left. The thick strip of duct tape over his mouth was caked with dried blood. His hands were zip-tied behind him and a length of nylon rope had been looped around his chest several times, securing him to the chair he was sitting in. He awkwardly turned his head to look at her. Gary waved his hand like a magician.

"Surprise!"

Ramey thought she was going to drop the bag of groceries at her feet. Benji raised an eyebrow and shook his head just as Judah stumbled through the door behind her.

"What is it?"

Ramey realized that her mouth was open. She clamped it shut and swallowed hard as Judah pulled up short beside her. She turned to see that his eyes were about as wide as she was sure her own were. Gary slid down from the kitchen counter.

"Well, here you go! Delivered as promised. I was gonna stick a bow on his head for you, but I couldn't find one in time."

Ramey's eyes narrowed as she realized that Judah wasn't so much flabbergasted, as simply caught unawares. She set the bag of groceries on the counter and slowly turned to him, letting the acid in her voice soak through every word.

"Judah. Is there something you want to tell me?"

JUDAH REACHED OUT to Ramey as she backed away from him.

"I was going to tell you."

Ramey crossed her arms over her chest. Even in the dim light of the living room, he could see her nails biting into her skin. From the expression on her face, the way she was working her jaw, drawing the edge of her bottom lip between her teeth, it was hard to tell if she was either scared or furious. Or both. Sometimes, there wasn't much of a difference with Ramey.

She cocked her head to one side.

"You were going to tell me?"

Ramey quit chewing on her lip and her eyes popped wide.

"You were going to tell me that I would come home to the man who shot and killed Lesser, who almost killed you, trussed up at my kitchen table like a goddamn Virginia ham?"

Judah let his arms drop to his side.

"Well. Not exactly all that."

Ramey glanced over Judah's shoulder, toward the light creeping around the edge of the hallway. She jutted her chin in the direction of the kitchen, where Alvin, Gary and Benji were waiting. Alvin and Gary were laughing loudly about something. Ramey dropped her voice down to a hiss and turned her blazing eyes back on him.

"What the hell is going on here? When I asked you this morning, you told me that you hadn't turned up anything on Weaver yet."

Judah turned slightly toward the kitchen.

"Well, technically…"

He was trying not to look at her.

"Judah, I swear to God. You even think about going there and so help me…"

Judah turned back to Ramey and gripped her shoulders. This time, she didn't back away. He dipped his chin slightly and met her eyes. Some of the fight was leaving them, but something else, something even more disquieting, was brewing there. Something he wasn't ready to see.

"I'm sorry. Ramey, I'm sorry. I should have told you."

She swayed lightly as he pulled on her shoulders, but then broke away from him.

"Should have was a long time ago."

Ramey pushed past him. Judah raised his eyes toward the ceiling and then shut them tight. He'd deal with her later. Right now, he had to figure out what to do with Nash. Judah followed Ramey into the kitchen and tried to take stock of the situation. Nash tied up in the chair. Benji glowering in the corner with glassy eyes. Alvin and Gary grinning like cats and popping tall boys. Gary shook his head and whistled when Judah walked in.

"Damn, Judah. We thought you'd be pleased."

Judah glanced over at Ramey, leaning in the doorway with her arms still crossed and the corners of her mouth still turned down. He turned back to Gary and grit his teeth.

"I didn't think you'd bring him here."

Gary shrugged.

"Went by the garage, but you'd left already, I guess. We figured you'd want to see him ASAP. I mean, I don't think he'd spoil or nothing, but you never know."

Gary smirked over the top of his beer can. Judah couldn't look back at Ramey; he knew she was seething behind him.

"You never hear of a phone?"

Alvin, obviously getting bored with the whole situation, cracked open another beer and held it out to Judah.

"Well, he's here now."

Judah shook his head at the beer. He walked slowly around the table until he was able to look at Nash straight on. In addition to the cut over his right eye, the left side of his face was already swelling in a patchwork of bruises and there was a thin red band of mottled skin circling his neck. His shoulders were slumped and his head cast down. Judah narrowed his eyes.

"And you weren't followed?"

Gary jumped down from the kitchen counter.

"Hell no, Judah. Plan worked like a charm. That Kristy girl was a sure thing. She called Alvin up this afternoon and we lit on over to Palatka. Nash was having himself a happy hour and he and his jarhead friend played right into the trap. She texted Alvin when she told Nash she'd buy a bump off him, but Alvin had already jimmy-rigged Nash's car and was waiting like a ninja in the backseat. Guy couldn't even move once Alvin got that extension cord 'round his neck."

Judah frowned. He had been distracted by the shock, by Ramey and then by the details of the story, but he tried to push it all from his mind now. The room fell silent around him and as he stared at Nash, everything slowly dialed down into pinpointed focus. Judah pulled out a chair and sat down in front of Nash. It was just him, this man and the weight of Lesser's death hanging between them. Judah leaned forward and took hold of a corner of the duct tape. He ripped it off and Nash gasped. Judah looked at the strip of tape dangling between his fingers and then he wadded it up and flicked it at Nash's face. It bounced off his cheek.

"You killed my friend."

Nash licked his split bottom lip and looked up at Judah.

"I'm sorry. Really. I wasn't trying to kill nobody. I was just being stupid. I didn't mean to shoot that kid."

Judah studied Nash, with his slumped, awkwardly tied body and his bloody face. He was disgusting. Pathetic. Abject.

"You're sorry."

Judah's voice was flat and he barely moved the rest of his body as he kicked his leg out. Nash toppled over backward, smacking the back of his head on the linoleum floor. The sound was sickening. Judah waited while Alvin and Gary hauled Nash up and righted his chair. He was vaguely aware that neither Benji nor Ramey had moved a muscle. Nash's eyes were bulging with pain and he seemed disoriented for a moment. Judah rested his palms on the thighs of his jeans and leaned forward.

"Who is Weaver?"

Nash shook his head slightly. The cut over his eye was oozing and he blinked through the strings of blood.

"I mean it, man. I'm sorry, I really didn't..."

Judah kicked again. This time, he could hear Ramey inhale sharply behind him. Alvin and Gary stood on either side of Nash's head, staring down at him. Gary put his hands on his hips.

"Want us just to leave him there? Can't do a damn thing laying there like a turtle on its back."

Alvin picked up his beer from the counter and cocked his head as he looked down at Nash.

"If you want him to quit whining, I got a welding torch in the Jeep."

Gary shook his head.

"Nah, use a car battery."

Alvin knit his brows.

"You know how to do that without killing him right away?"

Gary frowned.

"Well, I could try it, anyway. I saw this rerun of *24* the other night and they did this thing where they put a wire down the guy's pants and—"

"Weaver's my boss!"

Nash thrashed his head furiously from side to side. Alvin looked to Judah, but Judah only shook his head slightly. Alvin turned back to Nash.

"Nah, car battery won't work. Too much risk. What about a drill?"

Gary looked around the kitchen.

"Ramey, you keep a power drill charged around here? The pantry maybe?"

Nash raised his head up as much as he could. His fingers were curled against the sides of the chair as he hollered.

"Jesus Christ! Everett Weaver! He runs blow and shit all up and down I-95. Jacksonville to Melbourne. Sometimes guns, but he's smart. He's got a whole network buying wholesale coke and weed from the beaners, oxys and vikes from the clinics, marking it up, selling it everywhere on the coast."

Nash was panting, his voice trilling higher and higher as he spoke. Judah scowled and jerked his chin. Alvin and Gary lifted the back of Nash's chair and sat him up in front of Judah again. There was a smear of blood on the floor. Judah stared at it and then turned around to Ramey. Her eyes were guarded, but her mouth was set in a hard line.

"You got a cigarette?"

Her expression didn't change, but she finally uncrossed her arms and reached on top of the refrigerator. She took down a soft pack and slid out a cigarette. Ramey dug her lighter out of her pocket and lit it. When she handed it to him, he could see that her shoulders had relaxed just slightly. He turned back to Nash and took a long drag on the cigarette before pointing it in Nash's direction.

"Weaver send you to kill me?"

Nash's eyes went wide.

"What? No, no, that's not it. I promise. I know you don't want to believe me, but shooting that kid was an accident, I swear. I got this thing, like this anger management thing. They make me go to court-ordered meetings and everything. I'm serious. I got a problem. Honest."

Judah blew a stream of smoke in Nash's face.

"I can see that. So what's Weaver want with me?"

"What's Weaver want with you? Man, he wants to work with you."

Judah narrowed his eyes.

"And he sent you to tell me that? This guy I've never heard of?"

Nash was squirming.

"I'd told him before about Sherwood. About how the Cannons got this thing going out in the middle of BFE. The bookies running out of the honkytonk bars. The cigs and the booze and whatever. Good network, low profile, a chance for a lot of money to be made off the pill heads and tweakers. He'd already been talking about expanding west off the coast. Seemed perfect to match both sides up. But Sherwood didn't want nothing to do with Weaver. So, when he died and you took over, Weaver asked me to talk to you. See if you were interested in going in with him."

"That so?"

"I mean it. It's a good deal on both sides. A great deal."

Judah pulled the brown glass ashtray in the middle of the table toward him.

"And let me guess. You'd be the bridge between us."

Nash nodded emphatically.

"That was the idea."

Judah rolled the edge of his cigarette along the rim of the ashtray.

"A win-win-win, huh?"

Nash dropped his head.

"'Course, I guess you don't want nothing to do with me now."

"With you? No."

Judah took one last drag off his cigarette and then crushed it out.

"Where can I find Weaver?"

Nash shook his head.

"Well, see, it's not that easy. He's smart, like I said. Never in one place for too long."

Judah cast his eyes up toward Alvin and nodded. Nash began frantically twisting in his chair again.

"But I think he's in Daytona! Last time I talked to him, when I told him about you taking over the Cannons and all, he had just gotten to Daytona Beach. He's probably doing some business there. He usually stays a few weeks in one city before moving on to the next."

Judah leaned in close.

"You got a phone number?"

"No. He's always got different phones and shit. It's like, he calls you. You don't call him. But I can tell you some of his joints in Daytona. There's a couple of girly clubs he owns. And a few bars. I know the clubs: Stingrays and The Pink Pelican. You go there and I'm sure you'll be able to find him. He wants to work with you, remember? He wants to meet you."

Judah looked back over his shoulder at Ramey. She had a lit cigarette herself, but only shrugged her shoulders as she exhaled a stream of smoke. Judah turned around and glanced down the table at Benji. He was staring straight ahead and didn't seem to be following the conversation at all. Judah turned back to Nash and put his elbow on the edge of the table.

"How close are you with Weaver?"

Judah could see Nash weighing the question, trying to determine Judah's meaning. He spoke warily.

"Not too close."

Judah smacked his hand on the table and stood up. He nodded to Alvin and Gary.

"That settles it, then. Boys, he's all yours. You want to go all MacGyver on him, it's fine by me. But do it outside, okay? We already got enough to clean up in here."

Alvin put his heavy hand on Nash's shoulder and Nash almost shrieked.

"Okay, I lied. I lied! I'm important to Weaver. I'm somebody, goddamn it! You let these psychos kill me and Weaver'll never work with you. You'll have screwed up his dealings in Putnam County and he's not just going to forgive you for that. That's a lot of money you'll have cost him. Think about it, Judah! Just stop and think about it, for Christ's sake!"

Judah crossed his arms and regarded Nash, bloody, sweating, his eyes near about to bug out of his head. He knew what Ramey wanted him to do. Despite Benji's silence, he knew what his brother wanted, too. But Judah wasn't so sure either of them were thinking the way they needed to be. The Cannons couldn't afford to waver any longer. They couldn't afford to be weak. He couldn't afford to be weak. Judah looked down at Nash and considered his future.

"I am thinking about it."

Sister Tulah eyed the heap of Nesquik on her spoon before dumping the powder into her glass. She added another and then began to stir, watching the milk turn a creamy shade of light brown. The mixture had to be just right. She tapped the edge of the spoon on the glass and raised it so she could make sure the Nesquik had all dissolved. Satisfied, she grunted to herself and carried the glass into her study on the other side of the house.

She crossed through the empty dining room with its three tortured portraits of Jesus weeping for the sins of the world. Tulah stopped at the sideboard and inspected her collection of Hummel figurines, seeking out any motes of dust. Since Felton had moved out of the house to live next to his den of serpents, Tulah had been forced to hire a cleaning woman. She lumbered around the enormous walnut dining table and passed through the dark living room, pausing to lift up a few pieces of her displayed collector plates to check for dust underneath the wire stands. Sister Tulah scowled as she straightened the angle of her prized Bradford Exchange *Gone with the Wind* plate on the top shelf of the curio cabinet. Felton had known exactly how to clean each piece and how exactly to put it back. This new woman, the daughter of Sister Edith, hadn't paid enough attention to Tulah's precise instructions. She wasn't worried about the woman stealing from her, there was no fear of that, but she was concerned about her level of competency.

Sister Tulah sighed. If only Felton would come back to live in his room at the top of the stairs. Two weeks after the church fire, and after he had clobbered that beast Sherwood Cannon over the head with the cross, Felton had announced to her that he had bought another silly little tin camper and was moving out. At the time, she had sneered at him and told him to go ahead, knowing he wouldn't last a week. But apparently Felton's new setup was somewhat habitable and he seemed content to live in his sardine can and only bother with maintaining the church. Tulah pursed her lips. He was trying to make a statement. To gain some sort of independence from her, and Sister Tulah wasn't going to have it. As soon as she returned, she would take him in hand and lead him back down the necessary path of complacency.

Confident that everything was in its proper place, Sister Tulah entered her study and locked the door behind her. She settled herself into the oxblood wingback chair and placed the glass of settling chocolate milk on the massive oak desk in front of her. Tulah reached for a tall, dark green bottle sitting on the edge of the desk and squeezed the plastic bulb of the glass dropper. Being careful not to spill a single drop, she held it over her glass and let three clots of the sticky, oozing mixture splash into the milk. Sister Tulah quickly replaced the dropper and took up a long silver spoon, stirring the milk into a vicious whirlpool. She raised the glass to her lips and drank while the milk was still swishing around in the glass. With her eye closed and her face scrunched, she forced herself to swallow. When the glass was empty, she slammed it down, panting, and shoved it away from her.

There was nothing on earth worse than the taste of the Mithridatium. Over the years, she had tried to improve upon the ancient recipe, passed down from her grandmother, but in having to get the exact ratios of all fifty-two ingredients correct when she concocted the mixture, taste often fell by the wayside. A quarter of a gram one way or the other would have her convulsing on the floor and foaming at the mouth. Fiddling with the right amount of myrrh was one thing, but wolfsbane and arsenic weren't so forgiving.

Sister Tulah smacked her lips and tried not to retch as she reached under her desk and pressed a hidden lever. A drawer shot out and Tulah leaned over, picking through the layers of paper until she found the account ledger she was looking for. She opened the unassuming green record book to the page with the most recent entries and used her thick finger to trace down the columns of strange dots and dashes.

Ingesting the antidote every night for six months leading up to the second Sunday in August was essential if she wanted to survive drinking the Lotan, but none of it mattered if she wouldn't be able to actually attend. Sister Tulah had been faithfully paying her five thousand dollar tithes every month for the past three years, but now she had to make sure she had enough for the final offering. Regardless of the strength of her devotion, she still had to levy a hundred grand to secure her rightful place. Since Tulah had taken over the Last Steps Church from her grandfather, putting the money together had never been a problem. But the events of May had taken their toll. All those palms greased in Tallahassee and yet she'd still lost the phosphate deal when her fifty thousand was stolen, first by Sherwood Cannon and then from him, or so he had claimed, and she couldn't fork over the final bribe in time. In the grand scheme of things, fifty thousand dollars was a mere drop in the bucket, but the trail of damage left by it was considerable. Loaning money to that imbecile biker Jack Austin was the most foolhardy decision she had ever made and in the end she'd paid for it with her church, her eye and, ultimately, the mine that would have made her millions. And then, after all that, as if she hadn't lost enough in the fire, there were the never-ending payoffs to the sheriff and the fire marshal. To the local press to spin the story the right way. It was ridiculous how much money had flowed through her hands like water through a sieve.

And now there was this federal agent trying to stir things up. He had seemed innocuous at first, but Tulah could smell it coming. Agent Grant was staying too long in Kentsville and asking too many questions. He had even approached Felton, for God's sake, looking to poke holes in the account of Sherwood's death. Well, she was at an end with her indulgent ways, with the checks slipped between handshakes and boxes of cash left by back doors. When Sister Tulah had lost her eye, she knew she had lost some of her power over the people who feared her. They saw her bandaged face and the ruins of her church and thought she had loosened her iron grip on them. In the aftermath of the disaster, it had simply been easier to use the carrot in place of the stick. But if anyone thought she was going soft, they had another thing coming. Once she returned, she would remind them all of who she really was and what she could really do. And if Special Agent Grant was still poking around, she'd go for his throat first.

Sister Tulah scanned the rows and columns of code, adding up the math in her head. She took a stubby pencil from the silver tray at the edge of her desk and licked the tip of it before adding in three dots and two dashes at the bottom of the page. Brother Cary had called her that evening and given her another update on the one eleven account. She marked it in and then went over the column again. And then once more. Finally, she tossed the pencil down and clasped her hands together on the desk. It would be enough. Just barely, but enough. And the eventual return would be tenfold. Sister Tulah smiled to herself. She would be going to The Recompense. She would be going home to God.

"I WAS JUST trying to protect you."

"Don't."

Judah was hoping Ramey would turn to him, would at least look at him, but her eyes were fixed outside the second story window. The moon was heavy, almost full, and lighting up the backyard expanse of scruffy tufts of grass and patches of sandy dirt. The family who had rented the house before them, or maybe before, or before, must have had kids. A bent swing set frame, sagging beneath the stranglehold of greenbriers, stood back where the thick woods began to creep up toward the house and the moonlight glittered off the rusting metal. Judah leaned his shoulder against the wall, trying to catch Ramey's eye.

"I'm serious."

She still wouldn't look at him.

"Well, what do you know? I am, too. We're quite a pair, huh?"

It was hard, just standing next to her in the darkness of the bedroom. Ramey's palms were pressed against the glass, her fingers curling over the middle rail, and all he wanted was to put his hand on hers. To feel his fingers fall into place. Judah knew that hand, the white flecks under the nails and the way the pinky bowed out slightly. He knew her hands and he knew her body. The scars tracking across her lower stomach and left hip. The tattoo between her shoulder blades that she liked and the one on her ankle that she didn't. The chipped front tooth that had never kept her from smiling. He knew that she liked her coffee bitter and her whiskey straight. That she slept with her lips slightly parted. Had a soft spot for strays. Couldn't carry a tune to save her life. And didn't have time for bullshit.

Judah rammed his fists down into pockets. He knew all of these things, and so many more, but at the moment he didn't know Ramey's mind. Didn't know her heart. And it was his own damn fault.

"That we are."

Ramey drummed her fingers against the glass.

"Where is Nash now?"

"In the shed. Gary's keeping an eye on him."

Ramey turned to him, keeping one hand on the rail, picking away at a splinter with her nails.

"And you're really gonna do this?"

Judah pulled his hands out of his pockets, but still didn't reach for her.

"Look, I don't buy half of Nash's story—"

"I don't buy most of it."

"—but if I'm in any way on Weaver's radar, then I need to meet him. Size him up. See what's what."

Ramey's eyes narrowed.

"Why?"

"Why?"

"Yes, why. Why are you going to Daytona, trying to find some guy you know nothing about? Nash is lying about something, but who knows which part? This Weaver could've never heard of you; he could want to kill you. Shoot you on sight. You just don't know."

Judah shook his head.

"Ramey, I'll be fine."

Ramey's voice exploded in the darkness. She slammed her palms into his chest. Not as hard as she could, but hard enough.

"I know you'll be fine!"

Judah stepped back, more startled by her tone than by the blow. She went to push him again and he caught her wrists.

"Ramey."

There weren't quite tears in her eyes, but there was something. Frayed. Raw-edged.

"I know you'll be fine! You're always fine. But just tell me why the hell you're doing this."

Judah tried to keep his voice steady.

"With Weaver?"

"With all of it!"

She wrenched away from him and he let her go. Ramey stalked across the room, but then whipped back around to him.

"This ain't only about Lesser. Or Nash and Weaver for that matter. It's more than that."

Judah tried to keep his voice steady. He couldn't let her see him falter.

"No."

But Judah knew the answer was yes. And he knew that Ramey knew. And that flayed him down to the core. She crossed her arms and looked away from him.

"This is about you. You keep saying it's about others. Justice for Lesser. Taking care of Benji. Protecting me. Whatever the hell that entails."

Judah could feel his voice rising, matching hers. Both in volume and in spitting bitterness.

"It is about you! About all of you. What do you think I'm doing? Why do you think I'm doing everything, every goddamn thing I can to take care of this family?"

Ramey flung her arms out wide.

"I don't know!"

Judah suddenly brought his voice down, low and dangerous.

"Well, if you have to keep asking, I guess you don't know me at all."

Judah couldn't bear to look at her. She knew. She could see the lurking, hulking hydra of ambition and hubris, of penitence and doubt, coiling itself around his heart. But she wanted to shoot an arrow into the belly of the monster; Judah knew that its many mouths had already bitten him too deeply. He could not be released.

"I'm leaving in the morning. First thing."

He clenched his fists and walked away.

CHAPTER 7

RAMEY LET THE back screen door clatter and slam behind her. The top of the washing machine was open and she glanced inside as she walked through the laundry room. A bloody T-shirt, most likely Gary's or Alvin's, had been thrown onto a heap of dirty, greasy jeans and twisted up boxer shorts. Ramey didn't even stop. She went into the kitchen, washed her hands furiously and braced herself against the sink.

"This is ridiculous."

"You're telling me."

Ramey shook her hands and turned around to Benji. He was seated at the kitchen table, his pill bottles lined up in front of him like toy soldiers. Ramey leaned back against the edge of the counter top.

"I just held a gun on a man while he ate a PowerBar. Tied up. In my garden shed."

Benji picked up a bottle and popped the plastic top. He peered inside.

"Judah's a prince."

Ramey tried to blow a lock of hair out of her eyes and finally used her forearm to brush it away. She looked around for a dishtowel, but resorted to wiping her wet hands on her jeans. The .45 was digging into her back and she yanked it out, tossing it on the counter next to the toaster. She stared at it for a moment and then looked up at Benji in confusion.

"What?"

Benji replaced the bottle and picked another one out of the lineup.

"Leaving us here to deal with that murderer out there. While he's off with the good old boys, playing gangster at the beach. Just wait until Nash's gotta piss."

"Oh Jesus."

Ramey sat down at the table and put her head in her hands. She raked her fingers back through her hair.

"I am not cut out for this shit."

Benji shook a Vicodin into his palm and threw it hard against the back of his throat. He swallowed a few times and jutted his chin toward the backyard.

"That man out there, the one you just so kindly gave lunch to, killed my friend."

"I know."

Benji banged his fist down on the table and three of the pill bottles toppled over.

"My friend! Not Judah's."

"Benji..."

"And Judah was just sitting there last night, trying to be a badass. Acting like he really cared about Lesser."

Ramey pushed out her chair and stood up. She'd had enough of Benji's muttering, half-coherent rants to last a lifetime.

"I'm not listening."

Benji righted the pill bottles and put them back in line.

"Well, you should."

He looked up at her with a strange fire behind his glassy eyes.

"Somebody should. Judah may talk a big game about family, but he needs to start acting like we matter. The Cannons do shit together. We make decisions together. You, me and Judah. That's the way it's gotta be."

Ramey opened the refrigerator and stared aimlessly at the shelves. She didn't know what she was looking for.

"I'm not a Cannon."

"Might as well be."

Ramey slammed the refrigerator door closed. She was over it. So, so over it all.

"And you were never really involved with family business anyway."

"Neither was Judah. And yet look how far we've come."

She couldn't take it anymore. Ramey snatched up her keys from the dish on the counter.

"I've got to run up to the garage for a few hours. Think you can manage Nash?"

"Me?"

Benji shrugged.

"I ain't going out there. He's gonna have to be all by his lonesome. I got a packed afternoon of *Judge Judy, Oprah* and *Dr. Phil.*"

Ramey thought about it a moment, but finally just shook her head. She had to get out of there.

"Well, he's tied up pretty good. I don't think he's going anywhere."

Benji waved over his shoulder.

"Don't worry. The TV's right next to the window. I'll keep an eye out. If I see him running toward the woods, I'll call you."

Ramey frowned as Benji reached for another bottle.

"Fine. And quit taking all those pills. You don't need them anyway. God knows what that cocktail is doing to your insides. And your brain."

Benji twisted off the plastic cap.

"Yes, ma'am."

Ramey stared hard at the back of Benji's head as she watched him throw back a Xanax. He started mumbling to himself as he edged out of his seat and reached for his crutches. Judah, right before he left, had asked her to take care of Nash until he got back from Daytona. Ramey rolled her eyes and headed for the door. Compared to Benji, Nash was a piece of cake

CLIVE SAT UP straight. Then he slouched down in the chair, stretching his legs out. He put his hands behind his head and tried to affect a bored expression. No, that wouldn't work with this guy. He sat up straight again and smoothed down the front of his suit. He turned so that he was facing slightly away from the door and rested his forearm on the edge of the table. Professional. Yet, approachable. Confident. Clive glanced up at the controlled circuit video camera mounted in the corner of the interview room. He grit his teeth to suppress his embarrassment, but then realized that most likely no one was watching him. He was only ATF, after all.

Clive had made it a point not to mention Sister Tulah while at the county jail, and though he still didn't think he'd be invited to a barbeque anytime soon, the correctional officers hadn't given him the same hassle he'd received at the sheriff's office the day before. He'd kept quiet about the preacher, but talked up the Scorpions, whose apprehension was a tremendous source of pride. He'd good naturedly taken the jibes about federals not being the only ones who could handle unruly outlaws, but he'd been purposeful about soliciting opinions on the shootout and fire at the church. Everyone he asked thought the case was cut and dried: the Scorpions were the culprits, they had been caught and there wasn't anything else to do but pat themselves on the back and order an extra dozen frosted eclairs.

The door in front of Clive swung open and he jumped up, startled, forgetting his rehearsed pose. This was the first time Clive had ever interviewed a suspect on his own and he wanted to be sure that he did it right. He stood behind the table as an officer with droopy eyelids and a handlebar mustache led Jerry

Brown, Jr. into the narrow interview room. The officer loosely shook the man by the shoulder and sighed heavily.

"Cuffs on or off?"

Clive looked the inmate up and down. He was muscular, sure, and sporting more than a fair share of badly inked tattoos on his stringy forearms, but he still came in at five foot five and maybe one hundred twenty pounds soaking wet. Clive shook his head.

"I think we'll be okay."

The officer fumbled with the man's handcuffs. He gave the man a little shove toward the chair across the table from Clive.

"He cause any problems, you just holler. There's bound to be somebody out here can step in and do something. When you're done, just bang on the door. Somebody should be around to let you out."

Clive nodded and sat down.

"Thank you."

The officer gave a limp shrug and closed the door behind him as he left. The tattooed man eyed Clive with a look somewhere between amusement and disgust and then flung himself into the chair. He rested his forearms on the edge of the table and rubbed his bare wrists.

"Who the hell are you?"

"Mr. Brown, my name is Special Agent Clive Grant. I'm with ATF out of Atlanta."

"Mr. Brown?"

Clive took a deep breath.

"You go by Ratface, yes? Would you prefer it if I called you that?"

Ratface scratched his recently shaved head and snorted.

"I'd prefer if you'd tell me what the hell you want."

Clive narrowed his eyes at Ratface. The man sitting in front of him did indeed have a rodent-like appearance. His nose was long, but bumpy on the bridge as if it'd been broken one too many times and never properly set. He had dark eyes that were too close together and ears that stuck out awkwardly from the sides of his head. Clive didn't think there was too much going on upstairs, either, so he decided to try a different tactic. Clive leaned back in his chair and crossed his leg over his knee. He unbuttoned his jacket.

"What are you, kid, like nineteen?"

Ratface scowled at him. When he spoke, Clive could see yellow teeth flashing behind his thin, crusty lips.

"Twenty-two. And what the hell is ATF? I already spoke to so many of you pigs that it's starting to get lame-o. Can't you write shit down so you can remember it? Huh? Or they ain't teach you how to write in cop school? That it?"

Clive kept his smile to himself; it was obvious he was just dealing with an underdeveloped high school bully. This was going to be easy.

"ATF means I'm federal. I'm just looking into the fire, though. I don't care about the charges against you one way or another."

Ratface scratched his head again and then sniffed his fingers.

"Bullshit."

"It's the truth. I have no interest in you or what you did. Though it is pretty weak, I'd have to say, that you're taking all the blame. I've looked at the charge sheet. You're looking at murder one for Sherwood Cannon…"

Ratface smacked the table.

"That's a load of crap. They can't pin that on me. No way. Not when I ain't never even laid eyes on him."

Clive calmly continued.

"And yet, your buddies in here with you are both only looking at felony murder. A piece of advice for you: they're probably going to throw you under the bus. And then there's the missing Scorpions member."

Ratface shrugged, but Clive caught the slight twitch at the corner of his mouth.

"Don't know what you're talking about."

Clive tilted his head.

"Don't you? The Scorpions VP? Goes by the name Slim Jim. Man, where do you get these names from?"

"Why, you want one?"

Clive looked off to the side.

"Too bad you don't know where he's at. Info like that could probably put you in the judge's good graces come sentencing time."

Ratface stubbornly shook his head.

"Still don't know what you're talking about."

Clive glanced back at Ratface.

"Of course, I could be wrong. The cops don't seem to be looking for him too hard, so maybe they're not all that interested. And why would they be when they've got you to pin everything on?"

Ratface nonchalantly slung one arm over the back of his chair, but Clive could tell he'd struck a nerve.

"Oh, come on. Like I ain't heard that same spiel every time one of you assholes sits down with me. Trying to pit us against one another, blah, blah. Like you ain't know how it works with MCs. You ain't that stupid."

Clive leaned forward and smiled.

"And yet, you're not even a full member of the Scorpions, are you? And with your president dead, half your crew dead, the club dead for that matter, you'll never be one, will you? All your lifelong goals, flushed down the drain. Such a shame. You probably had such potential."

Ratface whistled, a little too loudly.

"Jesus, here you go again. You know, I heard all this shit before, too. You guys are like a broken record. Can't you even think of nothing different to say? Blah, blah, blah."

Clive figured he'd gone through the routine enough now to catch Ratface off guard. He didn't even allow for a pause.

"So, who's Brother Felton?"

He watched Ratface's eyes.

"Who?"

Clive was pretty sure Ratface was genuinely confused.

"Brother Felton? Sister Tulah's nephew?"

Ratface tilted his head.

"I think I saw him on the TV when that preacher bitch was doing interviews. Real window licker, right? Like he's got the brains of a squirrel, maybe. Or like a bug or something. Something stupid like that."

"So, who is he?"

Ratface gave him a blank stare.

"He's the guy on TV. Looks like a bug. Didn't we just go over that?"

Clive rubbed his temple; he was starting to get a headache.

"You've never spoken to him before?"

Ratface sat back, insulted.

"Not before. Not ever. I look like I would hang out with someone like Brother Felton? I didn't even know he existed until those news interviews started popping up with that one-eyed bible thumper acting all woe-is-me like, all boo-hoo my poor church and Hallelujah, and praise the Lord crap. Like ain't no one ever heard that routine before."

Ratface suddenly looked around the empty room.

"Don't I get a cigarette or nothing? For wasting my time in here with you?"

Clive ignored the request. He leaned forward, watching Ratface closely.

"How do you know Sister Tulah, then?"

"I ain't know Sister Tulah."

But Clive had seen the twitch in Ratface's cheek.

"Not at all? You'd never even heard of her before you tried to blow her church to high heaven? Come on, everyone I've spoken to in Kentsville knows Sister Tulah."

Ratface crossed his arms.

"Well, not me."

"But you were meeting Sherwood Cannon at her church, correct?"

Ratface groaned.

"How many times I gotta say this?"

Clive shrugged.

"I guess one more."

Ratface looked like he could spit on Clive.

"Listen, I ain't lied about this shit, not once from the start. Jack was meeting up with that turtle dick Cannon about a business deal."

He rolled his eyes at Clive.

"A legitimate business deal, asshole. Something about cars. I ain't know 'cause I'm just a prospect, remember? I clean out the shitter and make baloney sandwiches. I was just going along for the ride."

"And why did you meet up at Sister Tulah's church, of all places?"

"Jack said it was Sherwood Cannon's idea. So you'd have to ask him. But, oh wait, that's right, last I heard, he turned up extra crispy."

Ratface seemed to think about this for a moment.

"And no, I didn't kill Sherwood. Quit trying to trick me into saying I did. I ain't that dumb. Jesus."

Clive stood up.

"I never said you did."

Ratface scowled up at him.

"So, what, you ain't got no more questions? That's it?"

Clive circled around Ratface and pounded on the door.

"That's it."

Ratface sat staring straight ahead, probably trying to work it all. The door clicked, but before it opened, Clive turned around.

"Oh, and, Ratface."

Ratface twisted around in his seat.

"What?"

"If I were you, I'd use the next twenty years in prison to brush up on my vocabulary. You sound like a goddamn moron."

Clive opened the door and smiled at the listless officer as they traded places. "He's all yours."

JUDAH STOOD IN the empty parking lot and squinted up at the sign. It said Stingrays all right, in blue and yellow letters, and the Y was in the shape of a stingray. A smiling, cartoon stingray with googly eyes. There were fish tanks stacked behind the windows and a buy-one-get-one hermit crab sign taped to the glass front door. Judah put his hands in his pockets and waited for Gary and Alvin. They came up and stood on either side of him, silent for a moment as they took it all in, and eventually Gary cocked his head.

"Looks like a place where you buy fish."

Judah nodded.

"Yep."

"Like, *Finding Nemo* fish."

"Yes, it does."

Alvin, confused, narrowed his eyes at both of them.

"Nemo? What the hell's a Nemo?"

Judah squeezed his eyes shut. Alvin had refused to be seen in Gary's purple van, recently airbrushed with a mystical scene involving a wizard, a dragon and a topless warrior princess, and had instead kept Judah company in the truck while carrying on an excruciating, one-sided conversation about protein shakes, protein bars and protein powders the whole way down. Alvin wasn't much of a talker, but once he got going it didn't matter whether his audience was listening or not. The drive from Silas to Daytona Beach had only taken two hours, but they'd spent just about as long cruising up and down Atlantic Avenue, dodging giggling jaywalkers in string bikinis and muscle heads on crotch rocket motorcycles. Finally, they'd paid five dollars each to park and walked into the closest establishment: Eddie's Ink Spot. Eddie was busy tattooing a bright blue dolphin around the bellybutton of a girl wearing enough body glitter to hold her own New Year's Eve party, but he'd told them where they could find Stingrays. Judah supposed the asshole hadn't exactly been lying.

Gary put his hands on his hips.

"Nemo? You know, Nemo, Dory. The sharks. The stoner turtles. Don't you watch movies?"

Alvin glanced warily at Judah for confirmation.

"Turtles can get stoned? I thought I'd read somewhere that reptiles can't."

Judah smacked his forehead with his palm and walked toward the front door.

"Jesus Christ."

The inside of the store was mostly empty. Aside from the burbling aquariums piled up against the windows, each containing only two or three skinny neon fish darting around, there wasn't much else. A rack against the wall held packets of fish food and empty plastic hermit crab houses with brightly colored lids. A cardboard box in the corner was filled with plastic plants and chipped treasure chests and castles. *Half Price* had been scrawled on the box with a magic marker. The cement floor was dotted with blue plastic kiddie pools, some filled with water, some with sand. Judah walked over to the nearest one and looked down. Three sickly-looking goldfish were huddled against the rim.

A door on the back wall suddenly swung open and a woman came charging out, brandishing a newspaper in one hand. She had a potbelly stretching against her Bike Week T-shirt and heavy, dishwater-blond bangs that hung down almost to her eyelashes. With her round face and quick, jerky movements, Judah thought she resembled nothing so much as a bedraggled Shit-Zhou straight from the pound. She glanced briefly at Judah, but headed for the checkout counter.

"Don't worry, Oswald. I found it!"

Judah looked around the store. Aside from himself and Alvin and Gary, both tapping at the fish in the aquariums behind him, the place was deserted.

The woman thumbed open the newspaper and spread it across the counter. She began to read loudly in a nasally voice.

"Thursday, August ninth. Think about taking some time to do something relaxing. Go outside, enjoy nature or have a fun dinner with friends. Keep your eyes open, because someone special may be headed your way today."

The woman smoothed her stubby fingers across the newspaper and smiled.

"You hear that, Oswald? You need to keep your eyes open today."

Judah glanced around the store one more time and then cautiously approached the counter.

"Uh, ma'am? I was hoping you could help us with something."

She held up a finger to silence him.

"Hold on. Oswald is a Sagittarius and always needs to know his lucky numbers."

She squinted at the newspaper and drew her finger down the page.

"Here we go. Seventeen, thirty-three, two. Don't worry, I'll be sure to pick up a lotto on the way home today. You know I always do."

Judah thought about backing away slowly, but the woman abruptly closed the newspaper and folded her hands on top of it. She looked up at him through her fringe of bangs and blinked furiously.

"Yes? Can I help you?"

Judah just stood there, not sure what to do. The woman pointed to the tanks against the window.

"The tetras are on sale this week. No guarantee on them, but they're a good deal. Tell your friends to quit tapping on the glass, though. It upsets them."

Alvin and Gary jumped back and put their hands in their pockets. They slunk away to inspect the kiddie pool full of hermit crabs. The woman pursed her already puckered lips, making her faint mustache even more pronounced.

"Let me guess. You ain't here for the tetra sale."

Judah shook his head.

"Ah, no. But, um, could you tell me..."

He had to know.

"…who is Oswald?"

The woman looked at Judah as if he'd just stepped off an alien spaceship.

"Oswald? You got eyes, ain't you? He's right here."

The woman lightly caressed a round, glass aquarium perched on the edge of the counter. Judah came closer and peered through the cloudy water. The back of the tank had been painted black and it was hard to see inside.

"What am I looking at?"

The woman huffed.

"He's right there, in that crevice. No, right there."

Judah looked where the woman was pointing. A tiny octopus, its tentacles curled up around its bluish body, was resting between a rock and miniature treasure chest. The octopus opened an eye.

"Oh, I see. He's, um, cute."

The woman beamed at Judah.

"He sure is. And my name is Velma, by the way. And this is my store. And I'd put money on the fact that you're in the wrong Stingrays."

Judah sighed in relief.

"So there's another one?"

Velma picked up a ballpoint pen and started chewing on the plastic cap.

"Yeah. Let me guess, you're looking for the titty bar across town."

Judah nodded.

"Yes. I mean, not that we don't like fish and all. And Oswald, I mean, he's great. But yeah, we need to get to the other Stingrays. Can you give us directions?"

The woman sucked on the end of the pen and then pointed it toward Alvin and Gary.

"If you tell them to stop kicking the side of the pool. The crabs don't like it."

Judah whirled around and shot Alvin and Gary a threatening look. They backed away from the pool and stood aimlessly in the middle of the store.

Judah turned to Velma and raised his eyebrows expectantly.

"So, the other Stingrays?"

Velma chewed on the pen as she spoke.

"You'd be surprised at how many people come here looking for the strip club. I do half my business that way. They come through the door looking for pussy, but they leave with a goldfish. The goldfish ain't on sale today, though. Just the tetras. And I guess I could give you a deal on a hermit crab if you bought the whole kit."

Judah shook his head.

"No, we just need directions."

"That Stingrays club is something else, let me tell you. They actually got a dance floor set up on top of a shark tank. Got real baby sharks swimming in it. The poles are all screwed into the glass top and everything. My niece works over there and she says it's just wild. You're swinging on them poles and you look down and there's a shark underneath you."

"That's interesting. So, how do we get there?"

"I mean, I wouldn't mind giving that a try myself one of these days. Oh, you might think I'm past my prime, but they got all sorts over at Stingrays. I ain't even fifty yet and my niece, Mitzy, says they got one gal there who's fifty-five. The boys love it. You watch, I'm gonna try it one day. Just so I can look down and see those sharks."

Judah nodded impatiently.

"Yep. Well, good for you. You said it's across town?"

Velma put her hand on Oswald's tank and stroked it absently.

"Sure is. Just take a right when you pull out of here and go south on Peninsula until you hit Main. You know, the street with Joyland and the Boardwalk at the end of it. The Ferris Wheel. It's next to the Big Shark gift shop with all the bright orange and green fifty-percent-off signs in the windows. You can't miss it. There's so much neon popping off in that part of town it's like to blind you."

Judah turned to go.

"All the way south on Peninsula. Thanks."

"Can't miss it. You'll pass Razzles and Lollipops on the way, but don't get distracted. Their girls might be better, but they don't got no shark tank."

"Got it."

"Something tells me you're not looking for a lap dance, though."

Judah froze.

"What'd you mean by that?"

Velma shrugged.

"You boys look nice. Even if your buddies there can't keep their hands or feet to themselves. So, I'm just gonna toss this out there. If you're looking for Weaver, be careful."

Judah stared at Velma and spoke very carefully.

"Why would we be looking for Weaver?"

Velma shook her head.

"You just don't seem like the type looking to pick up an STD tonight. You look more like the hotshot type trying to get in on a deal or something."

Judah glanced over at Alvin and Gary, who were now keenly paying attention, and then looked warily back to Velma.

"You know Weaver?"

Velma tapped the pen against her teeth and shook her head again.

"I know of him. Mitzy's said a few things. I don't go in for any of that myself, but I take it he's into the drugs. You know, the bad ones. Some kinda kingpin, like in a movie. Sounds funny maybe, but let me tell you, he put one of Mitzy's friends in a dumpster last week because her boyfriend tried to screw him on a score. Who knows what happened to the boyfriend. Maybe they got a bigger tank somewhere and Weaver fed him to the grown-up sharks. From the things I've heard, it wouldn't surprise me one bit. So just be careful, okay. Like I said, you seem like nice boys. I'd hate to read about you in the papers."

Judah nodded grimly.

"We'll be careful."

Velma pointed at the tank beside her on the counter.

"And Oswald likes you. He wouldn't want to have to read about it in the papers, neither."

CHAPTER 8

BENJI WOBBLED AS he struggled to find the right key on the ring, jam it into the rusty lock and shoulder the door open. When it finally swung inward, Benji gripped the handles of his crutches and awkwardly edged through the door, leaving the keyring still jangling from the lock. Once inside, he had to stump around in a circle to close the door behind him and grope for the exposed light switch in the dark. By the time he flicked it, and the fluorescent panel above crackled to life, Benji was sweating. Just trudging through the soft, sandy dirt of the backyard had been a chore. He took a deep breath.

"Judah said that you killed his friend."

Benji twisted on his crutches and turned around in the cramped space of the garden shed.

"But he was wrong. You killed my friend."

Benji stabilized himself by halfway leaning against a rusting push mower wedged into the cobwebbed corner. He yanked the .45 out of the front of his waistband and leveled it at Nash's head. He thumbed the safety off and rested his elbow on the handle of his crutch to steady his aim. Benji hadn't fired a gun since he was fourteen years old, and that had been a bolt-action hunting rifle, so he took it slow. He had already loaded the gun and made sure there was one in the chamber, and now he adjusted his hold, squinted, and then stretched his fingers out again before curling them back around the grip.

In the chair a few feet away from him, Nash was flailing around as much as he could. He was completely bound to the back of the chair from his shoulders down to his waist, but he strained against the nylon cord. He tried to scoot and hop away from Benji, and the metal chair legs scrapped a few inches against the concrete floor, but it didn't matter. There wasn't anywhere to go. Tortured, muffled sounds were escaping through the duct tape sealed over Nash's mouth, but Benji barely noticed. He waited until he was good and ready and then he met Nash's terrified eyes.

"So."

Benji pulled the trigger.

The force of the shot knocked Nash's chair over and Benji watched impassively, his ears ringing, as Nash bled out from what was left of his throat. It only took a few seconds. Benji clicked the safety back on and stuck the gun back into his pants. He reached into his pocket and pulled out a pill bottle. Benji tapped a Percocet out into his palm and then crunched and swallowed it before hitching himself back up on his crutches and turning to go.

"NOW THIS IS more like it!"

Judah nodded in agreement as Gary swaggered around his van and clapped him on the back. Across the street, the Stingrays' marquee was lit up in pink neon and accompanied by flashing *XXX* and *GIRLS, GIRLS, GIRLS* signs mounted over the blacked-out windows. It wasn't even dark yet, but already there was a meathead bouncer sitting on a stool outside the main entrance. He lazily turned his head in Judah's direction, but there was absolutely no expression on his face. Judah glanced at Alvin, who was hanging back a little, surveying the scene.

"What do you think?"

Alvin grunted.

"Looks like the place."

"So, right or left?"

To the right of the main entrance, but still part of the same building, was Stingrays Package Lounge. Cardboard advertisements for ten different types of flavored vodka were pasted over the windows and narrow glass door. Gary didn't hesitate to answer.

"The club. Come on, guys, we go in the club."

Both Judah and Alvin turned and started for the liquor store. Judah could hear Gary grumbling behind them as he hustled to catch up.

"Gonna get nothing out of this trip."

Judah ignored him and cautiously opened the door to the store. It made him nervous that he couldn't see through any of the glass. An electronic tone went off as he passed through the doorway and entered the brilliantly lit space. He squinted his eyes against the garish fluorescent light, seeming to come from every direction and reflecting off every available surface, and slowly walked down a row of bottles. Gary and Alvin made their way down the row next to him and they met in front of the checkout counter. Aside from the clerk, who was watching their every move with beady, bloodshot eyes, the store was empty. Judah stepped up to the counter, every inch of which seemed to be taken up with cardboard displays of plastic lighters, energy shots and slender glass tubes encapsulating miniature silk roses. The clerk blinked at Judah, waiting. Judah jerked a neon green lighter out of a display box and held it up. The clerk nodded, but didn't stop chewing on his thumbnail. Judah slid him two dollars and casually scooped up his change.

"Weaver around?"

Judah had been hoping to catch him off guard, but the man seemed unfazed. The clerk finally bit off a crescent of nail and spat it out on the counter. He pointed in the direction of the club next door.

"Weaver don't talk to nobody 'less they spending cash in his club."

Judah should have known. He nodded to the clerk and jammed the lighter in his front pocket.

"Any way to get a message to Weaver while we're spending our money?"

The clerk shrugged; he was studying the thumbnail on his other hand.

"Try a girl looks like she can count higher than seven."

Judah didn't bother to thank him. They exited the blinding liquor store and after paying their ten-dollar door fee, slipped into the cool, smoky darkness of the club. The room was bigger than it looked from the outside and probably every inch of it would be taken up come nine o'clock on a weekend night. As it was, the cavernous, near empty space appeared suspended in time, as if only waiting for the sun to set and the party to start.

Several satellite stages were scattered around the club, but only the main stage in the back was lit up. It was indeed perched on top of an aquarium, though Judah couldn't tell if there were actual sharks swimming underneath the girl who was slowly shimmying up and down one of the poles above it. Judah looked to the other side of the room where a long, curving bar took up the length of the wall. He fixed his eyes on it.

"Boys, go spend some money. I need a drink."

Gary, followed a little reluctantly by Alvin, bolted for the stage and Judah headed to the bar. Of the fifteen stools, only two were occupied, both by men who looked like used car salesmen on their way home from work. One had a plastic Toys "R" Us bag on the seat next to him. Judah moved down to the far end and settled himself. Once he had a cigarette in one hand and a drink in the other, he'd be better off.

It took a few minutes, but finally a woman with glossy black hair cut into a severe bob strutted down the bar and stopped in front of him. She watched Judah ash his cigarette on the ground before pursing her glittery red lips and sliding a tin ashtray in front of him. Judah nodded.

"Thanks."

The woman crossed her arms underneath her silver bikini top and cocked her hip out, waiting. Judah smiled at her.

"Guy next door told me to find a girl who looks smart."

The bartender rolled her eyes and pushed at the bridge of her purple-framed glasses.

"Geez, I never heard that one before."

Judah tapped his cigarette on the edge of the ashtray.

"What's your name?"

The woman huffed.

"Sara. Now look, mister. You want a girl, you go to that side of the club. Join your friends. You want a drink, and only a drink, then stay where you are. Got it?"

Judah took a long drag on his cigarette.

"Whiskey."

Sara nodded and set a plastic cup on the bar in front of him. She scooped ice into it and then filled it halfway with Early Times. She pushed it toward him.

"Twelve."

"Jesus."

Sara snapped the silver strap around her neck and shrugged.

"Daytona Beach. You're paying extra for the sand in your glass."

Judah pulled a twenty from his wallet and laid it on the bar. He kept his hand on it, though, and leaned forward.

"Listen, Sara. I need to talk to Weaver. Do you think you could help me?"

Sara tugged at her bikini bottom and eyed the bill on the bar.

"Who?"

Judah groaned and pulled out another twenty. He set it on top of the first and leaned back, looking the woman in the eye. She snatched up the bills and gave him a wink before sashaying back down the bar. Judah hoped there had been some sort of agreement. He downed the whiskey and crushed the plastic cup between his fingers, popping a few ice cubes out onto the bar. Judah shook his head in disgust before making his way over to the main stage.

There were two girls dancing now, both with rippling stretchmarks, leathery skin and vacuous expressions on their pockmarked faces. Judah thought they could be sisters, maybe even twins. The one who had already unsnapped her red lace bra had Gary's full attention and he was leaning on the tip rail, feeding her dollar bills like she was a slot machine. The other girl kept trying to catch Alvin's eye, but he was entranced by the three small sharks swimming lazily along the bottom of the tank. Alvin, mouth open in wonder, nodded to Judah.

"Didn't know they made 'em that small."

Judah just shrugged.

"Who knew?"

Two more girls came out on the stage and the place slowly began to liven up. The cocktail waitresses on the floor were less attractive, but more friendly, than the bartender, and the drinks were still the same quality and price. Judah had his hands full trying to keep Gary from disappearing into a VIP room, first with a girl who looked about eighteen and six months pregnant and then with a woman who could have been the baby's grandmother. Between those two and the Rainbow Bright cocktail waitress who had taken a shine to Alvin, Judah knew they'd all be washing glitter down the shower drain for a week. He did his best to keep the girls at arm's length and his eyes wide open for trouble, but it wasn't easy.

Finally, he spotted Sara across the room. She was pointing at him and the man standing next to her, built like a tank, was nodding. Judah snapped Alvin and Gary back to attention as the man weaved his way across the club and came up beside Judah. He crossed his hairy arms over his chest, but kept his eyes on the girl crawling across the stage.

"You want to talk to Weaver?"

Judah nodded.

"Yes."

The man turned to him. He leaned his face in close and Judah could smell his hamburger breath.

"Well, come on, then."

The man led them down a corridor lined with private booths and through a dark hallway that smelled of Clorox. It made Judah's eyes burn. When they came to the end of it, another man, in a too-tight Affliction shirt with the sleeves torn off, pushed them against the wall and patted them down. Judah had been nervous about leaving the guns in the car, but now he was glad he had. The man jerked Judah's cigarettes out of his pocket and lit one for himself. He grinned around it and jerked his thumb up a flight of stairs.

"He'll see you now."

Judah snatched his cigarettes back and climbed up the narrow set of metal stairs. Alvin and Gary were close behind. At the top, yet another beefcake, this one with shaved forearms and oversized gold earrings in the shape of dollar signs, eyeballed Judah before letting them pass. Judah felt like he was being doused with slime every time one of the bouncers looked his way. Finally, they were let through the door and into Weaver's lair.

The room was almost like a separate, private club set directly on top of the actual Stingrays below. Only this place was brighter and the girls were less busted. A three-stool bar in the corner was backed by rows of top shelf liquor and magnum bottles of champagne. Red velour couches and plush armchairs were grouped together in clusters and occupied by women in spandex micro-dresses and men glistening with hair gel and bristling with gold chains and oversized watches. Everyone seemed to be drinking fuchsia martinis out of sugar-rimmed glasses. There wasn't a plastic cup in sight.

A man sitting on a white leather tuxedo couch against the far wall looked up when they entered. He slowly scanned Judah up and down and then jerked his head. Judah picked his way around the room, ignoring the stares and whispers, and stood before the man. He put his hands in his pockets and narrowed his eyes.

"Weaver?"

The man was sitting between two women, both of whom looked uncomfortable and bored, and as he leaned back he put his arm around both. He gave each a squeeze on their bronzed, bare shoulders and then shoved at them to move. They stood up and clunked away awkwardly in their platform stilettos. The man flashed his teeth at Judah.

"You wanted to see me?"

Judah nodded.

"Yes."

Weaver rubbed his palms together and then gestured to the black vinyl armchair on the other side of the glass coffee table. Judah slowly eased himself into it, trying to take everything in as quickly as he could: the lines of cocaine on the table, the heavy gold cross hanging low around Weaver's neck, his maroon tracksuit and spotless white Jordans. Weaver glanced up at Alvin and Gary, standing behind Judah, but dismissed them with a disgusted look. Judah decided to just hurry up and get it over with.

"Do you know who I am?"

Weaver scooped up a handful of Skittles from a giant glass bowl in the middle of the table. He tossed them all into his mouth at once and chewed as he spoke.

"I have no idea who you are."

Judah wasn't sure if had wanted Weaver to know him or not, but the man's lack of interest in him was unsettling. Judah leaned forward.

"My name is Judah Cannon."

Weaver swallowed.

"And?"

"And I've got your guy. Nash."

Weaver grabbed another handful of candy, but only rolled the pieces around in his palm.

"I don't think I know a Nash."

"Out of Palatka. Putnam County. He's sure been throwing your name around lately."

Weaver let the Skittles trickle through his fingers back into the bowl, but didn't say anything. Judah pushed ahead, not knowing what else to do.

"He's been saying that you want to use my connections. My network up in Bradford County. For your own operation."

Weaver licked his lips. His tongue was rainbow colored.

"Now, I think I'm gonna need you to draw me a map or something. That place ain't ringing a bell. That over there in redneck, screw your cousin, get her pregnant and smoke some meth land?"

Judah grit his teeth.

"A little ways north and west of here, yeah."

Weaver leaned back and stretched his arms out along the length of the couch.

"What'd you say your name was again?"

"Cannon. Judah. My father was Sherwood."

Weaver narrowed his eyes at Judah.

"Was, huh?"

Judah was tired of the game already. He dipped his chin slightly and met Weaver's glittering eyes.

"Was."

"How'd he die?"

"Got tired of living, I guess."

They stared at one another for a hard moment and then Weaver laughed obscenely. He smacked the leather couch cushion beside him.

"Happens to us all, I suppose. Anyway, you got something else? Something I care about?"

Judah kept his tone even.

"You care about my business?"

"Nope."

"You care about Nash?"

Weaver shook his head.

"Nada."

Judah stood up.

"Then I guess we're done."

Weaver stayed on the couch.

"I guess we are, my friend. Now get the hell out of my club and don't come back, you understand? Your trailer trash vibe is seriously cramping my style."

"No worries there."

Judah turned and pushed past Gary. He could hear Weaver cackling behind him, all the way to the door.

RAMEY COULDN'T BELIEVE her eyes. She was horrified and disgusted, yes, but mostly she was in shock. Only a few feet away from her lay the awkwardly twisted body of Nash, still tied to the chair as she had left him hours before, but now the chair was turned over on its side and Nash's throat had been ripped open. His dull eyes were staring straight ahead. There was dark, coagulated blood everywhere.

Ramey backed out of the garden shed, leaving the light on and the door open. She stood in the middle of the yard, the sun slipping away into twilight, the sky arching in a deep purple bruise above her, and wondered what the hell she was supposed to do now. She clenched and unclenched her fists as she looked around at the empty backyard, the line of trees, the shed before her, the house behind her. House, not a home. She tried to steady her breathing as she climbed the back steps and walked, stunned, into the living room. The TV was on with the sound turned down low. *Wheel of Fortune.* The contestant had just asked to buy a vowel.

"Oh my God, Benji. You didn't."

Benji wouldn't look at her. He was slumped deep into a corner of the couch, his leg thrust up on the coffee table in front of him. He kept his eyes on the spinning wheel on the television.

"He had it coming."

Ramey put her head in her hands and then rubbed her face with her palms. This was not happening. Judah gone. His brother now a cold-blooded killer. A dead body in the shed. She pushed her hair back out of her face and leaned against the wall, trying to think. Benji, slurring his words, didn't give her much time.

"And a car just pulled up in front of the house."

"What?"

Ramey jumped away from the wall and glanced out the front living room window. Benji craned his neck to see from the couch.

"And I'm pretty sure we don't know the guy getting out of it."

She turned to Benji.

"Shut up. Just stay here. Don't say anything, don't even move. I'll handle it."

"That's reassuring."

She crossed to the front door, forcing herself to appear calm, willing herself to breathe naturally. Ramey rested her hand on the doorknob, but the moment her fingers touched the brass it hit her. She had to tell Judah. She had to tell Judah before he talked to Weaver. Before he tried to bargain with Nash's life. Before he made a deal that he would have to go back on. Panic rose up in her like a wave as she heard footfalls on the front steps. There was no time. She yanked open the door and stepped out onto the rag welcome mat. Ramey quickly shut the door behind her and stood in front of it, barring it with her body. Ramey didn't even try to smile, but did manage to keep her voice a few notes below hysteria.

"Can I help you?"

The man in the suit stopped at the edge of the porch. He had a sheen of sweat across his forehead and he pulled a yellow silk handkerchief out of his pocket and blotted his face before speaking to her. Even that gesture was typical. Ramey had known the minute she had seen the man step out of his car that he was some sort of cop. He folded the handkerchief, tucked it away and took out his badge. He flashed it briefly before her eyes.

"Ma'am, my name is Special Agent Grant. I'm with ATF out of Atlanta and I'd like to ask you a few questions. Do you mind if I come in?"

Ramey crossed her arms.

"Yes."

Agent Grant seemed confused. He almost took a step back.

"Yes, you mind?"

"Yes. I mind. Out here is just fine."

Ramey didn't know what the ATF agent wanted, but she knew how it would play out. He would do his best to bully her, just because he thought he could. There was a thin line she was now going to have to walk: get him out of there as quickly as possible, while arousing the least amount of suspicion. Yes, he was all powerful with his shiny badge and his ego the size of Texas, but no, he couldn't come in. No, he couldn't have a look around the premise. Ramey suddenly realized, though, as she was trying to force a smile at Agent Grant, that she had left the shed door wide open. The light was still on. And the bloody remains of Nash were nearly in full view for anyone to see. Her heart was pounding.

Agent Grant didn't seem too ruffled, though, once he realized that she wasn't going to ask him in for a glass of sweet tea. He pulled a notebook out of his jacket pocket and flipped a few pages.

"All right. So just to be clear, I'm going to assume that you're Ramey Barrow."

"I am."

"And it's your name on the lease for this residence, but you don't live here alone, do you?"

Ramey raised her eyebrows.

"That one of your questions?"

He dropped the hand holding the notebook to his side and looked up at her.

"I just want to confirm that I'm in the right place. You live here with Judah

Cannon, correct? But it's your name on the paperwork."

Ramey smirked, keeping her eyes on the agent's.

"You know, even all the way out here in Bradford County, not all the women are barefoot and pregnant. Who'd have thought we were modern, huh?"

The agent glanced down at his notebook. Throwing that tone into her voice was risky, but she was beginning to sense that she had an edge on him. She knew that she made him nervous, and Ramey wasn't afraid to exploit that.

"Just makes Judah Cannon a little hard to track down, that's all."

Ramey put her hands on her lower back and looked away from him, down the length of the porch.

"Is there an actual question here?"

"Why? Are you in a rush, or something?"

Ramey gave him a saccharine smile.

"Well, I may not be confined to the kitchen, but I do have supper to keep an eye on."

"Fine. Is Judah Cannon here?"

"He isn't."

Agent Grant sighed.

"Would you like to tell me where he is, then? I already went by Cannon Salvage and there didn't appear to be anyone there."

Ramey shrugged.

"You must have just missed him. He's probably out running errands. And now, Mr. Grant, I'm sorry, but I'm gonna have to ask you to leave."

The agent slapped the notebook closed, but stopped her just as she had her hand on the door handle.

"Did Sherwood Cannon know Preacher Tulah?"

Ramey slowly turned back to him.

"Preacher Tulah?"

Agent Grant nodded.

"You know, the woman whose church burned down back in May? Who your boyfriend's father tried to kill?"

Ramey crossed her arms again.

"Yeah, I know how to change the channel to the news. And more than that, Judah and I already went through enough questioning when it happened to last a lifetime. But if you need to write it down for your own record, no, we didn't know anything about it. We weren't even in town."

She hated the glint that came into Agent Grant's eye. He knew something. Or thought he knew something.

"So, you're telling me that Sherwood's own son, just released from prison, didn't know what was going on?"

Ramey settled her eyes on his.

"Judah ain't his father."

The agent looked away from her stony glare and finally slid the notebook into his pocket. He glanced back at her and nodded curtly.

"Fair enough."

Ramey tried to smile again. She had to get him to leave. How much time had she already wasted with this guy?

"Anything else? Or can I catch my Stovetop before it burns?"

The agent opened his wallet and took out a business card. He passed it to her.

"When you see Judah next, you tell him to give me a call, okay?"

He started down the stairs, but called over his shoulder at her.

"Save me another trip. Because, trust me, I will keep coming back until I talk to Judah Cannon. You can put money on that."

Ramey held the flimsy card between her fingers and watched the agent cross the dirt driveway. His threat hung heavily in the air between them, but its significance was the furthest thing from Ramey's mind. She waited for him to get in his car and circle around. As soon as he disappeared around the bend in the driveway, she dashed inside and locked the door behind her. She squeezed her eyes shut and leaned back against the door, breathing hard. Benji grunted out a laugh from the living room.

"Well. I take it he wasn't selling Girl Scout Cookies."

Her eyes snapped open. She didn't have time for Special Agent Grant. She didn't have time for Benji. Ramey thought about her purse, thought about her phone inside it and how quickly she could get to it. She bolted for the kitchen. She had to call Judah. She had to tell him that Nash was dead.

CHAPTER 9

SLIM JIM PUT his hands on his hips and glowered at the motel room. He stood in the narrow space between the bed and bureau and slowly turned around in a circle. It looked as if a hooker's underwear drawer had exploded in the middle of a frat house kitchen. Lacy panties in Day-Glo colors were strewn about like confetti; matching bras hung from the bathroom door handle and dangled off the edge of the nightstand. More articles of clothing were balled up on the floor—his sweat-stained T-shirts, her mini-skirts, his tube socks, her bikini tops—and created an obstacle course from one end of the stuffy room to the other. Takeout pizza boxes, crumpled burger bags, half-crushed beer cans, empty liquor bottles, cellophane wrappers and cardboard chicken joint boxes, with greasy thigh pieces still lingering underneath the trash of paper napkins and straw wrappers, covered every other available surface, from the top of the TV to the wobbly table jammed in next to the rattling AC unit. Slim Jim stepped over a pair of strappy sandals and lifted up the top of a Styrofoam ice chest on the floor, wedged between the double bed and the wall, to inspect its contents. One lonely, empty, Milwaukie's Best can on its side, drowning in three inches of stagnate water. Two cigarette butts. A German cockroach belly up. He squashed the lid back on and pulled his dirt-streaked shirt over his head. Slim Jim wadded it up and hurled it into the corner before yelling as loud as he could.

"This place is a goddamn pigsty!"

The only reply was a thump back from the occupants on the floor above him. Slim Jim sat down on the edge of the rumpled bed and stared at the dark TV screen in front of him. Was this better than being back at home, looking over his shoulder every second of every day? Slim Jim wasn't so sure. He cared about Shelia, he did, though he hadn't exactly gotten around to telling her so. She was good to look at, even better in the sack, and when she kept her yapping opinions to herself, she could be pretty fun to party with. And he owed her. He knew that. Despite the barbarity of living in a shoebox that always smelled like a girl, and not necessarily in a good way, it was better than worrying about the cops. Or the Cannons. Or that goddamn bitch Preacher Tulah. Slim Jim flopped back and stared up at the popcorn ceiling. Maybe there were still a few cans of Schlitz in that case he'd left beside the bathtub. He was pushing himself up on his elbows when the phone rang. Not the prepaid cell in his pocket, but the telephone bolted down to the nightstand. Slim Jim stared at it like it was a snake. He cautiously lifted the receiver, listened and then groaned.

"Yes, I'll accept the charges."

Slim Jim scooted back against the headboard while the connection went through. The phone crackled and Legs' voice came through over the din of the county jail common room.

"Slim, it's Legs, man. How's life?"

Slim Jim could have strangled him.

"Damnit, Legs. I told you guys not to call me unless it was an emergency."

"Sorry, man. I know, I know."

Slim Jim rubbed his forehead with the side of his hand and grimaced.

"Tiny or Ratface had better be bleeding out on the shower room floor right now for you to be calling me."

There was a loud clanging in the background while Slim Jim waited for a response. Legs sounded put out.

"Well, fine. Jesus Christ, man, if you're gonna be like that."

Slim Jim sighed.

"No, it's all right. Just tell me what you want."

"That Shelia girl's got you all spun up, huh?"

"Don't I know it."

There was another pause and then Legs dropped his voice.

"Slim, I just thought you would want to know. Some guy came around this morning and questioned Ratface."

Slim Jim frowned.

"Some guy? What guy?"

"Said he was ATF. Federal. Looking into the fire."

"So what? Over the past three months, how many times have they pulled you guys out to question you? Come on."

"No, man, I think this was different. Ratface was really freaked out."

Slim Jim shook his head.

"Ratface is a pimple-assed squid who should've stayed in his garage and polished his bar-hopper. He never should've been with the Scorpions to begin with."

There was a grinding noise on the other end of the line and Slim Jim could hear Legs's muffled curses to someone. He waited, thinking about how much the call was costing him.

"Hey, sorry, Slim. These guys are assholes in here."

"You think? Speed it up, Legs."

"Oh yeah, right, okay. Just listen. Do what you want with it, but listen. Ratface said the ATF dude was acting like he was interested in the fire, but really, he was asking questions about how we knew the Cannons..."

"We already put all that on Jack."

"Hold on. And he was asking how we knew Tulah. Ratface said that was what the guy was hounding him about. Our connection to the preacher. You know, the connection we don't have."

Slim Jim cradled the receiver between his ear and shoulder and picked at a ripped cuticle. He was tired of the conversation already.

"So? Legs, what's your point?"

"You got mush between your ears, Slim? Are you so far away out there on the beach that you can't think straight?"

Slim Jim sat up. He could have punched Legs in the face. He didn't want anyone, not even the guy standing in line behind Legs for the phone, to know where he was. He tried to keep his cool, though. He had gotten lucky, Legs hadn't. He needed to remember that.

"Okay, Legs. Just keep to the story you've been telling all along. Don't worry about the Cannons. Don't worry about that crazy preacher. This ATF guy is just fishing."

"There's one other thing you should know."

Slim Jim squeezed his eyes shut

"Now what?"

"The agent brought you up."

Slim Jim swallowed hard.

"What?"

"Yeah, Ratface said that the ATF guy mentioned you. How you're on the run. Tried to get Ratface to, well, rat on you."

"He didn't say anything, did he?"

"Come on, Slim. Ratface knows I'd cut his balls off and feed them to him for breakfast if he said a word about you. He may be scared of going to prison, but he's a lot more scared of me and Tiny. We're keeping him in line, don't worry."

Slim Jim nodded.

"All right. I appreciate it, man."

"Hey, you just keep doing what you're doing. We're gonna need someone on the outside looking out for us, you know."

Slim Jim felt his gut twist. The rest of the Scorpions were only following the code, but he still owed them. It had been his idea to attack the church. And as a result, Jack and Toadie had ended up in the ground and the other three were awaiting trial, looking at ten plus years if it all went south. He was the only one who'd made it off scot free. For now, at least. Slim Jim hoped that what he was feeling came through in his voice.

"Thanks, brother. I mean, it really."

"Nah, man. No problem. What's family for, right?"

"Right."

The clanging sound had picked back up and it was hard to hear Legs now.

"Well, Slim. I gotta go. You take care of that old lady of yours, you hear?"

Slim Jim smiled to himself.

"Shelia ain't my old lady."

"Not yet. But take care of her anyway. She's putting up with your dumb ass. She deserves something. At least give it to her right."

"Now that I can do. And take care of yourself, Legs."

"Sure."

The line went dead. Slim Jim dropped the receiver and banged his head back against the headboard. One more thing to worry about now. Jesus. Though there was still no one to listen to him, he yelled anyway.

"There had better be some goddamn beer around here somewhere!"

He waited for the thump from above, but it never came.

JUDAH WAS SICK of Daytona Beach. He was sick of the candied neon signs, the thumping music blaring from every bar, the jackasses zipping between lanes on their buzzing ninjas, the families walking out in traffic with ice cream dripping down their arms and inflatable sea creatures in tow. Even the sunburned co-eds in thong bikinis, who winked and waved as they stumbled along the crumbling sidewalk in jelly flip-flops, held zero interest for him. He wanted to be home.

With a cold beer in one hand, a lock of Ramey's tangled hair in the other, and nothing else but the tree frogs and screech owls for miles in any direction.

Judah stomped on the brakes to avoid hitting a pack of club-goers, slick already with sweat, gel and glitter, crossing the street from one bar to another. A girl in a rebel flag print tube top blew a kiss to him. The much older guy tagging along at her elbow flipped him off. Judah ground his teeth. He could daydream all he liked about going back to Silas and sitting out on the front porch in the moonlight, but he knew that wasn't what was really waiting for him at home. Instead, he had his bitter, pill-popping brother and his pissed-off, and now mistrustful, girl to deal with. And Nash tied up in the shed. And Lesser in the ground. He had come to Daytona seeking answers and was driving away with none. He honestly didn't know if he should be thankful or not.

The van behind him honked at him to go and Judah glanced up at Alvin and Gary in the rearview mirror. He eased his truck into gear. They hadn't yet talked about what had happened with Weaver upstairs at Stingrays, but from the looks on their faces as they had walked away from the club in the descending violet twilight, he knew they were thinking the same thing as him: what the hell was that? Followed by: now what? Their eyes had been questioning, but Judah had only shaken his head as he yanked open the truck's door. They could pull over and talk about it once they cleared the Volusia County line.

Judah had barely gotten the F-150 into third gear when he had to stop for yet another light. Between the stoplights and the jaywalkers, he thought he'd never get off A1A. At least it seemed now that the bars, clubs and hotels were behind him. It looked like mostly gas stations and strip malls ahead. Soon, it would all peter out into familiar open highway. The light turned green and Judah stepped on the gas. Immediately, he had to switch over to the brake.

"Holy shit!"

It took Judah a few seconds to realize what was happening. At first, it just seemed as if an SUV had run the intersection. But then it all fell into place. The silver Range Rover had stopped directly in front of him and was blocking his truck. Two more identical vehicles had pulled up alongside, caging him in. In the rearview mirror Judah saw a fourth, up close behind Gary's van. They were trapped. Judah reached for the .45 beneath his seat and had it aimed at the passenger's side just as a man appeared at the open window.

"Stop right there."

The man raised his empty hands and grinned at Judah. His gold bottom grill flashed in the disorienting glare from all the headlights.

"Hey, amigo. I was you, I'd put that piece away and offer me a ride."

Judah kept the .45 aimed at the man's chest. He put his left hand on the steering wheel and, although he was trying to size the man up, he also tried to see what was going on around him. Horns were honking a little ways back, and on the other side of the intersection, but no one seemed to be doing much else. He spoke cautiously.

"Why would I do that?"

The man rested his fingers on the edge of the window and shrugged.

"You want to talk to Weaver. The real Weaver, right? And you don't want my friends and their AKs back there to blow you and your friends to rainbow sprinkles."

Judah's mind was racing. Real Weaver? Who the hell had he just talked to? The man twisted his jet black goatee between his fingers and then opened the front of his white Guayabera shirt.

"Plus. Kevlar, baby."

The man grinned again. Judah was trying to think it through, but did he even have a choice? He raised the gun slightly so that it was pointed at the man's head now. The man frowned.

"Come on, don't do this. Look around. You got kids, you got grandmas, all up on the sidewalk and shit. You want us to shoot up the whole street? You know we will."

Judah kept the gun pointed at the man, but nodded slowly.

"Get in, Paco."

The man slid into the passenger's seat. As soon as he closed the door behind him, the Range Rover blocking the intersection backed up and turned. The man raised his hand and pointed to the back of it.

"My name is Miguel, cracker. You'd better drive on."

Judah followed the SUV in front of him, intensely aware of the four other vehicles in their little convoy. He didn't put down the gun.

"So, we're going to meet the real Weaver now, huh? Who was that guy I was just talking to back at Stingrays, then?"

"Who, Travis?"

Travis. Jesus Christ. That explained some things.

"So, what, he likes to pretend he's Weaver? He's a front for the real guy?"

Miguel shrugged.

"I just do what Travis tells me to do. He does what Weaver tells him to do. It works out."

Judah nodded as he followed the SUV down a side street. It was hard to turn the wheel with the gun still in his hand.

"So, where are we going now? The Pink Pelican?"

Miguel snorted.

"Not unless you want to talk to Rufus."

The SUV turned again. Judah was losing his sense of direction. They were off the main drag, but he couldn't tell if they were heading toward or away from the water. The streets were lined mostly with laundromats, dollar stores and nail salons. They turned yet again.

"I'm guessing Weaver doesn't run out of strip clubs."

Miguel shook his head.

"Man, from what I hear, he don't go near them. I don't know which way he rolls, but he don't seem to like the mamacitas at the club. He'll take their dollars, but he don't want to look at no girls."

They turned one more time. The strip malls gave way to bars, seafood shacks and run-down motels advertising extended stays and free HBO. Judah could smell the ocean, but couldn't see it. At least he was more comfortable with the area. Less flash and more dive. Judah pulled into the sandy, mostly empty, parking lot of a bar and parked next to the Range Rover he'd followed. Gary's van came up beside him and then one of the tailing SUVs pulled in sideways, blocking them in. Judah cut the engine and glanced at Miguel.

"This Weaver guy's a bit of a control freak, huh?"

Miguel bared his gold teeth in a menacing grin.

"He just don't want nobody leaving 'til he says so. The jefe can do that. He can do whatever he wants."

Judah glanced at his side mirror. Three men had gotten out of the SUV behind him and were coming up to his truck. One had an AK-47 held down low at his side. Behind them, he could see a neon sign blinking the name of the bar on and off. The Salty Dog. Judah looked at the .45 still in his hand.

"I'm guessing I should leave this here."

"If you want to keep it. Same with your phone. It leaves this truck and it's ours."

Judah stashed the gun back under the seat and pulled out his cellphone. He held it up for Miguel to see and then tossed it into the cup holder. He looked out the window. Gary and Alvin were standing in the parking lot, with arms stretched out, already being patted down. He turned back to Miguel.

"Can I at least take my cigarettes?"

Miguel opened the passenger's side door and started to get out.

"You want to kill yourself with cancer, go ahead. Makes no difference to me. Now move."

RAMEY RACED INTO the kitchen and frantically searched through the purse she'd left sitting on the countertop. She pushed aside crumpled receipts, her wallet, the little .9mm she always carried with her now, and finally yanked her cellphone free. She flipped it open, punched in Judah's number and held the phone up to her ear. Ramey gripped the edge of the counter, listening to the rings. From the living room, she could hear the TV blaring. Benji had turned the volume up.

"And now here's your host, Alex Trebek!"

Ramey shut her eyes and counted the rings. After six, it went to voicemail. She hung up and immediately redialed. Six more rings.

"You have reached the voice mailbox of area code nine zero four..."

Ramey dialed again. There could be a million reasons why Judah couldn't pick up. He could be driving fast with the windows down, radio turned up, and couldn't hear the call. He could have put his phone on silent. He could still be mad at her from their fight the night before and was staring at the screen of his phone, trying to decide whether or not to answer.

Or Judah could be meeting with Weaver right then, telling him that they had Nash, alive, and trying to use him as a bargaining chip. Promising something they now couldn't deliver. Making a deal that he'd have to go back on, which would most likely mean hell raining down on them from Daytona Beach. Or he could be dead. There was still no answer.

Ramey ended the call and looked down at the cellphone she was gripping with both hands. She grit her teeth and then typed, *NASH IS DEAD*. She hit send on the text and raised her arm, ready to fling the phone across the kitchen, needing the force, the smash, something to give a physicality to the helpless frustration, and now fear, that was welling up inside her. She caught herself; she'd need the phone. Judah could call her back any second. She dropped it on the counter and picked up a half-full bottle of Jack Daniel's standing next to the sink. She gripped it by the neck and hurled it as hard as she could at the opposite kitchen wall, screaming as the glass shattered in all directions. She stood leaning back against the counter, digging her nails into her palms, and waited for Benji to call out some stupid quip from the living room.

There was only silence. And a spray of whiskey trickling down the wall.

IT WAS DARK in The Salty Dog, and smoky, just the way Judah liked his bars. It was the sort of dive that he felt at home in. The vinyl booths were ripped and worn, the row of bottles behind the bar were only dimly lit and Waylon Jennings was softly playing in the background. If he hadn't been sitting across from a man who looked like a complete psychopath, Judah might could have enjoyed himself.

The few barflies lingering over their warm beers had been shooed away when Judah, Alvin and Gary were brought through the front door. The man behind the bar, sporting gold-rimmed aviator glasses and a ponytail that looked like a drowned rat had latched onto the back on his head, had immediately declared The Salty Dog closed, ushered everyone out and locked the door. Aside from him, the goons who were more or less holding Gary and Alvin hostage up at the front near the bar, and a blonde he had vaguely caught a glimpse of, back in the shadows near the bathroom, the bar was now empty. Miguel and his entourage had been left outside. Judah was alone with Weaver.

Neither he nor Weaver had spoken yet. The man in the glasses had hurriedly brought over a bottle of El Dorado before scurrying back to the bar to watch. Judah was aware that all eyes were on him. He stared hard at the man seated across from him in the booth and made the first move.

"Everett Weaver."

"Judah Cannon."

The man with the long dark hair hanging heavy down the sides of his face picked up the bottle of rum and poured out two shots. His movements were slow, almost calculated, and Judah watched his blotchy, callused hands. The gnarled knuckles were faintly tattooed with the message to STAY DOWN. Weaver set the bottle back on the table between them and raised his glass.

"Will you drink with me?"

Weaver's voice was gravelly, almost as if the long, ropy scar on his left cheek, peeking out from behind the curtain of hair, had gashed all the way down into his voice box. His eyes were deep set and a watery blue, which, set against his tan, leathery skin, made them both surprising and terrifying. Judah raised his glass and they drank.

Weaver smashed his glass down with a sound that rang out across the bar and it was all Judah could do not to jump. He wasn't sure if Weaver was trying to intimidate him or was just naturally erratic. Judah waited while Weaver slowly folded his hands in front of him, letting the man take the full measure of him if he wanted to. Finally, Weaver tilted his head and spoke.

"So. I received a call that you were looking for me."

"I guess you did. I guess that punk at the strip club called you after I left."

There was only the vaguest hint of a smile at the corner of Weaver's lips.

"Yes. And Travis is a punk. But I would be wary of the way you speak to me."

Judah narrowed his eyes. While he was pretty sure by now that Weaver could back up any threats he issued, Judah refused to be bullied. It just wasn't in his nature, no matter how much trouble it got him into.

"Why? You gonna feed me to your sharks?"

This time, Weaver did smile. Though it was the sort of smile Judah imagined Weaver would give someone right before he shot them in the face. Judah pulled out his cigarettes and lighter, just to have something to do with hands. He fit a cigarette to his lips and glanced around for an ashtray.

"Mind if I smoke?"

"Yes."

Weaver was staring straight at him. Judah couldn't help it; he had to look away. He slowly and carefully inserted the cigarette back into the pack. He could feel it, the panic buzzing right behind his ear. A wasp, burrowing its way into his skull. He couldn't give in to it. Weaver poured out another shot, this time only for himself, and sipped it. He ran his oyster-colored tongue over his teeth and gave Judah a strange nod.

"You have Nash Conner in your possession. Is that correct?"

Judah raised his head.

"Yes."

"Is he alive?"

"He is."

Weaver blinked at him a few times. He sipped his shot of rum.

"And why do you think I care?"

The stab in the pit of his stomach was even worse the second time around. Apparently, no one gave a shit about Nash. Judah knew it was going to sound pathetic, but he had to try.

"He said you would. He killed a friend of mine, a kid…"

"I don't care."

Weaver rested his elbows on the edge of the table and leaned over, his hair swinging against his shoulders.

"I don't care about your dead kid. I don't care about Nash."

For the first time, it occurred to Judah that he might not be leaving The Salty Dog alive. There was a tremor in his chest, but he kept his voice cool and controlled. He knew that he was dealing with a wild, possibly rabid, animal and the only way to survive would be to show no fear. The wasp inside his head couldn't win. Judah forced himself to lean back and sling one arm over the back of the booth.

"All right. Then what am I doing here?"

Weaver cocked his head as he regarded Judah.

"When Travis told me that a man called Judah Cannon was looking for me, I became interested. It's not a name I've come across before. So, you should be telling me. What are you doing here?"

Weaver leaned forward.

"What are you really doing here?"

Without the Nash card to play, Judah didn't have much more left than the truth. He hoped it would count for something.

"Your boy Nash was running his mouth about you. Saying how you wanted to go in with the Cannons. You wanted to use our bars to push your product.

Use our people, our connections."

Weaver blinked lazily.

"Was he now?"

Judah nodded.

"I'm just here to find out if it's true."

Weaver picked up the shot glass again, but this time he didn't drink from it. He held it up to his right eye and looked through the rum at Judah.

"I'm going to presume you are the son of Sherwood Cannon."

Weaver downed the last of the shot and then thrust the glass away from him. It spun to the center of the table.

"Who, yes, I've heard of."

Judah nodded slowly.

"I am."

"And Sherwood sent you here to talk to me?"

"Sherwood's dead."

Weaver narrowed his eyes.

"And you've assumed his place?"

To admit it, right then, in that bar, at that moment, would anchor Judah firmly on the path he had been fighting ever since he had taken his first steps out of prison. He knew that saying it would change him. It would change everything. There would be no more wavering. There would be no turning back. Judah's eyes flashed.

"Yes."

"And you want to work with me?"

"I don't know."

"You don't know?"

Judah leaned forward.

"I don't know a thing about you. The way I see it, you're doing just fine over here. And I'm doing just fine over where I come from. Maybe we ought to just leave it at that."

Weaver closed his eyes for a moment.

"Maybe."

When he opened them, Judah didn't like what he saw.

"Or maybe not."

Judah knew it was time. If he was going to walk out the door tonight, he needed to do it then. He slid out of the booth and stood up.

"I think we're done here."

Weaver slowly turned his head and looked up at Judah.

"And I think I might need to keep my eye on you, Judah Cannon."

"You do that."

Judah turned his back on Weaver and headed toward the front door. Alvin's and Gary's eyes were wide as they watched him. He hoped they would have enough time to warn him if Weaver decided to shoot him in the back. But it was a word, not a bullet, that Weaver sent in his direction.

"Judah."

He stopped. He counted his breaths. One. Two. Three. Judah waited.

"Tell me. What would stop me from just coming in and taking everything the Cannons have?"

Judah took a step forward.

"Me."

CHAPTER 10

WEAVER SPREAD HIS hands out on the table and looked down at his gnarled knuckles and scarred fingers. They might not be pretty, but they could still pull a trigger for a dead-eye aim. Weaver listened as Judah Cannon walked out the front door of The Salty Dog, followed by the two clowns, tagging along behind him. Weaver could have eaten them for breakfast. But never mind. He waited until he heard the door slam, then bang open again. Weaver looked up from his hands. The Mexican who had brought the Cannon boy to him was standing patiently in the middle of the room. Weaver's own three men, casually lounging against the bar, eyed the man up and down. He could see one sneering in disgust as he whispered something to the man next to him. Weaver turned to the Mexican, who jerked his thumb over his shoulder.

"You want me to do something? Before he leaves?"

Weaver shook his head.

"No. I need him to go back to whatever hole he crawled out of."

The Mexican shrugged and turned to go, but Weaver narrowed his eyes and beckoned to him. The man came over to the table, but stood a respectful few feet away. Weaver liked this. He clasped his hands in front of him and rubbed the pads of his thumbs together.

"You're one of Travis' guys, aren't you?"

The man shrugged again.

"Yes."

"And your name is?"

"Miguel."

Weaver cocked his head. Miguel kept steady eye contact with him and Weaver liked this also. He leaned forward.

"Well, Miguel. You're my guy now. Understand? You report to me and me alone. You can let Judah Cannon go for now, but I want everything on him."

"Everything?"

Weaver raised his finger to Miguel and beckoned him even closer.

"Everything. Who he screws, who he loves, who his enemies are. Where he eats, where he sleeps. Where he can be found at any moment of any day. And who he considers family."

"Family?"

Weaver nodded.

"Who he would die for and who he would live for. Understand?"

"Yes, sir."

"And look into the whereabouts of Nash Conner. He's my dope man out in Palatka. I need to know how much of a liar this Judah Cannon is. Do this and I will make it worth your while."

Weaver flung his hand out toward Miguel.

"Now go."

JUDAH STOMPED DOWN the back steps of the house and crossed the yard to stand next to Benji in the moonlight. They watched silently as Alvin backed out of the shed, carrying the front part of Nash's body, now swaddled tightly in an old patchwork quilt, and Gary followed with the rest. Judah shook his head, but couldn't look at his brother. He watched as the quilt, blotchy with blood in some places, was jostled between them as they carried it toward Gary's van. Benji shifted on his crutches and his voice came out without a trace of emotion.

"I had to."

Judah grit his teeth.

"No. You didn't."

Benji stumped forward a bit, trying to get Judah to look at him.

"And what? You were just gonna let Nash go after you realized you couldn't use him anymore with Weaver? Tell him you're sorry and send him on his merry way?"

The quilt disappeared inside the van. Alvin slid the panel door shut and nodded briefly at Judah before climbing up into the passenger's seat. He and Gary weren't exactly thrilled about having to find a way to dispose of a body in the middle of the night. Like Judah, they were exhausted, but probably not as shaken. The weight of giving, as opposed to following, orders was beginning to settle upon Judah. He ran his hand through his hair as the van backed up and drove off, Nash's dead body bumping around in the back. Judah sighed and turned to Benji. He didn't want to fight anymore.

"I don't know."

Apparently, Benji didn't feel the same way. His mouth twisted in a sneer.

"Of course you don't. But you brought Nash here. You brought him into our home. Into her home."

Judah's eyes flashed.

"Leave Ramey out of it."

Benji hopped on his crutches until he was facing Judah fully. The play of shadows across Benji's face made his scars seem more visible, the damage even more pronounced. The word "monster" flitted across Judah's mind, but he quickly pushed it away. He needed to face Benji's scars. He was responsible for them. Judah forced himself to look his brother in the eye as Benji snorted a rough laugh.

"Why? You think Ramey'd have let Nash go? With the chance of him coming back at any time? You think she wants to live with that kinda fear every day? As if she don't have enough of it hanging over her already."

Judah spoke through clenched teeth.

"You didn't have to be the one to do it, though."

Benji suddenly flung his crutches to the ground, startling Judah. Benji stood before him, wobbling slightly, but standing nonetheless. He jabbed his finger down at his cast.

"Now, you listen to me. This leg, it's gonna heal. And the little kid brother you keep seeing when you look at me, well, he ain't coming back. He didn't get up off that asphalt. He's still lying out there in a ditch somewhere. The sooner you realize that, the better for both of us."

Judah bent over and picked up the crutches laying in the dirt. He held them out to Benji.

"I just didn't want to drag you into all this mess. This life."

Benji accepted the crutches, but shook his head as he jammed them under his armpits. His look suggested that he was pitying Judah, instead of the other way around.

"You didn't. The Scorpions did. And so here we are."

Judah knew Benji was right. The man standing before him, still healing from brutal skin grafts, smashed bones and a hundred and forty-seven stiches, was no longer the goofy towheaded kid who used to beg Judah to play Matchbox cars with him. Nor was he the easygoing charmer, buying everyone a beer, concerned only with having a good time. He was a Cannon now. A real one. And it broke Judah's heart.

"Yes."

Judah had to look away.

"Here we are."

He stood for a moment longer with his brother, listening to the night, and then he nodded once and turned away. He was almost to the back steps when

Benji called out after him.

"She's still got hope, you know."

Judah was brought up short. He slowly turned around.

"What are you talking about?"

Benji didn't move closer and Judah couldn't see his eyes as he spoke. But there was something cruel in his voice.

"Ramey. She still thinks you're a different kinda man. She's still holding out for a different kinda life with you. She still thinks there's a chance."

Judah's voice dropped and he dipped his head slightly. He tried to control himself.

"Quit talking about shit you don't know."

Benji laughed.

"And quit kidding yourself. You can see it in her eyes. She hasn't fallen like the rest of us. Not yet."

Judah clenched his fists at his sides.

"Benji. Stay out of it."

Benji raised his hands defensively.

"Fine. Ramey's your woman. Do what you like. Keep stringing her along. It's none of my business."

Judah turned his back to his brother and started up the stairs.

"You're damn right about that."

CLIVE POKED HIS fork at the remaining lump of meatloaf in front of him and then tossed his wadded up paper napkin onto the plate and pushed it away. He had his head in his hands when the waitress came by his booth.

"That bad, huh?"

Clive glanced up wearily at the nightshift waitress who couldn't have been more than twenty. There was a dark stain dribbling down the front of her light blue uniform shirt and he tried not to focus on it as he looked up at her. Her limp brown hair was pulled back with a plastic banana clip, and her face could use some makeup, but she had a welcoming smile. She was also one of the first people in Bradford County to be genuinely nice to him. He glanced at her left hand as she picked up his plate. Married. Of course. Clive smiled back at her.

"The potatoes were all right. Gravy was good."

"I told you there was a reason it was the dollar ninety-nine special. Next time you come in this late, just order some eggs."

Her gaze flickered across the restaurant and Clive's followed. Aside from a long-haul trucker, hunched over in a denim jacket up at the counter, the Pancake Hut was deserted. It was one o'clock in the morning, but as it was the only all-night place in town, Clive had figured that it would draw more of a crowd. He winked at the waitress.

"Will do."

"More coffee?"

She refilled his cup before waiting for a response. Ordinarily, he would have jumped to stop her. This meant more sugar, more cream, getting the ratio right, but instead he just watched her pour. Her wrists were so slender, it was a wonder they didn't snap against the weight of the coffee pot. He could smell the reek of grease coming off her.

"Anything else?"

"Just keep the coffee coming."

"You got it."

Clive watched her walk away, her oversized uniform shirt bunching up in the back. She disappeared around the corner into the kitchen and Clive turned his attention to his cellphone, sitting next to the steaming cup of coffee. He couldn't put it off any longer. Clive picked up the phone and dialed, reaching for the sugar shaker while it rang.

"Lopez."

She had been asleep. Clive couldn't decide if this boded well for him or not. Maybe she'd be too disoriented to really understand what he was saying and she'd just agree. Or maybe she'd be pissed that he'd just woken her up in the middle of the night.

"It's Grant. I'm sorry if I woke you up."

"For God's sake, Grant. Don't those hillbillies down there sleep?"

She was pissed. He'd have to be careful not to accidentally call her Vickie. Clive peeled open a creamer and dumped it into his coffee.

"More so than up there, let me tell you. There's probably only ten people awake here within a ten-mile radius."

Clive could hear muffled sounds, blankets and sheets being kicked around. He wondered if she was alone.

"Grant. What the hell do you want?"

He stirred his coffee.

"I need to talk to you about something."

"Are you serious?"

She sounded much more awake now. Angry, incredulous and awake. Not a good combination for her.

"Krenshaw was expecting that CAPA report this morning, but it never came in. What're you doing down there? What's going on?"

Clive blew on his coffee, but didn't sip it. He set the cup down and braced one hand against the edge of the table.

"There's something here."

"Something?"

He looked over his shoulder and then around the Pancake Hut again. It was still empty except for the trucker. Clive could hear snores coming from the man's direction. The waitress was nowhere in sight. He tried to keep his voice down anyway.

"Something I think needs looking into. I just need a few more days."

"Looking into? Are you telling me you still can't figure out how to write up the report? Really?"

"Of course I know how to write the damn report!"

Clive immediately looked around him, but there was no one to notice his outburst. The trucker was still snoring.

"I just need you to trust me on this, Lopez, and give me a few more days."

"No. Not until you tell me why. Not until you tell me what's going on."

Clive sighed. He'd have to give her what he had and hope she saw where he was going with it. Otherwise, she'd think he was off his rocker and order him back up to Atlanta where he'd probably spend the next year or so moldering away with the rest of the forgotten files. He gulped his coffee, scorching the back of his throat, and then began.

"All right, but you've got to just listen for a second, okay? Let me try to explain."

Lopez didn't respond, so he kept going, stumbling along.

"There's something just not right about this church case. I know Krenshaw thinks it's just open and shut, and the evidence on file probably points to that, but it's different down here on the ground."

"Different?"

"The preacher who ran the church, who still runs it, her name is Sister Tulah Atwell. And as far as I can tell, this whole town is hers."

He knew Lopez was shaking her head. She probably had that look on her face, the one she gave him that could make him feel like he was another species. Like she couldn't figure out how on earth he had managed to crawl his way back up the stairs from the records room. That look.

"I don't even know what that means."

Clive took another sip of coffee.

"It means that no one will talk about her. Everyone either praises her to high heaven or is scared to even admit that she exists. A real quick way to get ignored around here is to say her name with a question mark at the end."

Now Lopez would be rolling her eyes. Hard.

"So, folks don't want to be questioned about their preacher. This might surprise you, Grant, but that's actually pretty common."

He shook his head.

"No, this is different. And then there's the Cannons."

"The Cannons?"

"The man found dead in the church was Sherwood Cannon. If you go to the next town over, Silas, and mention the Cannons, people clam up just as fast as if you'd asked about Tulah here."

"So?"

She wasn't getting it. Clive groaned in frustration.

"It's like that Brad Pitt movie. The fight one."

"*Fight Club*?"

"Yeah. No one talks about the Cannons. No one talks about Tulah. Like it's an unspoken rule. It's strange, Lopez. I mean, it's almost creepy."

There was a long pause. Clive tapped the edge of his cup with his fingernail, waiting.

"Grant. Get your ass back up here. So the locals don't want to talk to a federal agent. So what? You've been off the street for way too long if you don't think that's normal. I don't know what you're getting at, but drop it. Creepy feelings don't move cases off the list."

He rushed before she could hang up.

"There's something else."

"Better be more than a feeling."

"It is."

It was the one real lead he'd managed to find; he'd spent all afternoon and most of the night on it. Clive hoped it would be enough to persuade her.

"I realized that I was getting nowhere with questions and interviews, so I started looking up public records."

She snorted a laugh.

"Public records? So you really do want your old job back, huh?"

"Wait, just listen. I was searching around, just trying to see what this preacher was all about. At first, I couldn't find a thing. Tulah's like a ghost. She wasn't on paper anywhere. But then I started noticing something strange. For a county this small, and this rural, there was an awful lot of land exchanging hands between 2006 and 2009."

"Okay, and?"

Clive pushed his cup away and took out his notebook. He started flipping through pages, looking for the names he had written down.

"I'm telling you, Lopez, it just wasn't making any sense. Pieces of land that had been in the same family for seventy years were being sold off to two different LLCs. Horizon Star Enterprises and Three Pillars Ministries. And by sold, I mean at a cost of twenty-five cents an acre. Then there were all of the land gifts and donations to a non-profit organization called Life Spring."

He could hear cabinets opening and closing and then the unmistakable sound of pouring cereal.

"Get to the point, Grant."

"I am, just listen. So, I did a lot more digging and it turns out that they're all dummy corporations. Horizon Star, Three Pillars, Life Spring. They don't exist, except on paper. The CEO of all of them is a woman named Rowena Morehead."

"Wait, let me guess. She also isn't real."

Clive picked up his coffee.

"Oh, she's real. Or was, anyway. It took me long enough, but I finally found a birth certificate listing Rowena Morehead as the mother of one Felton Halbert Morehead."

He could hear her crunching.

"Am I supposed to know what that means?"

Clive set his coffee cup back down, harder than he meant to. Hot coffee sloshed all over his hand.

"Felton! Brother Felton! He's Tulah's nephew. He uses Atwell, Tulah's last name, but he's actually a Morehead. So was Tulah. Rowena Morehead was her unmarried sister."

"Was?"

"She died over thirty years ago. But Tulah has been using her name and identity to front her companies, so that she herself is untraceable."

"So?"

Clive reached for the napkin dispenser.

"So, I also got out a map and started piecing together all of the property that was sold or donated to those three companies. The parcels all connect. If I'm right about this, it looks like Tulah has amassed a huge area of land out in west Bradford County."

"She's building a megachurch?"

He yanked out a poof of napkins and dabbed at the spilled coffee.

"I'm talking over seven thousand acres. That's pretty damn big for a church. She's still preaching in what's left of the building that burned and it's about the size of a studio apartment in Inman Park. These people, in this church, they're backwoods Christians. They drink poison."

"Poison?"

"There can't be too many of them, is what I'm getting at."

There was another pause. Finally, her voice suggested that she was beginning to take him seriously.

"You're wondering what all the land is for, then."

Clive nodded as he wadded up the wet napkins and shoved the soppy pile to the edge of the table.

"Exactly. I don't have a complete picture yet, but something is going on down here with this preacher. It's odd enough that an outlaw biker gang and the patriarch of a notorious criminal family have a shootout in Sister Tulah's church. But then the fire and police reports don't seem right, or at least complete, and everyone seems afraid to talk about her. And then this land business. Folks selling their family homesteads for pennies. I think…"

Clive took a deep breath.

"…I think she's got some kind of hold on this town. And everything that

I've found so far, it's got to be just the tip of the iceberg. I need some time to dig deeper."

She seemed to be thinking it over. Clive heard a slurp of milk and then the clanging of a spoon inside an empty bowl. When she finally spoke, she sounded only half convinced.

"Okay, I see where you're going. But this isn't really our jurisdiction. If it's anything, it's white collar. FBI. And the last thing Krenshaw would want is you handing them anything."

He'd come this far. Might as well tell her the whole plan.

"I'm thinking maybe of using the RICO angle."

Lopez burst out laughing. Clive grit his teeth; he'd expected it.

"You want to build a RICO case against this Sister Tulah? She's a preacher, not a mob boss. Maybe there's some kickbacks going on, some tax evasion with the land acquisition, who knows. But you want to link her up with organized crime? Are you out of your mind?"

Clive thought maybe he was. If he was wrong about Tulah, he'd be the laughing stock of the ATF. Again. Back to the records room, his career forever buried under an avalanche of humiliation. But if he was right. Well, if he was right, he'd make headlines.

"Lopez, please. Just a few more days. You've got to admit, I'm on to something here. It's been years since Atlanta ATF worked a real RICO case. If I'm right, and eventually the FBI picks it up, just imagine how you and I would look then? Give me a few more days. Let me see what else I can find."

"All right. Fine. I'll make an excuse, put Krenshaw off. But you've only got until Monday. Either call me Monday with something big, really big, like, RICO big, or you come on home."

"Yes, ma'am."

Clive set his phone down on the table and drained the last of his coffee. Four more days. He could find something, he could do it. The waitress came out from around the corner to shake the sleeping truck driver awake. Clive made eye contact with her, but she wasn't returning his smile as she slowly walked over. Clive held up his cup.

"More coffee?"

There was a strange look on her face. She regarded him for a moment, almost warily, and then reached into her apron.

"I'd better just give you the check."

Clive wasn't sure what had happened with the waitress, but he was too excited to care. Maybe she'd thought he was flirting with her and it had gone too far. Regardless, he needed to get out of there anyway. Now that he'd come clean to Lopez and had bought some time, Clive thought he might actually be able to get some sleep. He took out his wallet and laid a ten on top of the check.

"Keep it."

The waitress reached for it, almost cautiously, and then furtively stuffed the check and the bill into her apron. She started to go, but then quickly turned back to him. Her voice was hushed.

"I were you, mister, I'd be careful."

Clive leaned forward so he could hear her better.

"Careful? Of what?"

The waitress pursed her lips. Clive watched her twist her wedding band around on her finger. Finally, she cast her eyes down and whispered again.

"You know. Her."

RAMEY DIDN'T LOOK up as the front door opened and banged shut behind her. She raised the beer bottle over her head and her fingers touched Judah's as he took it from her.

"I'd get you a whiskey, but something happened to the bottle."

Judah sat down next to her on the front porch steps. Ramey watched him take a sip and then rub the sweating bottle back and forth across his forehead.

"I tell you. I could've done without today."

Ramey looked away. The moon was bright and fully overhead now, and she could see the leaves of the two live oaks in the yard twinkling as a low breeze rustled them. A whippoorwill called out, lonely and searching. Judah tapped her elbow with the bottle, but she shook her head wearily.

"You and me both."

Judah drained the beer and dangled it from his fingers between his knees. Ramey watched the moonlight glinting off the curve of the bottle's neck before picking up her pack of cigarettes. One left. It seemed a fitting way to end the day. She lit the cigarette, inhaled deeply and passed it to Judah. He seemed distracted as he smoked.

"An ATF agent at the door. A dead man in the shed."

Ramey nodded slowly.

"And Weaver."

She folded her arms on her knees and rested her chin on her right wrist. It was hard to look at Judah. He had only briefly recounted his meeting with Weaver, filling her in on the basics. That Weaver couldn't get give two shits about Nash. That it had seemed like Nash was lying in the first place about Weaver wanting the Cannons' business. Judah had been evasive, though, when she asked about whether or not he thought Weaver was a danger to them. His eyes had shifted. Ramey had known he was exhausted, riding home on the burn-out fumes of an adrenaline rush, but it was more than that. Something had happened in that bar between him and Weaver. Something he probably couldn't have explained to her, even if he had wanted to. But she knew it was there. Ramey knew that the man sitting next to her now was not the same man she had watched drive away that morning.

Judah passed the cigarette back to her and kicked his feet out onto the steps.

"You think Benji killed Nash to prove something to me?"

Ramey glanced over at Judah and realized that their thoughts were going in two completely different directions. She took a drag on the cigarette and raised her face to blow the smoke up into the night.

"Honestly? I got no idea. I don't know why any of this is happening."

Judah nudged her shoulder.

"Hey now. What's that supposed to mean?"

She glared at him.

"It means, we're in shit up to our elbows."

Judah shook his head more emphatically than he needed to. Ramey ground her teeth. If there was one thing she couldn't stand, it was Judah attempting to placate her. It was insulting as hell. Judah's voice was gentle, but firm. Like he was talking to a child.

"No. No, that's not true. Nothing's changed."

Ramey rolled her eyes and looked away from him.

"You really gonna keep trying that line with me?"

"Ramey..."

She bit her bottom lip before spitting out the words.

"You just had to go and kick that hornet's nest. You just had to."

Ramey felt his hand on her shoulder. She still wouldn't look at him.

"Are you talking about Weaver? Ramey, I had to know what was what with him. I had to know what we were dealing with."

"Sure."

"Ramey."

Judah gripped her arm and she turned to him sharply. His voice was low, strained, and he didn't let go of her.

"Everything I'm doing here, I'm doing for us. For our future. So we can step out of Sherwood's shadow and leave all that bullshit behind. So we can start new. Have a different life. An honest life. In a world where the Cannons are an honest family. You need to believe that."

Ramey looked down at his hand on her. She could feel the tension coursing through it.

"Oh, I do. All except that last part."

Judah let go of her and stood up. He stepped to the dewy ground and then turned to look at her. His shoulders were curving inward, his hands shoved deep down into his pockets. Almost as if he were protecting himself from her.

"What the hell is that supposed to mean?"

Ramey slowly shook her head.

"Judah, I don't know where you're taking us. But I know it's not to the place we talked about before. You keep thinking you're digging us out, but really you're just making the hole deeper. So deep, we can't even look up and see daylight."

Judah's voice was dangerously quiet.

"Sometimes you gotta do things you don't want to do, to get to where you want to be. You, of all people, should know that."

Ramey jerked her head up.

"Yeah, but Judah, I look in your eyes and I don't see a man balking at doing what needs to be done. Or even a man wrestling with it, confused about what he wants. Not anymore, at least. I think you know exactly what you want. And it ain't getting out of this life. It's going all in. Something happened tonight, with Weaver, and all the chips got pushed to the center of the table."

Judah scowled at her, but quickly looked away.

"It's not like that."

Ramey stood up. Her cigarette had gone out and she flung it over the porch railing.

"Listen. You want to keep lying to yourself, you go right on ahead. But don't you dare lie to me. Don't you dare. You're giving up on everything, everything we had a shot at, you and me. Just you and me. So at least be straight with me about what you're doing. About what you want."

Beneath her, Judah flung his arms out to the side.

"And just what is it that I want, huh? What do you think I want?"

Ramey looked down at him coolly. Her voice didn't waver for a moment.

"You want to be king of the mountain. You want to walk in the fire and not be burned."

CHAPTER 11

IT DIDN'T TAKE Clive long to discover why Sister Tulah wanted all that land. He'd spent more time trying to convince the prune-faced librarian behind the desk of the Bradford County Public Library to let him use a computer. First there was the skeptical, you're-not-from-around-here-are-you look that he'd already gotten used to, and then a flare of hostility, which he'd also come to expect. The woman, picking at her front teeth with the edge of a plastic bookmark all the while, had then gone to the trouble of hauling out the library's policy handbook and reading him the entire section on issuing cards, just to make it clear why she wouldn't give him one. No residency, no card. No card, no computer time. The woman had folded her sinewy arms and shaken her head adamantly. Clive had been forced to use the one means of communication that he knew worked with these people. He had taken out his badge. The librarian had begrudgingly allowed him a computer.

Sitting in a blue plastic chair designed for kindergarteners and fielding suspicious looks from the library's only other patron, a man in a battered fishing hat with a stack of *Reader's Digests* on his lap, Clive had begun to fit the pieces together. The swath of land Tulah had amassed in western Bradford

County appeared blank on the map, but was brimming with riches fifteen feet beneath the soil. Phosphate.

He'd had to look outside of Bradford County to find out about it, though. There was no mention of a potential phosphate mine anywhere in the *Bradford County Telegraph*. A tiny write-up at the bottom of page four in the *Lake Region Monitor* had given him his first clue, and then he'd started sifting through the archives of the *Florida Times Union*. The Jacksonville-based newspaper, reporting on more than the Restaurant of the Week and Senior Shout Outs, had given him the first solid evidence he'd yet encountered:

PRB Industries Considers Mine Operation in West Bradford County

The article was dated from 2006, about six months after Tulah had snapped up the first parcel of land in the area. There was an opinion piece on the controversy over phosphate mining in Florida, dated a year later, and then two more articles, specifically relevant to the mine proposal in Bradford County.

Despite Previous Opposition, Bradford County Board of County Commissioners Unanimously Approves Mine

Bradford Mine Permits Denied by State, PRB Industries Moves On

Clive clicked his pen and slumped against the back of the springy, plastic chair. It made sense. If the mine had been established, Sister Tulah would have been set to make a fortune by leasing the mineral rights to Peace River Basin Industries. He marveled at Tulah's ingenuity for a moment, but then the voice of Lopez crept into his brain. So what? Why did it matter? Where was the crime? Clive drummed his fingers on the edge of the table as he looked over his notes. The man in the fishing hat coughed loudly from across the library. He had discarded the *Reader's Digests* and was now flapping open a week old copy of *The Bradford County Telegraph*. He eyed Clive over the top of the newspaper and cleared his phlegmy throat again. Clive stilled his hand, but seeing a physical copy of the paper sparked something for him. If the mining deal had gone through, it would have the biggest thing to ever happen in Bradford County. Yet, there wasn't a single mention of it in the county's only daily newspaper. He searched the *Telegraph*'s website archives again for mining, phosphate, PRB, but still there was nothing. He tossed his pen down in frustration, trying to think.

There was another issue needling him, too. He could understand why Tulah's followers at the Last Steps Church were willing to sell their land to her at ten dollars a parcel, but what about the others? Clive groaned as he flipped back through his notebook for the long list of names he'd put together. He would have to do some serious digging. He looked up at the laminated sign posted above the row of three computers. *1 Hour Time Limit. This is the RULE!* Clive glanced across the room to the librarian who was viciously jabbing pencils into a plastic cup on the counter. If only his laptop internet hotspot would work; if only there was one single place within a twenty-mile radius that had Wi-Fi. Clive turned back to the computer, its struggling hard drive buzzing and sputtering away. Once, Clive had been in the position to pull out his badge and intimidate street thugs and drug lords. Now, he was using it to bully the local librarian. Clive sighed and slipped his wallet out of his jacket pocket. He opened it and propped his badge up next to the keyboard, where the librarian, or anyone else who wanted to bother him, could see it. He loosened his tie, clicked all the way back to 2006 and got down to business.

Slowly and painstakingly, with the newspaper headlines speaking for themselves, Clive pieced the puzzle together:

Daughter of County Manager, Presumed Kidnapped, Found Unharmed at Revival

Car Dealership Blaze Ruled Accident by Fire Marshal

Church Gifts Hospital New Equipment

Sheriff Admits Falling Asleep at Wheel, Driving Into Santa Fe River

Board of Commissioners Vote on Zoning Results in Turn-Around Decision

Kentsville Prayers Answered, Night Assaults at Pine Landing Cease

At first, Clive couldn't believe it. But the deeper he went, the more complete the picture became. He had been right; Sister Tulah didn't just intimidate the residents of Bradford County, she owned them. There was a pattern of extortion, sometimes violent, sometimes only menacing, that dated back at least fifteen years. Of course, Clive couldn't prove anything, but there were too many accidents, too many decisions changed, too many outcomes that just didn't add up for strings not to be pulled, for coercion and manipulation not to exist. If he was right, then Sister Tulah had the most important men of the county either in her pocket or at her mercy. It was no wonder everyone had sold their land to Tulah. No wonder they were all terrified of her. Clive reached for his cellphone. It was a textbook RICO case: a sprawling web of blackmail, bribery and racketeering, even if it was run by a grandma preacher in a flowered dress. Lopez was going to shit herself.

He dialed the number and pointedly turned his back on the librarian, who was now making disgusted faces and pointing at the *ABSOLUTELY NO PHONE CALLS* sign posted on the wall next to him. Three rings into the call, however, it dawned on him. He tossed the phone down and frantically thumbed back through the pages of his notebook. The library printer was out of ink, so he'd had to write down everything down by hand. He found the *Times Union* headline and then searched online for the article again.

"Although the Committee on Environmental Protection and Conservation had previously indicated their support of Peace River Basin Industries' proposed phosphate strip mining operation in Bradford County, yesterday's vote to refuse EPA and FDEP permits to the company tells a different story. This was a surprising turn of events, but the road to bringing PRB Industries to Florida has been a rocky one. While larger companies such as Mosaic have, in the past, pushed forward and appealed similar decisions with favorable outcomes, PRB Industries announced today that they will be withdrawing their proposal from further consideration by the state and instead will be exploring more promising sites in North Carolina and Idaho. State legislators participating in the vote had no comment on the matter."

Clive scribbled down the details in his notebook, but he still didn't understand why the permits had been denied to the mining company. It was another turnaround decision, but one that essentially destroyed all of the plans Sister Tulah had laid over the last five years. Clive kept staring at the newspaper article displayed on the screen, knowing there was something he was missing. When it finally hit him, he nearly choked. The vote had taken place only three months earlier, on May 13th. The Last Steps of Deliverance Church of God had burned on May 10th. Clive sat back in a daze. There had to be a connection between the two. If Sister Tulah could control local officials, who was to say that she couldn't manipulate state lawmakers as well? Something must have gone wrong for Tulah's church to be attacked and the vote to swing against her interests, but Clive was sure there was a link between the two. His hand was shaking as he went to pick up his cellphone, but he stopped himself yet again. This was huge. This could be everything for him. And he wasn't going to blow it this time. If Clive was going to try to fry a fish this big, then he'd better make sure he had the right pan first.

As soon as he saw the copperhead winding its way out of the thick underbrush lining the side of the path, Brother Felton knew it was the sign he had been waiting for. He had been on his way to the church, hurrying along the worn trail cutting through the scrubby woods that linked his small corner on the south end of the property to the church, the road and Sister Tulah's house. It was Friday, the start of the second weekend in August, and Felton knew that he would have to get the church as spotless as possible if he was to have any peace before Tulah left for The Recompense. Though she wasn't leaving until Saturday, he knew she would already be irritated, agitated and looking for someone to lash out at. Felton didn't know what exactly The Recompense was, as far as he was aware not even the Elders knew of its true significance, but the final preparations for it had commanded his aunt's attention for weeks. Felton was just glad he'd have a break from Tulah until Monday night. She only left her church once every three years for the event, and, especially this time around,

Felton was thankful for it.

He was about halfway down the sandy path, humming to himself, trying to ignore the itchy patch of sweat already seeping through the back of his shirt, when he laid eyes on the snake. Felton had the strange feeling, though, that it was more like the snake had laid its eyes on him. He waited as the copperhead purposefully crossed in front of him, knowing it was about to happen. Felton felt a tingling at the center of his palms and at the back of his neck, as if the very air around him had become galvanized. A metallic taste flooded his mouth and he clapped his hands over his ringing ears. A brilliant, scarlet light crept in at the edges of his vision and he felt a sharp bolt of pain shoot from his left to right temple. Felton squeezed his eyes shut, but didn't cry out. Just as soon as it had come over him, the pain dissipated, seeming to float away from his head like tiny particles of dust. He slowly opened his eyes. Everything he could see still had the strange red tinge to it, but he was no longer afraid. He dropped to his knees in front of the snake and the creature rose up until it was almost standing on the tip of its tail. Brother Felton stretched out his arms, beseeching.

"Tell me."

The snake's piceous eyes sparkled and its tongue flickered, testing the air, but Felton was not afraid. Everything surrounding him focused in on the snake, telescoping to the point of the snake's gash of a mouth.

"Rise up. Rise up."

Felton could feel the tears streaming down the sides of his face. He extended his hands out to the snake.

"Please. Tell me."

The snake flicked its tongue again.

"*Arise, shine; for thy light is come, and the glory of the Lord is risen upon thee.*"

Isaiah again. Felton recognized the scripture, but he still did not understand. He inched forward on his knees.

"What is my task? What must I do?"

The snake's narrow head weaved back and forth.

"Rise up. Find your voice. Find a way."

Brother Felton trembled.

"How?"

"Rise up. Rise up. Use the book. Use your voice. Find a way."

Felton felt a wave of vertigo crash into him and suddenly the snake dropped unceremoniously to the ground. Felton blinked a few times, but then stood up. He still didn't understand the message, but he felt shot through with an electric sense of clarity. The snake slithered away, but stopped just before disappearing into a tangle of low creepers. The snake turned its head in his direction and Felton nodded to it.

"I will. I promise."

The snake quietly slipped into the underbrush, but Brother Felton could still hear the rustling whisper of its voice.

"I know."

Judah shook hands with Bernie Tillman, who grinned and clapped him on the shoulder before half stumbling down the rickety metal steps. Judah stood at the top of the stairs, in front of the open door to the office trailer, and lit a cigarette. Bernie had just dropped off an envelope of cash in exchange for the load of catalytic converters Alvin would be driving over to High Springs later that day. The money wasn't half of what was brought in each week from the off-site businesses, but it was needed. With a little fuzzy math in the books, Ramey could wash everything out as long as there was something halfway legitimate to back it up.

Judah smiled around his cigarette and waved as Bernie backed his truck out onto the main road, but his face fell when he saw the shiny blue Charger turning in after it and pulling up in its place. Before the car had even stopped, Judah knew who was inside it. He shut the office door behind him and reluctantly came down the stairs. Judah stood on the bottom step, waiting as the ATF agent took his sweet time getting out of the car. He straightened his pastel tie, ostentatiously re-buttoned the jacket of his fancy suit and swaggered up to the office. It was all Judah could do not to roll his eyes; he knew every deliberate move the agent was making and why he made it. The law had been walking up to his door in the same way ever since he was still crawling around on the living room rug. Judah flicked his cigarette over the metal rail and came down from the last step.

"Special Agent Grant."

The agent stopped a few feet away from Judah and removed his dark sunglasses. He squinted through the brilliant afternoon sun, reflecting in a blinding sheen off the side of the office trailer.

"Judah Cannon. I'd like to have a word."

Judah stared blandly at the agent.

"You mean you'd like to question me about something."

Agent Grant raised his hand to shield his eyes from the sun.

"Yes. That, too."

Judah grunted and crossed in front of the agent as he headed around the garage to the back. He could hear Grant crunching through the dusty gravel behind him as he followed. If Judah was going to have to talk to this guy, he'd rather do it in his own space. And in a place where he knew Ramey had his back and Benji was at least another pair of eyes. The agent called out from behind him.

"Nice place you got here, this Cannon Salvage. It was your father's business, wasn't it?"

Judah ignored the comment. He turned the corner and quickly found Ramey's eyes. She stood up from behind the desk, but Judah jerked his head slightly in a warning. Ramey dropped the stack of papers in her hand and came around the desk, immediately crossing her arms. Benji, one hand keeping him steady on a crutch and the other up inside the guts of a Taurus on the lift, saw the agent, too. He tossed the breaker bar in the bucket of tools against the wall and reached for the other crutch. Judah walked past the lift and casually sat down at the poker table, pointing at a metal folding chair across from him and indicating that the agent should sit as well. Judah kept his eyes on Grant, but knew Ramey was just behind him, leaning against the desk, and Benji, for what he was worth, was just behind the agent.

Agent Grant was slow to sit down. He craned his neck, examining the garage around him as if he really cared.

"Wow, this sure is some place. Two lifts, huh? And a lot of space to work. What do you do with all the cars once you've finished with them?"

Judah knew the game. This was going to take forever. He jutted with his chin out the bay doors. The agent nodded.

"I guess that would make sense. But with all those stacks of cars out there. I mean, don't you ever worry they'll topple over one day?"

"No."

The agent turned back to Judah with a wide grin on his face. He looked over Judah's shoulder at Ramey.

"And we've met before. I guess you never told Judah to give me a call."

Judah kept his eyes on the agent.

"Oh, she did. We've just been busy. Livelihoods and all, you know."

Agent Grant turned to look behind him.

"And you must be the kid brother, Benji."

Agent Grant pointedly looked down at Benji's leg.

"Motorcycle accident, right?"

Judah was almost proud of the look of pure animosity Benji delivered back. A year ago, Benji would have been offering the agent a cold drink from the mini-fridge and trying to make small talk to ease the tension in the room. Now, his brother understood how things worked. He understood that unless a lawman was in your pocket or in your debt, he was firmly on the other side of the line. Judah waited until the agent turned back around and then he waved his hand toward the chair again.

"Agent Grant. Please sit and ask your questions so you can move along and get out of my garage. We do have work to do here."

The stupid grin fell from the agent's face and he pulled out the chair and sat down heavily in it.

"Yes, quite the operation you're running here."

Judah crossed his arms and stared at the agent.

"Your questions?"

Agent Grant fixed Judah with a hard stare.

"It's all above board, correct? Nothing illegal? Nothing that could get you into trouble? It's my understanding that you Cannons don't exactly like to follow the rules."

Judah leaned forward slightly.

"Excuse me?"

"Well, I guess it was your father who had the biggest record on the books. Goes all the way back to 1959. First arrested at thirteen for petty theft."

Judah didn't say anything. He knew where this was going and he didn't like it. He stared at the agent, waiting for him to continue.

"And you've got a record yourself, Judah. Just three months ago you were sitting pretty in the state pen."

Judah refused to show any emotion. He kept his tone even.

"I did my time."

The agent twisted in his chair to look at Benji.

"Your older brother Levi's got a rap sheet as long as Sherwood's, but you can look up my man Benjamin here, too. Arrested for marijuana possession, right? Twice, if I remember correctly. Though somehow or another, no prison time for you. And then this one."

Grant turned back around and winked at Ramey.

"Even this little lady has seen the inside of a holding cell. Many years back, but still. Drunk and disorderly. Looking at you, I just can't picture it."

From behind Judah, Ramey's tone was biting.

"Oh, you'd be surprised, special agent."

Judah had to put a stop to it now. If the bullying continued, either he or Ramey was likely to lose their tempers and do something foolish. And Benji was a powder keg. Judah had accepted this new version of his brother, but he wasn't sure he could control it. He smacked his hand on the green felt table top to get the agent's attention.

"All right. What do you want from us?"

Agent Grant turned away from the grinding stare he was giving Ramey and finally focused on Judah.

"I just want to make sure we all know where we stand with each other."

"I think we know where we stand. Now, get to it or get out."

The agent's eyes narrowed.

"Okay. If that's the way you want to play it. I want to know about your connection to Preacher Tulah Atwell."

Judah uncrossed his arms. He leaned forward, resting his elbows on the edge of the table.

"The only connection I have to Preacher Tulah is that my father was found dead inside her church. That's it. That's all."

Agent Grant frowned.

"But what was Sherwood doing in that church to begin with?"

Judah leaned back and slung his arm over the back of his chair.

"Jesus Christ, if I knew that, I'd be on TV with my own psychic show, now wouldn't I? Making millions instead of sitting here with you."

"So you don't know what connection your father had to the preacher? I find that hard to believe."

Judah dragged the ashtray over and dug around in his pocket to pull out a crumpled pack of cigarettes. He held one out to the agent, but Grant only stared at him. Judah shrugged, lit the cigarette and then leaned back again.

"Let me tell you a story, Special Agent Grant. It goes like this. When I got out of prison back in May, there was no one waiting to pick me up. I had to walk home. When I got back to Silas, two things happened right away. I got lit to the gills and she walked back into my life."

Judah jerked his hand over his shoulder toward Ramey.

"The next day, I woke up hungover. I spent the next few days or so trying to get my shit together. You probably wouldn't understand that, but it's what you have to do when you finally get out of the can. My girl and I, we decided to get out of town for a few days. Spend a little time just the two of us. We drove up to Valdosta on a Saturday. We checked into a motel. And the next day we turned on the TV and learned that Sherwood was dead. We came home. The end."

He stared hard at Agent Grant, who seemed to be considering his response. Finally, the agent put his hands in his lap and narrowed his eyes.

"You broke your parole going to Valdosta. No one seemed to catch that, huh?"

Judah took a long drag on his cigarette.

"Or maybe they gave me a break. On account of my father dying and all."

Ramey came up to stand beside him. He could tell from the taut way she was carrying herself that she'd had enough. She rested her fingertips on the edge of the table and leaned forward. Judah glanced up, though he already knew what the look on her face would be. She was shooting the agent daggers.

"Just what the hell are you hunting?"

Agent Grant only stared at her. She leaned forward even further.

"I mean, for Christ's sake, you're ATF. What do you want with us?"

A sly smile crept to the corner of the agent's lips. He leaned forward as well.

"Maybe I'm just asking the questions that no one else wants to ask."

Judah cut his eyes toward Ramey. He needed her to keep her cool. The agent was just trying to rattle her. Maybe he had something on them, maybe he didn't. But they certainly couldn't give him anything to work with. Ramey crossed her arms again and stepped away from the table as Grant cleared his throat.

"So, back to our Sister Tulah."

Judah shrugged in exaggerated nonchalance.

"Well, last I heard, she was still up in Kentsville, trying to put her church back together. Can't tell you much more than that."

Agent Grant leaned back in his chair and pulled the tip of his tie out of his jacket. He pretended to examine it, fingering the striped silk, before tucking it away. Judah knew this tactic, too. Was he supposed to be impressed? Envious? Judah would just as soon wear a noose as a necktie. He narrowed his eyes, though, as the agent reached into his pocket and drew something out. Grant rested his closed fist on the edge of the table.

"Well, let me ask you this, then. Do you want know what RICO is?"

Judah mashed his cigarette out in the ashtray, trying not to focus on the agent's hand. He stared hard at Agent Grant's smug smile.

"Yes. I do."

Agent Grant opened his fist and Judah caught a glint of brass. The agent pinched the small shell casing between his fingers and stood it upright in the center of the table. It looked like a .9mm.

"I want to be clear here, Judah. Clear as goddamn crystal. I want you to understand this completely. If I take down Tulah, I will take down everyone who has ever worked for her. Everyone who has ever committed a crime at her direction or taken a bribe from her hands. Even if they were only just a hired gun."

Judah glanced at the bullet casing, but quickly averted his eyes. He kept his gaze riveted on Agent Grant and hoped to God that Ramey was doing the same thing. Judah leaned back in his chair and loosely crossed his arms as he watched the agent dip into his pocket again. This time, he withdrew a slightly larger casing. He held it up to the light as if it were a precious gem. Judah still didn't say anything. The agent stood the second casing next to the first and continued.

"Do you understand what I'm saying? If I take Tulah down, I will take you down. I will take you down, your brother down, your lady friend here down. And, so help me God, I will take Tulah down."

Judah refused to flinch.

"Your point?"

The agent flicked his eyes up toward Ramey. Judah knew that the agent was trying to get to her. Grant was lavishing a self-satisfied gaze on her. The one that cops loved to give women. The agent was trying to tell Ramey that he might be an asshole, but he wasn't as big of an asshole as Judah. She could jump ship, come clean and maybe be treated a little less like dirt. From the way Agent Grant's brow knit as he looked away, however, Judah could imagine the expression on Ramey's face. Nobody could give you a go-to-hell stare like Ramey. Judah waited for the agent to focus his attention back on him.

"My point is this, Judah Cannon. You help me and I'll help you. You don't help me and, well, things are going to get pretty ugly around here in a hurry."

Judah leaned forward.

"So, you're trying to threaten me? Into helping you?"

"I'm giving you the chance to save yourself. You help me prove that Tulah is tied into your criminal activities and your help will be taken into consideration. We'll put together a substantial assistance deal or something. It will work out much better for you, and your family, in the long run."

Judah nodded slowly.

"That's your offer, huh?"

Agent Grant reached into his pocket again. He pulled out a shell casing, this one much larger than the other two, and slowly, carefully, stood it up next to the others. The agent glanced from the row of casings to Judah. His look was pointed.

"That's the offer. I'd take it."

Judah turned around to face Ramey. He knew she recognized the casings. Her .9mm. His .45. The .308 from the M-14 Hiram had insisted they take. To anyone else, the look on Ramey's face was stone cold. She would never let the agent see her sweat. But Judah had caught the flicker of panic in her amber eyes. In the twitch of her cheek muscle, in the lines around her mouth. What was she thinking? Her eyes had been fixed on the bullet casings, but when she raised them to meet his, Judah's breath caught in his throat for an instant. She narrowed her eyes, almost imperceptibly, and Judah smiled at her. Nothing could get to Ramey; she would always have his back. She would hold his secrets, their secrets, and take them down to the bottom of the sea with her, drowning alongside them if she had to.

Judah winked at her and turned back around. He looked over the agent's shoulder at his brother. Judah liked what he saw. Benji wasn't hunched over in an Oxy stupor; he was watching every move between him and the agent. He was listening. He was learning. Judah finally focused back on Agent Grant. He shrugged his shoulders.

"Well, it's kind of you, but I'm afraid we can't accept."

The agent stood up suddenly, knocking his chair over. The metal scraped against the cement floor. Agent Grant was furious and incredulous. Or, at least, he was pretending to be.

"Did you hear what I just said? Do you know who I am? I'm ATF, not the local law you're paying to look the other way. You piss off a federal and we're talking about a special response team coming in and tearing apart this little chop shop of yours. Helicopters. Battering rams. There won't be a single stick of this shack left standing. And don't you try to tell me that you had nothing to do with the shootout and the fire up at the church. I read the reports. I looked at the site. Unlike everyone else on the donut patrol down here, I can put two and two together. I know you were involved. I know it and I will ruin you unless you work with me on this."

Judah smiled and raised his hands helplessly.

"Sorry."

The agent's mouth hung open, but Judah kept going.

"So, good luck with all that."

He dropped his hands. And the smile.

"Now, get the hell out of my garage."

Agent Grant unbuttoned and then re-buttoned his jacket. He smoothed his hands down the lapels as if trying to calm himself. He looked as if he wanted to say something in retaliation, but couldn't think of anything clever enough. Judah waited calmly as the agent finally spun around and headed for the open bay doors. Just as he going, though, Grant stopped and looked back at Judah.

"You're going to regret this, you know."

Judah didn't dignify the comment with a response. The agent was trying to stare hard at Judah, but there was too much frustration on his face to pull the look off. Agent Grant stormed through the door and around the corner. Judah waited until he could hear the Charger's engine roar and then he sunk back into his chair. Benji swung toward him on his crutches.

"Jesus, Judah. Talk about throwing a stick of dynamite. What the hell was that?"

Ramey slumped into the seat next to him. She looked up at Benji and arched an eyebrow.

"A game."

Benji caught himself and leaned against the edge of the table. He pointed to the row of shell casings.

"And, what? Those are the pieces?"

Ramey shook her head.

"Something like that."

Benji picked up the .308 and turned it over in his hand a few times. His eyes were wide.

"What is this from? What the hell does that guy have on you?"

Judah controlled his voice. He was sure Ramey knew he had been shaken by the agent, but he couldn't let Benji know. He flicked the .9mm and .45, toppling them over.

"Don't worry, Benji, he's bluffing. He's found something, but he has no clue what it means. He's just fishing, like cops do. That agent doesn't have a damn thing on us. Not a thing."

Judah glanced over at Ramey; she was staring hard at the fallen bullet casings.

"Let's just hope it stays that way."

CHAPTER 12

Slim Jim watched Shelia struggling with the clasp of her lacy, purple bra. With her arms bent awkwardly behind her, she kept missing the tiny hook. Slim Jim sat up in the bed and leaned forward to help. His fingers were clumsy as he fumbled with it, but he finally got the damn strap attached. Shelia glanced over her shoulder at him before tossing her hair back and standing up.

"Thanks, Jimmy."

Slim Jim only grunted. He flopped back against the pile of flimsy hotel-issued pillows that Shelia had gradually been stealing from the cleaning woman's cart and watched her continue to dress. Shelia shimmied into a denim mini-skirt with rhinestone hearts bedazzled on the back pockets and then started kicking around the mess on the floor, looking for a shirt.

"So, what else did Legs say?"

Slim Jim was busy picking at a scab on his arm.

"Huh?"

Shelia found a white, ribbed tank top on the floor and shook it out. She held it up to the light to check for stains.

"Before, you were saying that Legs had called from jail, bitching about some ATF guy talking to Ratface."

Shelia pulled the tank over her head and walked to the sink to check herself in the mirror. Slim Jim grumbled and sat up, pushing himself to the edge of the bed. He half-heartedly looked around for his pants.

"He just said that some ATF guy was questioning Ratface about how we knew that fruitcake preacher."

"What's that got to do with you?"

Slim Jim glanced up at Shelia, who was turning this way and that in front of the mirror. When she piled her hair up on top of her head, he could see a black streak running down the back of her tank top. He gave her a lopsided grin.

"I'd get another shirt."

"What?"

"Another shirt. That one has a boot print on the back of it. I must've stepped on it."

Shelia twisted around, but still couldn't see the mark in the mirror. She yanked it off, looked at the print and then wadded it up and threw it at Slim Jim's head. He ducked and smiled. Shelia put her fists on her hips and pretended to glower at him.

"Well, at least you're good for something. I'm on a double. I would've walked around for twelve hours looking like somebody had kicked me."

"Hey, I'm here for you, babe. Whatever you need. You want to go again? I'm here for you."

Shelia was digging through a pile of clothes next to the TV stand. She picked up a black T-shirt with the bottom cut into fringe and smelled it. She raised her eyebrows over the shirt.

"No, I do not want to go again. I want to find something decent to wear so I can make it to work less than an hour late this time."

Slim Jim shrugged.

"Suit yourself."

Shelia slipped the shirt on and looked at herself in the mirror again. She slid the top over to expose one shoulder and put a hand on her hip.

"Better?"

"It'll do."

She twisted her hair up onto into a sloppy pile on her head and began applying mascara. As much as living with Shelia in such close quarters drove him crazy, Slim Jim did like to watch her get ready. There was something domestic about the whole act that he couldn't deny appealed to him. Slim Jim was forty-two and had never lived with a woman before. He had been engaged once, a long time ago, before he had patched-in to the Scorpions, but the girl had barely even stayed over. There was that, too, with Shelia. She didn't scamper away in the morning, stumbling out of bed to furtively collect her clothes and call a ride before he could get up and say good morning. Sometimes, Shelia lazed in bed with him, her face wiped clean of makeup, her breath as bad as his, and it was nice. She would snuggle up under his armpit and sometimes he would put his hand into her hair, still crunchy with gel, and they would talk. Or pass a cigarette back and forth. Or just lay there, together, like two people did, two people who liked each other and didn't have to talk about it.

"That's it? That's all Legs said? You'd think he wouldn't risk the call."

Shelia bent over and raked her hair down, wildly spraying it with an aerosol can. Slim Jim didn't want to talk about Legs or Ratface anymore, or the stupid agent asking questions, but he knew Shelia wouldn't give up until he told her everything. She was like that.

"I guess the ATF guy brought me up. Trying to mess with Ratface's head by saying he knew I'd run from the cops. It's fine, though. Ratface wouldn't never say nothing. It's not a big deal."

Shelia whipped her hair back and stood up straight.

"Sounds like a big deal to me."

Slim Jim sighed.

"Come here."

Shelia was rolling on deodorant. She looked over her shoulder at him.

"What?"

Slim Jim pointed to the edge of the bed next to him.

"Sit."

Shelia capped the deodorant and checked her lipstick quickly in the mirror. She padded over to him on bare feet and sat down impatiently.

"Jimmy, I gotta get going."

"I know."

He touched her arm. There was a streak of something—mascara, eyeliner, dirt, who knew—and he rubbed at it with his thumb.

"I just don't want you to worry, okay? We're gonna be fine."

The impatient look disappeared. Shelia lifted one leg up and twisted around on the bed to face him. Her neon yellow underwear flashed at him and it made him smile. Because she wasn't trying to be sexy, she wasn't trying to be anything. Shelia looked up at him in earnest.

"You sure?"

Slim Jim pinched her waist, but her expression didn't change.

"I'm sure. No worries, I mean it. All you need to worry about is making those tips tonight."

He winked at her and she grinned and shoved him before standing up to hunt for her shoes.

"Want to come by the bar later? Bring me some dinner? Nino's has half price pizza after nine on Saturdays."

Shelia smiled coyly as she balanced on one foot to slip on a dingy white tennis shoe. Slim Jim shook his head.

"Jesus, woman. Between the mess, the nagging and the constant asking for things, you're already acting like my old lady. I ain't even bought a ring yet."

He had never quite been able to bring himself to say the word marriage to her, just as the word love was something that he doubted would cross his lips anytime soon, but on mornings like this one, when the sex was good and the light was right, when he could watch her get ready for work and he felt that maybe, maybe, she did depend on him for something, Slim Jim thought that getting hitched might not be so bad after all.

Shelia smirked at him and flipped him off; he returned the gesture. She opened the motel room door, but quickly turned around to him.

"Pepperoni and sausage. And whatever else you want, but no…"

"No mushrooms or olives. I know, I know."

He smiled at her and waved her out the door.

BEFORE CLIVE HAD been sent down to the records room to rot, he'd sat through his fair share of stakeouts. Mostly, these had involved documenting drug handoffs on street corners and watching the doors of trap houses in The Bluff. He now wondered how many of his fellow ATF officers had ever spent time waiting for a nutso preacher's bovine nephew to waddle out of a Sir Clucks.

It was disappointing, but he was pretty sure working out a deal with the Cannons was a no-go. He knew there was something there, something between Sister Tulah and the Cannon family, but until he had more proof than Sherwood Cannon's dead body and a couple of unidentified shell casings, there wasn't much to go on. Clive thought that maybe if he had some actual evidence to present them with, the Cannons might cooperate. The Barrow woman seemed halfway reasonable, and he still thought he might be able to get her on board, but it didn't look like he'd be winning Judah over anytime soon. But was it even worth taking that route? He knew that Tulah and the Cannons were somehow tied together, but he didn't think it had much to do with bribing state senators for the phosphate mine. The Cannons just weren't smart enough to get in on a deal like that. No, if Clive wanted the big catch, then he needed information that would lead him to connections above Sister Tulah, not below her. And the only person he could think of who would possibly have information, and also be easily intimidated, wore polyester pants and seemed about as bright as a black hole.

He had thought to corner Brother Felton at the church again, he'd done a drive-by and seen the same gold Buick in the parking lot, so Clive knew Felton was there, but he was worried about running into Tulah. He'd instead waited down the road until he saw the Buick leave and then tailed it into town. Clive had now been sitting in the parking lot of the restaurant for an hour, waiting for Felton to emerge so he could talk to him alone. Clive couldn't understand how it could take so long to eat a plate of chicken, and he was just about to give up and barge in the place, when Felton finally pushed through the glass double doors. He was carrying a cardboard takeout container of food, swinging it along by the handle. Clive wasn't going to miss his chance. He jumped out of his car and followed him. He waited until Felton had gotten himself situated behind the wheel and then Clive came around the back of the Buick and rapped hard on the window.

For a moment, Clive almost felt sorry for the man. Brother Felton looked like a deer caught in headlights, the box of chicken still balanced on his lap, as he stared, wide-eyed and startled, through the glass. Clive motioned for Felton to roll down the window and after another moment of hesitation, he slowly did. Clive braced himself against the top of the car and leaned in.

"Remember me?"

Felton only blinked. Clive pointed to the box in his lap.

"The chicken here any good?"

Felton nodded. There was a crumb of biscuit on his moist bottom lip and Clive wanted nothing more than to tell Felton to brush it off, for God's sake. He stood up straight so that he didn't have to look directly at Felton's mouth.

"Last time we talked, we were just getting to know one another. I think I'd like to take that relationship a little further."

Felton swallowed and finally spoke.

"What do you mean?"

"Well, I was just poking around last time. Checking out the fire like I said, that kind of thing. But since then, it's come to my attention that something is rotten in the state of Denmark."

Felton craned his neck to look up at him.

"Huh?"

Clive shook his head.

"Never mind."

"Denmark?"

Clive pushed himself away from the car and squinted across the parking lot.

"It's from a play. It's a, seriously, never mind. Just forget I said that. Jesus."

"What do you want, then?"

Clive turned back to Felton.

"It occurred to me the other day, when I was thinking about this whole mess, that you were the only person who ever admitted to seeing Sherwood dead inside the church. And that we still don't know who killed him."

As he expected, Felton turned even paler than he already was. Clive thought it was laughable to even insinuate that Felton could have killed someone, but it sure did make him squirm. It didn't matter that the fact was obviously a lie, it only mattered that there was the possibility that the police could say it was true. Clive had seen the hint of that possibility, and all that could go along with it, work wonders in getting people like Brother Felton to cooperate. Felton fidgeted with the handle of the chicken box.

"I didn't kill Sherwood Cannon."

Clive shrugged.

"Never said you did. I'm just saying that some people might think so. If they really wanted to look into it."

Felton stared up at Clive and, for a moment, a glimmer of defiance flashed in his eyes.

"Why do you keep bringing this up?"

Clive didn't like the look in Felton's eyes and decided it was time to get to the point.

"Because I want something from you."

Clive leaned all the way over and rested his forearms on the edge of the window.

"Let me just be straight with you, Brother Felton. Because I think you're a good guy. I think you're a guy who tries to follow the rules. You probably drive the speed limit, don't you?"

Felton nodded warily.

"I thought so. You're the kind of person who likes to do the right thing, just because it's the right thing. Which is why I'm so surprised that you just go along with Tulah and all the wrong things she does."

Brother Felton frowned.

"What are you talking about?"

Clive had been expecting more of a reaction out of Felton.

"I mean, I know your aunt has done some terrible things. Illegal things. Bribed people. Threatened people. Maybe worse. She is a bad, bad person. She's hurt a lot of people. You know that, right?"

Felton slowly shook his head.

"I don't know anything."

"Oh yes, you do. So let me be clear here, Brother Felton. Because I'm tired of standing out here in this stinking, hot, cesspool of a parking lot. You're facing a choice. You should be thanking your lucky stars that I'm giving you one. And I'm only doing it because I like you and I think you're a good guy. You can either cooperate with me, help me, or you can go down with the ship and I'll just be waving at you from the shore as you drown."

"What?"

Clive stood back from the car. He opened his wallet and slipped out a card.

"I'm taking Tulah down. She's going to be arrested on so many charges it'll make your head spin. If you help me, if you give me the information I need, you won't be implicated. You won't rot in prison alongside her. If you inform on Sister Tulah for me, you'll be a hero. But if you don't, you'll be nothing more than just another lowlife criminal. And trust me, Brother Felton, I don't think you'd last very long in a supermax. Not very long at all. And it would be a sad, painful, humiliating way to leave this earth."

Clive flicked the card through the window.

"So, you just take some time and you think about that. You think about that and then you think about what it means to stand up and be a man. If you have it in you to do the right thing. And then you call me. Soon. Otherwise, I'm going to assume you chose to side with the devil on this one. Understood?"

The card had fallen down between Felton's legs, onto the floorboard. Felton stared at it, but made no move to pick it up. He didn't nod or say anything, but only sat there with his head bowed, clutching the soggy box of chicken. Finally, Clive smacked the roof of the Buick and walked away, shaking his head. He hoped it had worked; he needed Felton. Much more than he cared to admit.

FELTON HAD THE box of chicken ready. He held it up where Tulah could see it when she opened the front door. As he had guessed, she was less than thrilled than to see him.

"I brought you some chicken."

Sister Tulah stood in the front doorway to her house and pursed her lips. She didn't take the cardboard box from him, didn't even look at it. She did, however, turn and walk into the foyer without closing the door behind her. Felton carefully wiped his feet on the bristly *Christ is Lord* mat and followed Tulah inside. The house was filled with shadows, the heavy curtains drawn across every window as always. Tulah lumbered into the dark living room and clicked on the lamp next to her La-Z-Boy. Felton waited for Tulah to settle herself before sinking into the middle of a deep, leather couch. He set the box on the glass coffee table between them and nudged it toward her. Sister Tulah looked at it with disgust.

"Oh, how nice. You brought me your leftovers. You used to eat every meal in this house with me. You used to sit right in there, at my dining room table, eating food I worked hard to prepare for you, and you were grateful."

Felton didn't look where she was pointing. He remembered eating every meal with his aunt, but he certainly didn't remember her cooking it. Kraft macaroni and cheese was about the most homemade dish Sister Tulah had ever served. She clicked her tongue at him.

"But look at you now. All up on your high horse. Gracing me with your presence. Gifting me your leftovers, the scraps and bones you don't want to eat."

Felton nodded toward the box.

"That's a combo platter in there. The number three. There's a piece of sweet potato pie on top."

Sister Tulah's one pale eye bored into him.

"What do you want, Felton? I am sure you are aware that I'm leaving in less than an hour. I have a long drive ahead of me."

Felton glanced around the room. Not one stick of furniture, not one collector's plate or empty glass vase, had been moved since he had decided to live on his own. Of course, nothing had been moved really since he was seven years old, coming to live with his aunt and uncle for the first time. Uncle Walter had been dead for twenty-two years, but his corduroy armchair still haunted the corner of the room and no one was allowed to sit in it. Felton lamely turned back to his aunt.

"Can't I just come by for a visit?"

Sister Tulah clasped her hands in her lap and leaned back in the chair, rocking it a few times.

"Ever since you decided to leave me here alone and move into that tin can out in the woods, you only come to my door when you want something. Need something."

"That's not true."

"It is if I say it is."

Felton thought about reminding her that he had saved her life. That if he hadn't taken up the heavy cross and bludgeoned Sherwood Cannon in the head, Tulah wouldn't be sitting across from him right now. But he dared not. It was true that his confidence had been building since he had rescued Tulah in the church, but that didn't mean he still wasn't held in abject terror of his aunt. As he and everyone else should be.

Felton also considered telling Tulah about his conversation with Agent Grant in the parking lot of Sir Clucks, but held back. She probably knew the ATF agent was out to get her and most likely already had some plan concocted to take care of him. If he brought it up now, it would only be a distraction from his real purpose, which was going to make enough waves as it was. Felton rested his palms on the wide mounds of his knees and sucked in a deep breath. This was going to take all of his courage.

"I know you're leaving for The Recompense."

He looked up into Sister Tulah's eye. He was glad she was wearing the eye patch over the crater where her other eye had once been. Tulah's mouth twisted into a sneer.

"Well, whoop-de-doo for you. I hope you're not asking to tag along."

"No, of course not. I would never."

"Because you are certainly not worthy and, trust me, never will be."

Brother Felton nodded emphatically.

"No, I know, I know. That's not what I'm asking."

Sister Tulah pursed her lips.

"Well then, what? Get on with it. I have important preparations to make and I don't have time for your sniveling."

Felton rubbed the back of his neck, trying to think of the best way to frame what he wanted to ask.

"You'll still be gone tomorrow, and I was just wondering who was going to lead the services in your absence."

Sister Tulah huffed impatiently.

"I arranged for a visiting pastor to come up from Gainesville. I can't even remember the man's name, but he's done it before. Why?"

"Because, well, you'll probably have to pay him, right? For both the morning and evening service?"

Tulah sniffed.

"Yes, I suppose so. The Elders are taking care of it. Get to the point, Felton."

Brother Felton tried not to squirm.

"Well, I was wondering if you might think about letting me preach tomorrow night."

Sister Tulah laughed so hard she snorted and started coughing. Felton sat through it, his ears and cheeks flushed with embarrassment. He wanted to run from the living room, flee from Tulah's house and hide safely away in his camper, but he kept the image of the copperhead fixed in his mind. Finally, Tulah gained control of herself and wiped her eye.

"You're joking, right? I mean, you're not serious."

Felton sat up as straight as he could and spoke earnestly.

"I am serious. I want to preach on Sunday. Just Sunday evening. I feel called to do so and I think it would be a good time."

Sister Tulah hiccupped and echoed him mockingly.

"You think it would be a good time?"

Felton nodded vigorously.

"You won't be there, so I won't be hindering your message in anyway. And it will save you money since you won't have to pay that other preacher for both services."

"And you'll make a complete fool of yourself and the church will laugh you out of town. What's gotten into you, Felton?"

Brother Felton would have died before telling her about the snakes and how they had spoken to him. They were his signs. The messages had been delivered to him. And though he did not know exactly what he needed to preach about on Sunday, he knew that he must. The snake on the path had told him to rise up and use his voice. He would do so, and hopefully the Holy Spirit would handle the rest. Felton dipped his chin as he looked at his aunt. It would require Sister Tulah's blessing, however, to assume her place at the front of the church. There was no question of that.

"Please, Aunt Tulah. This is something I want to do. Need to do. Please."

Felton watched anxiously as Sister Tulah twitched her mouth back and forth, trying to decide. He cast his eyes down to the floor, waiting. If he had interpreted the sign correctly, she would let him. He believed it. Finally, Tulah reached for the box of chicken on the table. She pulled it to her and popped open the top.

"If it's that important to you, go ahead. You're going to look like an idiot, but at least I won't be there to witness it."

She pulled out the piece of pie sealed in cellophane and set it on the coffee table.

"And hopefully it will bring you to your senses and remind you of the humility and shame you should carry with you every day. I fear that you have lost your way, Brother Felton. But hopefully this failure will set you back on the path you need to follow."

"Oh, yes, thank you, Aunt Tulah! Thank you!"

Felton jumped up and banged his shins against the coffee table. For a moment, he felt filled with light. He thought of the snake. He was rising up. He was really rising up. And she wasn't going to stop him. Sister Tulah didn't even glance at Felton as he stumbled away; she was too busy unwrapping her pie.

CHAPTER 13

AT THE SOUND of the heavy door screeching open and slamming shut, Weaver slowly lifted his eyes from the warm glass of Cruzan he held slackly between his fingers. Miguel was late, and perhaps he had heard the rumors of how volatile the transgression could make Weaver. Or maybe he was simply being respectful. Either way, Miguel stood with his back against the door, a mixture of anticipation and caution playing out across his face. Weaver grinned, baring his teeth. Yes, he liked this guy. Miguel's roving eyes finally landed on him and Weaver tilted his head, beckoning him over.

Weaver watched Miguel cross the empty bar. It was late and The Salty Dog was closing down for the night. After botching two rum runners in a row, the Neanderthal bartender had been fired and sent home at Weaver's insistence. If he could ever get his hands on enough blackberry liqueur, Weaver would fill a bathtub with it, find the bartender, and drown him in it. The yappy blonde was still hanging around, standing at the far end of the bar, pigging out on a pizza with her washed-up boyfriend. Weaver didn't like the look of him. It was obvious from his tattoos, and the way his shoulders twitched, as if still missing the weight of a leather cut draped across them, that the lanky man had recently been part of a motorcycle club. Weaver had no use for bikers and even less use for quitters.

Aside from the misfit lovebirds, Frank was the only other occupant of the bar. He stood behind the register, counting out the till and keeping one eye on Weaver. He had dropped the cash in his hands when the door banged opened and now he carefully resumed his count, licking his thumb before peeling each bill from the stack. Weaver turned away from the bar and waited for Miguel to sit down across from him in the booth. He eyed the man.

"I am lonely tonight and surrounded by imbeciles. Drink with me."

Miguel shrugged.

"Okay."

The bar was small enough to be heard without it, but Weaver shouted anyway.

"Another glass!"

Weaver turned to watch Frank jump. He looked forlornly down at the money his hands, and Weaver knew he'd have to start counting all over again. Frank smacked the bar to get the blonde's attention and then he jerked his head. Weaver frowned.

"No. Not her. You."

He kept his eyes on Frank as the sweaty man carefully set the cash back in the drawer and brought over an empty rocks glass. He set it on the table in front of Miguel and scurried back to the bar. Weaver poured and raised his own glass to Miguel.

"Salud."

Weaver swallowed the warm, sweet rum and watched Miguel take a small sip of it. He laughed when Miguel set the glass back down on the table.

"Let me guess. You prefer tequila. Isn't that what you people drink? Or Corona. With a festive wedge of lime."

Weaver barked out a guttural laugh, but Miguel only looked at him blandly.

"I don't drink too much."

"And when you do?"

"Budweiser. Coors Lite. Whatever."

Weaver made no move to order the man a beer. He looked down at Miguel's hands, resting lightly on the edge of the table. His fingernails were clean. Weaver drained the rest of his rum and poured another inch into the glass.

"What are you doing here, Miguel?"

Miguel's eyes narrowed and he combed his fingers through his goatee.

"You asked for information on Judah Cannon. I have it."

Weaver shook his head.

"In good time. I mean, what are you doing in Daytona Beach? In Florida? In this country?"

Miguel picked at the top button of his tropical print shirt.

"I was born here. My parents came over the border to get a better life. The usual story."

"Bullshit."

Weaver rolled the glass between his palms.

"Tell me the truth."

"Why?"

"Because I'm curious."

"Don't you want to know about Judah?"

Weaver brought the glass to his lips.

"I want to know about you. I like you. You work for me now and I prefer to know the people I employ."

Miguel shrugged.

"There's not much to tell. My mother is gone. My father owes La Familia Michoacana. He'll never get free of them. He's a mule going coast to coast. Once, maybe twice a week, from Tampa to here and back. He drives a van. That's his whole life. Or, it will be anyway, until one day he gets caught by the police or shot."

Weaver sipped at the rum.

"But you do not owe La Familia anything."

Miguel cast his eyes down and shook his head.

"No."

"And you do not help your father with his debt."

"No."

Weaver nodded in approval.

"That's good. A young buck. Doing your own thing. Making your own way. Do you have a dream?"

Miguel leaned back against the black vinyl of the booth.

"A dream?"

"Yes, a dream. Something you wanted to be when you grew up. Something you still think you can be one day."

Miguel blinked at Weaver, hesitating only a moment.

"A professional DJ. Sometimes I spin sets at Stingrays on the slow nights. I'm pretty good."

Weaver finished his rum and shoved the glass to the middle of the table. He didn't move to refill it and he didn't respond to Miguel's dream.

"Did you find out what happened to Nash?"

Miguel seemed confused for a second, but quickly recovered.

"I think Judah was telling the truth. No one's seen him since Wednesday. One minute he was in some bar in Palatka and the next, poof, he's gone."

Weaver's face was expressionless.

"Did Judah kill him?"

Miguel looked up at the ceiling thoughtfully.

"Maybe. What else would Judah have done with him?"

Weaver considered this for a moment and then tilted his head slightly, keeping his eyes on the empty rum glass.

"Tell me about Judah Cannon."

"He lives in this town called Silas, in south Bradford County. Middle of nowhere. You drive through and it's like that zombie show. Except that everybody is the hick who sawed off his own hand to get away. There's only three towns in the whole county."

Weaver dipped his head as he listened and his dark, heavy hair closed in even further around his face.

"Go on."

Miguel ticked off the information on his fingers.

"He's been out of prison for three months and picked up business where his dead father left off. Low-key, some gambling out of a few bars. Nothing big. No guns, no drugs. He runs out of a chop shop. That's his base, right off the main drag. There's him, there's his brother, Benji, and his woman, Ramey. He's got an older brother, Levi, but no one's seen him since the fire where Sherwood died."

"Anyone else? Is there anyone else Judah would care about?"

Weaver was staring intensely at him and Miguel's brow furrowed.

"Well, there's the two guys who were with Judah when he came here."

Weaver shook his head dismissively.

"They're already roadkill. Anyone else?"

"The mother died when the boys were all kids. There's this ex-girlfriend, Cassie. He's not with her no more, but there's a daughter the woman used to say was his. Stella. The ex likes to change her mind about it, but it don't sound like the kid is really his."

Weaver steepled his hands on the table.

"And where is this woman and her child?"

"Colston. A little farther north. Halfway between Jacksonville and Lake City."

Weaver sat up straight and shook his head so that his hair fell away from his face. He drummed his finger on the edge of the table as he thought his way through the plan.

"They should probably be gotten out of the way first. I'll be up in Jacksonville this weekend anyway. I can just take care of them on the way down to Silas. I'd barely have to go out of my way."

Weaver was studying the faded letter D tattoo. He rolled his finger back and forth on the edge of the table as he looked at it. He raised his eyes when he heard Miguel cough uncomfortably.

"Yes?"

The man across from him seemed uneasy now.

"What are you planning to do?"

There was no change to Weaver's voice.

"Kill them all."

Miguel glanced around the bar, but Weaver didn't bother to follow his gaze. He stared hard at Miguel, waiting. Miguel finally dropped his hands into his lap and leaned forward. He whispered.

"A kid? A kid that's probably not even his?"

Weaver put both his hands on the table and spread his fingers wide.

"I'm not a monster. It will be quick and quiet with the child and the ex."

"And the other woman?"

Weaver looked into Miguel's eyes, watching the pupils dart back and forth.

"Do you think Judah loves her?"

Miguel nodded, his mouth open slightly with either confusion or concern.

"Yes."

"Then yes. And it will not be quick and quiet with her."

Miguel's face had twisted into a grimace. Weaver narrowed his eyes and leaned forward.

"You do not approve?"

It was obvious that Miguel heard the dangerous edge in Weaver's voice. He responded carefully, haltingly.

"I just don't understand. What did this Judah Cannon do to you? I thought you didn't even know he existed until two days ago."

Weaver considered this. It was a fair question. He reached for the empty glass in front of him and poured it full. He added to Miguel's glass as well, although he knew the man wasn't going to touch it. He gulped the rum and nodded once toward Miguel.

"You understand the expression 'sins of the father'?"

Miguel didn't answer, though his eyes were wary, and Weaver continued. He picked up the glass of rum and held it out in front of him, turning it around as he spoke.

"In 1971, I had a woman. Her name was Cherry. That was her birth name. She had hair the color of honey and she was mine."

Weaver took a sip of rum and set the glass down. He spun it around on the table.

"I was living in Jacksonville at the time, near the base. Navy recruits, coming and going, fouling the town. I tried to enlist for Vietnam myself, but no. They'd take any asshole with a dick swinging between his legs and an intelligence quota barely above that of a brick, but if you had a heart murmur, forget about it. Goddamn hole in my heart. The one I was born with."

Weaver pushed the glass away. It clinked against the empty bottle in the center of the table.

"I was living there, with Cherry. But she left me for a sailor. Didn't even tell me. Put a second hole in my heart. I saw her with him one night at a bar. Laughing. Touching. She didn't see me, but he did. He saw me looking over. Watching. He winked at me. He knew he had what was mine. His name was Sherwood Cannon."

Weaver stretched his fingers out before him again, feeling the knuckles pop. The cracks. The joints and fissures that had never healed properly.

"I was too much of a pussy to do anything about it that night. Scared of a bar full of uniforms. I thought I'd get Sherwood sooner or later, but he shipped out the next week. Sent to Da Nang. I prayed every night for him to end up a rotting corpse at the bottom of the South China Sea. Then I came to my senses and started praying that he'd make it back alive. So I could take care of him myself. Eventually, I moved on. Forgot about him. Began to build up what I have now. But with the arrival of his son, all that has changed. Sherwood died in a fire, not by my hand. The rage I am filled with can only be quenched in one way."

He raised his dead eyes to meet Miguel's. He couldn't tell if they were filled with pity or disgust. It didn't matter. The man shifted slightly in his seat.

"And the girl? Cherry? What happened to her?"

Weaver smiled.

"Oh. Her. I found Cherry the day after Sherwood Cannon left. I strangled her to death with her my bare hands and dumped her body in the St. Johns River. Filthy, lying whore."

Miguel's eyes were wide. Weaver looked into them and then gradually became aware of the heavy silence settling over the room like a soaking wet blanket. He glanced toward the bar. The blonde and her string bean boyfriend quickly turned away, keeping their eyes on one another. Frank immediately cast his gaze down at the pint glass in his hands. He began to dry it furiously with a rag. Weaver sighed and turned back to Miguel.

"So. Now you understand."

He didn't wait for Miguel to speak. In one fluid motion, Weaver stood up and pulled the Beretta out from its slot underneath the table. Miguel didn't even have a chance to be surprised before the bullet entered his forehead and shattered his skull. Weaver turned and found Frank next. The shot toppled him back against a row of bottles and sent them crashing to the floor, along with his slumped body. Weaver twisted around to the couple at the end of the bar. Both had hit the ground already, but the biker had been sitting on the outside of the bar. Weaver got him once in the side of the head and once in the gut when the shot flopped him back against the brass foot rail. He slid out of the booth and fired a few more rounds into the man, just for the hell of it.

The blonde had dropped behind the bar at the sound of the first shot and Weaver took his time advancing toward her. She was most likely wedged back between the coolers or something, cowering. Praying. Hoping that her sex would protect her. That he would have mercy on her. Weaver wanted to make sure he got her in the face. He moved toward the open end of the bar, opposite from where she had been standing before. He whistled at her, a few notes, as if he was calling a dog. Weaver couldn't hear a thing. He stepped to the end of the bar and swung to shoot down the length of it, but a searing, shattering pain bit into his kneecap and took his leg out from under him.

In the next few seconds, he heard the clink of metal hitting the cement floor and then saw the flash of the blonde's hair as she scrambled over him. He fired off a shot, but it only lodged into a ceiling panel. His left hand found her ankle, but she kicked, stomping her heel into his groin as she twisted away from him. Weaver let go and rolled halfway onto his stomach, aiming the gun out in front of him. He pulled the trigger until the clip was spent, but she had already made it to and through the door. Weaver flung the gun across the floor and yelled after her anyway.

"I will find you, you stupid bitch! Don't think I won't! I will find you and I will butcher you!"

His voice echoed across the empty bar. Weaver slowly hauled himself to standing and looked down at his leg. Blood was seeping through his pants and when he tried to put weight on it, his knee turned sideways. Aside from whatever gash he knew he would see when he cut his pants away, he was pretty sure his kneecap was dislodged as well. He gripped the edge of the bar to steady himself and then he noticed the rusty pipe wrench at his feet. He leaned over and picked it up, groaning at the pain shooting upward through his leg. He flipped the wrench over in his hand and whispered to himself.

"I will find you. And I will kill you. I will kill you all."

SISTER TULAH WHEELED her suitcase out of the Happy Holiday Inn lobby, but stopped abruptly when she passed in front of the entrance to the hotel bar on her way to the elevator. The sign staked out in front of the amber beveled glass doors read *Welcome Southeastern Better Business Association!* Tulah pursed her lips and adjusted her grip on the handle, trying to decide if she wanted to go in now or haul her suitcase upstairs first. It was nearing midnight, and if the raucous sounds coming from behind the doors were any indication, she was certain the festivities had already begun. Sister Tulah had to be sure all of the other twenty-three council members saw her before tomorrow night. She would stand for no rumors about her not being able to attend this year.

Tulah glanced down at the white Reeboks peeking out from underneath her rumpled, linen dress. She patted her usually perfectly pinned hair, now slightly mussed from the eight-hour drive, and adjusted the sweaty elastic strap of her eyepatch. She glanced toward the elevator, but before she could decide, one of the double doors swung to reveal a man grinning broadly at her.

"Tulah Atwell."

The man had a booming voice that contrasted sharply with his gaunt, almost skeletal, frame. His sharp cheekbones jutted up high in his face and his dark eyes bulged slightly beneath a wide, prominent forehead. Sister Tulah scowled at the man. In her eyes, he was a mongrel. It was known that he was a descendent of the so-called WIN Tribe out of the mountains of Virginia, a fact which set Tulah's teeth on edge.

"George Kingfisher."

Sister Tulah narrowed her eyes. Tomorrow night, it wouldn't matter that Kingfisher was the epitome of all that Tulah found repulsive about mixed-race breeding, but tonight they were both still living in the real world. And it didn't help that Tulah was painfully aware of Kingfisher's elevated status as the newest member of the Inner Council. She had heard that he was now the Ox.

Kingfisher held the door for her and smiled.

"Welcome to The Recompense, Sister Tulah. May the Fire and the Light be beneath your every step."

Sister Tulah bumped her suitcase over the threshold and maneuvered it awkwardly into the bar. She grunted.

"And yours."

"Come in, come in. We're so glad you're finally here. There was talk of you not returning this year. What with the fire and the scandal. What with…"

Kingfisher gestured toward Tulah's eyepatch.

"And your final tribute was almost late. It did not arrive until yesterday afternoon. There was concern that with the events recently befallen your church, you might not be able to afford to join us any longer. I mean spiritually as well as financially, of course."

Tulah glared at Kingfisher with her one pale, burning eye. There had never been any love lost between them, but this was going too far.

"Well, my tribute wasn't late. And I'm standing here, aren't I? Anything else you want to tell me that I already know?"

Kingfisher bobbed his head.

"No, of course. Welcome, Sister Tulah. Say hello, have a drink, enjoy yourself. We are so glad you are here."

He reached out and squeezed her arm. Tulah looked down at his long, bony fingers gripping her sleeve. In Kentsville, no one ever dared to touch her. Ever. She touched them. Sister Tulah held her breath until Kingfisher released her and turned to talk to a man with a bulbous red nose and a black bowtie. This was The Recompense, she reminded herself. Things were different, and she was by no means the most powerful person in the room. The fact rankled her, yes, but also filled her with pride. These were her people. The Order was where she truly belonged.

Tulah dragged her suitcase over to an empty seat at the bar and parked it next to her. She hefted herself up onto a stool and looked down at the paper cocktail napkin in front of her. Bamboozles. The Os had been replaced with two smiling orange balloons. She pressed her fingers lightly, almost reverently, against the napkin. The Day Recompense had been held at the Happy Holiday Inn in Cave Spring, Georgia since the early '70s. More than a decade before Tulah had secured her place in The Order. Bamboozles was the only bar she had ever had a drink in. She let her shoulders sag as she leaned against the back of the maroon leather stool. Sister Tulah nodded to the bartender when he came by.

"Glenlivet on the rocks."

She loved the sound of the ice cubes settling in the glass. Not until she had taken the first, tentative sip of scotch did she allow herself to survey the room. Even though she recognized every single face, she mentally ticked each person off. All twenty-three were present, so she was indeed the last one to arrive. But that was all right. At least she wasn't a sloppy drunk like Jim Rickson, head of Springwell Ministries, or a pig like Ona Sherpa, the uppity reverend from the Unitarian megachurch up in Charlotte. Ona was predictably standing guard at the buffet table set up against the back wall, her paper plate stacked high with toothpicked sausage balls and cubes of cheddar cheese. Tulah had heard a rumor that Ona had been chosen as the Crowned Woman, but she found that hard to believe. The honor almost always went to the svelte Pastor Linda McCormick or Sister Mary Matthews, who even now wore her black-and-white habit as she laughed nervously at the crude jokes flying around her. Sister Tulah rolled her eye. Aside from herself and the three other women in the room, The Order was, due to its nature, a boys' club.

Tulah rattled the ice in her glass and took another sip. She hated this part of the event. They weren't in their true forms yet, and there was an unspoken rule that business wasn't to be conducted until after The Night Recompense. Therefore, this little soiree was nothing more than a bunch of catching up and schmoozing: two things Sister Tulah had no patience for. Still, she was asserting herself and her right. Tulah had already caught a few curious glances and quickly averted eyes from the others, standing alone or corralled in small groups around the room. She was sure everyone had heard about the fire, had heard about her eye. Well, she was still standing. She could still prove her worth. Sister Tulah would show them all.

At the tinging of a metal fork against glass, the room began to quiet down. Brother Michael leaned over the bar and whispered something to the college-aged bartender, who quickly dropped the towel in his hands and hurried around the bar. He wedged his way through the crowd and exited through the double doors. Tulah watched as they were locked behind him. The tinging continued until the room was silent and all eyes were on the four Inner Council members, standing together in a line.

Kingfisher, being the most recent initiate into the Inner Council, took a step forward and raised his glass. Tulah noticed that it was filled with white wine. Of course. As if she needed another reason to despise the man. Kingfisher actually had the gall to find her eye and direct a smirk toward her before beginning his toast.

"To my fellow Morning Stars. To those who look with me through the Sacred Wall. To those who walk the path of the Fire and the Light, who stand fearlessly before the Wheels in the Whirlwind."

A few members cheered, but Kingfisher kept his glass raised. "Tonight we are friends, but tomorrow we meet as we are known to Him. You all have your roles, your tasks, you understand what you must do to honor Attar and prove your worthiness to be at His side when the Latter Rain is ushered in and the world is washed clean. Tonight we meet as we are to the others, but tomorrow we will be free of these worldly fetters as we stand before the God of our brothers Ezekiel and John."

Kingfisher looked over at the three men standing slightly behind him.

"To the Inner Council."

He then gestured wide, encompassing the twenty other members watching him.

"And to the Outer Council. To The Order of the Luminous Sevenfold Light."

He raised his glass even higher and every member did the same. Even Sister Tulah. The room erupted in cheers and the clinking of glasses. Sister Tulah nodded to a few of the men standing closest to her and then she raised her glass to her lips. It wasn't scotch on her tongue; she could taste the blood of the True God sliding down her throat.

SHELIA CLUTCHED THE yellow rubber handle of the screwdriver as tightly as she could, but her hands still wouldn't stop shaking. With her knees drawn up against her chest, her body wedged down into the narrow space between the wall and the untouched bed, she stared at the deadbolt chain on the motel room door. She knew it wouldn't hold. If Weaver's men found her, if they wanted to get in to kill her, the flimsy brass lock would snap off the edge of the door in seconds when they kicked their way in. Shelia knew this. She'd seen it happen before. This time, though, it wouldn't be a police raid or a jealous ex-boyfriend she could send away with either a blowjob or a baseball bat. These men would kill her. They would kick in the door and shoot her in the head and all she had to defend herself with was a goddamn Phillips head screwdriver.

Shelia tried to steady her breathing. She was pretty sure she had taken out Weaver's kneecap with the pipe wrench, so she didn't expect him to come after her himself, but she knew that within two minutes of her escaping through the door of The Salty Dog, Weaver had been on the phone, calling up his men, putting a hit out on her. Her first instinct had been to just run, as far and as fast as she could, in any direction away from the bar, but as soon as she cleared the parking lot, a heightened sense of calm had descended upon her. Shelia had made getaways before and she knew that losing her head wouldn't make her any safer or get her any farther away. It was a twenty-minute walk from the bar back to the Sundaze. Shelia, cutting through parking lots and alleys, had made it in five.

In less time than that, she was back out the door. Shelia had careened through the motel room, tripping over the mess, and slid on her belly to get halfway underneath the sagging bed. Feeling around blindly and frantically, she had located the roll of bills Slim Jim had taped to the underside of the box springs. Shelia had ripped it loose and scuttled back out and onto her feet. Her purse was still on a shelf underneath the bar, so Shelia had scooped up a wad of clothes from the floor and shoved them into a plastic grocery bag. She had pushed the wad of the cash into the middle of the clothes and then glanced frantically around the room. A baseball cap, the front airbrushed with two Ss inside of a pink heart, was wedged in between the overflowing trashcan and the TV stand. Shelia had snatched it up and squashed it down on her head. There was no time to change her clothes, but she had thought the hat would help. Shelia had finally turned in a circle, looking for a weapon. The knife she always carried was, of course, still in her purse back at The Salty Dog. Slim Jim's knife had been on him. She had squeezed her eyes tightly as she pushed him from her mind. Shelia hadn't seen where he had fallen, hadn't even seen his body, but she had heard Weaver's footsteps. She had seen the one shot to Miguel's head and the other to Frank's chest as he bled out next to her behind the bar. The rest of the shots must have been for Slim Jim.

Finally, her eyes had landed on the screwdriver sticking halfway out of a pair of Slim Jim's dirty jeans on the floor. It was better than nothing. Shelia had tossed it into the bag with the money and the clothes and bolted. She'd quickly been able to hitch a ride and had been on her way out of Daytona less than half an hour after Weaver had fired the first shot.

Shelia stretched her fingers and adjusted her grip on the screwdriver. Her hands were sweaty, but also still slick with rainwater. It had started to pour about halfway to Deland. The two drunk frat boys who had picked her up had pulled into the parking lot of a Love's truck stop and tried to make it clear why they had given her the ride. One had ended up with an elbow to the eye socket and the other with a heel to the dick. She had wound up running again, this time in the rain, her thin-soled tennis shoes sloshing through the mud as she slid down and then clambered up the side of a ditch. At least the boys hadn't gone after her. Following the highway, but keeping to the brush and the trees along the shoulder, she'd walked two miles until she came to the next exit. There was a gas station, a Denny's and a Motel 6. Shelia had wiped as much mud as possible from her legs and walked into the lobby with cash in hand. With a hefty tip to the night manager, no questions were asked and no paperwork had been processed. She was given a key to room number 10, the room she sat in now.

Every time a light from the highway panned across the thinly curtained window, Shelia tensed. Her dripping hair hung down in wet strings over her shoulders, but she didn't bother to push it back. She didn't bother to wipe her face either. Shelia had made it out of Daytona, made it almost to Deland, to this hotel room, where she was still alive, all without allowing herself to cry. There had been no time. Now, she clutched the screwdriver, rested her forearms on her bruised knees and let the streaks of mascara dribble down her face. James Raymond Ford was gone. He was gone, he had died in a bar, his body was crumpled up on the sticky cement floor and she would never see him again. Never catch his smile out of the corner of her eye. Never hear his braying laughter. Never feel his arm slung over her shoulder, his hot beer breath against her neck. Never. And unless she could think of some way to save herself, she, most likely, would be next.

CHAPTER 14

THE RABBIT FOLLOWING too closely behind her started flashing its headlights. Ramey scowled up at the rearview mirror, trying to keep her emotions dampened down to just aggravation. Maybe her Cutlass had a busted tail light, but it was only late afternoon and not even a Good Samaritan would be bothered enough by it to ride up on her and signal her. She didn't recognize the mint green car with the cracked windshield, so she doubted it was someone she knew. If it was an undercover cop, well then, budget cuts were worse than she thought. A wave of panic rose up inside of Ramey as her mind immediately shot to Weaver. Judah had reassured her yet again that morning, his head still mashed into the pillow, hair sticking up in all directions, dark circles settled in the hollows beneath his eyes, that Weaver wasn't a threat. That he had worked it out with Weaver, that he wasn't a problem, that she didn't need to worry. Just hearing those words from his lips made her skin crawl. Of course she needed to worry. If Judah was telling her not to, then he was either lying to her or lying to himself. She didn't know which was worse.

Ramey rolled to a stop at the corner of Central and Gains. If it was Weaver behind her, or one of his guys, she could gun it and try to outrun him. But then what? Judah was at the salvage yard, not two miles away, but she couldn't lead someone there. Ramey reached for the cellphone in her purse on the seat beside her and swallowed hard, preparing to steady her voice. She raised her eyes to the rearview mirror again, not wanting to make eye contact with the driver of the Rabbit, but wanting to be sure it wasn't someone she knew before calling Judah. Ramey couldn't believe her eyes when she saw the blonde behind the wheel. The woman flashed her lights again and waved, pointing toward the empty parking lot of a boarded-up Quincy's. Ramey dropped the cellphone back into her purse and ground her teeth. When the light turned green, she stomped on the gas and turned a sharp right into the parking lot. The Rabbit followed her and pulled up a few spaces over. Ramey yanked the keys out of the ignition and was halfway to the Rabbit before the other woman had even set foot on the blistering asphalt. Ramey barely gave Shelia a chance to stand.

The punch was hard and fast, knocking Shelia into the side of the Rabbit. Ramey kept her fist clenched, took a step back, then another step forward, then another back. She watched Shelia carefully steady herself against the door of the car and then raise her fingers to the corner of her bleeding lip. She looked at the blood and then cupped her jaw for a moment, keeping her eyes away from Ramey. Shelia seemed to be expecting another blow and had made up her mind not to defend herself. Ramey backed away in disgust and then shook out her stinging right hand. She could hardly speak.

"You."

Shelia kept her head down but turned toward Ramey. Her eyes were wide, still watery from the blow. She nodded slightly.

"Ramey, right?"

Ramey watched the thin line of blood trickling down the side of Shelia's chin. She crossed her arms and shook her head.

"You got a death wish or something, Shelia? Coming back into Silas like this? Judah or Benji see you and they're like to kill you. You know that, right?"

Shelia stood up a little straighter.

"That's why I'm standing here talking to you, not them."

"You think I don't want to kill you?"

Shelia ran her tongue along her bottom lip.

"I think want and will are two different things. Are you gonna hit me again? You can, if you want. I won't blame you."

Ramey realized that Shelia wouldn't. She was expecting it. Ramey scowled and then dropped her arms at her sides.

"No, I'm not going to hit you again. But you'd better have a damn good reason for being back in Silas."

Shelia stood up all the way now and dabbed at the blood on her face. She reached into the open driver's side door and pulled a paper napkin out of a crumpled Krystal's bag on the floorboard. She wiped the blood from her lip and chin and then wadded up the napkin in her fist.

"I thought I'd have a better chance of you listening to me than the boys."

"Listening to you about what?"

"Weaver."

Shelia pressed the napkin to her lip again and then pulled it away to check for more blood. Satisfied, she tossed the napkin to the ground and rubbed her fingertips together. Ramey stood in front of her, dumbfounded.

"Weaver?"

Shelia raised her eyebrows and nodded.

"Yeah. Tall, scary guy. Has a face looks like it was on fire and somebody tried to put it out with a fork. Complete whack job. Wants to kill your boyfriend. And you, by the way. And anyone else Judah's ever laid eyes on apparently."

Ramey had to look away for a moment. She set her jaw and stared out across the empty parking lot. Waves of iridescent heat were rising and quivering at its edges. Ramey wished she had a cigarette. She had left them in the car when she had charged toward Shelia with only bloodlust on her mind. Ramey turned back to Shelia, who was waiting, patiently, but expectantly. She spoke with caution.

"How do you know about Weaver? And Judah?"

Shelia pushed a clump of ratty blond hair back behind her ear and glanced away, her eyes on the road as she spoke.

"I was working at this place down in Daytona Beach. This bar my uncle owned. Or maybe Weaver owned it and my uncle only said it was his. I'd been there a few months and then this Weaver guy comes in about a week ago, starts using the place like it's his own private office or something. I didn't ask too many questions, but I got the impression from everything I heard going on around me that he's some bigshot boss on the east coast. Drugs, guns, whatever. A real professional asshole. Kinda like Judah's daddy was, but about a hundred times bigger, a hundred times more dangerous..."

Ramey blinked a few times, trying to take in what Shelia was saying. Shelia's voice had grown shaky and Ramey cut her off.

"What about Judah?"

Shelia stared down at the pavement and toed a loose chunk of asphalt with her filthy tennis shoe.

"Your man Judah came into the bar where I worked a few days ago. I don't think he saw me. I was certainly doing my damnedest not to be seen, that's for sure. But I saw him talking to Weaver."

Ramey was breathless.

"What happened? Between the two of them?"

Shelia shook her head and continued to prod at the crumbling pavement.

"It was like a standoff. I couldn't get too close because I was scared Judah would see me, but when Judah got up from the table to leave, he and Weaver were making threats at each other. The way guys do, you know? Like two rosters, puffing up to fight. Judah left, but I wouldn't say it was on friendly terms."

Ramey's heart was beating fast. She had known things weren't settled between Judah and Weaver, but Ramey forced herself to keep cool. That last thing she wanted was for Shelia to think that she wasn't completely in the loop with Judah.

"So, are you here to tell me something I don't know?"

Shelia jerked her head up and answered abruptly.

"Yeah, actually. It's what happened after that. I don't know how Judah took their meeting, but he should know that Weaver is coming for him."

Ramey narrowed her eyes.

"What's that supposed to mean?"

Shelia huffed.

"It means that after Judah left, Weaver told this guy, this Mexican dude, to find out everything he could. The guy came back to The Salty Dog last night and told Weaver all about Judah. Where he lived. About his family. About you. About some ex-girlfriend and a kid or something up in Colston. Weaver wants to kill you all. Is going to kill you all."

There was something about the way Shelia said it. Not all hysterical or dramatic. Without a hint of a scheme. She was stating it like it was a fact. As if it had already happened. Shelia's dark green eyes were flat and cold as she spoke, and this was perhaps the most terrifying of all. Ramey's voice came out as a croak.

"Why?"

Shelia gave a little shrug.

"Something about hating Sherwood like there was no tomorrow. He told Miguel this story, but we could all hear it, because the bar was closed and empty. I guess Sherwood stole his girl like a million years ago back in 1971. Up at the Navy base in Jacksonville or some shit. Weaver never forgave him. He's gonna kill Judah just because he's Sherwood's son. Because he's a Cannon. And the rest of you because he wants to kill Judah even deader, I guess. I told you, this man is batshit crazy."

The whole story sounded crazy. Ramey rubbed her temples and then slid her hands back through her hair. She coiled the length of it around her wrist and frowned.

"Why are you here, Shelia? Why are you telling me this? With the history between Judah and the Scorpions…."

Ramey hesitated, but Shelia didn't miss a beat.

"The Scorpions are all in jail or dead."

Ramey pursed her lips.

"We know that one of them disappeared. They didn't arrest one of them and he hasn't been seen in Bradford County for a while now."

Shelia dipped her head.

"Slim Jim. He came with me to Daytona."

Ramey raised her eyebrows.

"Slim Jim, then. It just doesn't make sense, you coming here to warn us…"

Shelia raised her head and interrupted Ramey again.

"Jimmy's dead."

"What?"

The lines around Shelia's mouth tightened and Ramey could see her jaw working, clenching. Shelia's eyes were suddenly glassy.

"He's dead. Weaver killed him. He killed him and he killed my uncle and he killed the guy who told him where to find Judah. He tried to kill me. He's going to kill me. And he's on his way right now to kill you. Unless Judah can stop him first."

Ramey didn't know what to say. She stood in front of Shelia, dumbstruck, trying to work it all out. She watched Shelia toss her head back and blink back any sign of tears. A smirk of contempt rose to her lips.

"So don't think I'm here out of the kindness of my heart. I didn't think there was much more to lose after what went down at that church, but now I've lost everything. Everything. I figure the only person Weaver hates more than me right now is Judah, so that's why I'm here. If Judah knows that Weaver has him in his sights, then there's a good chance Judah can take him out first. And I won't have to end up dead at the bottom of a river. You won't either, for that matter."

Ramey nodded slowly.

"Judah's not gonna want to believe this. Coming from you."

Shelia put her hands on her hips.

"Well, no shit, Sherlock. That's why I'm telling you first. You can make him believe it."

"And Benji. I don't think he'll ever forgive you."

Shelia snapped.

"He doesn't have to forgive me. He doesn't have to like me. But he won't have to worry about either if he's dead. You weren't there, Ramey. You didn't see how Weaver just shot everyone in the bar. Like it was a video game. Like they weren't even people. You've never seen anyone like this. You got to make Judah understand."

Ramey crossed her arms and took in Shelia's bedraggled appearance. Her skinned knees and loose, stringy hair. Her red, swollen eyes, the lids and lashes bare. The patchwork of bruises dappling her upper arm. It was hard not to believe her story.

"I'll do what I can."

Shelia turned and put her hand on the edge of the open car door. She turned to Ramey, before ducking down into the seat.

"If you can make him listen, I'll be here tonight. After dark, I'll wait around. If he wants to come and talk to me, I'll tell him everything I know. Every word of everything I heard. Anything that will help him. And if he won't listen, well, I'd appreciate it if you'd let me know that, too. So I can try running. Though I'm pretty sure Weaver would be willing to track me down to the ends of the earth. After he finishes up with you all, of course."

Shelia slid behind the wheel and looked up at Ramey gravely. Ramey nodded.

"Don't worry. If he'll listen to anyone, he'll listen to me."

THE BATHROOM MIRROR in room 124 of The Pines had become a web. Clive taped a final notecard to the bottom of the smeared, oxidizing surface and stood back in his bare feet and rolled-up shirtsleeves to take it all in. He took a sip from the Heineken dangling in his left hand and tilted his head. From this angle, it was all pretty impressive.

The bottom and sides of the mirror were cluttered with notecards, each with a name printed in black magic marker. Some had red stars in the corner of the card, others blue, others green. Beside many of the notecards were mini Post-it notes, scrawled with other names, with dates, dollar amounts and question marks. At the top of the mirror, taped up in a neat row, were four solemn cards, each with a name. Each with the abbreviation "Sen." in front of the name and a big red star in the corner.

All across the mirror, different notecards were connected to one another by thick lines drawn with a black dry erase marker. Some names had more lines coming and going than others, but every one of them had a line leading to the large piece of notebook paper taped in the center of the mirror. In tall, capital letters, Clive had scrawled the name SISTER TULAH. She was the one. She was at the center of everything. He finished the beer in his hand and then snatched up the cellphone balanced on the edge of the sink counter. He had to call Lopez now, before he chickened out. Of course, yet again, his timing was impeccable.

"Jesus Christ, Grant! I liked you much better when you were down in the basement. I only ever had to hear from you once every few months when you came up for air. You do know I have a life, right? You do know I have days off."

There were people chattering loudly in the background. Was she at a party? It was Sunday afternoon. The kinds of parties Clive imagined Lopez going to were not held in the daylight. The sound was getting fainter, it seemed that she was walking away for privacy, but he could still hear a kid shrieking in the background. And then something, a splash maybe?

"Where are you, at a pool party?"

A door slammed shut and then it was quiet except for the sound of Lopez's biting voice.

"Yes, as a matter of fact, I am. It's my goddamn nephew's seventh birthday. I'm surrounded by trolls in sundresses and their screeching brood whose entire mission in life, it seems, is to get pool water in everyone's drink by way of cannonballs."

Clive couldn't help but smile.

"So you should be thanking me for rescuing you."

"You're taking me away from the vodka, so this had better be good. I thought I gave you until Monday. Can't this wait until tomorrow?"

Clive looked up at the mirror, letting his eyes trace along the connected lines.

"I don't think so. I've found something here. Something big."

"You said that before. Your preacher lady, buying up land. Did you figure out if she's developing a commune out in the woods? Building a spaceship? Is she brainwashing all the holy rollers into drinking the Kool-Aid?"

"No. Phosphate mining."

"What?"

Clive cradled the phone between his ear and shoulder and pried the cap off another beer. It was time to make a move.

"The land. Sister Tulah, she was snatching up all the land, piecing it all together, so that when this phosphate mine opened up, she'd own all the land it was on. She was going to make a killing from mineral rights. An absolute slaughter."

"Okay."

Clive paced up and down the short length of the cramped motel room as he tried to make her understand.

"No, just listen. She acquired that land by coercion. Manipulation. Blackmail and God knows what else. She runs this town, I'm telling you. People signed that land over to her because they're terrified of her."

"Terrified of a preacher? Didn't you say she was old?"

Clive flicked the edge of one of the many photocopied newspaper clippings he had pinned to the peeling wallpaper by the door. If Lopez could only see Tulah, could see her pallid eye and the way her lips turned down at the corners. If she could her hear the menace lurking behind Tulah's every word, she would understand.

"The mine wasn't just coming here on its own accord. She orchestrated the entire thing. She forced people to sell her their land. Donate it, gift it, whatever. She forced the county commissioners to approve the project. To vote on tax breaks for the PRB mining company to come to Bradford County in the first place."

Clive took a long swig of beer. He knew it sounded crazy.

"She's like a spider, sitting in her church, but pulling all the strings...."

"Forced?"

Clive stopped pacing.

"Huh?"

"You said she forced people to sell their land? To vote a certain way?"

Clive set his beer down on top of the TV set and picked up one of the many piles of paper laid out across the top of the bureau. He began to shuffle through it.

"Yes. Forced. Threatened. There were kidnappings. Assaults. Businesses burnt to the ground. Who knows what else."

He dropped the stack of papers on the floor and began to rifle through others spread out on the stiff, paisley bedspread. Clive had spent the past two days amassing and organizing the documents. He'd bought the library a printer cartridge himself and had given the prune-faced librarian a hundred dollar bill in exchange for unlimited copies. The toner in the copy machine had just begun to run out when he'd finally left the library, his arms cradling two shopping bags stuffed with pages of tax records, board meeting agendas, transcripts and newspaper articles.

"This goes back years. Years. Tulah's been working on this phosphate deal since before I joined the ATF."

"Which wasn't that long ago."

Clive whacked a stack of papers against the corner of the TV.

"And before that, I'm serious, she was running the town even before that. I've got records here going back fifteen years. She had zoning ordinances changed to run this other church out of town in the early nineties. She had the tax code…"

Lopez drew him up short.

"You have proof?"

Clive dropped the papers in his hand and took a deep breath. He had known this was coming.

"I have connections. I have a pattern. Come on, I've been on this case for less than a week. I'm working out of the public library, for Christ's sake. The only one in the county. But there's something here. I know there is."

"You've said that."

"I'm telling you, she has this town by the balls."

Lopez exhaled loudly into the phone. He could feel her eyes rolling all the way across the state line.

"Grant."

"Yes?"

"Do you know what the letters in ATF stand for?"

"Lopez, you're not hearing what I'm saying. If you could see all these papers. If you could see the…"

Her voice was slow and patient.

"They stand for Alcohol, Tobacco and Firearms. Right? So, is this preacher lady smuggling cigarettes? Jacking semis full of liquor bottles? Is she selling guns to drug lords? Bombs to terrorists?"

Clive walked over to the mirror and stood before it. His beer clinked against the counter as he set it down.

"No. But these other things…"

"Are none of our concern, Agent Grant. And none of what you're saying falls under federal jurisdiction. It all sounds local to me. So if your morals are bothering you, drop a line to the sheriff and then get your ass back to Atlanta."

Clive was grinding his teeth so hard he thought his jaw would pop.

"She owns the sheriff. She owns everyone."

Lopez huffed.

"Well, she doesn't own you. Quit playing detective. You're a special agent, not a secret agent. And after this, you might want to reevaluate what the word 'special' stands for in your case. You are not undercover. You're not Jay Dobyns, for God's sake. You're not cool, Grant. You're a pencil pusher with a badge who got sent to do a job that no one else could be bothered with."

Clive stopped flipping through a file full of land deeds and inhaled sharply. He dropped the folder on the edge of the sink counter, stung.

"Lopez, that's not what, I mean, that's not how…"

She cut him off.

"Save it. And if this is all you've got on this preacher, then you've got nothing. I expect you back at your desk by tomorrow morning. Or I'm charging you with insubordination. Do you understand?"

Clive bit back everything he wanted to say. His eyes lingered on the four names at the top of the mirror; he hadn't wanted to bring them up yet. They were his very last cards. But at this point, he didn't have a damn thing else to lose.

"What if I said that Tulah controlled more than the town of Kentsville?"

"Grant, I don't care if she controls the goddamn western hemisphere! Shut it down. Get back to your desk."

Clive squeezed his eyes shut.

"What if I said that Sister Tulah had state senators in her pocket? What if I said that she bribed them to vote to approve a permit for the phosphate mine to operate here?"

Lopez was quiet for a moment. When she finally spoke, Clive could hear the tremor in her voice. The spark of curiosity. Of interest.

"Is that what you're saying?"

Clive gripped his sweating beer bottle and looked up at the notecards.

"That's what I'm saying."

There was now a tinge of excitement in her voice.

"And you can prove it? Because if you have some actual proof, we could go in on a joint RICO case with the FBI. Forget about just taking down some preacher. We could use this Sister Tulah against the senators. Talk about a case. It would be big. Huge."

Clive nodded along.

"I know. That's what I've been trying to tell you."

Clive could imagine the gleam in her eye. He knew she had been looking for a landmark case for years. She didn't advertise it, but Clive knew she wanted to make a name for herself almost as much as he did. Her voice began to crescendo.

"Who knows where it could all lead? What we could find? How big a corruption scandal? And if ATF establishes it, the FBI will have to settle for a joint case. Holy shit, Grant. This could be…"

"Career making. I know."

"But you have proof, right? Something solid to go on? Getting the go-ahead to pursue a case like this is going to be tricky enough as it is. I need something to give Krenshaw so he can take it all the way up to the special agent in charge."

Clive hesitated. If he said no, the moment would be gone. Lopez would never go for it again and he would miss his chance.

"Yes. Of course. I have an informant on Tulah. Two, actually."

Clive knew her eyebrows were raised, so he stumbled forward.

"Judah Cannon. The son of the man who was killed in the church fire. He's the leader of a small-time crime family in the town just south of here."

"And he'll talk?"

He was just heaping one lie up on top of another, but he had to build it up. He had to convince Lopez to give him more time.

"I'm pretty sure. But in addition to him, I've got an even better insider. One that's a sure thing."

"Who?"

Lopez sounded wary, so Clive tried to come off as confident as possible.

"The preacher's nephew. He's a total pushover. Scared of his own shadow. But he's been at Tulah's side like a sick puppy since he was a kid. He's our golden ticket."

"And he agreed to talk? He'll inform on his own aunt? You're sure he will?"

For once, Clive was glad he was talking to Lopez on the phone. If she had been able to see his face, she would have known he was lying through his teeth.

"Yes. He will. I'm certain of it."

"Oh, hell yeah, then."

Lopez sounded almost giddy.

"Oh man, this is it. This is really it, then. All right, I'll need a signed statement from this nephew to take to Krenshaw. We don't need an informant agreement or anything like that yet, but get me a signed affidavit from him with some info on Sister Tulah, okay? Just scan it and email me tomorrow. Or fax it, if they're still in the dark ages down there."

Lopez laughed glibly, but Clive was sweating.

"Tomorrow?"

"Is that a problem?"

Clive looked up at the mirror. He turned around to survey the motel room, strewn with papers. It was all just ideas. Conjectures. It meant nothing, really. It could all be blown away with one single breath from Atlanta. This was his big break. His chance to finally be a rock star agent and suddenly he had just been thrown in the deep end. Clive couldn't swim. He swallowed and closed his eyes.

"No, no problem."

"All right. This is going to be something, Grant. I can't believe I'm saying this, but I think you might have done okay here."

Lopez hung up, but it took Clive a moment to slowly take the phone away from his ear. He looked down at it in his hand and then let it drop to the carpet. He raised his head and stared up at the water-stained ceiling, his mind racing around in circles. Clive needed a miracle to make it all work, and if there was one thing he was sure of, it was that he didn't believe in God.

RAMEY KNEW WHAT she was walking into. She stood in the late afternoon sun, its low brilliance infinitely refracted in the burnished surfaces of the surrounding graveyard of cars, and steeled herself for a moment. Long enough to collect her thoughts, to think rationally, but not long enough to lose her nerve. Part of her wanted to just run into the garage, fling herself against Judah, listen to him as he held her and be reassured that it was all going to be okay. Feel his hand tangled in her hair, feel the strength he could envelope her with, find that quiet moment between them when it didn't matter that they always seemed to be taking on the entire world. When all that mattered was the sound of their breath as one.

But she was burying that part of her. It would stay buried until she could look into Judah's eyes and see the truth. Until she could trust him. Unconditionally. Ramey crossed her arms and dug her nails into her shoulders. Then she gathered herself, tossed her hair back and came around the corner of the garage.

Judah and Benji were sitting in the back, lounging beside the poker table in the fold-out metal chairs. They were smiling. Benji was in the middle of some joke and Judah glanced down at the worn green felt, his shoulders raised in a silent laugh, as Benji brought his palm down on the table, bringing the point of the story home. The sight sent a flare of anger through Ramey's chest. They were acting as if everything was all right. As if a homicidal maniac hadn't just etched their names on a bullet. As if nothing had changed and they were still only teenagers, sitting around the bonfire pit down at the boat landing. Benji cutting up, Judah just taking it all in, his head bent down slightly with that secret smile at the corner of his lips as he jabbed at the fire, sending a spray of sparks up into the night sky, rising along with the smoke to the stars. Many times when she had come down to the landing, seventeen, anxious, furious, mellow, half drunk, a little stoned, a girl on the edge of a knife, almost a woman who would never look back, she had stood just like this. Arms crossed. Lips parted. Stung. Waiting underneath the sweeping live oak branches for the boys to notice her.

She was Ramey Barrow, the girl who pulled the fire alarm during sophomore year just so she could get out on the football field and beat up the girl who had been bullying her sister. She was the girl who could walk into any classroom late with her head held high. Who outright accused her algebra teacher of trying to look down her shirt. Who could drink half the party under the table. Who walked alone at night, the handle of a switchblade gripped tightly in her fist. And yet, when she saw that look on Judah's face, that crinkle of the eye, that smile, disappearing behind the sparks and smoke, she had waited. Uncertain in the shadows. Knowing, but still not trusting, that the moment he raised his head and his eyes alighted on hers he would wave her over, make room for her on the overturned strawberry crate. They would sit so close, their shoulders and hips and thighs and knees touching in the darkness, but it would never be close enough.

Ramey uncrossed her arms as she stalked across the garage. Benji glanced down at her empty hands and shook his head in disgust.

"I thought you were picking up beer."

Ramey ducked underneath the lift.

"I didn't make it to the store."

"What? Seriously?"

Benji looked over at Judah in irritation, but Judah was staring intently at Ramey's face. His eyes followed her carefully as she pulled out a chair and sat down at the table. She reached for the pack of cigarettes in front of Judah and he held out his lighter to her.

"Ramey, what happened? What's wrong?"

She let Judah light her cigarette as she tried to figure out how to come out and say it. She'd been rehearsing the lines in her head ever since she'd left the Quincy's parking lot. Ramey lowered her eyes to the table and picked at a rip in the felt with her thumbnail.

"Weaver."

She looked up as Judah groaned and fell back in his chair.

"Ramey, we've been over this I don't know how many times in the past few days. Stop it, already. It's not a big deal."

He glanced over at Benji and shook his head slightly. Benji gave an irritated huff. Both of them were on the verge of rolling their eyes and Ramey suddenly had the impulse to turn the table over on them. She wanted to bang her fists, to scream. She wanted to burn it all down. The two of them could burn along with it.

Instead, she took a long drag on her cigarette to steady herself and then, ignoring Judah's skepticism and talking over Benji's indignation, Ramey related her encounter with Shelia. When she was finally finished, Ramey sat back and crossed her arms, waiting for their response. It was about what she had expected.

"You know that all sounds crazy, right?"

Judah whistled and shook his head as he looked away from her. Ramey watched his eyes narrow and his jaw clench. He seemed to be trying to process it all, trying to figure out what to say next. Benji, however, didn't hold back. He hadn't gotten past the fact that Ramey had spoken to Shelia in the first place. Benji smashed his fist down onto the table.

"Sounds crazy? I'm wondering if you're crazy, Ramey. You let that whore talk to you? She'd just as soon as bite you as tell you an ounce of truth. If she said the Earth was round, I'd argue otherwise. I can't believe you even listened to her. Did you forget that she tried to kill me? Did you forget all this?"

Benji smacked his ruined cheek a few times and Ramey turned away from him.

"Judah, I think…"

"No."

Judah shook his head again.

"Benji's right. Even if Shelia was there, at this bar in Daytona, and I'm not saying that she was, but let's say if. And if Weaver said those things, about wanting to kill me, why the hell would she come here to tell me?"

Ramey started to speak again, but Judah held up his hand to stop her. She could have smacked it away.

"Think about it, Ramey. Shelia is a liar. She's a liar and a manipulator. She set up that whole shootout at the church. She had to have been the one to tell the Scorpions that Sherwood was going to be there. She was with one of the Scorpions, for Christ's sake. Did you forget that? This is probably just another plan to get back at us. To still get that money from us somehow. Her old man probably put her up to the whole thing and…"

Ramey couldn't take it anymore. She mashed her cigarette out and interrupted him.

"He's dead."

This didn't seem to faze Judah.

"So, she's on to something new. She heard me and Weaver talking and she's figured out a way…"

"He's dead because Weaver killed him. Last night. He killed the Scorpion guy and he killed the guy who brought him the information about you and he killed the owner of the bar. He tried to kill Shelia. He's going to kill Shelia."

"Says her."

Ramey turned back to Benji. His knuckles had gone white where he was still gripping the edge of the table. Ramey spoke carefully.

"I think maybe Shelia's telling the truth here."

"Well, then, good. Weaver can kill her. Save me the trouble."

Benji was dead serious. The look on his face was chilling. Ramey turned back to Judah, but Benji wasn't finished.

"And you know what, Ramey. He can have you, too. Listening to that woman. After what she did to me. I can't believe you, Ramey. I just can't believe you."

Benji's voice was cracking now. Ramey looked at him, her mouth turned down, and Benji must have seen the pity on her face. He stood up awkwardly and banged his fist on the table.

"Fine. Screw you, Ramey. If this is the way it's gonna be."

Benji swayed for a moment and Ramey had to look away. She glanced up at Judah, taking in the scene before him. His eyes met hers, but she couldn't tell what he was thinking. Judah turned back to Benji and there was a strange, gentle note in his voice.

"Benji. Will you give us a minute here?"

Benji edged away from the table and jammed a crutch up under his arm. Ramey noticed that he was now using only the single crutch to get around. He looked at her as if he wanted to spit venom on her.

"Gladly. Maybe you can talk some sense into her."

Ramey almost called after him as he stumped away, but Judah touched her lightly on the arm.

"Let him be. It's not important."

Ramey turned back to Judah.

"One of these days, though, it will be."

Judah shook his head slightly. He kept his fingers on her arm.

"Listen, there's something else I don't buy about what Shelia told you. Why would Weaver want to kill me? I mean, nothing happened when I talked to him. I wouldn't say we parted as friends, but I figured, if anything, he'd come after the business. Want to tear it down, take it over or whatever. Why want to kill me? And you? And the others? It's too personal to make sense."

Ramey twisted in her chair so that she was facing him.

"It is personal with him."

Judah drew back from her.

"What do you mean?"

"I mean, Shelia, she said that after that guy gave Weaver the information on you, Weaver told this story. About how Sherwood had stolen his girl like forty years ago or something."

Judah frowned.

"Forty years ago?"

Ramey nodded.

"Yeah, back in 1971, I guess. Up at the Navy base in Jacksonville. For some reason, I always thought Sherwood had been in the Marines, like my dad."

Judah had a strange look on his face as he slowly shook his head.

"He wanted people to think so. The Navy was too cushy. He didn't want people to think he was a chickenshit taking the easy way out. And 1971..."

Judah's voice trailed off as he stared down at the felt top of the poker table. Ramey dipped her head, trying to catch his eye.

"What about 1971?"

She could see Judah's jaw muscles working as he clenched and unclenched his teeth.

"I'm just wondering how she knew. The Navy. 1971. How she knew the exact year Sherwood enlisted and went to Vietnam."

"You mean, how'd she know if she was just making it all up?"

Judah didn't say anything. Ramey waited, but finally reached for another cigarette and continued.

"According to the story Shelia overheard, Weaver had this lifelong vendetta against Sherwood over this girl. But since Sherwood is dead, and you just fell right into his lap, he's gonna make you pay instead. I guess killing you and everyone connected to you is his way of getting Sherwood back. It's like Old Testament revenge or something."

Judah slowly shook his head.

"That's just insane."

Ramey tapped the end of her cigarette on the table, but didn't light it.

"I think he's insane. Shelia said he shot those people in the bar, just out of nowhere. Like it wasn't nothing."

"And yet, she survived."

Ramey looked at the cigarette in her hand and then shoved it back into the pack. She sighed.

"I don't know, Judah. I just know what she told me. And I believe her."

Judah raised his head.

"You do?"

Ramey flung the pack into center of the table and turned toward him.

"Come on, Judah. You just said so yourself. 1971. The Navy. And she knew about Cassie and Stella, too. There's no way she's just making this all up. And think about it, why would she even want to?"

Judah looked away from her.

"Okay, but why come here?"

"She knows this guy wants to kill her. And he wants to kill us. It sounds like she thought that if she told us, warned us, we'd have a better chance of killing him first. She made it pretty clear that it was a decision born out of necessity and survival, not compassion."

Judah flicked his eyes back to her.

"Well, at least that part sounds honest."

Ramey bit her bottom lip as she looked at his downcast face.

"So, what do we do?"

Judah looked up sharply.

"Do?"

"Yeah. Shelia wants to meet with us tonight. She said she'd tell you anything you asked. Anything she could remember that you think would help. We need to come up with a plan, fast. We might only have a day or two before Weaver shows up in Silas and I think we need to hit him before he gets here. Maybe we can catch him off guard, maybe we can—"

"Whoa, slow down."

Judah gave her a slight smile that made Ramey's stomach turn. Something was wrong. It was that look again. That look telling her not to worry. Ramey dug her nails into the thighs of her jeans.

"What?"

Judah raised his eyebrows.

"I'm still not buying it. It's too, well, come on, Ramey. All right, so she knew some details. But the rest? Seriously, the whole story Shelia told you about Weaver sounds like something off a daytime soap. Men don't really act like that. Women just think they do. So just calm down. And if anything does come up again with Weaver, I'll take care of it."

Ramey stood up; she was shaking.

"You'll what?"

"I'll take care of it. Weaver's not going to just storm in here, guns blazing…"

Ramey slammed her palm down on the table.

"You're willing to bet your life on that? Or my life? Just because you're too goddamn stubborn and full of pride? Because you can't get your head out of your ass for five minutes?"

Judah's face went dark.

"You don't understand, Ramey. You're not the head of this family. You're not seeing the full picture of everything I'm trying to do here."

"And what is that? Die?"

She wished Judah would stand up and face her. She wished he would yell back, but he had closed her off completely instead. He spoke very slowly and firmly, his gaze fixed on the table in front of him. His fists were resting on the edge of it.

"Ramey, I will take care of you."

She crossed her arms and barked out a laugh.

"What does that even mean? Am I supposed to just blindly trust you?"

"It's been enough before."

He slowly looked up at her, crestfallen. But Ramey didn't miss the edge of a threat in his voice. She forced herself to hold his gaze.

"Well, it's not enough now."

Judah clenched his jaw and looked away.

"I don't know what else to tell you. Just let me handle things. If it comes to it, let me handle Weaver and let me take care of this family."

"In other words, let you be a Cannon."

"Yes."

"Fine. Be a Cannon. But you best remember that I'm not."

"Ramey..."

She couldn't take it anymore. She was done. Ramey turned on her heel and stalked out of the garage. Judah didn't go after her.

CHAPTER 15

TULAH PASSED BENEATH the Sickle's Door, a crumbling stone archway half buried underneath a web of suffocating kudzu, and silently entered the Forest of Anat. The moment her bare foot touched the dark, loamy soil, Tulah knew she had left her former self behind. She raised her head and peered up through the spidery canopy of hickory, oak and chalk maple branches. The full moon hung pendulously in the star-scattered sky, a lucent Charon, ferrying her across the threshold of time. She set her eyes on the wooded expanse before her, a snarling tangle of lichen-dusted trees and jagged limestone outcroppings, some barely visible in the beryl shadows, and felt the curving line of energy trembling beneath the earth, compelling her forward. Now that she had found the conduit, all she had to do was follow it to the source.

For three generations, since Reverend Benjamin Irwin had first been led by God to the Sacred Wall in 1904, the one-hundred-and-forty-four-acre Forest had been sealed and protected. To reach it, Tulah had driven west and then north from Cave Spring, veering off onto ever more narrow and nameless roads, until she had arrived at the unassuming cabin of the Keepers. The Bouman family had been guarding the Forest, running off the occasional naturalist or hiker and maintaining the perimeter, ever since Irwin had dedicated the site and appointed them the task. The Keeper who waved her through the high, wrought iron gate and took the keys of the Navigator from her hand was the same flat-faced, vacant-eyed man who had first welcomed Tulah to the Forest back in 1987 when she was a new initiate to The Order. The man had nodded to her solemnly, glanced at the sickle hanging among the folds of her long white robe and pointed left, down the rocky, serpentine trail that encircled the breadth of the Forest. Tulah had felt a secret thrill as she began her trek; never before had she been directed to the left. She had hoped this meant that her rank had improved this year. Each member of The Order arrived at the Keeper's gate separately, at a specific, pre-ordained time. No one was allowed to see or hear another once the journey had begun. They all must travel alone.

Tulah stumbled over slippery mounds of mossy stones and rotting logs, but she never once questioned her direction. Once inside the bowels of the Forest, she was no longer a preacher, no longer a woman. She was now, singularly, one of the Watchers. The darkness did not trouble her; she was following the Sickle's trail and could have navigated the Forest with her eye closed. At one point, a scintillant cloud of fireflies gently swarmed her, but she did not let herself stop in wonder. Tulah did not pause and scoop a handful of tangy water from the Chebar as she trudged across the swift and shallow stream, even though she was desperately thirsty. She trusted the carefully orchestrated timing, but was also cognizant of the moon climbing overhead, the earth spinning slowly toward dawn. Tulah knew that she must arrive in the Glade of Anat at the exact right moment. She had never failed before and didn't intend to start now. An hour passed, then two, and finally Tulah glimpsed the flickering glow of torch light seeping through the trees ahead. Tulah stopped and braced herself against the craggy trunk of a holly.

She caught her breath and adjusted the crowned mask over her sweating face. It was heavy, made of hammered steel and burnished copper, and shielded her forehead, nose and cheekbones. A narrow slit at eye level allowed her to see and the crown of the mask rose above her head in seven horns, encircling the loose gray hair straggling down past her shoulders. Before she had entered the Forest, Tulah had been apprehensive about being able to see through the mask with only one eye. Now, it seemed such a foolish thought. With the light from the Glade finally in her sight, it seemed folly to have been worried about anything. Tulah untied the golden sickle from her belt and grasped it tightly in her left hand. It was time.

All around her, Tulah could hear the rustling of other Watchers moving through the trees as they, too, prepared to step into the clearing. More torches were kindled, and then the low melody of the Angels' singing came to her ears, signifying that the moon had crested the apex. She wove her way through the last stand of ancient oak trees and finally emerged from the Forest, into the Glade, where she took her place beside the small Sickle stone and joined her fellow Watchers, under the glittering, revealed sky.

Without moving her head, which was forbidden until she was called, Tulah shifted her eye to look around the clearing of trampled earth as best she could. The Watchers, each standing next to a torch and their token landmark, were spaced out evenly in two parallel lines, forming a gauntlet running down the center of the Glade. Directly across from Tulah, dressed in an identical robe and mask, stood the Flaming Sword. On one side of the Sword was the Lamp and on the other was the Candlestick. She couldn't see who was beside her in her own row, but she was pleased to be standing even with the Flaming Sword. Her rank had most certainly improved this year and was quite a step up from her last appointment as the Key of Hell. In the sputtering torch light, Tulah tried to calculate exactly where she now fell in the hierarchy, but when a booming voice rang out through the Glade, Tulah's mind instantly turned from the thought. The Angel of Man had spoken. The Night Recompense had begun.

"Brethren! We are here on the Night of Nights. The Moment of Moments. When our true likeness shines forth. When the Wing and the Wheel and the Whirlwind rain down from the sky in a shower of sparks. When the Great

Cloud from the North sweeps over, when the Amber Brightness envelopes all the Land, when the air divides and the Spirit goes forth out of the midst of the Fire. We arrive for The Reckoning. We arrive for The Recompense. The Order of the Luminous Sevenfold Light arrives to celebrate and honor the Everlasting Reign of Attar."

Tulah let the sound of the Angel's voice fill her until she felt that she was nothing more than a million insignificant particles, floating heavenward in lazy ascension. Then a rush of flame replaced the voice and the tonal song of the other three Angels began again. Tulah gripped the sickle in her hand as the Angel of Man began the Calling. Tulah could not yet see the Angels and was forced only to listen. The first Watcher called was the Book.

"*And it was written within and without: and there was written therein lamentations, and mourning, and woe.*"

From somewhere near the end of the opposite row there was a stir of movement, and then a robed figure swished by Tulah like a ghost. The Watcher carried a rolled scroll in its left hand and its mask gleamed in the fire light. A few moments later, the voice of the Watcher responded to the voice of the Angel.

"*It was in my mouth as honey for sweetness.*"

Next, the Crowned Woman was called.

"*And there appeared a great wonder in heaven; a woman clothed with the sun, and the moon under her feet, and upon her head a crown of twelve stars.*"

The Watcher standing beside Tulah stepped forward and she was only able to catch a glimpse. It wore a crowned mask identical to the others, but from its raised hands dangled a circlet made of twelve silver stars. Over the susurration of the Angels, Tulah could barely make out the hushed response of the Woman, but Tulah knew the words by heart.

"*And she being with child cried, travailing in birth and pained to be delivered.*"

The Broad Arrow, the Seal, the Eye of the Lamb and Wormwood were all called and then the Glade echoed with the herald of the Sickle.

"Thrust in thy sickle, and reap: for the time is come for thee to reap; for the harvest of the earth is ripe."

Tulah stepped out into the gauntlet and turned, finally able to see the brush arbor at the north end of the Glade. The ground was soft and damp beneath her feet as she plodded forward, the golden sickle in her left hand at her side, her right arm stretched out, palm turned upward. She knew the Watchers on either side were looking at her as she passed, but Tulah was concerned only with what was before her: the Angels, the Fire Arbor, the Sapphire Throne and the Sacred Wall.

The arbor had been constructed of ash and hickory branches, twisted together and tied with ropes of vine to form an arch high enough to shelter the Angels standing beneath it. The branches were on fire, the flames sweeping high, filling the night with smoke, and sending a scattering of sparks drifting down onto the Throne. The hoary seat of Attar Himself. Its worn limestone arms and back were inlaid with thousands of star cut sapphires, still brilliant despite the spreading patches of dusky lichen and the lacework of choking creepers. A shallow bowl of iron, four feet across, rested on the seat and in the bowl blazed a brilliant indigo flame. On either side of the Throne stood the four Angels. Tulah stopped when she was a few feet away and held out the sickle to the Angel of Man. Her voice was clear and true.

"And he that sat on the cloud thrust in his sickle on the earth; and the earth was reaped."

Tulah looked at each of the Angels in turn. Like the Watchers, they wore long robes, though theirs looked as though they had been dipped in blood, and copper masks crowned with seven horns. Whereas the visages of the Watchers' masks were featureless, the Angels' each bore the likeness of the Spirit that had descended upon them. The radiant faces of an Ox, a Lion, an Eagle and a Man all beamed at Tulah and each Angel nodded to her in turn. She stepped to the Throne and held the sickle over the fire. The flames popped and spit, licking her wrist, but she couldn't feel her flesh burning. Tulah dropped the sickle into the bowl and bowed her head.

The Angel of Man stepped forward and took her by the shoulder, guiding her around the Throne to a wide, jagged rock face, jutting up out of the earth behind it. The surface of the rock was blanketed in kudzu and curved around the edge of the clearing until it disappeared back into the Forest. Tulah could hear a faint trickle of water as the Angel led her over to a rugged wall made of natural stones, piled up against the rock escarpment. One of the stones was missing, leaving a small opening in the center of the wall, but before Tulah leaned down to peer through, the Angel brought its mask close to her ear and whispered.

"*And he brought me to the door of the court; and when I looked, behold a hole in the wall.*"

Up until now, The Night Recompense had been ritual, an enactment and dedication to Attar, the True God. A test to determine if she was worthy enough for this moment. Tulah had knelt before the Sacred Wall seven times before and each time, a different prophecy was revealed to her. Tulah bent her head, aligned the slit in her mask with the crevice in the wall and looked.

At first, she could see only the flat blackness of the rock only inches away from her face. The space began to open up, however, and an amber light, tinged with a crimson glow, flooded toward her, expanding her view. Out of the center of the glow came a black shape, growing larger as it came closer, and once Tulah could see it clearly, she saw that it was a crow, flying toward her and swooping upward through a red sky. The crow landed on the branch of a dead tree and the tree turned to ash beneath the bird's spindly feet. The crow flapped its wings and flew back the way it had come, a speck that finally disappeared over the horizon, taking the vision with it. Tulah stood up, but did not think to interpret what she had seen. It was not for her to understand. The Angel of Man put its mask close to hers and Tulah whispered the correct response.

"*Upon his shoulder in the twilight, and shall go forth: they shall dig through the wall to carry out thereby: he shall cover his face, that he see not the ground with his eyes."*

The Angel nodded and stretched its right arm out, gesturing for Tulah to continue. She bowed her head and followed the curve of the rock face, back into the labyrinth of trees. She was ready to make the Descent.

FELTON WAS SWEATING. He gripped his Bible in both hands and rubbed his thumbs up and down the battered cover. Over the years, the leather had turned supple around the edges and along the spine, and there were two white streaks on the cover where the finish had been worn away completely. Felton bent the book back and forth between his hands and glanced over at Sister Mona, sitting stoutly at the piano and leading the Sunday night congregation in a round of "Come Sinners to the Gospel Feast." It was the fifth hymn of the night and the plastic tarp over the front door had ceased flapping with any latecomers' arrivals. Most seemed surprised to see Felton standing in front of the pulpit, but no one dared to raise a question. As always, they simply found their places and began to sing and clap along.

Felton tried not to make eye contact with anyone. He was afraid that one raised eyebrow, one stifled laugh, would cause him to lose his courage completely. He had stood on the low stage through the songs, not greeting anyone, not smiling, but simply tapping his foot along to the music and staring intently down at the Bible his hands. If he didn't get on with it, though, he knew he would lose his nerve altogether and never regain it. He stared at the back of Sister Mona's head, at the fat brown braid swinging down her back, and he cleared his throat. She didn't hear him and continued to bang away at the keys. He tried again, but against the piano, and the chorus of thirty-five souls, Felton's unobtrusive voice was simply drowned out. He counted the beats in the last verse of the hymn and made himself ready. He would have to begin before Sister Mona launched into another song.

"Brothers and Sisters!"

Sister Mona ceased playing, her hands poised above the piano keys. It was quite possible that she had never heard Felton speak so loudly. She craned her neck to look up at him and he nodded to her, indicating that he was ready. The rest of the congregation, after a few sidelong glances, settled themselves on the splintery benches. Felton had gone back to staring down at his Bible, but he was listening intently, waiting for the church to quiet, for all attention to be focused on him. He could feel the sweat seeping out from under his armpits and pooling against his lower back and he was glad that he had chosen to wear the maroon jacket over his dress shirt. It would make the wetness a little less visible. Felton took a deep breath. He had a burning urge to urinate. And then vomit. Instead, he lifted his head, cleared his throat and thought of the snakes.

"I'd like to start with the Book of Isaiah."

Felton shifted his weight back and forth and wiped the sweat from his upper lip before continuing.

"I mean, to be honest, Genesis is my favorite book, really. I like the part in the beginning, about how God created the earth and then made all the animals. How he made the birds and the great whales. All the animals and it was good. It was all good, in the beginning, like that."

He heard a snickering come from the side of the church and then the thwack of a child being smacked in the back of the head. Felton swallowed. He had turned his gaze back to the wooden floorboards beneath his shiny new loafers. He knew he was stuttering.

"And I like the part about Noah and the ark, too. Where he has to save all the animals from the flood. He has to put them on the ark to keep them all from drowning. Because most of them can't swim."

Felton kept his head down, but tentatively raised his eyes. The congregation was watching him placidly, as if they'd already given up on even being skeptical and were now just waiting for him to hurry up and bumble through it so they could get on home. Felton dropped his eyes again.

"But lately, I've been thinking about the Book of Isaiah. Like I said. Now this book is different. God is pretty angry with everyone the whole time. He doesn't see anything good at all around him. He's just mad at the Israelites through most of the whole thing."

Felton thumbed open his Bible.

"But with good reason."

From the back row of the church came a Hallelujah. Felton looked up, startled, but then quickly turned back to the Bible.

"Because the people, the people living in Jerusalem then, they weren't doing what they were supposed to be doing. They were doing all sorts of things they shouldn't have been doing, in fact, and God, he knew that. Of course. Because he's God."

Another Hallelujah pierced the air, followed by a murmured Amen. Felton opened his Bible to the place he had marked earlier and ran his thick finger down the tissue paper page.

"And so Isaiah, he has this vision, where God tells him everything. And Isaiah says, here, right at the beginning, he says, '*Hear, O heavens, and give ear, O earth: for the Lord hath spoken.*'"

Felton glanced up at the Amen that followed. A woman, Sister Bea, was standing in the back row of the church. She had her hand raised up in the air. Felton could hardly believe it.

"So, see, God tells Isaiah that he has to make the people of the city listen. And Isaiah tries. He tells them God thinks the city is like an unfaithful wife. The people have gotten so far out of control. They've come so far off the path of righteousness. It's like they don't even know which way is up or down anymore."

Felton stood up straight as he peered around the church. Two more women and one man were now on their feet. Felton found another passage that he had marked and as he read it, he was surprised at the gravity of his own voice. He was speaking with confidence. With authority.

"And so, Isaiah, he tells the people, he tells them, look, '*We have made lies our refuge, and under falsehood have we hid ourselves.*' Lies, brothers and sisters, lies. God could see that. He could see that the people of the city, they were living in sin. They were worshiping false gods. But most importantly, they were lying. To themselves and to God."

"Jesus save us!"

"Amen!"

"Lord forgive us!"

He was speaking with power. Felton closed the Bible; he knew the Book of Isaiah by heart anyway. He took a few steps forward and allowed himself to look out at the people staring up at him. From the expression on their faces, he couldn't imagine that they were actually looking at him. But he could hear his voice and the timbre it was carrying. Felton smacked the Bible against his thigh.

"And we're doing it right now, aren't we? Every day, it's something. Maybe it's just a little fib or maybe it's a big secret. Something bad, really bad, in your heart. But whatever it is, it's a lie. And God knows. God knows. He knows it all. And he is angry about it."

Felton rocked back on his heels and then pitched himself forward, right to the edge of the low stage.

"And let me tell you, God is clear, clear as day, about what will happen to you if you try to keep your secrets from Him. If you try to lie to him and to others and to the world about all the bad things you've done. 'Woe unto them that seek deep to hide their counsel from the Lord.'"

Felton could feel the rivulets of sweat running down the sides of his face, but he didn't bother to wipe them away. He was there, he was in the moment, and nothing could stop him. For all of his life, he had stood in that same church, looking up at his aunt, waiting for her to bring the Holy Ghost into the room. No one could invite Him in but Sister Tulah. And yet, now, here Felton was, standing on the other side, delivering the message of God, and he knew, he could feel it, that the Spirit had entered the church. And it was because of him.

"Woe to those who hide! Woe to those who keep their counsel from the

Lord! Woe to those who deny themselves the righteous path! Who creep around in the dark when they should be standing out in the light. Woe to them and woe to us all. May we all, may we all, be forgiven!"

It was because of him.

In the truck's headlights, Judah could see Ramey leaning against the driver's side of the Cutlass, arms crossed, jaw set, waiting for him. Judah sighed. This could not be good. He pulled his truck up in front of the house and cut the engine.

When did things get so complicated? Why, for God's sake, did they get so complicated? Judah rubbed his face and then ran his hands back through his hair. He glanced in the side mirror and could see Ramey, still slouched against the side of her car, her head turned away from him. In the glow from the porch light, she was so beautiful. She was always so goddamn beautiful. Even now, mad as hell, most likely aiming for a fight, she could take his breath away.

Judah twisted his hands around the steering wheel. Of course they were complicated. Weaver, Nash, Lesser, Tulah, Sherwood. The money and the guns and the fear. A month or so ago, he and Ramey had gotten drunk together. Silly drunk, teenage drunk. They had ended up in the bathroom, she in the tub, he on the tile floor next to her, an empty bottle of bourbon between them. Most of the night was a blur and had disappeared into a hangover's haze, but he remembered saying something to her about the future. Something stupid about kids. And he was pretty sure that at the time he had been more serious than not. He couldn't remember how Ramey had reacted or what she had said. The next morning, she was mopping up the soaking bathroom floor and he was loading bullets into his .45, on his way with Alvin to strong-arm one of their bookies.

She deserved better. Judah knew this. And if she could just hang on a little longer, he knew he could make it right. If Ramey would just calm down about

Weaver. If she would just calm down about everything and trust him. Judah scrubbed at his face again and then kicked open the creaking door of the truck. In the morning, everything would be better. He came around the truck to Ramey and saw the look on her face. Or maybe not. Judah had the feeling he was going to be sleeping on the couch.

"Ramey, I'm sorry I'm late. I know I texted you and said I'd be home earlier, but I had to—"

"Don't."

Her shoulders curved in slightly, almost as if she was shrinking back from him. Judah put his hands in his pockets and kicked at a tuft of brittle grass growing up through the sandy dirt.

"Are you still tore up about earlier? About the whole thing with Shelia and Weaver? Look, Ramey, you gotta understand—"

"I'm leaving."

Judah jerked his head up and met Ramey's eyes. They were dark. Veiled. He took a step back.

"What the hell is that supposed to mean?"

Ramey's voice was low. Not angry, but resigned. Defeated.

"It means I'm gone. It means I can't do this anymore, Judah."

It was like being sucker punched. Judah leaned over slightly, his hand on one thigh, bracing himself. He inhaled sharply and held his hand out to her, as if to ward her declaration off.

"Whoa, now. Let's just hold on a second. Let's just, let's just hold on. I don't think you know what you're saying."

She nodded and the corners of her mouth turned down. Judah realized that she was struggling, holding back tears.

"I do. You are everything, Judah. Everything. But I can't do it."

Ramey put her hands on her lower back and looked away from him, and now Judah realized that she actually was crying. Maybe she had been all along as she stood leaning against her car waiting for him.

"I just can't do it. This isn't what I wanted, this ain't what I signed up for. I can't live my life looking over my shoulder, being afraid every moment. Wondering which one of us is gonna get killed first."

Judah wanted to tell her that she was talking crazy, but that would be a lie. He woke up with the very same thoughts every day, only he had been able to build a little room and shut all those thoughts up and swallow the key so that he could do what needed to be done. What had to be done if they were ever going to make it to the other side. But maybe she couldn't do that. And the other side seemed to be receding further and further away every day. Judah stood up straight and nodded. He could handle this. He could fix this.

"Okay. All right, listen. Maybe you should get away for a little while. You know, get out of town for a week or so, until things cool down. I know it's been rough, so maybe just take some time..."

"No."

He was taken aback. There was something in her voice. A determination underneath the resignation. She was serious.

"You need to just forget about me, Judah."

Judah threw his hands up in the air.

"Forget about you? Why don't you just tell me to rip out my guts, rip out my heart, right here and now? It would be easier."

Ramey was shaking her head, but Judah almost couldn't hear her over the roar of paralyzing rage that consumed him.

"Judah. We've only been together for three months and—"

"Have you lost your goddamn mind?"

He knew he was yelling and he didn't care. It was all slipping away; it was all falling to pieces around him and he had no idea how to stop it.

"I've been with you my entire life, Ramey. You know that. You know me!"

The look on Ramey's face had become defiant now. She had stopped crying.

"I don't know who you've become."

Judah wanted to hit something. To shoot something. To smash the whole world up around him. He wanted to kick and bite and lash. He wanted to howl.

"Ramey, please, don't do this."

She shook her head and pulled her car keys out of her back pocket.

"I'm sorry. It's done. It's over."

"No."

"I have to go."

Judah stepped away from her. He turned and looked out at the woods, out at the night. He put his hands on his hips and opened his eyes wide, gasping, trying to get his face under control. When he turned back to her, she still had the keys in her hand. He stared at them.

"Where?"

"Away. From this life. From this family. From you. I'm not a Cannon, Judah. I never was. I never hoped to be. And you can't see that. I'm standing right here in front of you and you can't even see me."

She turned and opened the car door behind her. Judah reached out, wanting to grab her and hold her back. Wanting to yank her out of the car and press her to him and refuse to ever let go. But he just stood there, arms outstretched, with empty hands.

"No, please don't do this. Please."

Ramey slammed the car door and the engine of the Cutlass roared. He stepped back as the car circled around the yard. He watched her. She wasn't looking at him; she wasn't looking back. The car disappeared down the driveway and Judah screamed.

"Ramey!"

He clenched his fists and screamed again, his voice breaking in animal anguish.

"Ramey!"

But she was gone.

"AND ISAIAH, HE gives the people of the city God's message. He says, '*Behold, the name of the Lord cometh from far, burning with his anger.*' He tells the people that God's '*lips are full of indignation, and his tongue as a devouring fire.*' A devouring fire! But we need that, don't we? Brothers and sisters, we need a devouring fire. A cleansing fire. A fire to purify us of our sins, of our unfaithfulness, of our lies!"

Felton had left his Bible on the pulpit and was standing again at the edge of the stage, almost on tiptoe, with his arms outstretched and his head lifted high. He was vaguely aware that the congregation had been caught up by the Holy Spirit. No one was sitting; everyone was in the corybantic throes of some sort of ecstasy. Women were wailing and men were beating their hands against their heads and stamping their feet on the ground. Some were laughing hysterically, some were groaning and some were merely swaying while tears ran down their faces. One woman had fallen to her knees and lay slumped against the side of the piano as she repeated the same barking sound over and over. Sister Mona had taken to the piano again, though her eyes were now closed and she only beat out the same primitive, measured notes. And above it all, Felton was preaching at the top of his lungs. Words were coming from his lips in a torrent, but he had no real idea of what he was saying. Instead, his eyes were fixed on the brilliant white light that had appeared in the air just above the riotous congregation.

At first the light resembled others he had seen before when visited by the Holy Spirit. It was almost just a flash, like spots before his eyes, and then an echoing rush in his ears. He felt his body seeming to go in and out of an ether-like state, but then suddenly he could feel the wooden stage firmly beneath his feet and the spots disappeared from his vision. The light, however, was still there and had grown more substantial, more defined around the edges. Felton stared at it, watching it take form, elongating and coiling, until he was faced with an enormous pearl-white snake, hovering and undulating slowly in the air. The snake's head came around and its garnet eyes locked with his. When it spoke, its long, pale, forked tongue was only a few feet away from Felton's face.

"*Thus saith the Lord, Set thine house in order.*"

Felton stretched his arms out to the snake.

"What does that mean?"

The snake blinked lazily before speaking again.

"*Thus saith the Lord, Set thine house in order: for thou shalt die, and not live.*"

Felton could feel his whole body trembling.

"Am I doing to die?"

The snake slowly tilted its head. Its coils were rasping against one another.

"Rise up. I bade you listen and you listened. I bade you speak and you have spoken. Now I bid you to act."

"What must I do? Tell me, what must I do?"

The form of the snake began to fade, once more returning to mere light.

"Rise up. Set your house in order. Rise up."

The snake was gone. Felton stared up into the mesmerizing light until that, too, slowly disappeared. There was a whistling in his ears and he became aware that his mouth was filled with words. He had been preaching all along while he was talking to the snake that only he could see. Felton gazed out at the congregation; it was still in hysterics. He reached for the Bible on the pulpit and held it aloft in both hands. He knew now what he must do. He had listened. He had spoken. Now he had to act. He had nothing more to say to the church before him, so he simply fell to his knees with the book over his head and repeated the words of his destiny.

"Rise up! Rise up! Rise up! Rise up! Rise up!"

THE ROUGH STEPS cut into the side of the ravine were cold, their limestone surfaces slick with patches of pale green moss. There were no rails to steady Tulah as she tramped down the steep bank and more than once she tripped and slid, her bruised feet slipping off the stones and her fleshy toes digging into the layers of decaying vegetation on either side of the stairs. Though there were torches below, the fathomless darkness, punctuated only by nuggets of luminous foxfire, crept in around her and she could do nothing but trust that the True God would see her safely down. When she finally reached the bottom of the Valley of Anat, the front and back of Tulah's robe was soaked with sweat.

In the very center of the Valley, a low circular platform built of stone rose a few inches up out of the sucking mud and Tulah stepped onto it and found her place in the outer circle. Twenty symbols were etched on the circumference and Tulah set herself squarely over the crude drawing of a sickle as she waited for the remaining Watchers to make the perilous Descent as she had.

The walls of the Valley rose high over Tulah's head and were sheer in some places and stubbled with brambles and whip-thin birches in others. The bleached, peeling bark of the trees reflected the eerie beams of moonlight filtering down through the ravine. From somewhere outside the circle of torch light, Tulah could again hear the trilling of water and the rustling of curious night animals. Among the bloodless trees, Tulah was able to make out small figures carved in limestone and caches of bones, half buried under the years of sifting, fallen leaves. She clasped her hands in front of her and tried to focus on the light cutting through the shadows and not on what may have been lying beyond them.

Finally, the Ox, leading the other Angels in procession, made its way slowly down the steps and onto the stone platform. The four Spirits stepped through the ring of Watchers and assumed their marks at the edge of the inner circle, each one next to a tall, flickering torch. When they were all in their correct places, the Angels joined hands and raised their burnished masks. The Ox began to speak.

"Followers of The Order of the Luminous Sevenfold Light. Watchers of the True God of John and Ezekiel, who bow only to Everlasting Attar, who usher in the Latter Rain so that the Great War may be fought and the City may be built and the Chosen may find their place. Let us begin to Reap."

One by one, the Watchers were called again, this time by their Name of

Names, and each robed figure stepped forward and entered the inner circle. No one had yet fallen, though Tulah had seen it happen twice before. Once, the Watcher had crashed to the ground, writhing on the stones in agony until dead. The second time, the Watcher had screamed during the Reaping and so had been swiftly stabbed in the heart by an Angel. Both bodies had been unceremoniously dragged off the platform and thrown among the trees to rot. When Tulah was called, however, she was not afraid. The lightning of the True God was striking in her heart. She walked to the Angels with her arms outstretched and let herself be brought into the fold.

In the very center of the platform, a black star had been cut and burned deep into the stone, and there Tulah stood, waiting to be judged. If she did not survive, then at least she would die in the very place where Benjamin Irwin had witnessed the True God reach down and touch the earth. But she would not die. She would not fail. She would be at Attar's side when the Rain came and the world was rebuilt in the firmament. The Eagle stepped forward and held out the chalice of Lotan to Tulah.

"Assemble yourselves, and come; gather yourselves on every side to my sacrifice that I do sacrifice for you, that ye may eat flesh and drink blood."

The Eagle placed the cup in Tulah's hands and she looked down at the dark, curdling liquid. All four Angels were singing around her and Tulah raised the Lotan to her lips. She opened her mouth and poured the poison down her throat. Immediately, Tulah had the sense that she had swallowed fire. She could not see and could not hear, though she was vaguely aware that the cup had been taken from her hands. It felt as if her body was being torn apart in cauterized strips from the inside out, but Tulah controlled herself. She clenched her fists and thought of the Luminous Light. She would not move and she would not utter a sound. And then, almost as soon as it had come over her, the burning subsided and Tulah was left only with a bitter, acrid aftertaste in her mouth. The Mithridatium had worked and, along with her absolute faith, had kept her alive. Tulah's vision came back to her, though it was blurry, as tears streamed from her single eye. She choked out the response.

"*Ye shall eat the flesh of the mighty, and drink the blood of the princes of the earth.*"

The Angels bowed their heads; the trial was almost over for her. The last Angel, the Lion, took his place in front of Tulah. She loosened her robe, baring the top part of her chest, and then dropped her hands to her sides. The Lion held up the dagger for the other Angels to see and they began to sing once more. Tulah closed her eye. She was aware of the slashes, each blooming through her flesh about an inch below her collar bone, ripping through the scars from years past, but she felt them as if from a distance. She opened her eye when she felt the fingertips of the Angels touching her, pressing their fingers into the blood. She watched as they each bent and marked the star at her feet. The Angel of Man then touched Tulah's throat with two fingers, anointing her with her own blood. The thunder of its voice washed over her.

"*Thou shalt be for fuel to the fire; thy blood shall be in the midst of the land; thou shalt be no more remembered.*"

The Angels all bowed low to her and then stepped back so that she could leave the inner circle. Underneath the mask, Tulah's face was wet again, but this time for another reason. She had endured The Night Recompense. Her soul had been weighed and was not found wanting.

SHELIA STABBED HER cigarette out in the overflowing ashtray. The Rabbit was cramped, and smelled like day-old shrimp, but she thought it was safer to wait in the car where she'd have a better chance at getting away if she had to. The road just beyond the Quincy's parking lot was dark, with only an occasional car weaving past, some drunk on his way home from the bar, but otherwise the night was quiet. Too quiet. And Shelia still wasn't convinced that the best plan wouldn't have been just to run. She fit another Capri to her lips, but was suddenly blinded by oncoming headlights. Shelia squinted and flicked her lighter, waiting to see who was going to get out the vehicle and what they were going to do to her.

She watched the door of the car open and a woman get out. Shelia sighed in relief. It was Ramey. Shelia kicked open her own door and stood up as Ramey walked toward her. She waited anxiously for the Cannon boys to get out the car as well. Ramey stopped about five feet in front of her, but with all the shadows Shelia couldn't see the expression on her face. Her heart began to race again. Maybe Judah and Benji were still in the car, just waiting for Ramey to lure her closer so they could shoot her. Grab her and take her to God knew where, to do God knew what to her. Or maybe they had just sent Ramey to kill her. Shelia quickly eyed Ramey up and down. No purse. Her hands were empty at her side. Did she have a gun stuck somewhere in her jeans?

Shelia tapped her foot and took a last drag on her cigarette before pitching it across the pavement. She might as well get it over with. Shelia took a few steps toward Ramey and nodded warily to her as she looked around, keeping her eye on the car in front of her.

"Where's Judah?"

Ramey came closer and now Shelia could see that there was a strange look on her face. Cold. Distant. Resolute. Ramey shook her head slowly and then locked her eyes on Shelia's.

"He's not coming. Looks like all you've got is me."

CHAPTER 16

JUDAH PRESSED THE cigarette between his lips, sighted down the length of the rifle, took aim and fired. He dropped the gun at his side and squinted through the early morning light. He had missed his target by a mile.

"You sure you know how to use that thing?"

Judah could hear Benji behind him, clambering awkwardly down the bank and over the stagnant ditch. Judah had heard the Mustang pull up beside his truck, but was in no mood to talk to his brother. He kept his eyes on the length of field sprawling out before him, a rectangle of land choked with dogfennel and pokeweed. Once, many years ago, his mother, Rebecca, had grown vegetables in the field across the road from Sherwood's now vacant house. Field peas and okra. Tomatoes and hot peppers. Judah listened to Benji, stumbling and sliding along on his single crutch, but refused to turn around. Benji finally came up to stand beside Judah at the stubbly edge of the field. He was panting heavily.

"I can show you how, if you like. There's this thing you gotta do. It's called aiming."

Judah let a curl of smoke seep out of the corner of his mouth while he glared at his brother.

"Benji, you couldn't hit water if you fell out of a boat."

Judah raised the .22 again, taking aim at the Folgers can propped up on the split rail fence, but then lowered the rifle. He stared at it in his hands for a moment before tossing the gun into the soft, sandy dirt. Judah picked up the warm tall boy of High Life next to his boot and guzzled.

"Screw it."

Judah crushed the beer can in his hand and flung it up in a high arc across the overgrown field. He cut his eyes to Benji, who was watching the can sail through the air.

"Well, at least you quit drinking whiskey."

Judah shrugged.

"Finished what we had in the house. Liquor store don't open 'til nine, so I'm stuck with the Champagne of Beers. I think that might have been the last of the six-pack. You want to run up to the truck and check, though, be my guest."

Judah took a final drag on his cigarette and then flicked it down at his feet. He could feel Benji clocking his every move.

"Don't you think you should try sobering up, maybe? With it being daylight and all?"

Judah lit another cigarette. His mouth was immediately filled with the stale taste of ash. He couldn't remember how many cigarettes he'd smoked. Or how many packs. The cigarettes only tasted like dust now, but he kept on smoking them. Judah shook his head.

"No. No, I don't think that at all."

"Or how about sleep? You tried sleeping yet?"

Judah raised his head and stared up at the pewter sky. The sun was still low enough that it hadn't yet touched the field, but already the temperature was climbing. There was a film of tangy sweat on the back of Judah's neck, but he thought it was more from the alcohol than the heat.

"No. What's the point?"

Benji planted his crutch firmly in the dirt so that he was no longer swaying.

His mangled face appeared even more gruesome when he frowned.

"You're just gonna spend the day like this?"

"Jesus Christ, Benji."

Judah whirled on him, his fist raised, and met his brother's eyes. They were swept clear of the usual narcotic glaze. Judah didn't miss the irony. He unclenched his hand and let it dangle at his side.

"She left. You know that, right?"

Benji nodded cautiously.

"I saw her drive away last night. I saw her carrying a bag out to her car before that. She wasn't saying much."

Judah studied the end of his cigarette.

"Yeah, well, they never do."

Benji frowned again.

"You're comparing Ramey to any of the other girls who've run out on you?"

Judah stuck the cigarette in the corner of his mouth and spoke around it.

"I don't know. I don't know anything. She had every right to leave. In fact, it was probably the smart thing to do. What the hell do I have for her? What the hell have I given her but trouble and grief?"

"Come on. You made her happy."

Judah shook his head and gazed back out over the field. At the far end, the webs of dew were being to sparkle in the creeping sunlight.

"No. I don't think so."

Benji bobbed his head.

"You did. Sometimes these things just turn sour. You and Ramey, you were always like this. Even when you were kids. Fighting for each other one moment, against each other the next. Half the time, the rest of us couldn't tell if you loved or hated each other."

"There a difference?"

"And just think about it, even if she doesn't come back. Even if you never lay eyes on her again, just think about what you two had. How many people can say they've had someone like Ramey in their lives?"

A flush of panic raced through Judah, but he tried not to let it show on his face. He anxiously glanced over at Benji, but his brother was still staring thoughtfully at the field. Judah tried to keep the tremor out his voice.

"You think she's not coming back? Ever?"

"I don't know, Judah. I didn't hear what was said between you two. Did it sound final?"

Judah flung his cigarette to the dirt and ground it out with the toe of his boot.

"Maybe."

Benji heaved himself up higher on the crutch.

"I can't say, Judah. From what I know of Ramey, though, she don't say shit lightly. She doesn't threaten to do things she don't mean, and she doesn't do things if she's not convinced of what she's doing. Ramey just ain't seem like the type of woman who makes a show of leaving just so you'll get your act together and come after her with your tail between your legs. I've had about a million of those girls. And they're as far from Ramey as black is from white."

Judah clenched his jaw, trying to keep it together.

"So you think she's gone for good."

"I think you'd better start thinking that way, at least. And get over your rolling around in self-pity. Get your mind back in the game."

Judah squatted down and picked up the rifle. He brushed off the fine layer of dirt he'd accidentally kicked over the stock.

"What game? It's like none of that matters anymore."

He ran his fingers over the polished wood. Benji spat in the dirt next to the gun and Judah jerked his head up, catching the reprehension in his brother's eyes.

"Oh really? You know that Lesser's funeral was yesterday? Did you know that?"

Judah wrenched himself up to standing. He hefted the gun in his hand a few times.

"I did."

"Well, he saw what this family could be. The potential. The money it could make. The pride it already carried and how much more was ahead of it. Lesser believed in that. He wanted more than anything to be a part of that. He didn't want to just be some dumb dropout, selling slushies at the gas station for the rest of his life. He wanted to be part of something bigger."

"Not sure he got what he wanted."

Benji grabbed Judah's arm.

"When this cast comes off, which is in a few weeks by the way, and I've got my legs underneath me, I'm gonna belt you one in the teeth. When you least expect it. Because somebody's gotta knock some goddamn sense into you."

Judah looked down passively at Benji's hand, still gripping his arm.

"Ramey was pretty good at that."

Benji let go of Judah and shoved him in disgust.

"Well, she's not here no more. But I am. Gary is. Alvin is. Other people who rely on you. Other people who need you with a clear head, making smart decisions to get the Cannons back on track. Back to where they need to be."

"It's no use going back, Benji."

Benji threw his hand up.

"Well, then forward! Hell, sideways. As long as there's some kinda momentum. When you came back from Daytona, I could see it in your eyes. You were hungry. You wanted something more than just sticking to the line you've been walking these past few months. Maybe you were holding back for Ramey, maybe for something else, but it's time you put an end to all that. You've been feeding the fire of the Cannons bit by bit and it's gotten you nowhere. It's time to pour on the gasoline, brother. It's time to bring those flames to the sky."

Judah looked at Benji as if he'd never seen him before. The sun had finally crested the edge of the tree line and his brother was now fully in its path. Benji's face was flushed and his eyes were glinting as he stood up straight, barely using the crutch at all, and jabbed his fist into his palm. Judah turned away from him. His head was beginning to pound as his body slipped from drunk to hungover, and he didn't want to hear it. Enough with the Cannons. Forget the Cannons. All he wanted was Ramey. And she had left him. A pair of doves suddenly flushed out from the undergrowth and streaked across the field, their wings clapping as they rose up into the air. Judah brought the rifle to his shoulder and fired.

He missed. And he was glad. Judah lifted his head and watched the birds until they disappeared from view.

SISTER TULAH WAS not impressed. The Day Recompense had brought her nothing. Reverend Simpson had even gone so far as to suggest that Tulah not be expected to contribute to any of the proposed business deals shuttling across the Table all morning. In front of the entire Order, the Honorable Reverend had stuck out his droopy pink lip and intimated that pity should be taken upon Tulah and her enterprises, due to the recent decimation of her church. Pity. She could have wrung his scrawny turkey neck.

Tulah rolled up her dirty, white athletic socks and jammed them into a corner of her suitcase. The digital clock on the nightstand next to the lumpy hotel bed indicated it was only half past noon, but Tulah wasn't sticking around for the free buffet lunch. The Recompense was over. She was ready to get the hell out of Georgia.

It wasn't just her missing eye or the lurid tales of her church being consumed in flames from a biker's Molotov cocktail. In fact, she doubted those two elements had much to do at all with why she was spoken over like a child at the Table and avoided like a fat kid being picked for dodgeball when the Outer Council had broken into groups to discuss more specific, independent business interests. No, Sister Tulah knew exactly why she was being treated like a leper. It was her failure with the phosphate mine.

Needing a group to join when the Table adjourned, Sister Tulah had ended up listening in as two members from Alabama put together a juvenile plan that involved diverting donations from a non-profit ministry into an offshore shell company. Brother Robert had given Tulah a sloppy grin and made a joke about how they could always try bribing state senators if they wanted to go big time. The rest of the group, sitting at the small round table in the corner of the ballroom, had laughed, seeming to think this was the funniest thing since Jacob tricked Isaac. Brother Robert had even dared to nudge her shoulder and wink. He had winked. It was ridiculous; embezzlement was so easy she could have done it in her sleep. And Tulah certainly wouldn't have bored The Order with such an unimaginative scheme. If Brother Robert hadn't been a fellow member, she would have stabbed him in the cheek with her ballpoint pen. Instead, she had been forced to sit through the condescending jokes and sidelong glances. When the Inner Council, still seated at the large conference table at the front of the room, talking in hushed whispers to a chosen few, had finally stood and announced that the final hour had arrived and that The Recompense was officially over, Tulah had never been more relieved. Three years ago, she had sauntered from the ballroom, a check in hand, a finalized deal under her belt and gloated all the way to the buffet table. This year, she had hurried from the room, her head still held high, but her heart filled not with triumph, but with indignation. How dare they. How dare they all.

Sister Tulah crammed the tiny bottles of hotel shampoo and the sliver of papered soap into her toiletries case and zipped it shut. She flung it into her suitcase and glared around the tiny, stupid room. Tulah put her hands on her hips. She'd already packed the plastic packages of single-serving coffee and the stirring sticks from the tray beside the television. Coffee was a filthy, disgusting drink, but she was taking them out of spite. Tulah stomped over to the nightstand and yanked the drawer out. There was a thin pad of hotel stationary next to the Gideon Bible and she snatched it up and hurled it, fluttering, into her suitcase. She eyed the Bible and then took that as well, jamming it down onto the pile of dirty clothes and straining to zip the case shut. She had to brace herself, heave her torso on top of the case and then pull the zippers awkwardly from both sides. When it was finally secure, she shoved it off the edge of the bed. The other members of The Order were downstairs in the hotel restaurant, eating sticky barbecue ribs and swilling sweet tea. Maybe they were still laughing at her. Maybe they had already forgotten her. Either way, at least she wouldn't have to encounter them as she dragged her suitcase across the parking lot to her Navigator. They'd be too busy stuffing their faces with baked beans and potato salad to notice her departure. Sister Tulah kicked her suitcase in frustration. She pursed her lips and kicked it again. Then again, and was only stopped from continuing her tantrum by the sound of a sharp, precise rap on the door.

Sister Tulah stood up straight and pressed the back of her fleshy hand to her cheek to pat away the wetness. She couldn't understand why her eye was watering. Tulah smoothed down the front of her dress, her hands rippling over the puckered bandages underneath, before stepping around the suitcase. It had better not be housekeeping. She slid the deadbolt chain over and wrenched the door open.

"What?"

"Sister Tulah, I'm sorry to bother you in your room, but I wonder if I might have a moment of your time."

Kingfisher clasped his hands in front of him and tilted his head slightly as he regarded her. Tulah narrowed her eye suspiciously and didn't move to invite him in.

"Why?"

She couldn't read the expression on Kingfisher's face. He seemed to be sizing her up, but not in a cruel way. If he asked to come in, Sister Tulah would have to let him, but she made sure to block the doorway with her body and appear as hostile as possible. Dealing with Kingfisher's smug success was more than she could handle at the moment.

Kingfisher didn't take a step closer, however. He straightened his head and looked her directly in the eye.

"I have a proposition for you. One that I think you will find very, very appealing."

There was the slight hint of a smile at the corner of his lips, but she could tell that Kingfisher was serious. Her pulse began to race and she nodded stiffly, trying not to let the excitement and relief show on her face. A proposition from a member of the Inner Council. Sister Tulah opened the door wide and welcomed Kingfisher inside.

CLIVE HAD NOT thought it could get any hotter if the gates of hell themselves were flung open, but that was before he had begun his trek across the ashen wasteland of the Kentsville Town Park. His polished wingtips sank into the sandy, gray dirt, radiating the sun back up at him as surely as if it were blacktop asphalt. A dust cloud trailed in his wake as he trudged across the treeless expanse toward the lump of a man sitting at a concrete picnic table. Clive weaved his way through the cluster of playground equipment—a slide, a merry-go-round, a swing set—all made of rusting metal, blazing in the noon sun. He passed a row of tractor tires half buried in the dirt and a splintery balance beam. A blue jay landed on the beam and screamed at him before pecking at the flecks of cigarette butts on the ground. There was no sign of children. It seemed to Clive that there hadn't been any children in the park for a very long time.

Clive unbuttoned his suit jacket, wriggled out of it and slung the jacket over his shoulder as he approached Brother Felton. He glanced down at the concrete bench and thought of the backs of his legs searing. He decided to remain standing.

"You picked one hell of a place to meet up."

Clive shook his head as he scanned the playground.

"I mean, this is like Death Valley or something. Only with swings and a slide. You couldn't think of any other place?"

Felton slowly raised his head, as if just then realizing that Clive was standing next to him. There was an odd, placid look on his already dopey face. From their conversation that morning, with Brother Felton breathing heavily into the phone, his voice at a near squeak and his words rushed and cryptic, Clive had been prepared to deal with someone on the edge of hysteria. Instead, Felton appeared languid, almost peaceful, as he sat in his beige, sweat-soaked polo shirt, and gazed out at the deserted park.

"There is no one here."

Clive tugged at his tie.

"You got that right. You'd have to be crazy to bring the kids out here on a day like this."

Felton clasped his hands between his widely spread knees and nodded slowly.

"Yes. So, this is a good place to talk."

Clive was about to argue; his hotel room, with the air conditioner cranked all the way up, was a good place to talk. But he held his tongue. Felton hadn't said exactly why he wanted to meet with him, and Clive didn't want to blow it. He carefully laid his jacket on the picnic table and loosened his tie.

"All right, I'm here. And like I said before, I appreciate you calling. I was worried about not having heard from you yet. I like you, Felton, and I really, really didn't want to have to open up an investigation on you."

Felton shook his head.

"There would be nothing to investigate."

Clive put his hands in his pockets and jangled some spare change leftover from a drive-thru breakfast. He couldn't let Brother Felton know he was bluffing. He didn't necessarily want to bully him, but he couldn't let Felton get the upper hand either. Clive opened his mouth, ready to spill some bullshit about statute of limitations or something along those lines, but Felton held up a soft, pale hand to silence him.

"And there would be no need. I'd like to tell you of the illegal activities of my aunt, Sister Tulah."

Clive clamped his mouth shut and swallowed. Was Felton serious? He said the words without a hint of hesitation, without even an indication of conflict in his decision. Clive wanted to believe him, but the change of heart just didn't make sense. He cast his eyes warily at Felton.

"Really? That's certainly a change from the last time we spoke. You do some soul searching or something?"

Felton looked down at his clasped hands and smiled like a child who has a secret.

"Something like that."

Clive frowned.

"Did you decide that it wasn't worth it to be dragged down into the gutter with your aunt when we prosecute her? You're doing the smart thing, you know, looking out for yourself. That's all we can do in this world, take care of ourselves."

Felton shook his head, still with that blissful smile on his face.

"No. I'm not sure it's the smart thing. In fact, it's definitely not the smart thing. But it is the right thing."

Felton suddenly raised his head and Clive was startled to see the intensity in his eyes. The passion.

"God told me what I must do. And God is mightier than even Sister Tulah. I am only following the directive of the Lord. That is why I am here. That is why I will tell you whatever you want to know."

Clive tried to control his gloating smile. Now it made sense. These dumb-fool religious types. He should have used the God card from the beginning. Said that he saw a talking shrub burning up somewhere, telling him what Brother Felton needed to do. Clive reached for his jacket and took out his notebook and pen.

"Well, I'm not going to argue with God. Let's get started."

Felton suddenly looked concerned.

"You want to do it here?"

Clive clicked his pen a few times and scribbled on the corner of the notebook to get the ink flowing.

"No, no, of course not. I just want to confirm a few things with you first. Then we'll drive back to my hotel room, so I can type up the agreement and get an official statement of cooperation from you. It's just paperwork, a formality really. We'll do the initial interview there as well. In the AC."

Clive grinned.

"And then, depending on what you can give me, we'll go from there. It's going to be a process. But don't worry, we'll protect you from your aunt."

Clive wasn't sure Felton could be protected at all, but he'd deal with that concern later. Once the affidavit was signed and sent. Once he got word from the special agent in charge that the case was a go. Clive clicked his pen again.

"So, just a few quick things. Has Sister Tulah spent the last few years trying to bring a phosphate mine to Bradford County?"

Felton tilted his head, confused about the question, but then nodded.

"Yes."

Clive checked off the first bullet point on his list.

"And did Sister Tulah use coercion, intimidation, threats or bribery to obtain the land for the phosphate mine?"

"Yes."

"Did she use the same methods to get the mine approved in Bradford County?"

Felton nodded again.

"Yes."

With each affirmation, Clive could feel the anticipation building up inside of him. It was going to happen. The case was really going to happen. He flipped the notebook over to the next page.

"And did Sister Tulah employ these means in other instances? To persuade lawmakers on other issues or to gain favors illegally?"

Felton hesitated, but then Clive realized that he was just working his way through the language. Felton slowly nodded again.

"I think so, yes."

"Okay, and just one more. Did Sister Tulah bribe, or attempt to bribe, state senators into voting for an approval of environmental permits for the phosphate mine coming to Bradford County?"

"Yes. Definitely."

Clive made one last check on the paper and then flipped the notebook closed. He slapped it against his palm.

"And you can give us detailed information, correct? Names? Dates? Transaction amounts? Particularly with regards to the bribery of state senators?"

"Yes. Josten and Gripes. Kirkland. I think there was another. I won't be able to tell you everything. My aunt is very secretive and very cautious. But I've been listening from the shadows for a long time. I don't think she believes I know anything."

Clive reached for his jacket. He shoved the notebook and pen back into the inside pocket before draping the jacket over his arm. He nodded enthusiastically.

"Good. That's really good. You're going to be essential to this case, Felton. All right, now we head back to the hotel so you can sign those papers."

Felton stood up.

"Now?"

"Yes, now. We need to get the ball rolling on this."

"I can't."

Clive was already a few steps ahead. He slowly turned back to Felton. The idiot had better not be getting cold feet. He expected to see apprehension, maybe dread, in the man's eyes, but they were clear and untroubled. Clive frowned.

"What do you mean, you can't?"

Felton shrugged.

"I can't right now. Brother Lester and Brother Charles are on their way over to the church. We're working on the roof today. I have to be there."

"You're kidding, right? You can't just tell them that you're busy this afternoon?"

"Doing what?"

Clive dabbed at the sweat beading on his forehead. It was frustrating, but he realized that Felton was right. What else would he be doing? Making paper airplanes out of Bible pages? Brother Felton didn't live in a world of business meetings or coffee dates or things popping up out of nowhere. Clive understood how the town worked now. If Felton acted in any way suspicious, someone would report it back to Tulah. Clive groaned.

"All right. Good point. Can you meet tonight?"

"We'll be working into the late hours, I'm sure."

"Tomorrow?"

Lopez was going to be irritated that he couldn't send her the statement today, but she'd just have to deal with it. Plus, Clive had initial confirmation from Felton. That had to count for something. Brother Felton spoke slowly.

"Tomorrow. You know where the Hardee's is? The one across from the Dollar Tree?"

Clive nodded. How could he not? It was one of only two fast food joints in the whole town.

"Sure, I know it."

"I like the curly fries. I can meet you there in the evening. Around six. If you go in the back door by the bathrooms, maybe nobody will notice you. Bring your papers and whatever you need me to sign."

It wasn't ideal, but Clive figured it would work. Brother Felton had better be a goldmine of information for all the trouble he was going to for him. But then Clive checked himself. Without Felton, there was no case. He would have to keep reminding himself of that.

"Okay. I'll see you then."

Felton raised his hand like a man about to take an oath.

"See you then."

CHAPTER 17

THROUGH THE GLASS, Ramey watched the little blonde girl cruise a Hot Wheels car through an obstacle course of salt shakers, ketchup bottles and syrup pitchers. The girl flew the car over a pyramid of stacked creamers, her mouth opening and closing as she undoubtedly made whooshing and whirring noises. Stella. She had just turned six in July. Judah had casually, and then anxiously, mentioned this to Ramey when he had been trying to decide if he should send the girl a birthday present. They had been pushing a cart through the Wal-Mart up in Starke and Judah had vacillated back and forth as he absently picked up plastic water guns and Barbie dolls, trying to make up his mind. He was still pretty sure that Stella wasn't his. But maybe she'd like something from him anyway. Or maybe Cassie would just chuck the present before the kid could even unwrap it. He had picked up a stuffed alligator and squeezed it in both hands like he was going to strangle it. Judah had asked Ramey what she had liked when she was six. Had she liked stuffed animals? Ramey had patiently assented that she had. Judah had liked toy cars, of course. Did little girls play with cars? Ramey had smiled and nodded. Yes, they did. Yes, she had. Judah had finally said to forget it; he wasn't going to send anything. It would be too confusing for the damn kid, anyway.

Ramey leaned back against the driver's seat of the Cutlass and peered through the windshield. She was parked directly across the road from Gunner's Diner with a clear view of the restaurant. The front of the diner was all glass windows, and in addition to Stella playing with her cars in the back booth, Ramey could see Cassie behind the counter in a greasy, white apron with a spatula in her hand. She was waving it over her head and laughing with the two men sitting at the counter. Ramey watched Cassie and tried to take the measure of her: this woman who had stolen Judah away from Silas years before. Who had lived with him, raised a kid with him, cheated on him, kicked him out, taken him back. Cassie had barely written to Judah when he was in prison. It was hard to imagine how different things had once been. Judah had once played the role of a family man, cooking hot dogs on the grill, watching Care Bears on the living room floor with a two-year-old, far away from the clutches of Sherwood Cannon. And Ramey had once been a new graduate from nursing school, engaged, with a child growing inside of her. A girl. Her girl. Who would never be born. Who had never even had a chance.

Ramey shook her head and lit a cigarette. There was no point in dwelling on the past. Not two years ago. Not two days ago. The hardest thing Ramey had ever done was wake up in that hospital bed after the car accident and still want to live. Lying to Judah, telling him that she was leaving him, watching his face in the rearview mirror as she drove away, might have been the second. There had been no other way, though. She knew Judah wasn't going to change his mind about believing Shelia and she also knew that he would stop her if she said she was going on her own. Ramey and Judah hadn't spent a full night apart since he had walked away free from the state prison. Convincing Judah that they were breaking up had seemed the only way she could disappear for a few days with no questions asked. And she had known that Judah would either be too angry or too heartsick to go after her.

But she kept second guessing herself. It was a dangerous ruse, and that was without even taking Weaver into consideration. If all went well, if everything was charmed and went perfectly and she and Shelia did manage to kill Weaver and make it back to Silas alive and breathing, there was still no telling how Judah would react when he found out what she had done. Would he forgive her? Maybe in their time apart he would realize that it was easier without her. Maybe he would like feel like he could no longer trust her. Maybe he wouldn't even want her back. Ramey rested her elbow on the lip of the open window and ran her hand over her face and then through her hair. It was a risk. A gamble. But if she could stop Weaver from going after Judah, then, of course, it would be worth it to lose him. It would be worth her own life. It would be worth it all.

Ramey's cellphone rang just as she saw the vehicle pull in, and she knew what Shelia was going to say. She flicked her cigarette out the window and answered the phone.

"I see it."

Shelia, sitting in her Rabbit parked at the gas station on the corner, was breathless. Ramey could hear the alarm in her voice.

"The Escalade. The silver one that just pulled in."

"Yep. Just hold on, Shelia, let's see if it's him."

No one was getting out of the SUV parked at the end of the diner's side lot. Ramey's eyes darted back to the restaurant windows. Stella was tracing her Hot Wheels car along the window. Cassie was pouring coffee for the man at the counter wearing a red baseball cap. The man next to him had opened up a newspaper. An older woman, with a paperback in one hand and a fork in the other, occupied the booth closest to the door. Ramey looked back to the Escalade. There was still no movement. She glanced over to the gas station and could see Shelia in her car, leaning over the steering wheel as she watched the diner intently. Ramey shook her head.

"Maybe it's not him. Or if it is him, maybe there's too many people around. And it's only the afternoon. Maybe he's going to wait 'til tonight."

Shelia didn't respond, but Ramey could hear her breathing heavily into the phone. Ramey turned back to the SUV. The back passenger door slowly opened and Shelia's voice rose a notch closer to hysteria.

"There! That's him. That's Weaver."

Ramey gave the man a hard look. He was wearing dark jeans and a bomber jacket, despite the unforgiving heat. He had shiny black hair hanging straight down to his shoulders, but it was when he turned, and his hair swung away so that Ramey could see his face, that she understood. It was craggy, pockmarked, with a thick, jagged scar cutting down his cheek, but most of all, his face looked cruel. Dead. As if Judgment had already come upon Weaver and he knew he was marked for hell. He looked like a man with absolutely nothing to lose and only pain to give. Ramey now knew why Shelia was so terrified.

"It looks like he's going in alone. Ramey, can you see a gun?"

Ramey narrowed her eyes against the glare ricocheting off the windows, cars and pavement, but it was hard to tell.

"He's not carrying anything in his hands. But he's probably got a piece somewhere."

"Well, yeah."

Ramey watched Weaver closely as he stepped onto the sidewalk and opened the glass front door. What was he doing? Was he going to just walk in the restaurant and murder Cassie and Stella in broad daylight? Just like that?

"Shelia, go. You need to go now."

Ramey looked over to the Rabbit. Shelia was still sitting behind the wheel. Their eyes met and Shelia shook her head.

"I don't know, Ramey. I don't know if I can do this."

Ramey was afraid she was going to hear gunshots any second.

"Yes, you can. You can and you will. This was your idea. You found out where Cassie worked. You said we should come here and wait. Well, we did. And we're here. And he's here. You were right. So go."

Shelia didn't move.

"Yeah, but the rest of the plan. That was your idea, that was…"

Ramey didn't have time for it. She was worried that Cassie and Stella didn't have time for it.

"Shelia, so help me God, get your narrow ass out of that car and into the diner or I'm gonna come over there and shoot you. I will shoot you, I swear it, and save Weaver the trouble. Do you understand?"

Shelia hung up. Ramey threw the phone down and reached for the door handle, but then she saw Shelia slowly getting out of the Rabbit. She pulled at the hem of her fringed denim skirt as she jaywalked across the road, stopping traffic in her high-heeled sandals. She was headed for the diner. Ramey watched her cross the side street and enter the restaurant. Weaver had sat down on a stool at the counter, though Ramey couldn't tell what he was doing. Shelia was standing just inside the doorway, adjusting her red suede halter top. As soon as Shelia flashed her smile, Ramey reached for her purse. And the .9mm inside it.

SISTER TULAH CLASPED her hands on the paper-strewn desk in front of her and wrinkled her brow. Sometimes it was hard, even for her, to tell the Elders apart. She thought the man standing in front of her desk was Menahem, but he could just as easily have been Zechariah. The Elder hanging back in the doorway of the office, though, was most certainly Elah, the youngest of the four men. His crooked harelip scar gave him away. She glanced at him briefly, but then ignored him, addressing only the hunched old man before her.

"Tell me."

The man's wrinkled cheeks stretched as the puckered hole that was his mouth opened and closed. When he spoke, the rest of his body, including his head, remained completely immobile.

"*Give me now wisdom and knowledge, that I may go out and come in before this people: for who can judge this thy people, that is so great?*"

Tulah almost groaned. She was definitely talking to Menahem. All of the Elders communicated exclusively through Bible verses, but some were more expansive than others. If allowed, Menahem would probably recite the entire Book of Ecclesiastes if she asked him whether or not he thought it was going to rain. Though she had gotten back to Kentsville the night before, Sister Tulah was still tired from The Recompense. She had slept most of the morning and hadn't gotten a chance to attend to business until the afternoon. She hadn't even spoken to Felton yet. In driving up to the furniture store, she had only passed by the church and caught a glimpse of her nephew, sweeping the front walkway.

A malicious grin spread across Sister Tulah's face.

"Felton. Start with Brother Felton. Just how disastrous was his attempt at sermonizing Sunday evening?"

There was no expression on the Elder's face and no emotion in his voice.

"*How is Sheshach taken. And how is the praise of the whole earth surprised. How is Babylon become an astonishment among the nations.*"

Sister Tulah pressed her thin lips together tightly. That was certainly not good. The last thing she needed was for Felton to astonish the congregation with the prowess of his preaching. She would have to get a full account later. If Brother Felton hadn't managed to make a fool of himself, she would have to find another way to humiliate him. Tulah brushed Felton from her mind and turned to the more pressing issue at hand.

"And what about our little ATF friend? Is that noisome fly still buzzing around?"

"*That which the palmerworm hath left hath the locust eaten; and that which the locust hath left hath the cankerworm eaten; and that which the cankerworm hath left hath the caterpillar eaten.*"

It took her a moment to figure out the meaning behind that one. She adjusted her eyepatch and pursed her lips.

"So, he's still around. Is he doing anything besides asking questions he shouldn't and attempting to dig up information that is best left buried?"

"*When thou art departed from me to day, then thou shalt find two men by Rachel's sepulcher; and they will say unto thee, The asses which thou wentest to*" *seek are found."*

Sister Tulah leaned forward on her elbows. She knew that the agent had been asking the locals about her and she knew also that he had spent several days at the library, most likely researching her affairs. But this? Actually meeting with someone? Tulah was livid. No one in the town would dare willingly meet with an ATF agent who was looking into her.

"Who? Who was the other man? Who's talking to the agent?"

"He shall neither have son nor nephew among his people, nor any remaining in his dwellings."

The chair beneath her creaked as Sister Tulah fell back into it, stunned. Felton. Could he honestly be talking to the special agent? Her mind raced back to the last imbecilic move her moronic nephew had made without her knowledge, when he had enlisted Sherwood Cannon to rob the Scorpions. His motive had been to triple Tulah's money and she had believed him. There had been no other reason for him to attempt such a risky and foolhardy venture. Tulah shook her head. Brother Felton had gotten too big for his britches lately, but he would never willingly betray her. There had to be an explanation. Perhaps Felton had gotten it into his softshell brain that he could somehow trick the ATF agent. Pull one over on him. Sister Tulah banged her hand down on the desk and crumpled a paper up in her fist. Whatever his reason, it was one more headache she'd have to deal with. But after she took care of the ATF agent. Getting rid of Special Agent Grant was the number one priority. She looked up into the reflective lenses of the Elder's dark glasses.

"Don't go near Felton. I'll deal with him accordingly. But I think it's about time we rid Kentsville of a certain annoying pest, don't you?"

The Elder bowed his head in assent. Sister Tulah heaved herself to standing and braced herself against the edge of the desk. She was tired. If she ever, ever got all of her business taken care of, she needed to take a break. Tulah leveled her gaze at the Elder and spoke.

"And number thee an army, horse for horse, and chariot for chariot: and we

will fight against them in the plain, and surely we shall be stronger than they."

The Elder bowed his head deeply.

"And he hearkened unto their voice, and did so."

Sister Tulah's mouth stretched into a wide, grotesque grin as she waved the Elder away.

"Good. Now go and make it happen."

SHELIA DIDN'T GIVE herself time to think twice. She was vaguely aware that the two men at the far end of the counter had raised their heads at the sound of the bell on the door tinkling, but she didn't look in their direction. Nor did she glance at Cassie, standing behind the counter, flipping eggs on the flat top grill. The only person Shelia had eyes for was Weaver, and he hadn't bothered to look up. Shelia tugged at her skirt and pushed out her chest before sitting down on the empty vinyl stool next to his. She leaned her elbow on the filmy counter and ran her fingers quickly through her hair. Her heart leapt up into her throat, threatening to choke her, as Weaver slowly turned to face her. His voice was low and guttural.

"You decide to save me the trouble of hunting you down?"

Shelia had spent most of her life charming men, and at this point, instead of allowing herself to consider what she was actually doing, she let instinct take over. Shelia popped her eyes wider and smiled, her lips curling upward in a sultry promise.

"You wouldn't actually hurt me, would you?"

Weaver's expression didn't change.

"You have no idea what I'm going to do to you."

Shelia's eyes flitted away to the counter and then back up at Weaver. She kept that same smile on her lips.

"Well, what if I offered you something better?"

"Better than watching the light fade from your eyes?"

Shelia kept up the one-sided game. Her only hope was that Weaver really did think she was as dumb as she looked.

"Could be better. I know of a lot of fellas who think it's a pretty good time."

Weaver laughed loudly and brought his palm crashing down on the counter, rattling the silverware setups. Cassie turned with a plate in one hand and gave him a reproachful look before setting the eggs and bacon down in front of the man wearing a baseball cap. Shelia watched a ripple of determination pass over Weaver's face and knew that she had only seconds to snap his attention back to her. She needed to make the promise of her death more appealing than Cassie's. Shelia laid her fingers lightly on Weaver's gaunt, hairy wrist.

"How about I make you a deal, sugar? How about we go on back to the john and I make you feel like you've never felt before?"

Weaver's frost blue eyes darted back to her.

"What the hell are you talking about?"

He hadn't pushed her away, though, so maybe he was considering the possibilities. Maybe he believed she was stupid enough to think she could make a bargain for life. Here she was, offering herself up, Bambi to be slaughtered, and she'd even let him knock her off somewhere where it wouldn't make too much of a mess. Weaver could kill her quietly and then come back out and figure out how to take out the mom and the kid. Shelia raked her nails lightly over the back of his hand. Come on, come on. He had to go for it.

"You know what I'm talking about."

Shelia lowered her eyes flirtatiously and started to get up from the stool. Weaver suddenly had her wrist gripped in his hand and it was all Shelia could do not to gasp. He jerked her closer to him.

"All right, sweetheart. Let's see what you've got."

He let go of her bruised wrist and stood up. Shelia quickly glanced around the diner; no one was giving them a questioning look. If anything, they probably thought she was just another lot lizard making a quick buck. Weaver was ahead of her and Shelia noticed with a wry smile that he was favoring one leg. Just beyond the cash register was a short hallway leading back to the kitchen and single bathroom and Weaver disappeared around the corner of it. Shelia brushed her hand against the side of her skirt, feeling for the tiny penknife she had jammed into the narrow denim pocket. It was useless, but reassuring. She came around the corner, trying to calculate how much time she had, how much longer she would be able to keep it going.

Weaver had her by the throat before she could even work it out. In one rapid movement he had her up against the wall of the dim hallway, one hand over her mouth, the other squeezing her windpipe. She was out of time. Weaver brought his face close to hers and Shelia stared up into the beast behind his eyes and was no longer afraid. Ever since she was sixteen years old, Shelia had known that she would die this way, at the hands of a man who was looking down at her with hatred or disgust, at a man who thought he had power over her and wanted her to know it. But she did not know it, did not believe it, and never would. Even in her last moment of breath, Shelia knew that she held all the cards.

RAMEY HAD BEEN trying to keep her back to the diner's windows, but the moment she caught a glance of Shelia disappearing down the hallway behind Weaver, she spun and bolted through the front door. The bell jangled furiously, but Ramey didn't bother to silence it. She went straight to the counter and leaned over, waving frantically at Cassie to come to her. Cassie warily set down the coffee pot in her hand and approached Ramey, glancing back and shrugging to the men at the other end of the counter.

"Can I help you?"

Ramey grabbed Cassie's shoulder and pulled the woman toward her so she could whisper loudly in her ear.

"Get your kid and get the hell out of here. Now."

Cassie was struggling against her.

"What the…"

"Now!"

Ramey shoved her back and yanked the gun out of the back of her jeans. Everyone around her froze at the sight, except for the little girl, standing in the center of the diner, with a bright green stuffed alligator hitched up under her arm. Stella didn't freeze. Stella screamed at the top of her six-year-old lungs and Ramey lurched into motion. There was no chance of surprise now; she just had to get to Weaver as soon as possible. Ramey careened around the corner of the hallway only to come face-to-face with Weaver and the barely struggling Shelia in his grip. She raised the .9mm and fired.

Confusion exploded around her as the three of them grappled in the narrow confines of the hallway. Weaver already had his Beretta out, and while she had been able to get the one shot off and hit him somewhere in the shoulder, she'd been forced to duck to avoid the bullet coming for her. Ramey saw Weaver bend forward in pain as Shelia rammed her knee between his legs, and she halfway regained her balance enough to take another shot. He still had Shelia by the throat, but was able to twist away so that the second bullet skimmed past him. Before she could fire again, though, Weaver had let go of Shelia for a moment and slammed his body into hers, forcing her against the opposite wall. Ramey fired again, but the bullets only went into the ceiling as Weaver grabbed her forearm and smashed it repeatedly into the wall. The bones in her wrist and hand cracked and she couldn't hold on to the gun. It fell clattering to the floor.

Weaver grabbed by her the back of the neck and shoved her to the ground, slamming her face into the floor. He kicked her once in the stomach and then brought the Beretta around to aim. Ramey was blinking blood and grit out of her eyes, but even through the chaos she saw the gun coming toward her. She tried to scramble to her feet, but then the Beretta was on the ground next to her and Weaver was howling in pain. Ramey looked up to see Weaver clutching at the side of his head and Shelia spitting out a bloody chunk of flesh. Weaver turned away from Ramey and punched Shelia squarely in the face. Ramey heard the knock of her head against the wall and then Weaver was limping past her. Ramey tried to grab for his legs, but was having trouble seeing straight and her fingers only grazed fabric. She heard the swinging of the kitchen door at the end of the hallway and focused on the sound. Ramey pushed herself to her feet and stumbled after him.

There was still blood in her eyes, but by the time she made it through the door, her vision was partially coming back. Enough for her to duck the flying skillet meant for her head, anyway. She slipped on the wet, greasy floor, but launched herself at Weaver, standing in front of an industrial refrigerator in the back of the kitchen, his face and neck splattered with blood from the ragged remains of his ear. He reached for another pan and Ramey dodged this one too, but tripped on one of the rubber floor mats. A shockwave of pain snapped through her wrist when she caught herself against the edge of the stainless steel countertop. A rack of baking sheets clattered to her feet as she braced herself up with her elbow and kept after Weaver. She didn't have a gun. He didn't have a gun. He'd been shot in the shoulder. She'd been kicked in the ribs. Her wrist was fractured. His ear was dripping blood. She kept going toward him, her mind and body out of synch, the desire to stop him, to end him, driving her muscles forward. She was led by her rage, by her instincts, by her loyalty, by her fierce and near-feral love.

Weaver, however, was led by the wasteland inside him and his pure disregard for human life. Ramey was a fighter. Weaver was a killer. She was able to get in a few deep scratches to his face, but then her back was against the wide refrigerator door and his elbow and forearm were pressed against her throat. She kicked, she clawed, she spit, she tried to bite, but he was too heavy, there was too much of him against her, and in his free hand she saw the wide blade of a chef's knife flashing. She tried to twist away, but there was nowhere to go.

And then he was screaming. The knife fell to the ground and Weaver followed it, sliding down against Ramey's body. He seemed stunned for a moment and then Ramey saw the long prongs of a carving fork sticking into his lower back and behind him, Shelia, her mouth bloody, eyes wide.

"Ramey, come on, let's go!"

Weaver had already begun to flail around on the ground, grasping for her legs. Shelia jumped over him and grabbed Ramey by the shoulder, dragging her toward the back door. Ramey tried to resist.

"No, Shelia. He's not dead. He'll still come after—"

"We have to go, now!"

Shelia kept pulling on her and finally Ramey heard the sirens. She heard their wailing echo and the screams from the front of the diner and, finally, her own ragged, wheezing breath. Ramey stopped struggling and turned to follow at Shelia's heels as they ducked out of the back of the diner. It was over. For now.

CHAPTER 18

No one at The Ace in the Hole would drink with him. Judah had spent the last two hours alternating between trying to engage someone, anyone, in conversation and brooding silently over his Budweiser. Maybe it was this capricious behavior, or the fact that he had blown in through the door on a clear mission to get drunk, slamming his wallet and keys on the bar, scraping his stool back as loudly as he could, shouting at the new bartender, Linda, to start pouring and erase his memory forever. Maybe it was Ramey. He hadn't spoken to anyone about her leaving, but from the look of pity Linda gave him as she poured his beer, she had to know. Everyone had to know. This was Silas. There had probably been whispers of Ramey's departure in the night before the sun had risen the next day.

Judah cleared his throat and pushed his sticky, half-full beer glass away from him. Linda put down her Sudoku puzzle and came over to him, resting her meaty palms on the edge of the bar and giving him a sour look.

"What now?"

Or maybe the look hanging on Linda's fleshy jowls wasn't pity, it was worry. Linda owed the Cannons money. She was Gary's stepmother's sister, or cousin maybe, Judah wasn't exactly sure, and could set up bets like nobody's business. She also had a baffling scratch-off habit and went through reams of the cards, scraping away with her lucky quarter while sitting in her Pinto outside the 7-Eleven.

"Jack."

Linda shrugged and reached for the bottle and a glass while Judah turned to the man sitting at the other end of the bar. Whitey Jones owed the Cannons money. Linda slid the glass over to him and held up a metal scoop.

"Ice?"

Judah turned back to her sharply and put his hand over his glass protectively.

"Jesus, no. And you'd better not offer water, neither."

Linda dropped the ice scoop into the bin below with an unnecessary clang. She picked up her Sudoku book and stalked away from him. Judah tasted the whiskey, it was better, but like everything else, still tasted like ash in his mouth. He swiveled around on his barstool. Percy and Kyle Sutter, sitting together at one of the bar tables, both wearing jeans caked with dried cement, both staring vacantly at the Miller Lite bottles in their hands, owed him money. Judah let his gaze wander the room. Tom Hawkins owed him money. Tom's girlfriend, Margie, owed him money. Or her brother did, anyway. Chris Collins didn't owe him money. But he wasn't in the Cannons' good graces either. Judah sipped the whiskey and squinted toward the hunched man, sitting sullenly by the door. Judah couldn't remember what Collins had done to put him on the shit list. Ramey would have remembered. If she were sitting next to him right now, she would have whispered it in his ear. Judah shook his head and gulped the whiskey. Ramey wasn't there. She wasn't whispering to him. He turned back around and stared absently at the row of liquor bottles beneath the bar mirror.

So maybe that was it. Folks didn't want to drink with him because they were afraid of him, not because they pitied him. Judah spun his glass around on the bar, trying to make sense of this new revelation, and wondered if that was why Sherwood had steered clear of The Ace and of Limey's, the bar on the other side of town. The VFW had been Sherwood's haunt, a place where unspoken rules kept business on the other side of the door.

Judah drained the glass and held it upside down for Linda to see. She grumbled, stuck a cardboard coaster in her book to mark the puzzle she was working on and poured more whiskey.

"Should I just leave the bottle here?"

Judah shook his head. He had woken up that morning, shirtless, his jeans covered in mud and, strangely, cat hair, on the steps of his front porch. He had found his shirt underneath an azalea bush, balled up and coated with vomit that smelled like licorice jellybeans. He had been at Alvin's trailer, drinking Jager with the boys and some girl named Kristy who he felt he should have known, but he couldn't remember much more of the night. Judah wanted a bartender with her hand on the bottle. Someone who would cut him off before his lights went out. He watched Linda walk away and then smiled bitterly to himself as he raised the glass to his lips. Who was he kidding? He was Judah Cannon. The entire bar owed him something. Nobody was cutting him off against his will.

He had just started in on his third whiskey when a woman sat down at the bar only one stool over from him. Judah glanced up as she reached for a stack of cocktail napkins and began dabbing at her wet arms. She smiled when she saw Judah watching her.

"Just started raining."

Judah didn't say anything and the woman quickly looked away. He watched her order a Coors Lite from Linda and then dig around in the oversized purse she had set up on the bar next to her beer. The woman was a brunette, her hair cut short at the neck, her eyebrows plucked a little too thin, and Judah couldn't figure out if he knew her or not. Between the whiskey and the dim, neon lights surrounding them, it was hard for Judah to tell. When she found what she was looking for in her purse, a pack of menthols, Judah offered her a light. She smiled and leaned toward him, holding her cigarette out to his Bic.

"Thanks."

"Sure."

The woman dramatically blew out a plume of smoke. She was looking straight at him now and Judah could tell that she was young, maybe only twenty-two, twenty-three. Her lips were painted a dark shade and she smiled coyly at him.

"I'm Ginger."

"Really?"

Ginger raised a sharply arched eyebrow.

"Yes, really. Why?"

Even as he spoke, Judah regretted it.

"Nothing. It's just, is that your real name?"

She frowned and clicked her darkly painted nails together around her cigarette.

"Yes. My real name. Let me guess, though. You think I'm one of those types of girls."

Where was someone to kick him in the shins when he needed it? Oh. Yeah. She had left. She was gone. Judah shook his head and forced Ramey from his mind.

"No, no. I'm sorry. That was a stupid thing to say. Sometimes, I just open my mouth and I don't even know what comes out."

Ginger smiled impishly at him.

"It's fine, don't worry about it. You wouldn't be the first. Or the hundredth, for that matter. It's the curse of having a daddy who was obsessed with *Gilligan's Island*."

"No, it's not fine. At least let me buy you a drink."

She pointed with her cigarette at the full beer bottle in front of her.

"I have a drink."

Judah picked up his whiskey and slid over to the barstool next to her.

"Well, let me buy you the next one."

He held out his hand.

"I'm Judah…"

"Cannon."

She took his hand and squeezed it.

"I know who you are."

Judah let go of her hand and turned back to his drink.

"Oh. I was thinking that maybe there was one person around here who didn't."

Ginger laughed. Judah glanced down and saw that she had turned slightly and her bare knee was brushing against his jeans.

"Of course I know who you are. I work over at the Clip 'N' Curl next to Winn-Dixie. I do Cleo's hair. You know, Alvin's sister."

Judah already wanted the girl to stop talking. He didn't know Ginger, but she was determined to prove a connection to him.

"And then my cousin, well, he's not really my cousin, but close enough, Danny, he's done a few things for you, I think. I don't know what all exactly, but he said you were real nice. For a Cannon."

Judah looked closer at Ginger. Maybe only twenty-one. There was something both sweet and calculating behind her spidery lashes that unnerved Judah. He couldn't tell if she was talking to him because she genuinely liked him or because he was a Cannon and she liked the idea of him. He sat with her through another round and the less he spoke, the more Ginger must have felt the need to fill in the awkward pauses with conversation. By the time he finished his fourth whiskey, the room was spinning, he knew the names of every one of Ginger's pet rabbits, most of the names of her favorite songs, her detailed astrological chart, his chart, Benji's chart and for some reason her hand was resting high up on his thigh. Judah stood up.

"I gotta go."

He pushed his empty glass toward the sticky bar mat. Linda glanced up, but Judah quickly shook his head at her. Ginger blinked at him, confused. Her lipstick was thinning out.

"What're you talking about? I thought you wanted to come back to my place. Meet my bunnies. I said I'd show you my crystal collection."

Judah stuffed his wallet and phone down into his pocket and snatched up his keys. Had he indicated that he'd wanted to go back to Ginger's place? Possibly. His side of the conversation had been mostly grunts and nods, while his mind had been a million miles away. He turned to Ginger and saw the sting in her eyes, the way her bottom lip was turned down at one side. Damnit. Judah put his hand on her shoulder and squeezed it.

"Listen, Ginger. You're great. Really."

He let go of her and took a step back.

"But someone else owns my heart. Always will."

Ginger nodded slowly.

"Ramey."

Judah nodded back. Of course the girl knew about Ramey. He gave Ginger a last smile and turned his back on her. He pushed through the bar's front door and stumbled out into the rain. Ramey. Who owned his heart. And had taken it with her when she left. He started walking.

WHEN THE CAR behind him flashed on its high beams, slicing through the darkness, Clive knew it was all wrong. It had been wrong since the moment he had set eyes on Sister Tulah, since he had arrived in Kentsville, since he had crossed the Florida-Georgia line a little more than a week ago. And it had most definitely been wrong since night had fallen and it had become apparent to Clive that Felton wasn't going to show up. He had waited in the back booth of the Hardee's for two hours, and then spent another in the parking lot, still in the hopes that maybe Felton had only been delayed. Or was wavering. But finally, the realization had sunk in. Brother Felton was not coming. There would be no informant. He had been played.

Clive slowed, trying to see who was following him so closely, but between the glare of the bright lights and the blur of the pouring rain, he couldn't tell who was behind the wheel of the SUV on his tail. Clive gripped the wheel and turned his attention back to the dark road ahead of him. There were no houses, no street lights, only the slippery wet asphalt unrolling before him in the swath of his headlights. Clive had no idea where he was. Or where he was going.

In one last ditch attempt to find and speak to Felton, Clive had driven down to the Last Steps Church. He had slowly cruised past the church twice, but there had been no lights and no cars. The building had appeared empty and there was no sign of Brother Felton. Clive had turned around and headed back into Kentsville, his mind on his cellphone, beeping again in his pocket, yet another text message from Lopez, he was sure, wondering what the hell was going on. He had been thinking about her, and about Krenshaw, about the special agent in charge, and if he would ever see the light of day again after they sent him back down to the records room, and not concentrating on the road ahead of him. When he came upon the orange construction barrels and the detour sign now blocking the main road back into town, he had simply turned and followed the arrows onto a road that veered off to the left.

The vehicle behind him nudged his bumper and Clive sped up. The SUV matched his speed and kept close to him. Clive tried to swallow his panic and pressed down harder on the gas. It could be teenagers, playing a prank. It could be a drunk asshole. It could be anyone. Clive knew it wasn't just anyone. He kept increasing his speed, trying to keep the Charger steady on the slick pavement, but then, out of nowhere, he was blinded by dazzling lights. Another SUV was barreling toward him, and in the few remaining seconds, Clive understood what was about to happen. The SUV behind him swerved to his left and boxed him in, and the vehicle in front of him kept coming. Even if he slammed on his brakes right then, he'd be smashed head on. Clive couldn't tell what was to the right of him, but he didn't have time to think. It could have been a tree, or a telephone pole, but it didn't matter. He wrenched the wheel over, hard to the right, and skidded off the road just as the oncoming SUV went roaring past him.

He flipped only once and was surprised to open his eyes and see the hood of his car submerged in a drainage pond. The headlights were still on, glowing eerily beneath the water. Clive unbuckled his seatbelt, but couldn't shove the door open, so he crawled through the window and landed face-first in two feet of water. The sludge beneath him sucked at his knees and elbows, but he pushed himself up and stumbled out of the weeds and muck. His mouth was full of blood, and he hacked and spit. The coughing made the sharp pain in his head worse and he shook it, trying to clear away the disorientation. He began to clamber up the steep bank toward the road, his feet sliding back with every step, but when the bright lights of crisscrossing headlights flashed on above him, Clive stopped. He tried to find his balance as he looked up at the silhouettes of the four men above him.

Clive couldn't see their faces, couldn't see anything but their shadows against the headlights, but he knew who they had to be. Clive immediately reached for his holster, but it was empty and slick with grime. The Glock had probably fallen into the muddy water, but he had no time to turn back and try to find it. At first, Clive thought one of the men was coming down the bank to him and he glanced around frantically for a stick or a rock, anything to defend himself with, but the figure didn't move past the shoulder of the road. He only stared down at Clive and then tilted his head and spoke.

"And though they hide themselves, I will search and take them out thence; and though they be hid from my sight at the bottom of the sea, thence will I command the serpent, and he shall bite them: thence will I command the sword, and it shall slay them."

Clive looked up at the man and did not understand exactly what the words meant, but he knew enough. He heaved a strangling sigh of relief as the four men disappeared into the rain. It was not his time to die. Not this night. Not this moment.

JUDAH DROPPED HIS cigarette into the black water swirling beneath him. The rain had finally ebbed to a drizzle, but Judah was soaked through. It was two miles along the back roads from The Ace to the Wake Creek Bridge and Judah had gone the whole way with his head down, tramping through the snarling weeds and brush or, once he cut over to Bligh Road, simply walking down the center line of the crumbling pavement. No one used Bligh Road anymore; it began and ended with nothing and nowhere. Occasionally, fishermen threw lines off the bridge hoping to reel in a redbreast or stumpknocker, and every now and then teenagers would still rendezvous down on the banks to smoke and drink, fall in love and battle it out, but even those trysts were becoming a thing of the past. Judah hadn't seen a single car on the road and he was damn sure he was the only man standing on the bridge under the faint glow of the orange streetlight, arms crossed on the narrow metal railing, staring down into the abyss. He didn't want to jump; he wanted the creek to rise up and swallow him whole.

"Judah!"

He jerked his head up and spun around. For a fleeting second he thought of his .45, under the seat of his truck, still parked at The Ace, but he knew that voice. He couldn't see her, but he could hear her, and the ringing sound caught in his throat and pierced him somewhere back behind his lungs. His hands were shaking as he watched her step out of the mist at the end of the bridge.

"Ramey."

It wasn't a question; it wasn't an assertion. It was a feverish calling of hope. Judah couldn't move. Ramey's skin and clothes were wet and her hair was down, impossibly tangled over her shoulders. There was a hitch in her step and as she came closer, Judah could see that there was something wrapped around her right wrist. She kept walking steadily toward him, not running, not smiling, with a strange look of determination and desperation on her face. When she had almost reached him, Judah realized that what he had thought was just a dark shadow under her eye was actually a smear of blood. She walked straight into him and pressed the length of her body against his. Only then did he raise his arms to hold her.

Ramey leaned into him and Judah gasped as he tried to crush her closer. He didn't know why she had returned, but he was terrified to let her go. He remembered the blood, though, and gently pushed her away. He gripped her by the elbows and looked down into her upturned face.

"You're bleeding."

It was more than just blood, though. Even in the tenebrous light, he could see the bruising all along the left side of her face. The cut above her eye had been taped closed with thin strips of gauze, but the cut below was bare and slowly seeping blood in watery tendrils down her cheek. Ramey raised her fingers to her face and gently touched it.

"Did it open up again?"

Judah held her face gently in his hands.

"You need a doctor."

Ramey dropped her hand back to his waist.

"I need you."

He pulled her to him again with a trembling ferocity and pressed his face into her wet, matted hair. He could only whisper.

"Are you back?"

"I'm back. I was never gone. But yes, I'm back."

"I don't understand."

He released her and stepped back.

"I thought. Jesus, I thought—"

"We found him."

Judah shook his head.

"No, I don't understand. You left."

He could feel it now, rising up inside of him. The hurt, the anger, the shame.

He had driven her away; he knew this. But yet here she was, standing before him, bloody and bruised. And he was merely broken.

"Ramey, I don't understand."

Ramey swallowed. It looked as if she were biting back a night's worth of words, but her eyes softened and she dipped her head.

"Judah, I'm sorry. It was the only thing I could think of. The only way that I could get away quickly. Without questions. Without having to convince you. There wasn't any time and I knew I couldn't get you to listen. We had to act fast."

It still didn't make sense.

"We?"

Ramey wiped some of the blood off her cheek with the back of her hand.

"Shelia and I. We found Weaver."

Judah took another step back from her.

"What the hell?"

"Shelia was telling the truth. She found out where Cassie was working up in Colston, at this little diner. I saw Stella, she was there, too. And so was Weaver."

"What?"

Ramey held out her hand.

"Just listen. Weaver was there, I'm sure, to kill them. We attacked him."

"You did what?"

"Let me finish!"

Judah clamped his mouth shut, but his mind was racing. What the hell had she done? What the hell had she done because of him? For him? Ramey waited another moment and then continued, speaking slower this time.

"We attacked him. We tried to kill him, but I don't think we did. We left him on the floor of the diner's kitchen. He's banged up worse than I am, at least I got a bullet in him, and Shelia stabbed him with a fork, but he was definitely still kicking when we ran."

Judah blinked.

"She stabbed him with a fork?"

A corner of Ramey's lip curled up.

"Yes, a fork. She stabbed him like a hunk of roast beef."

"Jesus."

He reached out and put his hands on Ramey's shoulders.

"But you're okay?"

She nodded.

"I'm okay. Though, I can cross getting a boot in the stomach off my bucket list now."

She was grinning up at him, trying to make a joke, but Judah wasn't laughing. Only one thing mattered to him now: he was going to kill Weaver. He was going to destroy him.

"You think he's headed this way?"

The smile disappeared from her face.

"Yes. I think Stella and Cassie are safe for now, I warned them as best I could, but he's gotta still be coming for us. Maybe tonight, maybe tomorrow. He's in bad shape, but that's not gonna stop him. I saw his eyes, Judah. He's not going to stop until his body matches the state of his soul. He will hunt us all down until he's in the ground himself."

Judah nodded.

"Okay then."

A look of relief passed over Ramey's face.

"Okay then."

Judah frowned.

"Ramey, what you did, all of it, was crazy and reckless and stupid and brave as hell. And I know it's because of me."

Ramey tilted her head.

"Don't give yourself all the credit."

"No, that's not what I mean. I just mean, I know what you risked. With us. With Weaver. I'm sorry. And I'm grateful."

He pulled her to him one final time. The rain was coming down harder again, and he blinked the water out of his eyes as he dug his fingers into her back.

"I will make this right, Ramey. I will make this right. I promise."

CHAPTER 19

CLIVE CRAMMED HIS suitcase into the miniature backseat of the clown car and slammed the door shut. The candy apple red Chevy Aveo, dropped off that morning by a rental car company, was perfect. Just perfect. The exact type of failure-mobile he needed to announce his departure from Bradford County. Clive hadn't even bothered to ask the slick joker who handed him the keys if there was any other car to choose from. He knew there wasn't. Not for him, anyway.

Clive had spent most of the morning on the phone with Lopez, trying to defend himself, but it hadn't gotten him anywhere. In fact, he was pretty sure he'd only made things worse. If they could get any worse. Clive knew he would never get out of the records room now. He'd stay down in that tomb forever and grow as moldy as the carpet. Of this, Lopez had assured him. She would lock him down there and swallow the key herself. Lopez had been furious, shouting at him over the phone as she tore into a breakfast sandwich. Clive had been able to hear the wrapper crinkling between obscenities and bites. Lopez had already gone to Krenshaw and proposed the case and now she would have to go back and explain that, yet again, her agent had wasted time, money and resources, not to mention a company car. Clive had made her look like a fool and she was never going to forgive him. Never. When he had tried, nearly sputtering, to explain himself once more, to remind her of the evidence he had found—the land deals, the phosphate mine, the mismanaged crime scene—her cruel, sharp laughter had silenced him. On top of the absurdity of his delusions about a granny preacher mob boss, he was now claiming to have been threatened, and almost killed, by a posse of geezers spouting Old Testament gibberish. Lopez must have asked him at least twenty times: had he lost his goddamn mind?

Clive opened the front door of the Aveo and shook his head in disgust. It was six hours back to Atlanta and he would be driving the whole way with his knees up around his ears. At least he would be leaving the wretched, scorched earth of backwoods Florida, and that was all that mattered. Even if he was skulking away with his tail between his legs, at least he was leaving the miserable place behind. Clive hoped the whole damn state would just fall into the ocean already. He wedged himself behind the steering wheel and cranked down the window by hand. Clive was just about to pull the door shut when he saw the glittering black Lincoln Navigator parked in the empty lot across the street. Its tinted driver's side window slowly lowered and he was forced to behold the face of Sister Tulah Atwell one last time.

She was smiling. Grinning wide, sickeningly wide, and she wasn't wearing her eyepatch. The craggy divot where her eye should have been only intensified the grotesqueness of her smirk. He would never be able to forget Tulah's face. Her nauseating smile would haunt him all of his days. Its image had settled in the bottom of his stomach like a slimy bezoar and he would never be rid of it. Sister Tulah. The woman who had beaten him. The woman who had ruined him. And knew it. And enjoyed it. Relished it. Clive turned away and started the car. He couldn't stand to look at her a moment longer.

Clive bounced over the crumbling threshold of The Pines' parking lot and navigated his way out of downtown Kentsville, following the signs to the highway. The weight in his stomach grew heavier and heavier, even as he put distance between himself and Sister Tulah. When he braked at the crossroad for Highway 301, her bloated face flashed before his eyes and Clive took his hands off the steering wheel. He needed to go north. Back to Atlanta, to his immaculate, climate-controlled apartment. To his twenty-four-hour gym and protein shakes, his double-espressos and wireless internet. To his shame, yes, but also to sanity. An F-250 pulled up behind him, its diesel engine rumbling, but Clive couldn't seem to make himself turn. A long, loud honk came from the truck and Clive glanced up in the rearview mirror. A man in a rebel flag netter was giving him the finger. He pounded on the horn again, but Clive ignored him. He turned his attention back to the crossroads. A black SUV had pulled up at the stop sign opposite him. For a moment, he thought it was Sister Tulah, that she had taken a shortcut somehow, just to really see him off. But no, there was a man behind the wheel and a man in the passenger's seat and both were wearing dark, wraparound sunglasses. Clive almost laughed. He shook his head and smacked his palms against the steering wheel. He didn't care. There was one last possibility, one last shot, one last Hail Mary attempt to salvage the case, and he had to take it. He had to. Clive turned right and gunned the engine. Tulah's bulldogs could follow him if they liked. He was heading south. Toward Silas.

WEAVER WAS COMING. Ramey could feel it in her bones. Before nightfall, it would all be settled. She ran her thumbs along the rim of the coffee cup cradled in her hands and continued to stare out the high picture window above the front door. From her vantage point at the top of the stairs, she could see halfway down the muddy driveway until it curved around to join with the main road. How many nights over the past three months had she had sat in this very spot, sometimes with a cup of coffee in her hand, sometimes a beer, whiskey, a cigarette, as she waited for Judah to come home alive.

"How many cups is that?"

Ramey rested the cup on her knees and turned as Judah sat down beside her on the top stair. She gave him an exhausted smile.

"Three? Four? I started counting over once dawn broke."

Ramey wasn't sure if she had slept at all. At some point, after the fight between Shelia and Benji, after the raucous arrival of Alvin and Gary, hopped up on cocaine and who knew what else, after the discussion and decision to stay put, wait it out, let Weaver come to them, Ramey had dragged herself up the stairs and fallen into bed. The night had been punctuated by the clicking of ejected shells and the slamming of magazines. Shotguns being racked over and over in apprehension and preparation. Bottles clinking. The back screen door clattering open and closed. At one point, Judah had collapsed beside her and murmured into her hair. Slung his arm over her bruised hip. Inhaled and exhaled alongside her.

She started to hand the coffee cup to him, but Judah shook his head.

"I lost count completely. At this point, I'm probably too jittery to shoot straight."

Judah rubbed at his bloodshot eyes and raked his fingers back through his disheveled hair. Ramey watched him for a moment before turning back to her vigil.

"It's going to come down to that, ain't it?"

Judah nodded wearily and Ramey sighed, resting her chin on her hand.

"This is exactly what I didn't want. A war on our doorstep."

She glanced down at the 12-gauge on the stair just beyond her feet.

"I mean, Jesus Christ. Who are we, Judah? Who have we become?"

Judah only shook his head and rested his hand on the small of her back. He knew. And she knew. There was no more running from it. There was no more trying to pretend otherwise. The line had been crossed. Perhaps they were simply, finally, becoming the people they had always been marked to be. Ramey kept her eyes on the window.

"And there's no going back, is there?"

Judah's voice was very quiet.

"No. I don't think so."

And there it was. Ramey set her cup on the stair below her and sat up straight, working her shoulders out, as she pulled and tied her hair back. Shelia walked past the bottom of the stairs on her way from the living room to the kitchen and Ramey nodded to her.

"Well, at least those two quit trying to kill each other."

Judah finally cracked a smile.

"Yeah, at about three thirty in the morning I think. They might have started up again, but I haven't heard any screeching or hollering yet."

When Shelia had first come through the front door last night, Ramey had been positive that Benji was going to strangle her. He went so far as to lunge at Shelia's throat before Judah stepped in front of her and announced that, at least while she was in their house, Shelia was under his protection. Benji's eyes had just about popped out of his skull, but there wasn't much he could do. Shelia and Benji had spent most of the night glaring viciously at one other in seething silence, with an occasional bout of yelling and cursing thrown in for good measure.

"Shelia did save my life, you know. With Weaver."

Judah glanced over at Ramey.

"She's still responsible for what happened to Benji."

He stood up and stretched.

"But at this point, they can work it out for themselves as far as I'm concerned. I just don't have time for—"

"Judah."

Ramey jumped up and pointed toward the window. A lone red car was coming down the driveway. Benji called up from the living room.

"Judah! There's a car!"

Judah turned to Ramey.

"Weaver?"

"I don't know. That's certainly not what he was driving before."

Judah called down the stairs.

"Hold on! Just wait a second. Just, oh, for God's sake."

Ramey watched the car roll to a stop and Special Agent Grant awkwardly squeeze his way out. She turned to Judah, her eyes wide, mouth open in disbelief. Judah shook his head as he bounded down the stairs.

"You've got to be kidding me."

Ramey charged after him and they nearly smacked into Gary, swinging around the corner from the kitchen.

"Who the hell?"

Judah pushed past him.

"ATF. We'll get him out of here. Just stay watching the back door."

Ramey cautiously stepped to the edge of the living room window and looked out. Agent Grant was standing by his car with an uncertain look on his face. Ramey turned around. Shelia and Benji were both craning their necks, trying to peer over her shoulder through the window. Ramey looked at Judah, standing by the couch, scratching his forehead with the barrel of his .45, and Alvin, now coming out of the bathroom with his fly unzipped and a shotgun gripped in each hand. Ramey took a deep breath, trying to calm down everyone else in the room as much as herself.

"It's okay. I can talk to him, I can get rid of him."

Judah frowned and looked past her, through the window. He flipped the .45 in his hand and held the grip out to her. Ramey eyed the gun, but shook her head. Judah pushed it toward her.

"Are you crazy? Take it."

"Oh, and that won't look suspicious? He's ATF. I think he'd know if I was carrying a firearm out to greet him."

Ramey turned around to look out the window again. Agent Grant had started walking toward the house. Ramey put her hand on the doorknob.

"Just give me a minute. I'll take care of him."

Judah looked worried, but jerked his head toward the agent.

"Do it."

CLIVE DIDN'T THINK the old men in the SUV had followed him after all, but he couldn't be sure. He turned and looked anxiously over his shoulder, back down the driveway. From where he was standing, he couldn't see the road, and that made him nervous. Clive shook his head; he had to get a grip on himself. Ramey Barrow was coming down the porch steps with a look on her face like she was about to spit nails, and he needed to be focused on her, not worried about the Meals on Wheels brigade rolling up behind him.

Clive took his sunglasses off, trying to appear more personable, but raised his hand up against the glare of the midmorning sun. He did his best to smile.

"Hello there, again."

For a moment, Clive thought Ramey was going to barrel right through him. Her arms were crossed, her head tilted down just enough so that her eyes had to slice up through the air at him. He almost took a step back, but she drew up short, cocked her hip out and threw her head to the side, her wild hair glinting with copper from the sun. Her voice was tight and clipped.

"I thought Judah made things clear the other day."

Clive dropped his hand and turned slightly so that he wasn't completely blinded by the sun. Ramey moved so that she was still standing close in front of him. Even though it was obvious that there were no other cars in the driveway save his own, Clive made a point of looking around the yard.

"Is Judah around?"

"No."

Clive turned back to her.

"Is he up at the salvage yard?"

Ramey's teeth were biting into her bottom lip.

"Yes."

Clive knew she was lying. He also knew that falling back on the bullshit routine wasn't going to work this time. He needed her. He needed the Cannons. Clive put his hands on his hips and stared down at the scrubby tufts of grass at his feet.

"Listen, Ramey. I'm not here to play games."

"Oh really? You just gonna stick to threats this time?"

Clive looked up at her sharply.

"No, I'm not here for that either."

She stuck out her chin defiantly.

"Then what? You just got nothing better to do? Want to come up on the porch and play some checkers?"

Clive smoothed down his tie, trying to figure out how to say what he needed to say. Finally, he just blurted it out in a rush.

"Tulah. Is there anything you can give me on her? Anything at all?"

Ramey laughed and shook her head.

"Man, you're like a dog with a bone."

Clive put out his hand.

"No, listen, that's not what…"

She stepped close. Too close. Her eyes looked like they wanted to carve him up.

"No, you listen. I can't help you with Tulah. But I can tell you what you're gonna do. You're gonna get in your car, and you're gonna turn around and you're gonna leave me and my family alone, do you understand?"

"Ramey, I mean it. I'm not threatening you. I'll make sure you're all granted immunity, whatever you want. Just help me out here, okay? Help me. I'm asking."

Clive knew that he sounded desperate. No, he sounded pathetic, just as he had earlier on the phone with Lopez. It made him sick. He made himself sick. Clive kicked savagely at the clump of grass, but when he looked back up at Ramey, he saw something in her eyes. Something. The flicker of a waver?

It wasn't disgust and it wasn't pity, as he had been expecting to see. It was, maybe, uncertainty? Her jaw was clenched, but no longer out of anger. When she spoke, her words were softer, but they still held the same finality.

"Agent Grant, you need to go. Now. Understand? You need to go."

Ramey began to turn away from him, but hesitated. She seemed to be waiting for him to do the same. But he had seen it, that second of doubt on her face.

"Ramey, just hear me…"

Out of the corner of his eye, he caught a flash of movement. Clive didn't see the man, only the gun, and he crashed into Ramey, slamming her down into the dirt. He had heard the shot, and then the cacophony of ones that followed, but the first one stuck with him, one long, shattering note that seemed to go on forever. He had twisted when he fell and the whole world above him was caught up in shadows. The shadow of a tree limb, the shadow of a cloud, the shadow of the sun, the shadow of a bird, sweeping gently over him, ascending on outstretched wings. Clive listened to the sound of that single bullet, its echo still resonating in his ears, reverberating now somewhere in his chest, and he knew. He would be a shadow now, too.

ALL HELL WAS breaking loose. Shelia had been standing at the edge of the living room window, cigarette in hand, while keeping an eye on Ramey and reporting her progress with the ATF agent back to Judah and Benji. She screamed when she heard the first gunshot and saw both Ramey and the agent hit the ground. More shots followed, coming from both the front and back of the house, and then there was the shattering of glass, but Shelia stayed crouched down by the window. Judah was behind her, yelling his head off at Alvin and Gary to get to the back, and Benji had grabbed her ankle and was trying to drag her behind the couch for cover, but Shelia watched for Ramey. The agent had flopped on his back and wasn't moving, but Ramey was scuttling on her knees and elbows, trying to stay low and make it around the car. Shelia waited until she could see Ramey hunched down behind the wheel well, trapped, but alive, before she let Benji pull her behind the couch.

"Jesus Christ!"

She got to her knees just in time to catch the shotgun Judah tossed in her arms. He pointed to Benji, sprawled out awkwardly beside her.

"You stay with him, you hear? You stay with him!"

Judah was out the front door before she could say anything. Shelia turned to Benji, now struggling to get to his feet with a rifle gripped in one hand. Shelia jammed her shoulder up into his armpit and he braced himself against her. He was trying to get to the window.

"For the love of God…"

Benji let go of her long enough to smash one of the window panes with the stock of the rifle. He jammed the barrel through the hole in the glass and turned to her.

"Just shut up already and cover me."

JUDAH CROUCHED DOWN behind the porch steps and realized that he was about to make an impossible decision. To his left, not twenty yards away, was Ramey, pinned behind the Aveo, without a weapon or a way to run. He could see her, but he couldn't get to her. The windows above her had been shattered by bullets coming from two men with assault rifles at the edge of the woods. Ramey's hair was dusted with glass and her face was streaked with dirt. He had to look away; there was so much fear behind her wide, wet eyes.

Ahead of Judah, also at the edge of the woods, but closer to him, was Weaver. He stood stock-still like a golem waiting to be brought to life, his hands at his sides, one fist clenched and the other gripping a gun, until suddenly he grinned at Judah. A savage, inhuman smile. The smile of one who has come to slaughter. Weaver raised his hand and the shooting from the two men further down the tree line abruptly ceased. Weaver was waiting and Judah understood.

He turned back to Ramey. Did she? Ramey was panting and holding her already injured wrist to her chest, but she raised her head up. Everything was there, as it always had been, and at least he could take those eyes with him. She nodded once and mouthed the word.

"Go."

Judah nodded back and turned to Weaver. The man's smile fell and he turned tail, disappearing into the woods. Judah followed.

The underbrush snagged his clothes and whipped at his face and hands, but Judah charged headlong, crashing through the stands of palmettos and dodging around scrub pines and turkey oaks as he kept Weaver barely in view. Weaver's men hadn't fired when Judah crossed the yard, but now he could hear gunshots again. He tried not to think about Ramey, trapped behind the car, or the others still in the house. Judah kept his eyes on the black flap of hair he could see flashing through the trees ahead. Weaver was the only one who mattered.

Weaver had a lead on him, but Judah knew he was gaining. Weaver was limping, at times staggering against the trees, but Judah couldn't get a clear shot. He fired off three rounds, but they all went wide. A tangle of kudzu snagged him and for a moment Judah was caught up as he tore at the vine, trying to wrench himself free. When he looked up, Weaver was gone.

Judah ran into the small clearing just ahead of him and frantically spun in a circle, searching in all directions.

"Weaver!"

Judah stopped for a moment, listening. The gunshots coming from the house had ceased and now he could hear only the hum of insects, the screaming calls of birds and his own ragged breath. Judah turned in a circle again, the .45 held out in front of him, but he wasn't fast enough. He heard the crash through the palmettos behind him at the same moment as he felt the blow to the back of his head. Judah dropped to the ground like a stone.

He was disoriented for a moment and realized, as he rolled and pushed himself to his knees, that the .45 had been slung from his hand in the fall. Judah lurched to his feet, his fists clenched against the throbbing pain in his head and neck, to face the man pointing a Beretta straight at him. If Judah was going to die, he was going to die on his feet. Weaver coughed out a wheezing laugh. He was without a shirt, but wrapped around the waist and chest with bandages. Blood was seeping through the gauze wrapped over the bullet wound in his shoulder and Judah smiled bleakly at this. That was where Ramey must have shot him. Good for her. He could see where she had scratched his face pretty badly, too. His right ear was taped up with more gauze and even just standing, he was favoring one leg. Weaver laughed again and spat at Judah's feet.

"Well, those girls made a mess of me, huh? I'm a regular Egyptian mummy standing here. But they couldn't quite finish me off."

Judah didn't say anything. He was trying to lift his head up all the way, trying to stand up tall in front of the man about to kill him. Weaver's face darkened.

"Maybe you thought you'd be the one to do it?"

Judah looked Weaver in the eye. His voice was steady.

"Yes."

Weaver laughed again. A dispassionate, merciless laugh, and Judah swayed but kept his feet under him. He was not going to fall. Weaver would have to put him down.

"Well, I'm not sure how well that's going to work out now, all things considered..."

The shot came from behind Judah and barely missed Weaver, but it was enough. Weaver turned his head as the bullet whizzed past and Judah lunged forward, tackling him to the ground. They rolled over one another and Weaver ended up on top, crushing Judah with his weight. Weaver was trying to bring his arms up between them, to get the gun to where he could aim, but Judah reached around and pounded his fist into Weaver's back, right where Shelia had already stabbed him. Judah could see the shock come over Weaver's face, and as his body went slack for a moment, Judah wedged his arm between them and jammed his knuckles into the man's bullet wound. Weaver thrashed backward, half-howling, half-snarling, and Judah kicked hard, finally twisting around so that Weaver flipped and Judah was on top of him. Weaver was still clutching the Beretta and he brought it around to try to shoot Judah in the side, but Judah knocked his arm back and reached for his own .45, caught in the damp, fallen leaves and slippery pine needles. He got his fingers around the gun and, even as Weaver bucked beneath him, lashing his head back and forth, Judah was able to bring the barrel around to Weaver's temple. He didn't stop for a dramatic pause, he didn't look into Weaver's eyes, he didn't say a word. Judah pulled the trigger and was done with it.

What was left of Weaver's head fell backward onto the mess of blood and leaves, and Judah rolled off of Weaver's body. He lay heaving and panting, staring up at the canopy of tree branches and the bright sun filtering down over him. Judah caught his breath and waited for Ramey to come out of the woods, lay down her gun beside him and put her hands on either side of his face, pressing her forehead to his.

Judah waited, but Ramey didn't come to him. He listened, but the woods were quiet again and Judah sat up in a panic, his head throbbing, his chest still heaving.

"Jesus Christ, little brother. You gonna lay there all day like sleeping beauty or what?"

Eyes wide, almost uncomprehending, Judah staggered to his feet and clasped the outstretched hand of Levi Cannon.

CHAPTER 20

FELTON RAISED HIS head and squinted up into the searing, white firmament. He did not see the lowering sky or the compass of sparrows wheeling above him. He saw only God.

"*The voice of him that crieth in the wilderness, Prepare ye the way of the Lord.*"

Felton whispered under his breath as he lifted his feet high to step over the nubs of cypress knees breaking through the skin of brackish water surrounding him. He steadied himself on the long tupelo branch he had cut down into a staff and continued to mutter.

"*Make straight in the desert a highway for our God.*"

The mud sucked at his shoes and legs, and the insects tore at his hands and face, but he did not feel their sting.

"*Every valley shall be exalted.*"

He stumbled on a root underneath the water and his pack swung heavily to one side, but he caught himself. Felton continued.

"*And every mountain and hill shall be made low.*"

On either side of the shallow waterway, cypress trees shrouded in Spanish moss rose up around him, but their canopy didn't quite cover his path and the bare skin on Felton's balding head was already blistering in the unforgiving sun. This, he did not feel either.

"And the crooked shall be made straight."

A white heron swooped down in front of him and landed on a half-submerged rotting log, but Felton did not see it.

"And the rough places plain."

The air echoed with the sound of woodpeckers drilling into trees, and somewhere in the distance was the faint bellow of an alligator, but Felton did not hear it.

"And the glory of the Lord shall be revealed."

He did not smell the tannins in the water or the rotting vegetation. He did not hear the songbirds. He did not feel the sweat. He did not see the swamp, stretching endlessly ahead of him for forty miles, leading him up into Georgia.

"And all flesh shall see it together."

Felton did not know where he was going, but it was no matter. God would guide him. The right hand of the Lord, the pale serpent in the sky, would deliver him. Felton had listened. He had risen. And now he would wander, until the time was right, until his spirit was broken and reborn. Until he was called again.

"For the mouth of the Lord hath spoken."

THE SHOOTING HAD stopped, but Ramey stayed crouched down behind the Aveo's front tire until Benji opened the front door, holding a rifle over his head like a goddamn trophy. He shouted across the yard to her.

"We got 'em, Ramey!"

Ramey shouted back to him.

"What?"

Benji hobbled out the door. Shelia, behind him, handed him his crutch and he stumped over to the porch railing.

"The men shooting at you. I got one of them, and the other ran off down the driveway."

Ramey cautiously stood up and looked around the yard. Aside from the two dead men, one of them the ATF agent who she had to quickly look away from, it was empty.

"I heard shots coming from somewhere else."

Alvin, supporting Gary, stumbled through the door and collapsed on the porch swing. Gary had a bloody dishtowel pressed hard to his side, but he seemed to be okay. He was grinning like a lunatic, at any rate.

"Taken care of! We got the two who were out back. You're gonna need a new rug in the laundry room, though. There's a mess of blood all over the floor."

Were they all insane? Or just high on survival? Ramey slowly walked across the yard.

"And Judah?"

Everyone's face suddenly fell. Ramey charged up the porch and grabbed the rifle Benji had stood against the railing. He reached for her arm, trying to stop her.

"What are you doing?"

She pulled free of him.

"What does it look like I'm doing? I'm going after him."

Ramey turned to Alvin, who was already on his feet, reloading. Benji tried to stop her again.

"You don't know what happened. You can't just run out into the woods after Judah. We got his guys, but Weaver could still be out there."

Ramey pushed past him.

"Exactly."

She started down the porch steps, but drew up short when she heard branches snapping loudly and then caught the flash of Judah's white T-shirt as he emerged from the woods. There was blood on his neck and collar, but from the way he was walking, forcefully, purposefully, he didn't appear to be hurt. And there was someone coming out of the trees behind him. She raised her hand to her mouth.

"Oh my God."

"Levi?"

Benji cried out from behind her as he stumped down the steps. Judah and Levi came up to stand in front of the porch and Benji pounded his oldest brother on the back.

"It's you. Jesus Christ, man. Where you been for the past three months?"

Levi shrugged his broad shoulders and shook his head.

"It's a long story. A very long story. But I'm here now."

Ramey narrowed her eyes at Levi and noticed that he avoided looking in her direction. The last time she had seen him, he was beating the shit out of Judah in the back parking lot of The Ace. And she had pointed a gun at him to make him stop. She turned to Judah, looking for a sign, but he was ignoring his brothers. He was staring hard up at Ramey as he stepped onto the bottom stair. She crossed her arms and met his eyes.

"Weaver?"

"Dead."

Judah slowly looked around him, as if seeing everyone for the first time, and Ramey realized that perhaps he was, in a way. There was something changed about him. His eyes. The set of his mouth. The way his gaze lingered on Shelia at one end of the porch and Alvin and Gary at the other, as if assessing their worth. Their place. And the way he looked at her. Not as his girl. Not as his woman. But as his queen. A sharpness stole into Ramey's heart, at once thrilling and terrifying. It was sealed; things would never be the same.

Judah trudged up the steps and slid his arm around her waist. He pressed his head against her collarbone for a moment and then continued to the next step above her. She reached out and grabbed his wrist.

"Judah. What now?"

He turned around and stared out at the mess with her. Agent Grant's body still lay where it had fallen. There was another dead man sprawled in the dirt about halfway down the driveway and Ramey supposed that Weaver's body was still somewhere in the woods. Judah's smile was grim.

"We take care of this. We move forward. We keep going."

Judah dropped his eyes to Ramey.

"Because this is who we are."

Ramey understood, and she echoed him, but she still wasn't sure that she believed him.

"This is who we are."

SISTER TULAH RECOGNIZED the handwriting on the outside of the envelope. The childish block letters spelled out the recipient of its contents: *Attn: ATF Special Agent Clive Grant.* She stared at it, creased down the middle from where The Pines manager had folded it to stick in his shirt pocket. Tulah had already checked the back: when the greasy little manager had handed the envelope to Tulah through the window of her Navigator it had still been sealed.

The envelope now sat squarely on the thick leather blotter in the center of her desk. She settled herself comfortably in her oxblood chair and clicked the green-shaded lamp on. The bottle of Mithridatium was gone, replaced now by stacks of file folders and ledgers. The Recompense was over. It was time to get back to business. Sister Tulah took up her silver letter opener and slit the side of the envelope. She tapped the pages out and carefully unfolded them. It was as she had feared. And worse.

The list of transgressions was long, going back to the early nineties. There were dates, names and estimated dollar amounts. Locations. Transactions. Quotations. Most were accurate, some were not, but it was enough to put her and about twenty other people in prison for life. The last page was signed, swearing all of the information to be true. The signature, scrawling almost off the page, cauterized itself into Sister Tulah's mind.

Felton. She had never confided in him, not once, but what she held in her hand was more than a decade's worth of eavesdropping and snooping. Listening at closed doors. Scurrying about, with his head down. His tail between his legs. All the while, remembering. Tulah had not thought he had it in him: a backbone for betrayal.

She folded the pages and slid them back into the envelope. Tulah would decide what to do with them later. She would decide what to do with Brother Felton later. The Elders had been searching for him since the previous night, but so far there was no word. No trace. It was as if he had vanished. Sister Tulah would find him, though. She would find him and she would skin him. She would cut him into a thousand pieces like the snake that he was and she would trample the remains into the dust.

Tulah unlocked the middle drawer of her desk and pulled it out. She unlocked a second compartment, underneath the false bottom of the drawer, and she tucked the envelope inside it. Tulah withdrew its only other contents: a folded piece of hotel stationary. She locked the drawers back up and held the crumpled slip of paper greedily between her fingers. On it was the name of the man George Kingfisher wanted dead. His proposition to her was very clear. The Eagle was dying of pancreatic cancer and would not survive to the next Recompense. If Sister Tulah fulfilled her task, the Mark of the Angel and the seat on the Inner Council would be hers.

Tulah smiled. She would ravage the man and more. She would ravage his kin. Especially his kin. She would steal the last breath from each and every one of them and they would all ride the pale horse home. Sister Tulah opened the folded paper and let her eyes fall on the two words written in a beautiful, delicate hand:

Levi Cannon

It was time to reap what had been sown. It was time indeed.

END

ACKNOWLEDGMENTS

Always and forever, thank you to Ryan Holt for igniting the spark that started it all. And for your patience, your honesty and your unwavering belief. You never let me walk away and you never let me fall. You have my heart.

Thank you to Janet Sokolay, for endless support and encouragement, and for being my irreplaceable first reader.

So many thanks to everyone who breathed life into *Walk in the Fire*, with special thanks to Jason Pinter, Jeff Ourvan, Georgia Morrissey, David Joy, Natalie S. Harnett, David Swinson, Erica Wright, Eric Beetner, Kent Wascom, and Erik Storey.

Also, thanks to everyone who supported the first year of *Lightwood*, including Taylor Brown, Brian Panowich, Chris Holm, Beth Gilstrap, Jeff Zentner, Alex Segura, Jeffery Hess, Patrick Millikin and so many more. Thank you to everyone who read with me, hosted me, sold my books, came to events and put up with me in general. Drinks on me.

And thank you readers. The books are for you. Thanks for coming along for the ride.

ABOUT THE AUTHOR

Steph Post is the author of *Lightwood* and *A Tree Born Crooked*. She is a recipient of the Patricia Cornwell Scholarship for creative writing from Davidson College and winner of the Vereen Bell Award. Her short fiction has most recently appeared in *Haunted Waters: From the Depths*, *Nonbinary Review* and the anthology *Stephen King's Contemporary Classics*. She was a finalist for The Big Moose Prize and has been nominated for a Rhysling Award and a Pushcart Prize.

Visit her at www.StephPostFiction.com and follow her at @StephPostAuthor.